SACHAEL DESIRES

SACHAEL
desires
MELODY WINTER

Sachael Desires Copyright 2015 by Melody Winter. All rights reserved. No part of this publication may be reproduced or transmitted in any form or by any means, electronic or mechanical, including photocopy, or any information storage and retrieval system, without permission from the publisher, except in the case of brief quotations embodied in critical articles and reviews.

Cover design by Ashley Ruggirello
Cover art Copyright 2015 bumimanusiastock on DeviantArt.com

Electronic ISBN: 978-1-942111-32-0
Paperback ISBN: 978-1-942111-31-3

This is a work of fiction. Names, characters, places and incidents are either the product of the author's imagination or are used fictitiously, and any resemblance to actual persons, living or dead, business establishments, events or locals is entirely coincidental.

REUTS Publications
www.REUTS.com

To Pete, my husband, who copes with my diva tantrums and feeds me chocolate when necessary.

PROLOGUE
Fire

ORONTES

Orontes pounded his fist into the van's steering wheel. He would find Estelle, and he would kill the Sachael she loved.

He stared at the house in front of him, the skyline of Ravenscar reflecting in its windows, his own eyes alternating between glossy and glazed, narrow and focused. None of this should have happened.

He was missing something, some part of the bigger picture. Estelle was definitely a Sachael—of that, he was sure—but he still needed evidence in order to convince Lilith. It mattered that others believed him—he wasn't crazy. He knew the truth.

Narrowing his eyes at the small croft house, *her* house, he gripped the steering wheel harder, his knuckles white with tension. Anger rolled beneath his skin and heat flushed through his body. He removed his hands from their tight grip of the steering wheel and cracked his knuckles one by one. The one day he had needed to leave The Sect, place her in the care of others, she'd managed to escape.

His son wasn't the only person who would die today. The other members of The Sect, the cowards who had deserted Pactolus on the beach this morning, would be dead as soon as he returned to the organization's headquarters. He rubbed the venom bullet bracelet around his wrist. Oh, how they'd suffer—just as his son did. If they had any sense, they would have left, gone into hiding, live in fear of the day he would find and kill them—and he would, eventually. He'd find each and every one of them. But there were other people to find first.

The shrill, melodic ring of his phone disturbed the silence, but he ignored the noise emanating from his pocket. He was in no mood to talk to anyone, not after the last call he'd received, alerting him to Estelle's escape and Pactolus's death.

Thankfully, the ringing stopped, but only for a few seconds. Feeling the vibrations of the phone against his thigh, he growled and hastily grabbed the small metal contraption. He checked the screen to see who was calling.

Lilith.

Screwing his eyes shut, he ignored the call, but his thoughts centered on the woman he'd saved all those years ago. He needed to see her. He wasn't with her when she was told of Pactolus's death. How was she coping with the news? He didn't think she'd care about Estelle's escape; she'd never wanted her caught in the first place. But their son was dead, torn apart by a group of Sachaels on the beach. Sachaels. His hate for them intensified. This had become personal. How dare they kill his own flesh and blood? Snarling, he gazed, unfocused, through the windscreen. He wouldn't rest until he'd found the Sachaels responsible and dealt with them in his own special way.

His punched the steering wheel again and threw his head backward onto the headrest. Estelle. Did she have anything to do with Pactolus's death? A sly smile crept across his lips. He wouldn't be surprised if she was responsible—killed him even. He'd witnessed how much stronger she had become each time he visited her. She'd stood up to him, unlike others, who cowered whenever he was near. Many were fearful of his size, anger, and strength. He pictured her in his mind, as he always did, with loose curls framing her face, her jewel-blue eyes fixed with a determined expression as she questioned him. He'd loved their dance of words, the way she pushed his buttons. He'd enjoyed teasing her, predicting her reactions. As he pulled his hand across his face, his fingers lingered on his lips, remembering the time she had responded to his kiss. He would never forget that moment.

"Oh, Estelle," he whispered. "You may have escaped this time, but it won't happen again." It was a promise to the smiling vision in his head.

There was nothing he could do to alter the events of the morning. All of his plans, his intentions to take Estelle away when he returned, had unraveled so easily. Could nothing run smoothly when he wasn't there?

Focus, he needed to focus.

He would sort this, would plan every last detail. It only made him more determined.

The next time he went after the Sachaels, he would be better prepared—he wouldn't need to be close to them to inject the venom, he would fire a bullet from the gun he'd invented. It had taken months of design, and many more of experimentation. But the gun meant many things—increased power, greater speed, accuracy, and the ability to kill many Sachaels quickly.

He'd spent enough time at the beach. He should have gone straight to The Sect's headquarters, but he'd needed to see the place his son was murdered and close this chapter of missed opportunities. Stepping from the van, he took a deep breath. Ravenscar held many memories for him. It was where he first saw Lilith all those years ago. Where he'd spied on Estelle and her father—witnessed her grow into the woman he now wanted.

Unfortunately, the place now held an unpleasant reminder as well.

Orontes slammed the van door shut, the action so forceful that the vehicle shook. He strolled casually to the back of the van before unlocking the doors. Grabbing the full can of petrol and a handful of rags, he focused on the task at hand. The lighter was already in his pocket.

Walking to the house, he cautiously scanned the surrounding area, searching for any potential witnesses. The last thing he needed was interference from nosey passersby.

Taking a deep breath, he lingered in the doorway. He stepped back a few paces and charged, shoulder first. The door crashed inward, slamming into the wall. He strolled into her house and systematically worked through the interior, splashing the obnoxious-smelling liquid onto the floor and furniture. Entering her bedroom, he glanced at the rumpled sheets on her bed and smirked. He'd lost count of the numerous times he'd envisioned her soft, young body rolling around in a bed. And she was always with him, their limbs entwined as he showed her what a loving man he could be.

A growl developed in his throat as his gaze wandered across the bed and onto her nightstand. The shell. The shell the Sachael had left her—the Sachael who had ruined all his plans. Without hesitation, he picked it up and threw it against the wall. The fragments scattered on the floor, and he laughed. The sound was hollow, empty. There was nothing funny about this, nothing at all. He took another deep breath, drawing in her lingering scent. This was the first and last time he would sense her presence here. When he left, he'd not be able to return.

Like a thief with limited time, he pulled open her bedside table drawers. He found nothing of any use to him in his quest to prove what she was. Just some trinkets, some bits of fabric, and the pictures sitting on top of the table. He glanced at each framed photograph before selecting the one he would keep. The visions of Estelle in his head were crisp and fresh, but he knew that they would fade with time. This photograph would be a constant reminder of what he had lost, of what he would never give up searching for. He broke the glass in the metal frame and ripped the photo from its surrounding. He ran his finger along the face of the woman it depicted—Estelle. He tore the picture in half, severing her from her father, and placed the photo in his back pocket. Rummaging through her bedside table again, he pulled out a colorful patterned scarf and held it to his nose. Closing his eyes, he stood still for several seconds, breathing in her unmistakable scent. Once again, his mind wandered, his memories fresh, clear, and as beautiful as the sun rising in the morning. Her voice called in his head.

"*Orontes.*"

Turning sharply, he expected to see her at the door. She wasn't, of course she wasn't, but the action snapped him from his reverie nevertheless. He picked up the half can of petrol and splashed the liquid onto the floor and furniture. Walking backward, he moved outside.

He took another glance around, looking for movement in the distance. Satisfied that there was no one to witness his act, he reached for the lighter in his pocket and flicked the flame alive before throwing it to the ground. A line of fire snaked its way to the house, not halting, not pausing, not caring. The smell of petrol permeated the breeze, overpowering and acrid. Orontes took several steps back, unable to tear his eyes from the open doorway of the house.

Within seconds, the house was alive with orange, dancing flames. As they spread through the interior, they engulfed everything, the fire spitting and roaring like a hungry wild animal. Orontes's skin prickled with the scorching heat, but he watched, hypnotized by the ferocity of the inferno.

Even though he would have been content to stay and ensure the building burned to the ground, he couldn't. Above the roar of the fire, he heard his phone ring again. Cursing the disturbance, he pulled it from his pocket, wishing he had thrown it from the window earlier. He viewed the screen—Lilith again. This time, the letters lit against a reflected backdrop of burning building. He canceled the call before jumping back into the van.

He needed to see her, ensure she wouldn't do anything stupid. She wasn't the frightened seventeen-year-old he'd first met anymore, and he knew her love for Pactolus was never as strong as the love she felt for her first child. She denied it, just as she denied her true feelings for the Sachael who stole him from her. But she was a vulnerable person, strong in many ways, but weak with her endless love for a man who had treated her appallingly.

"She'll be fine. She always is," he muttered to himself, more from hope than anything else. He turned the key to start the engine.

The van roared to life, and he steered it away from the cliff top. Without glancing back, he drove up the steep dirt track to the country lane. Peak Hall was on his left, a hotel now, no longer Lilith's family home. In his head, he still heard her bombastic father's voice. Orontes sneered when he remembered the same man, begging for his life several months later. Such a pity he threw himself from the top of the cliff on that bright, sunny afternoon, a desperate cry for help as Lilith turned eighteen.

Such a pity he didn't cope with his daughter growing up.

Such good fortune that Lilith had inherited everything.

He would not be beaten—not by the Sachaels, not by Lilith's father, not by anyone.

Eyes fixed forward, he drove fast.

When he arrived at the Sect's headquarters, the imposing building appeared normal. He parked the van outside the main doors before rushing into the building.

"Where is she?" he shouted into an empty hallway. An unexpected chill ran through his body, and he shivered. There was no one to see, but he had still expected an answer. His bare feet thudded across the wooden floor as he made his way to the bottom of the stairs. "Lilith!"

It was strangely quiet, and, as he placed his foot on the first step, prepared to go upstairs to her room, he knew the cold feeling sweeping through his body, reaching every nerve ending, had nothing to do with his surroundings. It was because Estelle wasn't there. He was used to feeling her presence, even when she'd been locked in her room and he was in his; he couldn't shake her influence on him—the hold she had.

"Lilith!" he shouted again, ignoring the chill. Instead, he concentrated on Michael's betrayal, and the slow way he would torture him for his part in Estelle's escape, in the murder of his son. Another man to add to his list—a list that was growing longer by the minute.

There was still no answer to his call. He turned into the hallway before making his way to the office at the end of the corridor. He wanted Michael's personnel file. He suspected the traitor would return home, even if it was only for a day or two. His downturned mouth turned into a snide sneer when he envisioned Michael's surprise at his arrival. He'd make sure he got there first, was there to greet him.

Polished wooden floors, dim wall lights, and the smell of old leather assaulted his senses as he strode into the office. The smell made his stomach wrench. It overpowered the scent of his body, the reminder that he was a man from the sea. Living on land was no substitute for his true existence.Lilith was sitting on the floor, leaning against the side of a filing cabinet. She was crying, but at least she was alive.

"What are you doing?" he asked, his voice soft as he stepped toward her, avoiding several crumpled pieces of paper strewn about her outstretched legs. Her eyes were fixed on the sheet of paper held in her shaking hand—one with a photograph of Michael clipped to it.

Orontes glanced at the other scrunched balls, picking a few up to read. They all referred to Michael. Lilith had found the records before him.

"They said he was with them," Lilith whispered. "He helped her escape. He watched as they killed Pactolus."

Orontes crouched in front of her, concerned at her blank, level emotions. "I'll find him. I'll make sure he suffers for what he did."

Lilith continued staring blindly at the floor, not lifting her gaze. "I trusted him."

"I've told you before. You shouldn't trust anyone."

She nodded, although the gesture was slight.

He took the piece of paper from her hand, strode toward the desk, and quickly read through the detailed information.

Name: Michael Irvine

Current age: 22

Home Address: Rackwick Bay, Hoy, Orkney Islands

Mother: Morag

Father: Mitch (Deceased)

Driving License: Clean

Scanning the rest of the information, he huffed. He hoped there were only a few houses on the small island of Hoy. He wasn't keen on traveling so far north—it wasn't safe. Sachaels weren't the only creatures in the water up there.

Placing the single sheet of paper on his desk, he turned to Lilith. The wetness of her tears still lingered around her eyes. While he wanted to offer her comfort, he didn't know how affection would be received. He'd distanced himself from her since Estelle's arrival and was certain she'd noticed.

Lilith slowly stood, wiping her face with the back of her hands. "I didn't know if you'd come back."

Not missing the cold edge to her words, he frowned at her. "Of course I would. Why wouldn't I?"

"She's gone. You had no reason to return." Her voice was stronger, determined.

He snarled, not needing to be reminded that Estelle wasn't here. The powerful warmth, the calmness, had disappeared.

"Did you hear me?" Lilith snapped. "I said she's gone. You didn't need to come back."

"I heard you," Orontes retorted. "But I didn't come back for her, did I? I came for you. Just like I always do."

"If you weren't so obsessed with her, none of this would have happened!" she shouted, striding toward him. "Pactolus would still be alive. This is your fault. I told you there was no need to bring her here—that your theories were ridiculous. We could have caught the Sachael without this happening."

"I still believe the girl is a Sachael."

"They don't exist. You know that. All the time she was here, you managed to prove what, exactly?" She sneered, turning her back on him and facing the window.

Orontes sighed, not wanting to argue with her, not now.

"Then you really shouldn't have gone along with my plans, should you?" he reasoned.

"I was humoring you, as I always do." She spun to face him, her arms folded across her chest.

He caught the sarcasm in her voice.

"Humoring me?"

"Yes. No one else would put up with your numerous obsessions. The octopuses, the bullets. The other women."

Her voice cracked as she spoke, but Orontes would never confirm her thoughts. Lilith was a separate part of his life. What he did away from here was none of her business.

"Other women?" he asked, raising his brow, feining surprise at her question.

"Yes. Don't deny it. I know you go to see them when you disappear from here."

Orontes smirked, not denying her accusation, but not confirming it either. "I hardly think that's fair, Lilith, do you?"

"Fair?" She dropped her arms to her side and surveyed Orontes with a frown.

"You say I have other women, yet you have only ever loved one man. I never stood a chance against him—a memory."

Lilith glared at Orontes. "I tried!" she shouted. "I tried to love you."

"Tried?" His voice was loud, his anger matching that of Lilith's. They'd been here so many times before. But all they did was hurt each other with their accusations.

Even though she was significantly smaller than Orontes, she stepped up to him. "I can't cope with the competition any longer. I don't want to compete for your attention. Not now. You'll go again, leave me. Only this time, you're chasing a girl who's young enough to be your daughter." Her words were spat at him before she turned away, her shoulders rising and falling quickly.

Orontes wanted to tell her she was wrong, but he couldn't. He was already planning to leave. He wanted to find Michael, ask him a few questions before he killed him. Then he'd find Estelle.

"I need to find Michael," he said firmly.

"Because you think he'll lead you to her." She was distant, detaching herself from the situation. It was something she always did. Protected her heart when she thought it about to break. Her vulnerability reminded him of the seventeen-year-old he'd fallen in love with all those years ago, and he rushed to her as she turned around.

He cupped her cheek in his hand. "Not because he'll lead me to her. But because I hope he will lead me to the Sachael responsible for killing our son."

Pulling her into his arms, he sighed heavily. He hated their arguments, hated the cruel words that sprang from both of them. This was not the time to fight. As she relaxed into his comforting hold, he held her tight.

"I'll find him, Lilith. I promise, I'll find him."

Lilith sniffed. "I told you what they did to Pactolus. How they tore him limb from limb. Why?" she asked, turning the focus of the conversation away from Estelle, from his suspicions of what she was.

Orontes shrugged. He had witnessed the way Sachaels killed his kind. Their army was known for its brutality.

"Did the other members not help him?" he asked.

"No." The word was muffled, spoken into the salty, cold, musky smell of his t-shirt as she grasped a handful of the cotton material, clinging to him.

"Petrol?" she questioned, not moving, keeping her body close to his.

"Hmmm . . . I had some loose ends to tie up."

"Such as?"

"Nothing for you to worry about," he said, reluctant to discuss the subject any further. There was no way he would tell her what he had done. It didn't concern her. "Have the cowards who were on the beach gone, or are they still here?"

"They've gone," Lilith said with certainty.

"Good." Orontes patted her shoulder. At least he wouldn't need to waste time dealing with them before he left. They could wait, wondering when he'd turn up. They'd always be looking behind them, running in fear of their miserable lives. He'd catch up with them at some point.

"I didn't tell you . . . the lab," Lilith whispered, as if fearful of his reaction.

"The lab? Why? What's happened?" He was already pushing her away, her tight hold faltering.

"The octopuses. They're dead."

He was sure he saw her smile as he turned away, but dismissed it. She called to him as he charged from the room, but he didn't turn around.

Storming along the corridor, heading toward the back of the building, he fought the rage that was building, threatening to overpower him. As he swung open the heavy white doors, his anger exploded.

"What the hell happened to them?" he demanded. The ten large tanks, each one containing twelve Blue Ringed Octopuses, were not empty, but filled with the floating, lifeless forms of his pets. They drifted on the water's surface, eerily bathed in the artificial glow from the fluorescent lights.

The two men in the laboratory didn't answer him, too afraid to meet his eyes. One of them glanced at the log book he was writing in, the other continued taking stock in the room where the venom was stored.

"I asked what happened?" he repeated, glaring at the man writing.

"I . . . I don't . . ."

Orontes snarled, striding to the nearest tank and gently tapping his fingers on the glass. Nothing happened. The octopuses' usual reaction was to scurry and hide between the rocks and sand at the bottom of the tank. They didn't move. Shaking his head in disbelief, he systematically walked to each tank, repeating his action. He waited for a few seconds each time for any sign of movement, hoping at least one of them was alive.

He lingered over the last tank, sniffing the air above it. Moving his face closer to the water, he drew in a deep breath.

"Bleach," he murmured, and then, as if to confirm it to himself and the men in the room who were ignoring him, he repeated the word louder. "Bleach! They were killed with bleach." Spinning on the spot, he glared at the man who had attempted to answer him earlier. "Did you see Michael wandering around with the container in his hand? Did you see him pour it into the tanks?"

"No," he answered, his voice shaking.

"And why wasn't he stopped? He wasn't allowed in here." Orontes paced the laboratory, convinced this was Michael's doing. "Is the venom contaminated?" he asked the man in the store room.

"No, the vials I've checked are clean."

Orontes glanced at the tanks again before marching from the room. Long, heavy steps took him upstairs and to the left of the building—the rooms where the men he trusted would be. This whole tragedy wouldn't have happened if he'd stayed. Michael wouldn't have dared to take Estelle to the beach without him. He didn't understand why nobody had stopped him. No one had questioned him. Not even Pactolus.

"Stupid half-bred idiot," he growled.

Eight familiar faces turned to him as he opened the door to the games room. The television was immediately switched off, and the two men playing pool stopped their game. These men were the ones who had returned this morning after the phone call from Lilith. They were Oceanids.

"Ten minutes, and we're leaving," he informed them.

"Leaving? Again?"

"Yes. We'll be in the water."

"But you're not allowed in the water. Hebrus banned you."

"And you think he will stop me?" Orontes snapped. "You can stay here if you want, but you'd better not be here when I return."

What did it matter whether he was banned or not? Orontes didn't care for Hebrus's rule. He never followed it; although, this time, he would be in the water for considerably longer than the quick swims he occasionally went for. He smirked. Hebrus would never stop him. He'd never even know.

"Where are we going this time?" another man asked, already jumping to his feet, ready to leave.

Orontes fought a smile, confident with what would greet him when he arrived.

"The Orkneys," he growled. "I need to visit Michael."

ONE
Home

ESTELLE

Safe. We were safe—for now. But who knew how long it would last? Orontes was not likely to just let me go. He wouldn't let any of us go, not after what had happened on the beach at Ravenscar. It would only be a matter of time before any safe place would become one of danger. We'd have to keep moving, keep one step ahead of him.

I leaned against Azariah, watching Michael swing his mother around in his arms, his wet clothing clearly forgotten in his excitement to see her. Their laughter carried to us on the gentle sea-born breeze, and I smiled sadly.

"He missed her so much," I said, feeling a twinge of sadness at my rushed departure from Ravenscar, from my own mother. When would I see her again?

"Not as much as I missed you," he replied.

His arm tightened around my waist, and I pushed my gloom away as we walked toward Michael's enthusiastic reunion. I was happy for Michael, really happy. He was home—where he belonged. But as I took in the finer details of where we were heading—a small stone croft house—I couldn't help but compare it to my home in Ravenscar. There were differences, of course, between the two, but the similarity still made my heart twinge with longing. Michael's home was in desperate need of repair. The thatch roof was blackened, and a small area of it was non-existent. A wisp of grey smoke snaked from the chimney, the tendrils twisting back on themselves, pulled by the fresh morning breeze. The house was only one floor, and the two windows visible from this side were tiny. I had always viewed my home as small and basic, but this was far less pleasant.

As Michael placed his mother back on the ground, I noted that she was a petite woman, the top of her head only reaching his chest. Her cheeks flushed as she rested her hands on either side of Michael's face. She wore a long skirt that skimmed the clumps of grass growing randomly in the yard, and the top half of her body was wrapped in a dark brown shawl, which she pulled tightly around her shoulders as she finally looked in our direction. She ran her fingers through the sides of her hair, tucking wiry grey strands behind her ears. But when she turned, and her gaze caught Azariah, she froze.

"It can't be," she gasped as we approached, her hand shaking as she let it fall slowly to her side.

"Mum?" Michael asked.

I frowned and turned to Azariah. He shrugged.

"Do you know her?" I said, quiet with my words, not wanting her to hear my question.

"No." He shook his head. "I have never seen her before."

The tiny bit of color in the woman's face had drained away. Not even her rosy cheeks kept their weathered tinge. She stumbled sideways, and Michael grabbed her shoulders, turning her so she focused on him. He spoke gently, cupping her chin in his hand. "What's wrong? Are you feeling okay?"

"He . . . he . . ." Her head lolled to the side and she slumped forward, falling into Michael's arms as Azariah and I rushed to help.

"It's okay," Michael said, but his eyebrows were drawn together as he held his mother. "I just need to get her inside."

Azariah stepped back, away from Michael, who was trying to reposition his mother into his arms.

"What has happened to her?" he asked.

"I think she's fainted," I told him, recognizing the situation.

"Fainted? Why?"

"I have no idea," Michael said, done sweeping his mother into his arms and striding into the house with her as if she weighed nothing at all. "But when she recovers, I hope she'll tell us." I expected Azariah to follow, but he remained where he was, staring at the door.

"What's wrong?" I asked, surprised by his reaction.

"Will she be all right?" He nodded toward the open door, his eyebrows drawn together as he struggled to focus on me.

"Yes, it's just that your appearance seems to have shocked her."

His eyes widened. "I have caused her to be unwell?"

I shook my head. "No. She just fainted. Does no one ever faint in Saicean?"

He rubbed his face with his hands and shook his head. "The men are brave and would never faint if shocked. To do so would potentially end their lives, if they were in the ocean. Her body completely shut down."

"Not quite."

I smiled, wanting to reassure him. "Come on, I bet she's already talking to Michael."

"Are you sure?" He ran his hands through his hair, his gaze now fixed on me.

"Azariah, she will be fine. Stop worrying." I reached for his hand and led him into the house.

"We're in here!" Michael shouted from a room to the right.

I screwed my nose up at the smell of the damp, dingy interior. The stone flags on the floor offered no cushioning under foot. The curtains in this room were closed, but I was still able to see what little amount of furniture lurked in the shadows. Much like the exterior of the home, the inside was in need of repair.

"Turn the light on, please?" Michael asked. "It's too dark in here."

I turned to the light switch on the wall and flicked it. Nothing happened. I tried again, but still no light flooded the room. Glancing at the ceiling, I noticed why. There was no light fixture, only a bare wire. The natural sunlight was the only way to light our surroundings. I stepped to the window and pulled the dusty curtains open. The room flooded immediately with the rising sun's rays. They illuminated the floating airborne dust, the tiny flecks drifting in random swirls. The cause of the musty smell became apparent; one of the walls was wet, and a vein-like pattern of green and brown growing mold fanned across the ceiling. In the other corner of the room, near the smoldering fire, was a bundle of blankets and a mattress. Sparsely decorated, the only items of furniture, apart from the make-do bed, were two single wooden chairs, a tall-backed and overstuffed chair, and a side cupboard.

Michael's mum was sitting in the cushioned chair in front of the smoldering fire. Michael crouched on the floor in front of her, tucking a blanket across her knees. She was slowly regaining consciousness, her movements slow as she reached for Michael's hand. From what Michael had told me about her, I'd always presumed she would be roughly the same age as my mum, but as I examined her thin, worried face, she could have passed for a woman of sixty, if not older.

Azariah took a sharp intake of breath as he stepped fully into the room. Walking straight to the old wooden sideboard, he picked up a solitary picture frame and blew on the glass before running his fingers over it.

"Why didn't you tell me?" He directed his question at Michael, shooting him an accusing stare.

"Tell you what?" Michael said, still attending to his mother and not seeing Azariah's glare.

"What's wrong?" I asked, noting Azariah's stiff posture and tight hold on the picture.

He brought the frame to me, tapping the glass. The man in the photograph was dressed exactly like Azariah. He even looked like Azariah. From the angle of the photo, you could only see part of his back, but I was pretty sure I made out the edges of a Sachael mark. I frowned. It made no sense.

"You?" I asked, dipping my head in his direction

"No, how can it be?" Azariah snapped. "I told you I never came to land before I left you the shell." I stepped back, surprised by his sharp tone.

"It was just a question," I mumbled, looking around the room for something to focus my attention on.

Azariah moved quickly, kneeling next to Michael and in front of his mother.

"Who is this?" he asked softly, in direct contrast to how he had spoken to me, and placed the framed photograph on her blanket-covered knees.

Michael shifted, twisting to see what Azariah had placed on his mum's knee. His eyes widened. "Who?"

His question went unanswered as his mother raised her hand slowly, touching the side of Azariah's face.

"You're not him, but you look exactly like him. I never thought there'd be another . . . that there were more . . ." She paused but continued touching his face, studying the contours of his features with her fingertips. "Who are you?"

"I am Azariah, and this is Estelle." He looked at me, and she followed his gaze. I ignored Azariah, but smiled at Michael's mum as I walked to the side of her chair. She looked so fragile now that I was close to her.

Azariah placed one of his hands over hers as it rested on his face.

"Is this Michael's father?" he asked, lifting the photograph closer to her face, watching her expression closely.

She nodded, barely glancing at the photo, seemingly hypnotized by Azariah.

"You never told me you had photos of him," Michael said, pushing himself up from his crouched position and breaking the silence of the room. He shuffled back from his mother and stared incredulously at her. "Why didn't you tell me?"

"Only that one," she said, her words quiet as she looked up at him.

"Why did you never show me? I asked about him so many times." He waved his hand at the photograph, and his gaze drifted between his mother and the photo, never settling on either for long. "I know nothing about him apart from the fact he died before I was born." His voice became louder.

"I couldn't tell you. You'd never have believed me." Her gaze softened as she caught Michael's gaze. There was no anger in her response, just a calm statement of the situation.

Azariah stood slowly. He watched Michael for a few seconds and rubbed his chin with his fingers. "Michael," he said softly, placing his hand on the other man's arm. "I think your father was a Sachael."

"No way. Mum, tell him." He pushed Azariah's hand away and stared directly at him. "Just because this photo shows a man dressed in a pair of shorts like you all wear, doesn't mean he's one of you."

"Take a closer look, Michael," Azariah said. "Really *look* at the photograph." He lifted the picture toward Michael, who snatched it from him.

"It's true," Michael's mother said. Her words were quiet, like a confession. But saying them had clearly been like a huge burden lifted from her, as her next words were said with a lightness that defied the seriousness of her secret. "I didn't want to tell you. You had no need to know. But what Azariah says is true. Your father was a Sachael."

"No. No, I don't believe you." Michael pushed one hand through his hair. He stood rigid, shaking his head and taking in the details of the photograph. "I don't believe any of this," he snapped, looking to his mother. "Why didn't you tell me?"

"How could I?" His mother shifted in her chair and reached toward him with shaking hands. Michael stepped forward and crouched down beside her chair. Her eyes filled with tears as he looked up at her.

"I asked what happened to him," Michael said, "so many times. Where he was? What he was like? You always refused to answer me." His voice was quiet, edged with the sorrow of never knowing a father. I could relate to that in some way. Losing my father when I was twelve had had a dramatic effect on everything I did, everyone I met. But to have never known him, to have never spent any time with him and then be confronted with this? I sniffed as quietly as I could, fighting my own tears. I lowered my gaze to the floor, not wanting to witness Michael's sorrow or eavesdrop on such an emotionally charged conversation. They both had so much to say to each other. And his mother needed to explain why she'd kept his father a secret.

"I had to keep you safe," Michael's mum whispered.

"Safe?" he mumbled. "What were you trying to protect me from?"

I frowned at her words. Why had she needed to keep him safe? Had she met Oceanids as well?

"Did he tell you about The Sect?" Azariah asked.

Michael's shoulders stiffened, and he glared at Azariah. His mother turned her attention to Azariah and gave him the same angry look her son had. "I have never heard of The Sect. But he told me of others in the ocean who didn't like his kind. He said it was dangerous for him to travel alone. He chose to live away from the water with me, and our son. I was five months pregnant when he. . . . One evening, on the night of a full moon, he went into the sea . . ." Her voice trailed off again, and she turned back to Michael, grasping his hands tightly as tears trailed down her cheeks. He shifted even closer, leaned across and pulled her into a hug.

"He never came back, did he?" Azariah's voice was full of compassion and understanding.

She shook her head, her wet eyes filling with even more tears. "I know he would never have left me. Menelaus loved me."

Menelaus. The name sounded familiar. I'd heard it before. I glanced at Azariah, about to ask, but when I saw his stiff posture and the gap he had created between himself and Michael's mum, it clicked. Menelaus was one of Azariah's brothers. One who had been killed by The Sect.

Azariah held his hand out to Michael. "Photograph. Please."

Michael huffed and handed it to him.

"Menelaus," he said, staring at the photograph in front of him. "You are certain that was his name?"

She smiled a tight smile, her eyes still glistening with tears. "Yes. That was his Sachael name. I called him Mitch."

This whole situation was unbelievable, but it also explained the closeness I'd felt toward Michael when I was a prisoner. It wasn't because he was my guard; it was because he was a land Sachael—one with no knowledge of what he was, just like Daniel. The image of Daniel, lying on the floor of my room at The Sect's headquarters a week ago, dead, flashed in my mind, and I quickly forced it away. The memory of his begging, scared eyes, of the blood trickling from his mouth, wasn't an image I cared to linger upon. At least he was finally gone.

"I don't believe this," Michael mumbled before rising to his full height. "I'm sorry. I need some air." He ignored all of us as he rushed outside. Azariah's gaze followed him. He appeared torn, as if he couldn't decide whether to stay and find out more about Menelaus, or follow Michael.

"I'll go," I offered.

Azariah nodded, turning back to Michael's mum.

"Would you, please, tell me more about Mene—I mean Mitch . . . ?" Azariah asked softly, his voice fading to a low murmur as I headed toward the door.

"Michael!" I called, stepping outside and looking for him through the laundry pegged on the line.

It didn't take long to spot him. He was leaning on a fence across the yard. I hurried toward him, desperately trying to think of what I would say when I caught up with him. But I couldn't find the words. How could I? This news had shattered him. He looked a lonely figure leaning on that fence, his head dipped toward the ground as he kicked at the earth beneath his feet. He slumped further when I came to stand next to him.

"I'm sorry," I said. They were the only words I could think of to say.

He sighed heavily before lifting his head.

"She should have told me," he mumbled. "I mean, let's forget everything else I've discovered since I met you, but for God's sake, I was in The Sect."

"Michael, I—"

"She should have told me!" he shouted, but it wasn't directed at me. It was said to the expanse of blue ocean that flowed away into the distance.

I followed Michael's gaze across the land and out to sea. It held so many secrets. Ones that people knew, and ones that would never be discovered. The sun wasn't far above the sea's horizon, slowly rising in the morning sky. It held the promise of a new day, an exciting beginning. Not just for me. For Michael as well.

"She should've told me," he repeated, quieter now, the anger gradually washing away.

"Did you ever tell your mum what you were involved with?" I asked, squeezing his hand.

He shook his head.

"I think she kept his secret from you because she didn't understand. She was trying to protect you. My father never told me, either, remember?"

He still didn't look at me. It was as if he was waiting for the sea to give him the answers he so desperately sought. "Maybe he had his reasons," he said.

"In the same way your mother had hers."

Michael sighed. "I don't understand any of this."

"I don't think any of us do."

I glanced toward the building behind us. Azariah would want to know everything about his brother. I contemplated going back inside to make sure everything was okay, but I didn't want to leave Michael alone. I wanted to be here for him as he analyzed what he had just found out. Michael picked at a splintered piece of fence, concentrating on pulling the loose wood free. "My life's turned as crazy as yours," he said. "I've discovered my father was a Sachael, I have a mad Oceanid chasing after me, and I've been dragged through the water for the past few hours by men who swim in the sea." He shook his head, as if denying the insanity of it all. "I mean . . ." He frowned, his jaw slackening. "Oh, shit . . . I . . . my father was a Sachael . . . that means that I'm . . ."

He pushed himself away from the fence. His hands were on the top of his head as he wandered in a small circle and looked up at the sky.

"I don't believe this!" he shouted. "I'm a Sachael, aren't I? I'm a Sachael!"

I was at a loss of what to say to him.

"I can't be a Sachael!" Michael exclaimed before leaning on the fence next to me again. "I just can't. I hate everything about them. They're cruel, and vicious, and nasty. And I'm meant to be one of them? Never!"

"Michael," I said, reaching for his arm. "You don't have to be like them. Just because you were born a Sachael doesn't mean you have to behave like one."

He looked at my hand. "Well, you would say that, wouldn't you? You're one too." His face was flushed, his eyes hard.

I flinched at his ferocity, but quickly composed myself. "And do you think I'm nasty, cruel, and—"

"You know I don't." He looked away.

"And Azariah?"

"He has yet to prove himself. I know you're convinced he's not like the others, but what about his father, his brothers, all of the ones we don't know?"

I understood what he meant. His concerns were also mine.

"I can't change what I am," I said, at last finding some clarity in all the confusion. "I can ignore it, but I can't change it. You can do the same. Ignore that your father was a Sachael, live on land, pretend to be a human. You've done it for twenty-two years, just keep doing it." My words were sharp, harsher than I'd intended.

He sighed, a growl of frustration hovering around the edges of his breath. "I can't. My father was a Sachael. I owe it to him to be what am truly am. I'm sure he'd have brought me up to be like him. He'd have taught me about life as a Sachael, about everything he knew. I have to know more. I *want* to know more. It's just . . . this whole situation. It's crazy."

He looked out over the water again, and I followed his gaze.

"No crazier than the life you were previously living," I said. "And if you don't want to ignore what you were born as, then who says you have to live like they do. Azariah doesn't follow their rules. Perhaps together, you can persuade others. I mean, Azariah's not the only one. Your dad sounds like he was going to stay with your mum. And Azariah told me his other brother, Ammon, didn't believe in the way they lived either."

"So they're not all evil prats." The corner of his mouth lifted, a half attempt at a smile.

"Not all of them." I nudged him with my elbow.

"I should have guessed I was a Sachael," Michael said quietly, focusing his attention back on the piece of fence he'd pulled at earlier. "I've always been obsessed with the ocean. It used to calm me as a child, you know? I sat for hours on the sands, wanting to paddle in the water and just . . . stay there. But even as a child, I recognized that paddling in the sea wasn't enough—I always wanted more. I never knew why I felt that way. When I found out about Oceanids, I actually wondered if I was one of them."

His familiar grin made a quick appearance, and I chuckled at his admittance.

"I wonder what Orontes would make of that?" I said.

"Well, it would be better than him thinking I was a Sachael. He would have killed me if he'd known. I'd have experienced one of those horrendous venom bullets of his."

"Not anymore," I added, remembering that he'd destroyed the lab before we left.

He turned to face me, a grin pulling at his mouth as he pushed his hand into his pocket and lifted out the three golden bullets he'd stolen.

"I meant what I said earlier. I'll wear these as a necklace, and then, if I ever have the misfortune of meeting Orontes again, I will have the venom, and I will kill him. Although, I hope I never see him."

I recognized the fear in his voice. He knew Orontes would kill him if he found him. I was positive he'd not kill me, though. He had other plans where I was concerned. I shivered as I recalled his obsession. But it wasn't fear for myself that worried me, it was the fear for Azariah and Michael. The two men who meant the world to me would be ripped from my life, killed in an impossibly cruel way. I had no doubt that Orontes would make them suffer. He wouldn't give either of them an easy death if he ever caught up with us.

The silence between Michael and me stretched on for minutes as we both stared across the bay. Both of us were lost in our internal thoughts, our memories, and our fears of what was to come. But I'd been here before, feeling this way—scared, and yet excited. Melancholy, yet optimistic. My mother always said that life was an adventure, that it was for living. I smiled as I thought of her, and pushed my negative thoughts aside.

I closed my eyes and took a deep breath. Azariah said he would keep us safe. I had to believe him.

"I don't think Orontes will get close to us again, not now. Azariah won't let him," I said, nodding at the sea. "Not with all those Sachaels in the water."

Michael narrowed his eyes at the unseen men in the sea. "I think they are for your and Azariah's protection, not mine."

"Hey, he made sure you came with us, and he brought you home. He didn't want to leave you."

"But what are his plans now? He won't want to stay here long. I'm sure this is the first place Orontes will look for me, and Azariah knows that." He pushed away from the fence and kicked at the gravel beneath his feet. I linked my arm through his.

"I'm sure Azariah has it all worked out," I said. "Let's go and see what he's up to."

As we walked back toward the house, Michael groaned. "Look at this place. It's a mess. There's a hole in the roof. I really should stay and fix it. Do the jobs that need doing. She obviously can't manage on her own."

"Isn't there anyone nearby who can help her?" I squinted into the distance, attempting to locate any other buildings in the area. There weren't any.

"No. She moved here for a reason. She didn't want to be near others. She always said she didn't trust anyone. I understand why now. She had a lot to hide."

As we neared the house, several chickens strutted across the yard toward us, clucking loudly.

"These need rounding up," Michael said, scratching the back of his head and frowning. "The fence is broken. It's one of the first things I need to fix, otherwise they'll eat Mum's vegetable garden."

I nodded my agreement.

Azariah immediately looked to me and smiled as I opened the door, before turning his attention back to Michael's mum. He was still sitting on the floor, exactly where we'd left him, but he'd obviously moved at some point. The small fire in the hearth had been replaced with a large roaring one that heated every corner of the room. It lit every surface with a warming orange glow.

Azariah stood and held his hand out to me. I hesitated for a brief moment before walking to him. I still hadn't forgotten how he'd snapped at me earlier.

"I am sorry, Estelle. I fear I have ignored you since we arrived." He placed his arm around my waist and kissed my cheek. All traces of his earlier frustration had disappeared. "Morag and I have had an interesting talk."

"Morag?" I asked, turning to Michael's mother for the first time since coming back into the room. My breath hitched, and I stared at her. She looked like a different woman.

"Yes, dear, I'm Morag." She chuckled. The sound spurred Michael toward her.

"Mum? You're laughing?"

She nodded, looking first at Michael, then me, and then finally to Azariah.

"Yes, yes. It's wonderful, isn't it?"

Michael shook his head, a deep frown line visible across his forehead. "But when I left, you were upset; you were crying." He turned to Azariah. "What's going on?"

The glow of the roaring fire danced in Azariah's eyes. He held his hand out to Michael, as if wanting him to shake it. I grinned, remembering the way Michael had shaken his hand when they met on the beach for the first time a few short hours ago. Azariah had appeared amused at the gesture, but here he was, offering the same hand of friendship to Michael.

Michael cautiously took Azariah's hand in his.

"Welcome to the family," Azariah said. "We are related. Not only was your father a Sachael, he was also my brother."

TWO
Family

Michael's mouth fell open, and he jerked backward as if he'd been struck. "What? Mum, is this true?"

"Yes." She smiled at Michael as he strode to her chair.

"But . . . but how? Azariah must be roughly the same age as me. How can my father be his brother?"

"I am twenty-five," Azariah confirmed. "Menelaus was quite a bit older than me. I was only a few years old when he died. My memories of him are limited, but my father always said I look exactly like him."

Michael kept his focus on his mum, but eyed Azariah warily. "I wasn't talking to you," he mumbled.

"It's true," Morag said, leaning forward in her chair toward Michael. "Menelaus was Azariah's brother. We have a family, Michael."

I stepped away from my position at the door and wandered to the small window. I glanced at the yard, the fence where Michael and I had just been, and the ocean beyond. This was one secret it had given up, but there were many more still to discover.

"Azariah's family is also our family. He is your uncle!" Morag chuckled excitedly.

I turned around just as Michael placed his hand to his brow and rubbed his forehead. His eyes were closed as he shook his head.

Azariah turned to face me as silence descended on the room, but he quickly returned his focus to Michael and his mum. The quietness unnerved me. I didn't mind it when I was outside, but inside, surrounded by four walls, it reminded me of being locked up. I focused on the door, and for a brief moment, I saw myself back in the room at The Sect, Orontes's large figure blocking my only escape. I breathed deeply, filling my lungs with clean air. It wasn't real. I screwed my hands into fists, feeling their clamminess. A cold shiver ran down my back, and I forced myself to take the slow, measured breaths that always helped me quell the panic. I shook my head, physically forcing the image from my mind.

"There's not even a glimmer of hope to hang on to, is there? You are certain he's no longer alive?" I focused on Morag, welcoming the sound of her voice. It broke my impending panic.

Azariah sighed before turning to face her. "I am sorry, but my father would know. If Menelaus was alive, he would have found him." His voice became quieter as he spoke, and I knew he was thinking of Elpis. I didn't like the reminder of his death, and I was sure it would be worse for Azariah. I caught his gaze, and he immediately strode across the room to be with me. The days after Elpis's death were hard on both of us, and the revelations that had followed had nearly torn us apart. Azariah's face was etched with obvious sadness, and I reached for his hand and squeezed it tightly.

"I understand," I whispered.

He nodded, but didn't speak.

Michael appeared to have gone into shock, but his mother's expression was the exact opposite—complete tranquility, full of understanding and acceptance. I knew that type of melancholy relief. It came with finally having answers, even if they weren't the ones you'd hoped for.

"So, he's definitely dead?" Michael said softly, once again crouching down in front of his mother.

She nodded as she studied Michael's face. It was the same look my mother had given me in the days after my father's disappearance. It was the look a mother gave her child when she knew the words she had to offer were not what anyone wanted to hear.

"Tell me how he died," Michael said, reaching for her hands.

"I went to the beach in Wick every day after Mitch disappeared," Morag began. "I always hoped he would return. Only he could stop the nightmare I was living in his absence. I sang to him, to the waves, every time. He'd always loved my voice, so I knew that if my singing didn't entice him from the water, he surely wasn't coming back. He said that it was my singing he fell in love with. That my voice was what drew him from the water in the first place. How could it fail to make him return to me if he was alive? I suppose a part of me always knew what had happened to him. But not knowing for sure tore me apart. Was he injured somewhere? Had one of his enemies attacked him? Without answers, I hung on to the thought that perhaps, one day, he would be able to return. That my fears were unfounded. That I'd be wrong."

I raised my hand to my mouth, holding in a gasp at what she'd said. She had still hoped he would return. It was exactly what my mother thought. Suddenly, everything she'd done began to make sense. She had insisted on the room with the sea view so she could watch for any sign of my father. She still lived with the hope he would return for her. Could he still be alive? Was there any chance of it at all? Azariah's hands slowly rubbed the top of my arms. His gentle palms offered reassurance, understanding—a comforting gesture I hadn't realized I needed.

"I know what you're thinking," he whispered.

I swallowed heavily as my emotions took hold. I couldn't think that way. I needed to accept that my father was dead. He wouldn't have left us if he'd had a choice. He'd loved us too much.

Azariah kissed the top of my head before pulling me against his chest and wrapping his arms around me. I sniffed quietly, unable to hold in my tears as I rested my cheek against his shoulder. I gazed through the window at the sea. I couldn't help but wonder what else it's turbulent currents were keeping from us.

"And then *he* started visiting me," Morag continued. The anger in her voice was startling, a direct contrast to the soft-spoken words of before.

"Who?" Michael and Azariah said together.

"A big man. He was tall. He claimed he wasn't the same as Menelaus, although he also came from the sea."

I turned my head, my tears instantly stopping as I caught Michael's eyes. I swallowed nervously. Michael nodded, an unspoken confirmation of the question I hadn't asked, looking anxious as he turned to his mother.

"Mum, did this man have long blond hair?"

Morag nodded. "He frightened me, even though he was nothing but kind. I didn't like what he was saying. He stood there beside me, at the edge of the water, telling horrendous stories about men like your father. He insisted that I didn't know anything. That your father had lied about his love for me, and that he would save me and my child from him."

Azariah flinched, but her words were no surprise to me. I'd already heard much worse from Orontes.

"It's definitely him," I said quietly.

Michael nodded his agreement. "It has to be. That story is exactly what he told me when he recruited me."

"Orontes?" Azariah questioned.

"Yes," I said. "I wonder if he was part of The Sect all those years ago."

"The Sect?" Morag's brows drew together, and she dipped her head forward, toward Michael.

Michael's eyes looked glassy, the tendons on his neck standing out; I could see the faint pulse of his heart as it beat under his skin. Was he panicking? He'd been a part of The Sect, the very group of men who'd wanted his father dead—who wanted all of us dead. He'd said so outside. Nevertheless, he needed to explain this to his mother. She deserved to know the truth.

"Talk to your mother," I told him calmly. "You need to tell her everything."

It wasn't my place, or Azariah's, to tell her.

"Why don't Azariah and I give you some time alone?" I stated, with a sympathetic glance at Michael. This wasn't going to be an easy conversation for him.

I took Azariah's hand and led him toward the door.

"Just one thing," Azariah said, pausing and turning back to Morag. "What did this man do when you gave birth? Was he there, waiting for my brother to return as he'd expected?"

"No." Morag shook her head. "Michael was born here. I left Wick to get away from that man's visits. I didn't trust him and feared what he would do to my child. I never believed that he'd save him. When Michael was born, I suspected he was a Sachael, just like his father. He had the mark on his back. I needed to protect him from those who wanted to harm him."

"That's why you didn't like me even paddling in the ocean?" Michael sank to the floor in front of his mother. He took her hand in his, and she smiled at him.

"Every time you went to the beach, I worried. But you were a child, fascinated with the water and its treasures. It was my mistake in choosing to live so close to the sea, but I couldn't move away from it completely. There was always the chance that Menelaus would return."

"You have a lot to talk about," Azariah said softly, before he slowly turned and took the few steps remaining for us to be outside.

"I feel so sorry for Morag," I said, as the brisk, fresh air swept around us. "She reminds me of my mother. Neither of them has ever gotten over the loss of the man they loved."

"It seems we are hard to forget."

I silently agreed. He reached for my hand, entwining our fingers as we walked across the yard. This was the first time we had been alone since we arrived on Hoy, and I leaned into him, wanting more than just his hand for comfort. A soft chuckle escaped him and he released my hand and placed his arm across my shoulders. I slipped my arm around his back, relaxing in the closeness we now had.

"Although, I would like to add something to that," Azariah continued. "When a Sachael falls in love, he would never recover from losing the woman he loved, either. I have faced that situation—weeks of worry, with you snatched away from me. If something had happened to you . . ." His words trailed away, and he shook his head as if ridding himself of memories he struggled to forget.

"But it didn't. I'm safe."

I squeezed my arm around his waist, hoping to ease his worries. I needed to have contact with him, feel his skin against mine, however innocent the touch. It made him real, not just another dream. I tilted my face toward him, studying his profile against the brightness of the sun. He was here, we were back together. I could hardly believe it. Being in his presence relaxed me, made me calm. And it wasn't just his Sachael magic. There was a tightness in my stomach, a longing to be next to him, and an unstoppable urge to throw myself on him. I was giddy, stupidly happy that he was here. I didn't want to let him out of my sight.

"Come on," I said excitedly, slipping away from his hold and grabbing both his hands. I walked backwards, leading him across a lush green patch of grass. "Let's explore a bit."

We made our way around to the back of the house, and Azariah caught sight of the chickens.

"What are those?" he asked, grinning with nervous curiosity, not taking his eyes off them.

"Chickens."

"I have never seen such a creature before. They are strange looking." His pace slowed, but I tightened my hold on his hands and pulled him across the yard where the chickens strutted and scratched the earth.

I grinned. "Wait until you see cows and horses."

Azariah huffed a slightly uncomfortable chuckle, moving quickly across the yard as the chickens strutted toward us. I giggled at his antics, realizing there would be many things for him to experience and see now that he was living out of the water.

At the side of the yard was a wooden gate that led to the fields beyond. There'd be no chickens in there to worry him. Our destination sorted, I released one of his hands and shifted next to his side, keeping a tight hold of the one hand I still held.

"It's beautiful here, isn't it?" I said, as we approached the gate.

"It is. Unfortunately, we will need to move tomorrow. Orontes will be looking for us, and he will bring many men with him in his quest to kill Michael and me. I have no doubt that he will still be obsessed with you." He sighed loudly. "I suspect Michael's home will be the first place they will look for him, and us."

Orontes. The images in my head danced to life every time he was mentioned, bringing varying stages of panic with them. I pushed them aside, easily this time, determined not to let any thought of Orontes spoil my time with Azariah.

Azariah released my hand and opened the heavy wooden gate. We were greeted with a golden carpet of flowers. The field was full of buttercups; their intense yellow glowing in the morning sun. It was stunning.

"The colors are as bright as the ones in Saicean," Azariah said, his eyes brightening at the sight.

"Tell me what it's like there," I said, moving through the gap between the fence and the gate. "Are things really different? What will I be the most shocked about?"

Azariah laughed loudly as he shut the gate. "Probably my father."

"Seriously," I insisted. "I want to know what it's like." I tucked my hair behind my ears, desperate to hear more about the world he was from. The world I was meant to become part of.

"I am being serious. My father is a frightening man. He does not like to be challenged."

"But you've challenged him." Why did it always come back to his father?

"Yes, but I had a very strong reason to do so." The full force of his gaze hit me. Eyes sparkling with hidden desire pinned me to the spot.

"And what was that?" I asked, my voice weak, breathy.

"You." He smiled, releasing me from his gaze before gesturing to a corner of the field. "Let us go and sit over there."

Azariah turned away, and I followed his lead across the field. Once at the spot he had chosen, we both sank to the ground, and Azariah leaned back, lying on the blanket of yellow. He placed his hands behind his head and gazed at the sun. I breathed deeply, enjoying the relaxed atmosphere between us. It was as if the time I was kept away from him never existed. Time had moved on, but we hadn't.

I picked one of the buttercups and placed it under his chin.

"What are you doing?" He grinned, his curiosity stirred.

"It's something my father used to do with me," I explained. "If the flower makes your chin glow yellow, then it's a sign you like butter."

"Butter?"

I laughed as I dropped the flower. "I can't believe you've never heard of butter! It's made from milk, from cows."

He smiled even more, shaking his head. "I think there are lots of things I have never heard of concerning life on land. There are many strange customs and activities here." He pushed himself up onto his elbows before picking a buttercup and placing the flower under my chin. "You did not say if the flower showed whether I like butter or not. This is telling me you like it. I can see the yellow glow."

I nodded. "You do like butter, even though you've never tasted it. The flower never lies."

I giggled as I shifted my position to lie beside him. He dropped back down onto the flowers, and I rested my head on his chest.

One of his hands curled around my waist, his fingers circling my skin, while the other played with my hair. I closed my eyes, reveling in his touch. It was these small gestures that I'd missed the most. The way we were so comfortable around each other. It was as if we'd never been apart.

"Saicean is a beautiful world," Azariah said, his voice distant, lost in the memories of his home. "The colors are bright and vivid, exactly as your father painted them. The seven moons constantly light our sky, and the lake in Saicean has the clearest water I have ever seen. It glistens in the glow from the moons. Some of us live in caves—homes carved into the sides of our world. Some are grand; others are quite basic. And others live in wooden huts dotted throughout the slopes leading down to the lake."

"It sounds amazing," I said lazily. The effect of Azariah twisting my hair between his fingers, and the warmth of his touch on my skin made me feel sleepy, almost as if I was being hypnotized. I trailed my fingers over his chest, circling them across the taut surface as he continued talking.

"I cannot wait for you to see it. But the most important thing about Saicean is that it is safe, Estelle. When we get there, we will be free from this constant threat hanging over us."

"I'd feel safe with you wherever we were," I told him, turning my head to look directly at him. "Nothing can touch us now that we're together again."

Azariah smiled before lifting his head to place a gentle kiss on my forehead. "Your faith in me is flattering, but unfounded. My father would never have let me attempt to rescue you by myself."

"But you brought all the others. No Oceanid would dare attack that many Sachaels."

He slowly pulled himself into a sitting position, his action forcing me to sit up as well. The buttercups tickled my feet, and the breeze made itself known again, carrying the fresh saltiness of the sea in its airborne dance around us. But I felt like I was in a bubble with Azariah, one that no one could burst.

A deep frown wrinkled Azariah's forehead.

"I have so much to tell you. I do not know where to begin." He was serious, speaking slowly, choosing his words carefully.

"I thought you'd already told me what I needed to know." I was instantly confused. The bubble I had visualized popped. Had he kept things from me? Why? And more importantly, what?

"I have told you what you needed to know, but not everything you should know."

It was my turn to frown. I picked at the flowers growing around me, stripping petals from each flower, not looking at him. How quickly my calmness disappeared. My stomach twisted, and a new fear developed within me. Now what was he going to tell me? His obvious apprehension made me surmise that it would be something I didn't like. I frowned in concentration as I pulled another petal from the buttercup. I didn't want to feel like this, on edge, jittery every time he mentioned something new.

"My father would only let me travel to Ravenscar to rescue you if I brought an army of Sachaels with me."

"An army?" I dropped the buttercup and looked up at him. "Those men in the bay?"

He nodded.

"They are but one of his armies, ordered to protect you, and me. They are swimming off shore at this very moment, ready to risk their own lives for ours. My father hates that I am bewitched by you, but now that he knows you are a Sachael, he is cautiously optimistic for our future."

"Do all Sachaels have armies?" My fear had gone and was replaced by curiosity. This was nothing serious. It was good news. We had people to protect us—an army, even.

Azariah shook his head and looked away. "No, but my father does. He gave the order for the men in the bay to come with me. Sometimes, it can be useful to have Kaimi as a father." He grinned as he turned back to face me, but the gesture wasn't genuine. I eyed him suspiciously, and he chuckled—nervous.

"What else are you hiding?" I said, my brows furrowing with accusation.

He didn't answer me straight away, and I widened my eyes, waiting.

"I'm not hiding anything from you, Estelle." He leaned toward me, and his smoldering expression returned. "All you need to know is that we are safe. I am in charge of the army while we are on land. Once we travel to Saicean, we will not need them."

One of his hands settled comfortably around my waist again, while the other trailed slowly up my neck. I sighed deeply, relaxing as his gaze followed the journey of his fingers. He wasn't being fair. He was still withholding information, but he knew how intoxicating his touch was to me.

"Never take this off, Estelle, never," he said, as his fingers curled around the single pearl of my necklace. "Whatever happens, keep wearing this. It is my link to you."

"And what link do I have to you?" I murmured. "What have you got of mine that links us?"

"This," he said as he placed his palm over my chest. "I have your heart. And I promise I will treasure it for the rest of my life."

His eyes drank me in, and I wanted to drown in their gaze as they rested upon me. My heart beat faster, my chest rising and falling under his hand. The moment was perfect, so perfect. I wanted him in every way imaginable, needed to feel his body on mine, to chase away the shadows haunting my mind with his love.

"Azariah," I whispered. "Please . . . make love to me."

A bewitching smile pulled at his lips. "I will, I promise. But not now, not here."

"But it's perfect," I said as he moved his hand away. Why was he refusing me?

"Estelle, any moment I am alone with you is perfect. I am not refusing your request completely. I am only asking you to wait a little longer." He scratched the back of his neck, glancing away for a brief second before returning the full force of his attention on me.

I returned his gaze, unwilling to back down. I didn't understand. Did he need to be the one who instigated the moment? Was that the problem?

"Believe me, I am more than eager. But I will not rush this with you. What we have together is so special. I want us to be in Saicean. I want us to be safe. If I make love to you now, I will not be alert enough to sense danger approaching. I do not want a few quick, snatched moments with you. I want a whole evening with you in my arms, immersing myself in your scent, your body, your very being. Please, let us wait a little longer. We have a tough few months ahead of us."

"Months," I gasped, straightening up. "All the more reason for us to grab this opportunity while we can. Azariah, please, I need this."

"No. Estelle, please. This is how it has to be for me."

I couldn't speak. I'd lost the ability to even think. His words were not what I wanted to hear, but I had to agree that they made sense. The idea of spending a whole evening making love. . . . I smirked before realizing that, unfortunately, it would be a very long time in the future.

I sighed heavily, but nodded my concession. "Okay."

He was serious, watching my every move, my every breath. "Thank you for understanding."

"I understand, but I don't like it," I told him, shifting my body so that I faced him.

He grinned at my stubborn response.

"And don't expect me not to ask again, or try to persuade you otherwise," I added, grinning as he slowly shook his head, his laughter continuing.

"I would be disappointed if you did not try to change my mind," he teased, leaning forward and capturing my lips with his. His hands meandered up my arms before caressing my neck, and I shivered in delight as his thumbs rubbed my gills behind my ears. "Do they still hurt?" he asked.

I shook my head, only slightly, but it was enough of a response. They were still sore, but they didn't hurt, and the feel of his fingertips caressing such a sensitive area far outweighed any discomfort.

We continued kissing slowly, savoring our blissful moment. I trailed my hands over his body, purposely skimming his chest with my fingertips before moving lightly across his shoulders. I followed his action, touching the raised red line in the crease of his ear. He moaned with pleasure as he continued to kiss me, and I gasped in surprise when he pulled me onto his body before rolling on top of me. Breaking our kiss, he gazed down at me. I returned his intense look, breathing heavily. His eyes flitted from my lips to my eyes, as if he was undecided on whether to look at me or continue kissing me, and when a smile spread across his face, I grinned.

"Maybe I was a little hasty with my decision to wait until we get to Saicean," he said.

I grinned even more and kissed him. My fingers curled into his hair as his roamed along the sides of my body, slipping under my t-shirt. I relaxed as he slowly caressed my bare flesh. Maybe he *had* changed his mind.

"Estelle! Azariah!" Michael's voice pierced the air. We both froze. Azariah groaned, his head sinking down next to mine. I smiled, realizing he hadn't moved his hands from their position on my body. But the moment was short-lived, as he then slipped them out from my t-shirt and propped himself up on his forearms, hovering over me.

"I should not have let myself get carried away. I apologize."

I kissed his nose before giving him an exasperated pout. "You'll do no such thing, Mr. Sachael. I happened to like what you were doing. I grant you permission to do it again, whenever you want."

He kissed me one more time, and then pushed himself off me. Sitting up, he waved at Michael across the field.

"You do realize that when we leave here in the morning, Michael will be with us constantly," he said. "How do you endeavor to find the solitude we need to repeat such an action?" Azariah sounded hopeful, as if he actually did want a solution to his question.

I trailed my fingers across his arm, thinking of a response. "There'll be times when we're alone. Michael won't be with us constantly. He'll give us time to ourselves," I said as I sat up next to him.

"Perhaps."

I pulled my t-shirt into place before running my fingers through my hair, trying to tame the scrunched up mess Azariah's fingers had created. "Do I look decent enough?" I asked. "We can't have Michael thinking we've been up to anything."

His smile faded.

"I like it when you look ruffled," he explained.

I immediately fluffed my hair, undoing what I'd done to fix it.

"Consider me ruffled." I laughed, catching his shocked expression. He shook his head, trying not to laugh as Michael approached us.

"Hey, Uncle," Michael called as he stood a short distance away.

I laughed even more as Azariah growled at Michael's statement.

"Mum needs our help. There's a bit of work for us to do here. She needs things fixed, and the chickens rounded up; they've escaped."

Azariah shuddered. "I'll help you with whatever she needs fixed. Estelle can sort the chickens."

I smirked at his reply. Did the chickens really worry him that much?

"Sounds like a great idea," Michael said before casting a sly smile at me. "What exactly were you two doing out here?"

"Talking," Azariah immediately responded, too quick.

"Right." Michael smirked before turning his back to us and starting to walk away. "Yeah, well, finish 'talking' and come to the house whenever you're ready to help out."

"We will be with you shortly," Azariah called after him.

"No, we won't." I grabbed Azariah, catching him off guard as I pulled him close for another kiss.

"Estelle, no, I . . ." His sentence remained unfinished as our lips met. He didn't pull away or rush the kiss, but as soon as our lips parted, he backed away from me. I stared at him as he scrambled to his feet.

"I know you think I am a man of honor, capable of showing great restraint and living by my high morals and words. But I am fast losing all sight of being honorable with you. My restraint is crumbling, and my morals are dissolving faster than I can swim."

Tipping his face to the sun, he sighed, hard and heavy, before turning his attention back to me.

"I retract my earlier decision about waiting until we get to Saicean. It will not be possible to resist you for that length of time."

My pulse quickened. He had said the words I desperately wanted to hear.

But then reached his hand out to pull me up from the carpet of buttercups, and his eyes refused to meet mine as I searched for clarification of his statement.

"Come on," he said, shooting me a nervous smile as he strode after Michael. "We need to help Morag."

He didn't wait for me, and I followed slowly, not willing to match his exuberant pace. How could something so perfect be pulled away so quickly? I stared at the back of the man who had stolen my heart and contemplated what our future held for us. Lies and half-truths seemed to float around and punch us in the face when we least expected it. Azariah may be used to that—I wasn't. This wasn't how I wanted to live, on the run and hiding from someone who had his own agenda for all of us. I kicked at the flowers beneath my feet before lifting my head and taking several deep breaths of the salty air around me. It was time I grew up, time I faced whatever awaited me.

I was a survivor, and, like Michael, I owed it to my father to find out more about what he was. I was a Sachael, a fearless creature from deep in the ocean. It was about time I started to behave like one.

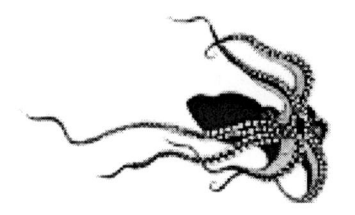

THREE
Fixing

The rest of our day was busy. Michael and Azariah worked to mend the leaking roof on the house, while Morag and I dealt with the interior. There were pools of water in the kitchen and the bedroom, and the only hospitable room was the one we were in earlier, which explained the mattress and blankets I'd noticed in the corner.

I hated seeing how Morag lived. Everything was in a state of disrepair. It wasn't just the house. There were also broken fences and dilapidated walls around the exterior of her home.

She'd gone beyond struggling-to-manage and had clearly given up.

There was so much work for Michael and Azariah to do that it took most of the day. It was hard, manual work, demanding all of their physical strength. I lost count of the number of times I found myself staring at Azariah as he worked alongside Michael. His bare torso was on constant display, and I knew I should be used to seeing him in just his shorts, but my time away from him had only increased my desire. The dark, dirty smears covering his chest made him even more appealing, and I sighed wistfully over his earlier decision. I was never able to observe him unnoticed for long, though; he seemed to have an inner sense, alerting him to when I was ogling his body. And I reveled in his attention, loving the silent interactions between us.

Morag insisted she make a nourishing, thick soup for us all to eat when Michael and Azariah had finished working, so I helped her collect vegetables from the small garden and engaged her in small talk while we prepared them.

"Morag," I said, chopping the herbs we'd picked—fresh basil and coriander. "Will you be okay when we go?" She was the thinnest woman I had ever seen, the layers of clothes barely disguising her body.

"Yes, you have no need to worry about me, dear. I know you'll travel away to keep safe. And I am well aware that Orontes may call to see me. I may look fragile, but I have a fierce heart . . . and a big gun." She nodded in the direction of a large upright cupboard. "He won't get any useful information from me. Azariah has promised he will keep Michael safe. I believe him." She stirred the pan containing the vegetables we'd cooked earlier, and then turned the temperature dial to a low setting.

"But Orontes—"

"I'll be fine," she said, wiping her hands on her apron. "I have a few friends on the island. And when you leave, I may visit one of them. It would make sense for me not to be here when Orontes arrives."

I nodded. It was the right decision. A confrontation with Orontes, whether she had a gun or not, was best avoided. That familiar shiver ran down my spine, the one that always accompanied the mention of his name. We needed to get away from here as soon as possible. Azariah was right. Rackwick Bay would be the first place Orontes would visit when he discovered our escape. Cold fear swept through me as I recalled Orontes's threatening words, his promise of a life together beneath the waves. I knew he didn't have any real feelings for me, that they were all based on the attraction between Oceanids and Sachaels, but that didn't make them any less dangerous.

"I'll go and stay with James," Morag said, shifting the prep board away from me and tipping the chopped herbs into the simmering mixture in the pan. "He'll more than welcome a woman who can cook, and I think he's quite fond of me."

I smiled as I listened to Morag's chatter and busied myself with washing the dirty pots we'd stacked up in the sink.

"Does he live far away?" I recalled looking for other houses earlier, but not seeing any.

"Just a five-minute drive. He supplies the propane gas canisters that run the stove. He pops down once a month."

"So he's seen how you live? Couldn't he have fixed the roof for you, or sorted the fence?" I didn't understand how any man could visit and leave without helping her.

She tutted at my question and reached for a spoon to stir the soup. "He's in a worse state than me. He can hardly walk, never mind climb a ladder."

"But you said he brought the gas canisters. They're pretty large, and they look heavy."

"He doesn't lift them off the van. I do." She laughed. "He'd never manage it."

I sighed. I didn't think I could ever live like she did. But then I realized I'd been prepared to do exactly that only a few months ago. Wasn't Ravenscar similar to here? There were no houses near where I lived, either. They were all a good walk away. And I'd have stayed there quite happily, living a reclusive life next to the sea.

"This soup is nearly ready," she said. "Why don't you go and tell them it's time to eat?"

I removed the last of the soapy dishes from the sink and placed it on the draining board before heading outside. Even though the day was ending, the sun slipping low in the sky, it was still bright, and I had to shield my eyes from the hazy glare. I could only see Michael, leaning against the same fence we'd stood at this morning.

"Where's Azariah?" I asked as I approached.

"He went to the beach."

I scanned the area but was still unable to see him.

"I'm sure he won't be long," he said, probably picking up on my concern.

I continued to look for him, anxious about his safety. Even though there was an army of Sachaels in the bay, I didn't like that he had gone there alone. He'd only seen Orontes from afar; he didn't know how strong he was.

"Hey," Michael walked over to me, placing his arm across my shoulders. "Don't worry. He'll be fine."

I rested my head against his shoulder. "It's going to be like this from now on, isn't it? All this worry and fear about getting caught?"

He sighed before answering me. "Yes. It seems so . . . but we'll be fine. We just have to be careful and keep one step ahead of Orontes. I think that's why Azariah's gone to the beach. He mentioned Chanon before he wandered off."

I nodded. It was difficult to forget the man with the damaged face. I wondered if Chanon was the leader of the army. His wounds signified that he had been in at least one ferocious battle, and Azariah had trusted him to travel with Michael when we swam here.

I pulled away from Michael's hold, turning my back to the sea before jumping up to sit on the fence. I tried to forget about the constant worry hanging over us. I didn't want to dwell on Orontes and what lay ahead of us, but it was hard.

"Your mum says the soup's ready," I said, focusing on something different. "It smells delicious."

"She always did make good soups," he said, leaning over the fence. "Although, I remember her putting chicken in them." He looked to me and grinned before pushing himself away from the fence. He turned and rested his back against it.

I glanced over my shoulder at the path leading to the beach. Azariah was coming back. I tried to assess whether he had good or bad news based on his posture. As he approached, his determined walk turned into a jog.

"Did you speak to Chanon?" I asked as he jumped over the gate.

"Yes. I have news I need to share with you and Michael." He stepped over to me, brushing up against my legs.

"Is something wrong?" Michael asked, stepping away from the fence.

Azariah nodded. "We need to leave as soon as possible. Orontes is on his way."

"It'll be a while before he gets here, then. It's a heck of a journey by road and ferry," I said, longing for the comfort of at least one night in Azariah's arms, safe and warm. We could leave tomorrow, first thing. Orontes would still be miles away.

"He's swimming here, Estelle, not driving," Azariah said.

"But he's not allowed. He's banned from the water. He told me Hebrus banned him years ago." I stared at Azariah, confused.

"Seems he has no regard for Hebrus's orders." Azariah shot his gaze to the sea, his customary frown making another appearance. "It doesn't surprise me."

I jumped down from the fence. "We need to leave, then. Now!" If Orontes was swimming, then he'd be here a lot quicker than by road. Azariah grabbed my hand, halting my rushed escape to the house. "Chanon says he will be here by midday tomorrow."

"What do you mean? How does he know? How do you know? No, scrap that. How do any of you know what Orontes is doing? He could be five minutes away. I can't believe we haven't already left!" I pulled against Azariah's hold, ready to run. I had no idea where I'd run to, but we couldn't stay here.

Azariah smiled at my torrent of questions and pulled me to his chest. He kissed my forehead. "Oh, Estelle, do you think we would still be here if there was an immediate danger to you? To any of us? I left some of the army in the water at Ravenscar so they could alert us to Orontes's movements once he was in the water."

"But how do they get their messages to you? I know you are faster than Oceanids, but surely not that fast?"

Azariah rubbed my shoulders.

"You still question our speed?" His smile turned into a full grin before he brought his fingers to my forehead and tapped my skin. "We speak to each other through our minds. It is how we communicate in the water."

"Telepathy?" My head buzzed with this newfound information. Telepathy in the water—it made sense. Sachaels were designed for a life in the ocean, swimming freely as they traveled. Of course they would need to communicate with each other.

"Well, sort of. We can block our thoughts if we choose. It would be too noisy in our heads if we heard everyone. At the moment, the Sachaels in the water are only communicating this way if it is news that affects us. Chanon is acting as my ears while he is in the bay and I am on land. He listens to what the others at Ravenscar are saying. Orontes left a short time ago. Apparently, he didn't look happy."

I stared at Azariah, my expression one of sardonic disbelief. "Are you surprised? After what we did?"

"You always said he'd come here first," Michael reasoned, chewing on a fingernail. "Where do we go? The sea isn't the safest place to be at the moment, if Orontes is in it. I don't fancy him charging up behind me in the water."

"As much as I do not like the idea, we will travel over land," Azariah replied, dismayed by his own suggestion.

Morag joined us, looking concerned at our topic of conversation.

"But how?" I exclaimed. "We'll not get far by walking. Surely we need to put a bit of space between us and here, and fast."

"I can help with that," Morag offered. "My old van. The one I used to drive when we traveled to the other islands, Michael. You can take that. It's not fast, but it will be quicker than walking."

Michael grinned at his mother. "Brilliant!" he said before pulling her in for a hug.

Azariah's eyes widened at her suggestion. "A van?"

"Clothes!" Michael suddenly exclaimed, releasing his mother from his arms "We all need at least one change of clothes."

"Clothes? Surely you do not expect *me* to wear them?" Azariah snapped.

"Of course I do. They'll spot you a mile off dressed like that. You don't blend in. You'll need to wear normal clothes when we're traveling." He turned to his mother. "Mum, can you grab some clothes for Estelle. I'll sort myself and Azariah. He's pretty much the same size as me; we'll share."

"Of course. I've got some spare jumpers and cardigans. They might be a squeeze, but I'm sure they'll be okay." She hurried back inside with Michael following.

Azariah rubbed the back of his neck before twisting the cord on his necklace.

"I never expected Orontes to move this quickly," he said. "Perhaps coming here was not my best idea."

"Of course it was," I said, moving in front of him, "Look at what you've discovered. We'd not know any of it if we hadn't come here." I pulled him into a hug. I hated seeing him like this. Everything he had done, he had done to keep us safe. We were leaving now. It was the right decision. We'd all be long gone by the time Orontes arrived.

"I know. But do you think any of it matters if you get caught? I would prefer to know none of it and be safe somewhere with you."

"But what about Michael? Surely you wouldn't want him to have to fend for himself."

His piercing blue eyes stared into mine.

"Estelle, you are my priority. Never think otherwise. I will kill anyone who tries to harm you in any way. I hope I do not ever need to prove it to you, though. I hate speaking about this to you," he whispered. "You see me for what I am, and it concerns me. You may not like what you hear."

"I understand." It was the truth. I did understand, but I didn't like it. He sometimes sounded like a completely different person to the one I thought I knew.

"Everything will work out. It is only two weeks until the next full moon." He shifted his gaze to look over my shoulder at the same time I heard Michael and his mother talking behind me. I turned around to see Michael carrying two stuffed duffel bags. A pale blue jumper flew through the air toward us, and Azariah caught it.

"Put it on!" Michael shouted.

Azariah screwed his nose up at the item of clothing but did as directed. I was stunned when I saw him in the jumper. The color of it intensified that of his eyes, as well as his tanned skin. The deep V-neck hinted at the body underneath, a tease of toned muscles.

"I've found some old sandals for you as well. You can't go around barefoot," Michael said, coming to stand before us, his mother a few steps behind.

"I am." I motioned to my feet. Why couldn't we wander around with bare feet?

"I think I will forego the kind offer of footwear, and join Estelle in her expression of bare feet. Perhaps you should do the same?"

I chuckled at Azariah's words. I loved the way he spoke, but sometimes he sounded so formal.

Michael tutted at our united agreement, dropping the duffel bags on the ground.

"Let's have a look at the van," he said before turning his back on us and walking to the barn.

Azariah picked up the bags from where Michael had dropped them, and we followed his rushed stroll across the yard. We were right behind him when he unlocked the heavy doors. He swung them open before running inside and pulling a grey plastic sheet free from the vehicle underneath.

"I cannot travel in that," Azariah protested. His eyes were wide, and he stepped backward as he took in the appearance of the white van. I didn't blame him for his reaction. I wasn't too keen on the state of the vehicle either. There were numerous areas of rust covering the bodywork, and in parts, the outer shell was completely missing.

"Does it actually move?" I said, turning to Morag.

"Yes, I travel to the Mainland in it when necessary. But I don't go often." She patted the van like others patted their family pet.

"It's perfect," Michael stated, rushing to the driver's door.

"The keys are in the ignition. There should be at least half a tank of petrol in it," Morag said as she continued to run her hands across the front of the van.

Michael turned the key, and the van spluttered to life. Several loud bangs blasted as it backfired, and Azariah stepped even further away from the rumbling white monster.

"It'll be okay," I reassured him. "And it's the only way for us to travel safely."

"Safely? The sea would be a better choice for me. I would much prefer to take my chances out there than in this . . . this . . . van."

"Are you two coming?" Michael shouted above the roar of the engine.

Azariah gave a nervous smile. "It seems I have many new things to experience while I live on your land. I hope they are not all as worrying as this," he mumbled.

"It'll be fun," I said, grabbing his arm and guiding him to the passenger side of the vehicle. "Count it as one of those land experiences you were talking about earlier."

Michael revved the engine as we approached the passenger door and grinned at Azariah. Unfortunately, Azariah didn't share his humor and clenched his jaw, frowning at Michael.

He dropped both duffel bags on the ground before lifting his hand to the silver door handle of the van and pulling. His angry expression changed to one of satisfaction as the door swung open.

"I never expected it to be so easy," he said. "Are all vehicles the same?"

"They're all similar," I responded, picking up the bags and heading to the back of the van. I opened up the back doors and threw the bags in before banging them shut and returning to Azariah. He dipped his head as I jumped into the front seat.

"I would have put them in the back if you'd told me that was where they were going," he said as he climbed in next to me.

As soon as Azariah pulled the door shut, Michael released the handbrake next to my leg. The van lurched forward and onto the dirt-covered track before slowly heading toward where Morag stood.

"This is a nightmare," Azariah said. "I have never experienced the feeling of something mechanical carrying me around before. I cannot say that I like it."

"Oh, behave." Michael chuckled as he yanked the handbrake back on and switched the engine off. He jumped out and hugged his mother, whispering words to her.

"I'm sure we won't be traveling for long," I reassured Azariah.

"I hope not, Estelle. I am concerned as to how fast this thing will go."

"Not as fast as you can in the water."

"That is true." He placed his arm across my shoulder, and I snuggled into his side.

Michael sprang back into the driver's seat, closing his door behind him. Azariah frowned and leaned across me and Michael toward the open window. "I insist you come with us, Morag. It is not safe for you to stay here. Orontes is on his way."

She shook her head. "I'll be fine. James will be calling soon. I'll invite myself to stay at his place for a while. Well, until this all blows over anyway."

"James?" Azariah glanced at me.

"The gas man," I explained.

Michael chuckled, as did I.

"I have no idea what you are on about, Estelle," Azariah said. "But as long as Morag is safe, then I am happy."

"And I have my gun," she said, nodding at me. "I know how to use it, and if Orontes gives me any problems, I'll fill him with lead."

Michael laughed even louder, but I didn't share his enthusiasm.

"And you're sure James will call tonight?" I asked.

She nodded. "He's always on time. I could set my watch by him." She glanced at her wrist and grinned. "He'll be here in exactly half an hour. Now, you all get going so I can pack a few things before he arrives. And don't forget these."

She stepped up to the van and handed two large flasks through the window.

"The soup," she said. "When you eventually stop for the night, you'll have something warm to eat."

Michael took the flasks from her before placing them on the floor at mine and Azariah's feet.

"Thank you, Morag," Azariah said. "It has been a pleasure to meet you."

"And you, Azariah, Estelle. Thank you for telling me things I had long ago given up hope of ever knowing. And thank you for bringing Michael home, even for a short time. You must take care of each other. And when you can, when it is safe, please come back and visit."

"We will." Azariah sounded confident it would happen.

Morag stepped back from the van and pulled her shawl around the top of her shoulders. The frail-looking woman who greeted us when we first arrived had returned. I closed my eyes and prayed that James would be here as she expected.

Michael started the van up again and we moved forward. Azariah's arm tightened around my shoulders as Michael drove us along the bumpy track and toward the road.

"Where exactly are we heading?" Azariah asked.

"Melia's," Michael responded, pulling a piece of paper from his pocket. "Mum kept the letters she sent me. Apparently, she moved six months ago, but I've got her new address."

"Melia?" Azariah asked.

"His ex-girlfriend," I clarified, stunned that Michael would want to see her after the way he'd explained the end of their fiery relationship.

Azariah raised his eyebrows at my explanation. It seemed I wasn't the only one who was unsure of Michael's choice. I wondered how she would greet the arrival of her ex-boyfriend and two strangers.

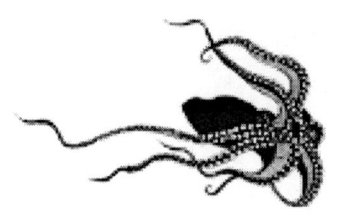

FOUR
Run

The van rumbled noisily as we traveled the narrow roads winding between the steep hills of Hoy. We saw no other traffic, no twinkling headlights of other cars as the evening began to settle in. Azariah shifted in his seat, looking increasingly uncomfortable as we headed away from the sea. He was hunched up, as if trying to make himself as small as possible. His hands kept curling into fists and then straightening, and he constantly scoured the view from the front and side windows. I took in the views outside; it was a beautiful, but barren landscape. I only saw one house, and that was far away in the distance. I focused, like Michael, on the road ahead, but regularly looked up to Azariah, who was showing no signs of his nervousness disappearing.

"Where does Melia live?" Azariah asked, his words clipped as he turned to Michael.

"On the Mainland," Michael said. "At the Bay of Skaill. Have you heard of it?"

"No." He shook his head. "Which part of the Mainland is it on?"

"The west side. It's a beautiful sandy bay. Mum took me there when we traveled the islands. There's a tourist spot—the Skara Brae." Michael chuckled. "I can't believe Melia's moved there. It's so quiet."

"And how exactly will we get there in this van? I presume we have water to cross."

Michael nodded and shot Azariah a grin. "We catch a ferry."

"We are to travel on a boat?" Azariah sat upright, his eyes wide.

"Hey, it's okay. At least you'll be out in the open," I said, shifting in the seat and stretching my legs out in front of me.

"How else do you think we get there? Swim?" Michael chuckled again, and then shook his head. "No, don't answer that."

Azariah slumped back into his seat and reached his arm across my shoulders. I sank into his hold, but it wasn't comforting. He was tense, his muscles hard and unforgiving.

I wrapped my arm around his waist. "We're getting away from Orontes, and that's what matters," I said. "We'll get settled for the night, and then you can go into the water."

He pulled me closer, kissing the top of my head.

"That's the reason I'm rushing," Michael said, tutting as he looked at the dashboard. "I wouldn't usually drive this fast, but we need to catch the last ferry to Stromness. Otherwise, we'll be staying on Hoy for the night. I don't know about you two, but I want to put as much distance as possible between Orontes and us. Not getting away from Hoy would be a big mistake."

As if to accentuate his point, the van found another lease of life, roaring loudly.

"How long before we get to the ferry terminal?" I said, understanding the rush. Michael wasn't the only one who wanted to get as far away from Orontes as possible.

"The ferry leaves from Moaness at half past nine. That's in twenty minutes."

"And how long will we be traveling for?" I heard the unease in Azariah's question.

"Not long. Look, there." Michael grinned as we turned a corner on the road and pointed toward the windscreen. Before us was a stunning view of the sea, an island clearly visible in the distance. I spotted what I presumed to be the port of Moaness, and, more importantly, the ferry. Its bright lights twinkled in the subdued light of early evening.

"The ferry ride is about half an hour," Michael said, sounding like a tour guide. "But that depends on the roughness of the sea."

"It is calm this evening," Azariah stated.

"Do you think that's far enough for us to go?" I asked, catching Azariah's gaze. "Maybe we should travel further." I didn't like the idea of only being half an hour from Orontes.

"We're heading to Melia's, remember? Her home is a fair distance from Stromness. We won't arrive there until late."

"Maybe we should stop somewhere for the night, then," Azariah offered, his voice flat, uncommitted.

"Where?" Michael asked, flicking a quick glance at Azariah.

"Is there a beach we can stay on?" I asked, slipping away from Azariah's arm and leaning forward in the seat. I searched in the glove compartment for a map.

"Yes," Azariah agreed, instantly brightening and straightening up in his seat. "Do you know of any beaches that would offer us some form of protection? A hidden bay, perhaps?"

Michael frowned, nodding at the creased and crumpled map I'd found. "I'll have a look at that when we get on the ferry. Are you sure you don't want to go straight to Melia's?"

Azariah smiled. "Far be it for me to assume anything about your relationship with Melia, but I feel your appearance will be enough of a shock to her. The fact that you will be turning up with two strangers, and at such a late hour, is not an ideal situation."

"You said she had a fiery temper," I added. "She might still be mad at you for breaking off the relationship. Have you given that any thought?"

Michael grinned, switching the transmission into a lower gear and slowing the van down. "I'm sure she'll be fine."

As we descended the hills in the center of Hoy, we were met with a series of twisting roads which led to the small port. There were no cruise liners or large vessels here, just the one ferry, bobbing gently in the water, waiting for us. There was only a smattering of houses along the road that ran to the port, and Azariah's body became less tense, his muscles relaxing as we traveled alongside the water.

"I'll go and buy the tickets; let them know we want to go to Stromness, not Graemsay," Michael announced, bringing the van to a halt next to a shabby looking hut which I presumed was the ticket office. He pushed the van door open before jumping out. He whistled cheerfully as he walked to the office

I turned to Azariah, concerned.

"Are you okay?"

"Me? Yes, of course I am. I am not the person who has been locked up for weeks"

"I don't need reminding," I mumbled. I stared straight ahead and wrapped my arms around myself.

"Do you want to talk about it?" Azariah's hand was on my arm, and he dipped forward as if trying to catch my attention.

"No, not yet. I'm not ready. I want to concentrate on being free, on being back with you." I was trying to forget what had happened. Why was he reminding me?

"I understand." His fingers caressed my cheek, and I closed my eyes, reveling in his touch. "But, just so you know, I will kill Orontes for what he has done. When things are sorted with Michael and you are safe in Saicean, I will lead the army protecting us now, and we will track him down and kill him."

I froze. My mouth instantly became dry, and my stomach felt like a rock had settled in it. It was too dangerous. Any Sachael sent to deal with Orontes—even an army of ten, twenty, thirty men—would be killed. And if Azariah was with them . . . I shook my head, tears threatening to spill from my eyes, the first ones since my escape.

"The bullets. You can't. He'll kill you!" My voice trembled as I thought of the outcome.

He pulled me against his side. "He has to catch us in order to inject us with the venom, and I can assure you, he will never catch any of us. How many more times do I have to tell you how fast we are? Orontes is slow in the water, too big to twist and turn like we do. Speed is what makes us powerful. It is our best form of attack, and of defense."

I picked at invisible fluff on the thin, pale blue jumper covering him, forcing my tears aside. If I started crying, I doubted I'd be able to stop.

"I will never stop blaming myself for your capture." His eyes were soft and full of concern. "I should have stopped them from taking you."

I shook my head. He couldn't do this to himself. It wasn't fair to either of us. I sat up straight, ready to drill my point home.

"Azariah, please, you mustn't blame yourself."

Azariah closed his eyes. "I do not deserve your forgiveness."

"There's nothing to forgive." He nodded, but I saw the anguish behind his eyes.

"I love you," I said, resting my hand on the side of his face. "And you're here with me. We're getting thrown into all sorts of situations, but we'll get through each and every one of them because we love each other. He nodded again, and I leaned forward to kiss him. The moment was interrupted by Michael springing back into the van

"On we go," he exclaimed as I broke my kiss with Azariah.

"Yes, indeed," Azariah said. "On we go." His eyes locked with mine, not sharing Michael's enthusiasm. I sank back into my seat, and Azariah laced his fingers through mine as the van rumbled to life. He kissed the side of my head and whispered to me: "Forget it, Estelle. We need to move on."

Michael maneuvered the van onto the ferry carefully, parking it in between two other vehicles already on board. It was a small boat, but had enough room for several parking spaces, if the drivers were careful. Tonight, there were only two cars and our van. There were no crowds, just a few passengers and the crew.

As soon as Michael cut the engine, Azariah opened his door and jumped out onto the deck. He waited for me to join him before leading me to the side of the ferry. He stood behind me, his arms wrapped around my waist, hugging me as we surveyed the water. It was wonderful to feel the breeze on my face as the ferry traveled across the short stretch of water between the islands. The rich blues and soft pinks of the evening sky offered a beautiful backdrop to Hoy as we left it behind. Azariah didn't look back, though—he looked forward, lifting his head and breathing deeply, inhaling the salty air.

"I know you'd like to be in the sea," I whispered. "I'd like to be in it as well."

"I am missing it so much, and only after one day."

"I'm sorry," I said, placing my hands over his. I couldn't help but feel it was my fault he was on land with me, and not where he should be.

"Shhh . . . I meant what I said earlier. I have made the decision to stay with you, and I would not have it any other way." He tightened his arms around me.

"But you're risking so much." I turned in his hold so I was facing him.

"Am I? I think I would be risking more if I was not here with you. How many times can I tell you that without you, I was lost and desperate? I had no idea what to do with myself."

He stroked my cheek with the back of his hand before leaning closer and gently nudging my lips with his. His kiss was slow, sensual, and full of unspoken passion. When we slowly parted, he smiled at me, resting his forehead against mine.

"It is not much longer until the next full moon. We will soon be in the water together." His voice lightened, just as it always did when he spoke of the next full moon. To him, it was the ultimate goal, the end of this journey and the start of a new one—life in Saicean.

"And then we return to Saicean?" I said, trying my best to hide the unease in my voice. I still didn't want to go. My original fears, the ones I'd had before I was caught, were still there. But it wasn't safe to be in Ravenscar at the moment. In hindsight, it hadn't been safe for a long time. And now, all my reasons for staying there had been snatched away. I couldn't visit my mum, paint on the beach, or hang out with Azariah like I'd done in the past—not now, perhaps never again. And with Orontes after us, maybe Saicean was the safest place to be.

"I see you two love birds are hiding in a quiet corner." Michael was back, grinning as he patted Azariah's shoulder.

"It was quiet until you found us," Azariah replied. "Although, I would hardly say we were hiding."

Michael completely ignored Azariah's barb and waved the tatty looking map at us.

"I've found the perfect place to spend the night. It's slightly out of our way—not on a direct route to Melia's—but I think it's exactly what we need. I'd much prefer a building to stop in, though. I don't much fancy spending the night on a beach when there is a chance Orontes will find us, but this one is ideal." He rested the map on a nearby pillar and frowned in concentration as he ran his fingers across the paper.

Azariah glared at Michael before we wandered over look at the map. "You are foolish to think a building would offer you any great protection from Orontes. In fact, a beach is by far the safest option. With the other Sachaels guarding the water, he would find it difficult to penetrate their watchful guard over us. On land, he has no one to overcome, just us."

Michael frowned, jabbing the map with his finger, ignoring Azariah's serious warning. "This is where we are heading, a bay, slightly east of Finstown."

"It's on the north coast of the Mainland," I noted as I squinted at the map. It was perfect; well, as perfect as it could be in our situation. The Mainland of Orkney was shaped like the letter *u*, and Finstown was on the inner curve of the bottom. Hoy was the island beneath the Mainland, and for Orontes to get to us from Hoy, he would need to swim around one of the sides. It was a considerable journey.

"Exactly," Michael said. "Orontes will never find us. He'd need to swim right around the Mainland one way or the other. It'll be safe for tonight."

Azariah nodded his agreement before turning his back on Michael and looking out over the edge of the ferry, watching the water. I wrapped my arms around his waist, resting my head on his back. Michael huffed before walking to the van. He stayed there for the rest of the journey, not encroaching on Azariah and me as we hovered near the edge of the ferry, watching the water and enjoying the simple pleasure of the spray splashing our faces.

All too soon we had to climb back into the van, and Azariah's cheerful mood disappeared Michael told us the journey across land would take about twenty minutes, but he was unfamiliar with the road, and so drove carefully and a lot slower than he had on Hoy. It was a relief when the sea came into view once more.

"We're here!" Michael shouted enthusiastically, slowing the van before bringing it to a stop.

"At last." Azariah sighed. "Please, both of you, excuse me. I must head to the water to contact Chanon. He needs to know where we are."

He leaned toward me, kissing my cheek before pulling the jumper off over his head and leaving the van. I slowly shifted myself along the seat and jumped out as well. As soon as I was free, the sound of the ocean filled my head. The gentle roar of the distant depths calmed me, and as the dry saltiness of the air touched my lips, I breathed deeply. I felt alive, drawn to the ocean and its hidden wonders. The air whipped around me, and tiny particles of sand speckled my skin. I stayed next to the van and rubbed my arms as I watched Azariah walk toward the water. His figure was silhouetted against the soft light thrown onto the surface of the water. Glancing to the narrow arc of the moon, I puzzled over why the night wasn't completely dark—the moon didn't offer any significant amount of light.

"Michael?" I said, twisting back to the van and leaning across the seat toward him. He was studying the map he'd showed us earlier. "Why's it not really dark?" I asked. In Ravenscar, even in summer, nights were always completely dark, not like this was tonight.

He looked up at me. "Long days in summer, short days in winter. It's the northern position of the Orkneys. We refer to it as the 'simmer dim,' a constant twilight. It never gets completely dark in the middle of summer, as the sun is only just dipping over the horizon. It'll be in the sky a lot earlier in the morning than it was back in Ravenscar."

"Amazing," I said, glancing once more at the sky before turning my attention back to Azariah. He was in the sea now, the surface lapping at his waist as he stood completely still. Placing his hands palm down on the water, he tipped his face back before sinking below the surface.

"I'll sleep across the seats in the front of the van; you two can sleep in the back," Michael said as he climbed from the van and came around to stand at my side.

"Sleep in the back of the van? Seriously?" I didn't fancy being shut up in any confined space, never mind on the hard and unforgiving metal base of the van

"Why not? There are a couple of blankets in the duffel bags. You two can cuddle up together all night."

It was reassuring to think we could hide out in the van if the weather ever became unbearable. But the sky was clear tonight, and I didn't think Azariah would want to sleep in the back of the van any more than I did.

"I think Azariah has plans for us to sleep on the beach," I told Michael.

"Whatever, you can sleep where you want. I'll be in the van. It'll be pretty cold out here all night. The wind whips around the islands here a lot more than back at Ravenscar."

"We'll be fine." I wanted to be alone with Azariah on my first night of freedom. I'd spent several weeks sharing a room with Michael, and I needed tonight to be different.

"You can sleep in the back," I said. "Stretch out those long legs of yours. It'll be more comfortable for you than lying across the front seats."

I wandered to the back of the van, intending to grab one of the blankets from a duffel bag but diverted my gaze as I caught sight of Azariah walking toward us. I grinned at his perfect physique. I doubted I would ever tire of seeing him walk out of the sea. He was a vision, pure and simple—stunning.

He was also carrying two long sticks which both had several fish skewered on them. Michael came and stood next to me, rubbing the back of his neck as Azariah approached.

"Food," Azariah called out, waving the sticks toward us. "I presume you two are as hungry as I am. These will go nicely with the soup."

Michael screwed his nose up at the fresh fish.

Azariah chuckled before looking along the beach. "There's some driftwood along the shoreline. May I suggest we light a fire? I will eat my fish as they are tonight, but perhaps you would like yours cooked?"

Michael huffed before heading off to collect the wood Azariah had indicated.

"Did you catch those?" I asked, eyeing the shiny silver fish.

"No, Chanon caught them earlier when he knew we were on the move. He passed them to me. He assumed we would be hungry."

"He's out there? But you only called him a few minutes ago." I shot my gaze to the sea, narrowing my eyes, trying to see Chanon and the other Sachaels, but there was no one to see.

"He was listening, waiting for my call to alert him to where we were. They are out there now, circling the water and keeping watch. I have told Chanon of our intention to go to Skaill Bay tomorrow. He will inform the others when it is time."

"Is Chanon second-in-command? You only ever mention speaking to him," I said, pushing my hair away from my face. The breeze Michael had mentioned was making itself known.

Azariah nodded slowly. "Yes. He is a formidable guard, and I have known him all my life. I trust him more than any other Sachael I know. He saved my life when we were young, and I know he would do so again. I hope I do not put him in such a dangerous position that he has to prove me right, though." Azariah stabbed the fish-laden skewers into the sand. A serious expression touched his features. "When Chanon spoke to me this morning, did you see his scars?"

"Yes. I noticed them, but only briefly. I didn't want to stare."

Azariah dropped down onto the sand and began to clear an area for the fire. He didn't look at me as he said, "Orontes gave him those scars."

"Orontes." I gasped.

"Yes. I did not know it was him until I saw him on the beach at Ravenscar with you. Both Chanon and I recognized him instantly, as, unfortunately, we have both met Orontes before. I had hoped I would never see him again; our first encounter ended badly. But we were younger then, boys, not the strong grown men we are today."

"What happened?" I crouched next to him and rested my hand on his shoulder.

Azariah glanced across the bay, watching Michael as he collected armfuls of wood.

"We were both sixteen, looking for oysters on the ocean floor. I was attacked first, and it was only through Chanon's fast actions that I was not killed. He saved my life that day by putting himself between me and Orontes. Unfortunately, he bears far more visual scars than I do for his trouble."

"You have scars? Where?" I had never noticed any marks on his skin.

"On my thigh." He patted his left leg. "Orontes attacked me and then Chanon with something so sharp it left the angry red scars you now see on Chanon's face. I can assure you it looked a hundred times worse when it happened. Luckily, his vision was not affected."

I caught the lilt in his final sentence and chose to question him further.

"And if his sight had been affected, what would have happened to him?"

Azariah sighed, looking away. "My father would have had the authority to banish him from Saicean."

I sprang up from my crouched position. "Kaimi would have banished him? He would have forced him out into the ocean to fend for himself?" I was shocked, angered by such a heartless action. "Your father sounds more like a monster than Orontes at times. He seems to have too much power. He organizes the armies, but doesn't anyone control him?"

"He is governed by set rules, and he is a good man."

"I fail to see how." I kicked at the sand, unhappy that the mere mention of his father had us disagreeing with each other.

"You should never compare him to Orontes," Azariah said, his voice solemn, his words spoken as if in warning. "He has allowed me to be with you. He does not approve of my choice to stay on land, but it is because he is concerned for my safety. Believe it or not, he is also concerned about you. Allowing us to be together, and instructing an army to stay and guard us, is not the action of a monster. It is the action of a man who cares deeply, but does not always know how to show it."

"I disagree. I think he is cruel and heartless."

"Estelle." Azariah raised his brow at me. "No more disrespect of my father."

"You have just admitted what he would have done to Chanon, the man who saved your life. He is cruel, and he is heartless."

"No," Azariah spoke softly. "I will not ever think that about my father. I also think you need to meet him before you make such wild assumptions."

"Well, I doubt he'll like what I say to him." I huffed, crossing my arms over my chest.

A smile graced Azariah's face, breaking the tension between us, but he didn't respond to my statement. I watched his expression, trying to work out exactly how he did view his father. He obviously loved him very much. He also had a lot of respect for him. But Chanon was also an important person in his life—one he thought highly of. I remembered when Azariah first mentioned his father to me. He'd painted him out to be some sort of tyrant, almost as if he was afraid of him. But now, he was almost standing up for him and his bullish behavior. What had changed?

"Can I ask you a question?" I said, dropping my arms to my side. I was confused and needed clarification. But I was unsure of how he would react.

He looked up at me, pushing his curls away from his face. "You may ask me anything you wish, and I will answer as truthfully as possible."

"You said you trust Chanon with your life."

"Yes."

I pinned him with my gaze, not willing to let him look away from me and avoid the question. "So, where was he when we were attacked by The Sect that morning in Ravenscar?"

"He was there." He didn't look away.

"Then why didn't he come to help us?" I dropped onto the sand next to him.

"He was in the shallows," he said, pulling a fish from one of the sticks. "He drowned the two men I dragged into the water. Neither of us had any idea they would bother you." He sighed. "He was incredibly angry that they took you."

"Really? I get the impression he doesn't like me."

Azariah stopped removing the fish and grinned. "Of course he does. Whatever gave you that idea?"

I shrugged. I had no real evidence. There was just something about the way he'd regarded me back at Rackwick Bay, and the way he'd dismissed me—as if my presence annoyed him.

"Stop thinking about it." His serious tone resurfaced once again, and he pushed the stick of fish to the side. "I assure you he harbors no ill feelings for you. I would never allow it."

I raised my brow at his last comment. Was this how his father spoke?

A loud cough alerted me to Michael's presence, and the clatter of dropping wood that followed caused me to turn away from Azariah. Michael was back, crouching over the driftwood and arranging a pyramid of twigs from what he'd collected.

"You gonna help?" he grumbled, turning to Azariah.

"With what?"

"Lighting the fire. I can't do it."

Azariah shifted to his knees, pulling his knife and a triangular piece of flint from his pocket. Within seconds, the sparks he created had lit the tinder. It was an action that reminded me of my father. It was exactly the way he had lit the nighttime fires on the beach at Ravenscar. And just like that, I became lost in memories of the evenings spent curled up in his arms as I listened to the comforting crackle of the wood, relaxed in the heat thrown toward us by the flames.

It wasn't long before the fire was burning strongly, lighting our small area of the beach with its orange glow. Azariah prepared the fish, gutting them with his knife before placing them back on the sticks to cook.

The fish and soup provided us with a decent, tasty meal. But Azariah didn't eat the soup, he only ate the fish and didn't seem bothered by the small portion.

"You should have had some soup," Michael said, draining the last of the tasty liquid from the flask.

"I was not as hungry as you obviously were," Azariah responded.

"Is fish all you eat in your world?" Michael screwed his nose up.

"No, we eat much more. We have hunters who gather different types of mollusks, as well as fish and larger sea mammals. You will not go hungry in Saicean." Azariah's mood lifted as he spoke about his home.

"Don't tell me you eat the meat raw, like you do the fish." Michael pulled a face, and Azariah laughed.

"We do generally cook our food. The herring we ate tonight required no cooking, though."

"I know I have seven submergences to do first, but do you think I'll like it there?" Michael was serious, his usual humor gone.

Azariah stared into the fire, not responding immediately. "I think so," he said eventually. "It is different to living on land. Life is simpler, organized. Everyone knows their place and their worth."

Michael nodded.

"It is safe as well. Orontes will never get into Saicean." Azariah reached for my hand before slipping his arm around my waist. "We'll be safe when we get there."

Michael leaned forward. "I presume you two will go to Saicean straight after Estelle's done her submergence. But I can't go, can I?"

Azariah responded immediately. "Unfortunately not. You know how keen I am take Estelle there. But I promise that we will ensure you are safe before we leave you. I intend to do your first submergence with you. Teach you what to say and do."

"I'd appreciate that," Michael said, a small smile pulling at the corner of his mouth. "And you'd better come and find me when I've done my seventh submergence. Mark it on your calendars!"

"We will, we promise," I said. Azariah nodded and offered Michael a smile.

The fire crackled as a thoughtful silence fell around us. It was the only sound, apart from the gentle crash of waves breaking on the beach. After some time, Michael rose slowly to his feet.

"I need some sleep. Are you two staying out here all night?"

"Yes," Azariah confirmed.

"Well, goodnight then."

"'Night," I said. "Sleep well."

Our combined mood was relaxed, yet tinged with an ever present fear of the situation we all faced. Azariah's earlier words had only confirmed the danger that seemed to be a mere step behind us. We had to keep moving, keep running away from Orontes. I still had numerous fears about going to Saicean, but I kept reminding myself that it was the only safe place to be, and, at the moment, that was all that mattered.

After fetching two blankets from the duffel bags, I rolled one of them into a makeshift pillow that stretched out behind Azariah and myself. When we had settled on the sand, I pulled the other blanket over us. Wrapped up in the comforting warmth of the fabric, I snuggled into Azariah's side and hugged him. He turned to his side and faced me before pulling me flush against his body. The softness of his lips covered mine in a demanding kiss. I relaxed in his hold and shifted my leg over his, drawing him even closer.

"Estelle," he breathed as he broke the kiss. "We need to sleep. Tomorrow will be another tiring day."

I pouted my response, but quickly tried to cover up a yawn. I was suddenly aware of just how exhausted I was. So much had happened in the last twenty-four hours. This time yesterday, I was falling asleep at The Sect, petrified for the morning in case my planned escape didn't work, but also excited about seeing Azariah again. I'd been locked up last night; tonight, I was sleeping on the beach. I sighed with contentment, wrapped in Azariah's strong, comforting embrace.

My eyelids fluttered shut, heavy with sleep. Even though I was naturally tired, I knew Azariah was forcing sleep upon me. He'd done it in my dreams many times, and now, he was doing it as he lay next to me. It was exactly the same as I remembered. "Don't do that," I muttered.

"You need to sleep. I am trying to help. I will be here all night; we are safe. No one will bother us."

"Are you sure?"

"Estelle, you can sleep without fear. Trust me."

I was with Azariah, in his arms—just like the last time we'd spent a night together. It was as though the last month had never happened. I could let go, give in to my exhaustion. I was safe again. But as I drifted toward sleep, vivid images of Orontes crossed my mind, the ones I wanted to forget. I stiffened, quietly panicking until a sudden wave of tranquility settled over me. But instead of fighting Azariah's calming influence, this time, I welcomed it.

Familiar visions of the sparkling, jeweled sea filled my mind. My breathing became as steady as Azariah's, and I sank into a deep, comforting slumber.

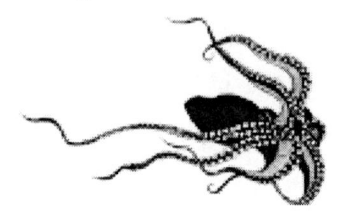

FIVE
Reunion

I woke to a gentle kiss upon my forehead. It had been a long time since my morning started in such a pleasant way. For the past few weeks, it had been Orontes's loud, unwelcome growl which was my greeting to the morning. This was bliss, and I smiled before tilting my head toward the softness of the lips kissing my forehead.

"Morning," Azariah whispered. "Did you sleep well?"

I nodded before opening my eyes. Azariah was sitting beside me, his legs stretched out in front of him and his eyes focused on my face, watching my reaction.

"I slept wonderfully, as you should know. Thanks to you and your calming influence."

"I have no idea what you are referring to." He at least had the decency to grin at my accusation, though he was trying to be coy by deferring.

"Liar."

Reaching up to his shoulders, I wrapped my fingers around the back of his neck and pulled him closer. He didn't hesitate, dipping his head nearer to mine.

"Michael's stirring. He will be awake soon," he whispered.

"I don't care."

I slid my fingers into his hair, dragging him closer, and gasped when he shifted his position to lay on top of me, settling his body against mine. His hand slid leisurely along my arm as his soft, warm lips pressed a kiss on the corner of my mouth.

"I could wake you up every morning like this," he whispered, pressing delicate, open-mouthed kisses along my neck and onto my shoulder. I slid my hands from his hair, running them down the center of his back before slipping them under the waist of his shorts and pulling his body harder into mine.

"I promise I'll not complain."

As his lips searched for mine, he moaned inwardly. I knew the sound was a warning he would stop—he always did. As expected, he broke our kiss and rested his forehead on mine.

"I am so tempted by you that it is taking all my willpower not to drag you away somewhere private and finish what we have so wonderfully started."

"You wouldn't have to drag me," I said breathlessly. "I would come willingly."

"And you think I do not know that?" His lips gently rubbed against mine as he closed his eyes. He sighed heavily before rolling to my side and placing his hands over his face. "I thought I was stronger than this, that I could resist." Groaning in frustration, he turned to me. "You must help me, Estelle. Stop me from rushing into anything."

I stared at him, not answering. What he was asking was impossible. I couldn't stop myself from wanting him.

"You have no intention of stopping me, have you?" There was an edge to Azariah's question, and the full force of his gaze hit me.

"I don't know why you fear it so much," I said, shrugging off his seriousness and wiping grains of sand from the blanket. "Would it really be such a bad thing if it happened?"

"No, of course not." He shifted upright before inclining his head toward the sea. "But look, look closely."

My gaze followed his.

"What am I looking for?" I asked, scanning the water.

"Can you not see their heads?"

"Whose heads?"

"The heads of the army. They are watching us."

"Where?"

He rested his head next to mine, trying to get the exact view I had.

"There." He pointed at what looked like a group of rocks in the water at the edge of the bay.

"That's them? I had no idea they would be so close."

"They come close because they are curious. You have to understand that they have never seen a female Sachael before. I am very lucky to have found you first. I will not have any competitors for your affections." Once again, his words took on an air of arrogant authority—one I was seeing more often. One I wasn't sure I liked.

My shock at the nearness of the Sachaels in the bay was replaced by intrigue over what Azariah had just told me. "What do you mean, you 'won't have any competitors for my affections'?"

"I would not have to fight for you."

"Fight? You'd fight for me?"

"Most definitely."

I frowned. "But if I'm the first female Sachael, how do you know you would end up fighting for me? It's never happened before."

"It happens with the Oceanids. The men have fights over them. Sometimes, one of them will bring a particularly beautiful Oceanid back, and the others want her for themselves. They fight each other as a way to show her who is strongest, and therefore who deserves her."

I was shocked. It seemed primitive, men fighting to show off, to impress a potential mate.

"Does she not get to choose?"

Azariah widened his eyes. "She would naturally choose the strongest Sachael."

"Why?" I shifted on the sand, crossing my legs and turning to face him.

"Because that's what Oceanids do." He continued watching the Sachaels in the bay.

I screwed my nose up, not understanding his complete confidence in Oceanid behavior. There was only one thing I was sure of: my feelings for Azariah. "You would not have to fight for me," I said. "There would be no need. I was yours from the moment I picked your shell up from the beach."

He turned to face me, his expression serious. "I know."

I frowned again as he jumped to his feet. Sometimes, I struggled with his confidence. It was as if he'd anticipated how I would react from the moment we first met. I huffed. Did I know the real Azariah, or only the parts he wanted me to know? He'd admitted that he'd killed people—male Oceanids—and he spoke about the Oceanid women as if they were completely besotted with Sachaels. But surely not every Oceanid felt an undeniable attraction. I recalled the way Orontes had reacted to me. Was that the Sachael-Oceanid attraction? I'd always presumed it was, but was it?

"I see Chanon has dared to venture from the sea," Azariah said, scowling at the approaching figure. He held his hand out to me. "Let us see what news he has for us."

I hesitated for a few moments, not willing to be so quick to do as he said.

Chanon walked toward us, his gaze switching between Azariah and me as I stood. His friendly expression for Azariah changed to one of annoyance when his eyes met mine, and a deep frown settled on his forehead. I contemplated what Azariah had said about Chanon; that he'd been furious with himself for not saving me from The Sect. But the hard set of his narrowed eyes didn't fit with what Azariah had told me. Undeterred by his glare, I took the opportunity to stare back at him, to study the scars Orontes had caused. The three sore-looking red marks ran deep across his cheek and above his eye. It was a miracle, just as Azariah had said, that his sight wasn't affected. I couldn't begin to imagine what they must have looked like at the time of the attack.

A smirk pulled at Chanon's lips as he caught me staring at him, but when he reached us, his attention was on Azariah.

"The men are restless. The Oceanids are traveling along the north coast of Scotland, and they want to attack. It seems Orontes's visit to Rackwick Bay was not successful in gaining any knowledge of your whereabouts."

"Morag wasn't there, was she? She left before he arrived?" I was desperate to hear that she'd made it, she was safe. An image of her frail body crumpled on the ground flashed in my mind, and I grabbed Azariah's arm to steady myself. My stomach flipped. "Please tell me she'd left."

Chanon didn't speak to me. He continued looking at Azariah as he replied. "The woman had left, yes. There was nobody there. As I said, the Oceanids have moved along the northern coast of Scotland. They must have assumed your journey would take you that way."

Azariah nodded. "Good."

"And the men? How do you intend to curb their desire to attack the Oceanids?" Chanon insisted.

"Send five of them to deal with the Oceanids," Azariah said, not even a flicker of hesitation preceding his order. "The rest are to remain here with you."

"Where's Orontes?" I asked. If he was still with the Oceanids, then any Sachaels sent to deal with them would be at risk from his venom-filled bullets. Azariah couldn't just dismiss them—Orontes wouldn't hesitate to use his prized possessions. He could kill all five of the Sachaels without even really trying.

"He was with the Oceanids," Chanon replied, still looking at Azariah. "But he has headed back along the east coast with two others. I presume he is returning to Ravenscar."

"Did they have the bracelets? The ones with the bullets?" I asked.

Azariah raised his brow. "Estelle. Stop worrying. The men will be fine." He switched his attention back to Chanon. "Tell the men to show the Oceanids no mercy. They must kill them, and then travel to Skaill Bay. That is where we shall be heading shortly. I will see you there tonight."

I reached for Azariah's arm, needing him to listen. "But if they have the bracelets—"

He placed his hand over mine and turned to face me. His eyes were hard, his mouth a thin line. "They are in no danger.

You need to trust me. I informed you yesterday that the Oceanids would not get near a Sachael. Do you honestly think I would send the men into a potential trap, or to their deaths?"

"No, but—"

"Estelle!" His voice rose. "Enough. Do not question my authority over the army. It is not your place to do so."

I stepped away from him, shocked at the change in his demeanor.

"Five men," he said, focusing on Chanon. "Tell them to go immediately."

"As you wish." Chanon nodded his head. I caught the sideways smirk he gave me before he turned and walked back to the sea, and I kept my gaze fixed on him until he disappeared under the water. I didn't want to look at Azariah. I was finding it hard to even think straight. It was difficult to reconcile the man beside me, who had just ordered the death of Oceanids as easily as ordering a meal, with the man who had whispered words of love to me a few moments ago.

As if sensing my quandary, Azariah took my hand in his.

"Michael is awake," he said.

"What?" I pulled my hand away from his. "You think you can just change the subject, and I won't notice?"

Azariah cocked his head to the side and frowned at me.

"You did it a lot when we first met." I shook my head. "You're not doing it now."

Azariah closed his eyes and sighed. "What is it that you wish to know?"

"There's nothing I want to know. But you just completely ignored my concerns about the Sachaels and the venom bullets."

"I told you that the men would come to no harm. Do you think I do not know how to organize and instruct them? Are you questioning my authority?"

I widened my eyes. "Seriously?"

Azariah rubbed his jaw. "I am struggling to understand why you have chosen to argue with me."

"I don't want to argue with you. I had, *have* genuine concerns. You tell me that Sachaels are in no danger from Oceanids. But look what happened to Elpis."

He straightened and scowled at me. "That was different."

I repeated his words from yesterday. "Sachaels are quick, they evade their enemy with their speed. That's what you told me. But it can't always be like that, otherwise Elpis would still be alive."

"He was betrayed, Estelle. He was left alone to fight them. He was a boy. He stood no chance against that many." His voice rose as he spoke. But I refused to be quiet. I had real concerns about sending the army to fight Orontes's Oceanids. I had seen firsthand what the venom bullets could do. Why did he not appreciate how deadly they were?

"So, if even one Sachael dies because of your order—"

"He will not. No one will die apart from the Oceanids."

"But—"

"Estelle!" he shouted. The scales on the back of his arms rose, looking sharp and angry. "I do not want to argue this point with you any further. You are, however unintentionally, questioning my decision and my authority. Whatever I instruct the army to do will not be questioned. Not by you, not by anyone. Understand?"

I scowled, silenced by his angry stare rather than his words. It was the first time he had shouted at me; the first time I'd seen a glimmer of his fierceness, of the warrior underneath. Of the true Sachael he was.

He sighed loudly, his tense shoulders dropping.

"I apologize." He stepped toward me and offered a slight smile. "I have never had anyone question my decisions before, let alone a woman. The Oceanid women in Saicean would never challenge me."

"Perhaps you'd be better off with one of them, then." I looked away, catching sight of Michael emerging from the back of the van and stretching his arms above his head. He was yawning.

"Estelle." Azariah's voice was softer, and his hand brushed against my arm. I risked a tentative look at him. The sharpness of his scales had disappeared along with his anger. "I do not want any of them. I only want you."

"Well then, you need to get used to me disagreeing with you. You should know that I won't always just accept what you say. If I have an opinion, I will tell you. And I certainly had no intention of disrespecting you. But I will challenge you. I'll push you, I'll annoy you, and I will probably infuriate you."

Azariah nodded, a smirk pulling at the edge of his mouth. "It will take some getting used to. I am not used to being challenged by anyone."

"Well, consider this morning your first lesson." I narrowed my eyes, but couldn't stop the grin that covered my lips.

"Come here," he said, grabbing my arm and pulling me toward him. I stumbled into him, and he wrapped his arms around me.

"Did we just have our first fight?" I asked, resting my head against his shoulder.

"I think we did."

Leaning back, I put a small distance between our upper bodies so I could see his face as I asked one last question. "You need to tell me more about Saicean. How should I behave when I get there? Are there any rules I need to follow?"

Azariah grinned even more. "There are rules, but you will not be expected to follow them. You are a female Sachael and, as such, will be treated like royalty."

I placed my head back on his chest.

"But I expect you to always do as *I* say," he added.

I was about to push away from him, tell him that I'd do no such thing, but I caught the rumble of a laugh building in his chest. I punched him lightly on the arm. "Stop it."

"Oh, Estelle," he said, rocking side to side with me. "I do not think you will ever do exactly as I say. But please, do not question me in front of Chanon or any of the other men in the army. They are not used to it, and I cannot let them see any sign of weakness from me, which includes you questioning my decisions."

"But in private, I can tell you what an idiot you are?" I lifted my head to look at him, smiling, and he chuckled before nodding.

Michael's loud yawn made us both turn toward him.

"Morning, you two," he called. He scratched his chin, rubbing at the growing stubble.

We ambled toward him, hands locked together.

"Did you sleep okay?" he asked, lifting his hand to disguise another yawn. "I had the best sleep ever."

"We slept very well, thank you." Azariah hid a smirk.

"Can we go now?" Michael shut the back doors of the van before making his way toward the driver's side. "I'm starving, and I know Melia will cook us a huge breakfast when we get there."

"Won't she be at work?" I asked. It was odd that she'd studied at University, but had returned to live in the Orkneys.

"She doesn't work. Never has," Michael replied, but didn't explain any further.

As soon as Azariah and I climbed into the van, Michael started the engine.

We traveled for a few minutes, heading out of Finstown and retracing our journey toward Stromness.

"How long have you known her?" Azariah asked. I guessed he was as unsure about her as I was.

"About six years."

"Where did you meet her?"

Michael laughed. "What is this, Az? Twenty questions?"

"'Az'?" I stiffened. It was what Elpis had called him.

"Well, his name's so unusual. I like the shortened version."

"It is better than 'Uncle,'" Azariah replied, his mood turning somber. He took a deep breath before continuing to quiz Michael. "I was curious as to how much you know about her. About Melia."

"I know what I need to know." Michael's tone was one of closure. It was clear that he didn't want to discuss his ex-girlfriend. "Petrol station," he announced as he swung the van off the road and onto an old garage forecourt. He tapped a dial on the dashboard display. "We need petrol."

As soon as Michael left the van, I turned to Azariah. "Why all the questions about Melia?"

"Her name, and the reaction you said she had when they broke up. She sounds unpredictable, wild and unreasonable. It all makes me think she is an Oceanid."

"Really?"

He nodded, his gaze on Michael through the front windscreen of the van. "I am concerned that she may not be trustworthy."

"Or that she'll not be happy to see Michael?"

Azariah smiled. "Oh, I have no doubt she will be pleased to see Michael. He is a Sachael."

I widened my eyes at his statement. "But he's a land Sachael. He hasn't even completed a submergence."

"She will still have an attraction to him that will defy all logic. It is too strong for them to ignore." He watched

Michael through the window of the van. "Look at him. He is ridiculously excited about seeing her again. I have no doubt it is because she was a very generous lover. He will be hoping for a passionate reunion."

I didn't think my eyes could open any wider. "Really?"

"All the Oceanids are . . . how shall I put this?"

"Don't," I murmured, screwing my nose up and holding up one hand to stop him. "I get the picture."

Azariah seemed convinced that Melia was an Oceanid and, as such, would welcome Michael with open arms. I wasn't so sure, but if he was right, and it was because Michael was a land Sachael and the attraction was built-in, then surely her attraction to him, a full Sachael, would be greater than it was for Michael. I didn't like that thought at all. I rested my hand on Azariah's thigh, silently promising myself I wouldn't let her anywhere near him. Just as Azariah had written the word "MINE" in the sand at Ravenscar for Orontes to see, I would ensure that Melia had no doubt Azariah was taken.

When Michael returned to the van, he was grinning. Even when driving, the grin remained. Maybe Azariah was right after all. They must have shared a very physical relationship.

The van rumbled along for another half hour, spluttering and gurgling as Michael increased the speed. As he turned the van a sharp right, the bay of Skaill opened up in front of us. A large sweeping curve of endless golden sand came into view, and after traveling along a road that ran parallel to the sea, we stopped outside a two-story brick building. Michael pulled the handbrake on, and I reached for the scrunched up blue jumper.

"Put it on," I murmured at Azariah.

"We're here." Michael sprang from the van. His eagerness to see Melia was impossible to ignore.

"I thought you said it would be Melia who wouldn't be able to resist Michael," I said as we left the van. "His reaction is what you expected from her, not him."

"Have you ever met a female Oceanid?" Azariah answered, tugging the jumper into place.

"No. Well, not that I know of. Why?"

Azariah raised his brow and looked over my shoulder. "Well, I am confident there is one standing in the doorway over there."

I turned around and was momentarily stunned by the woman who had answered the door. There was a blur of movement as she slapped Michael across the face. I flinched as she hit him, but watched open-mouthed as Michael straightened himself up and laughed, rubbing his cheek. Seconds later, she flung herself at him, practically knocking him to the ground as she wrapped her legs around his waist. She was a flurry of lustrous blonde hair and long limbs. They kissed passionately. It was obvious that she was pleased to see him, despite the hard slap.

Azariah took my hand, leading me toward the entwined couple. It was several seconds before either Melia or Michael became aware of our presence. Surprisingly, it was Melia who turned toward us first. She stared at Azariah, her lips forming a bee-stung pout.

"Michael." Her voice was clear, sweet, and sultry, hinting at her smooth Scottish accent. In that moment, I completely understood why the Sachaels took them as their wives—even their voices sounded appealing. "You have brought people with you. Friends?"

Michael could barely contain his joy as he eagerly introduced us. "Melia, this is Azariah, and Estelle."

"We are pleased to meet you." Azariah spoke formally.

"Likewise." Her eyes never left Azariah as she invited us inside.

"I'm starving," Michael said as he stood behind Melia, kissing her neck. "Have you any food?"

"Of course I have." Her gaze still rested on Azariah, but he was preoccupied, looking around the room we'd been led into. He surveyed every surface, from the framed photographs on the walls to the arrangement of silk threads on the table. Next to them was a velvet cushion with pins in it. It looked like she had been creating a delicate piece of lace when we arrived.

"Come and see what I have for you," she suggested, taking both of Michael's hands and leading him out of the room.

"What do you think?" I whispered to Azariah. "You're sure she's an Oceanid?"

He nodded. "Most definitely. See the lace? It is one of the most complicated designs, made with the finest of threads. Ianira enjoys making lace of this sort, as do all the Oceanids in Saicean."

"Do all the Oceanids look like her?"

He lifted his gaze from his inspection of the lace and frowned at me.

"Blonde hair, vivid green eyes, and her voice—"

"They all have naturally blonde hair, but some of them color it. I appreciate their beauty, but they are nothing compared to how I see you, Estelle." His eyes locked with mine, and I swallowed loudly. His gaze was overpowering at times, particularly when he looked at me with such intensity. How did he do that? It wasn't fair.

A loud giggle from the kitchen was followed by Michael's familiar laugh.

"And you doubted whether she would be pleased to see him?" Azariah raised his brow and then continued looking around the room

"I don't like the way she looked at you," I said, moving to a sideboard that had numerous picture frames on it.

"I did not notice. Perhaps I am used to the attentions of Oceanids. They are quite common in Saicean." He wandered back to the cushion where the lace was and studied it again.

The picture frames contained photographs of Melia and Michael. She was usually wrapped around him, but both of them were smiling in every one. There were only a couple of other random ones—photographs with two other people, a man and a woman who looked to be the same age as them. But I froze when I saw the photo of a familiar face. I stared at the image, unable to look away. Pactolus was on one side of Melia, Michael on the other. Just the sight of him stirred memories I wanted to forget.

"Definitely an Oceanid," Azariah mumbled.

I snapped my eyes away from the photo. "Do they live with you and your father?" I asked.

He stepped toward me, his eyes lingering on the same photograph that had unwillingly caught my attention. "The Oceanids?"

I nodded.

"Some of them do, but none of them have access to my room. I am often surrounded by them when I go to the lake, though."

"Surrounded?"

"Yes." He grinned at my astonishment. "They would like me to choose them as my wife."

"Your wife?" I scowled. I didn't like the thought of others fawning over him. I didn't want to become a clingy female, constantly questioning him and worrying about what he was doing, but I couldn't deny the surge of jealousy running through my veins. "I thought the Oceanids in Saicean were already with Sachaels?"

"Not all of them. They see me as young, unattached."

"Handsome, kind, considerate . . ."

Azariah grinned. "If you say so."

"So what do they do to try and get your attention?" I needed to know, even though I doubted I'd like the answer. I wanted to know what would confront me if I went to Saicean.

"Many of them make their intentions very clear. I tend to be polite to them, engage in small talk, but always return alone."

"And their intentions . . . ?"

"Sex," Azariah stated, appearing to have no problem with the subject we were discussing. "They make it quite clear what they want. They think their sexual tricks will persuade me to want them. I am well accustomed to their advances, and their attempts to seduce me."

"But you ignore them?" I hated what he was telling me. I couldn't help but compare myself to these unseen Oceanids. If they all looked similar to Melia, they would be incredibly beautiful.

"Yes." His lips curled into a smile. "Estelle, are you jealous?"

I shrugged.

He closed the small gap between us and placed his hand under my chin.

"You have no need to be. It is they who should be jealous of you. They could never compete with you for my affection. Never." His lips grazed mine. "You have nothing to fear, Estelle. Your beauty is far greater than any Oceanid's. Never doubt my love for you."

Another loud laugh filtered through from the kitchen, and he straightened, looking toward the door.

"Let us see what they are doing. Perhaps if you spend time with Melia, she may become a friend."

I scowled. "I doubt it. I think she has her eyes on you."

"But I am not interested in her." He motioned toward the door with his hand

Just as we were about to move toward the kitchen, a loud moan sounded out. I glanced at Azariah, shaking my head, indicating that it was probably best if we didn't disturb them.

"It tastes wonderful," Michael's voice said. "Az, Estelle, come and try this fresh orange juice."

As we entered the kitchen, Melia was laughing at Michael. He had emptied one glass of orange juice already, and she was pouring him another.

"You always did like orange juice, but I cannot remember you being so vocal about it."

I raised my eyes heavenward at their interaction.

"Michael, why don't you bring your luggage in from the van while I chat to Azariah," Melia suggested. I didn't miss the way she excluded me, and caught the flutter of her eyelashes as she glanced at Azariah.

"Sure," Michael agreed. "Are we okay to stay?"

She directed a sugary sweet smile at him. "Of course."

Azariah watched Michael head outside before turning his attention to Melia.

"Why have you chosen a life on land?" he asked politely.

"I have no idea what you mean."

Azariah smiled and nodded. Her response seemed to be exactly what he'd expected.

"I know you are an Oceanid," he said. "What I do not understand is why you are living out of the water."

"It's personal." She turned away, her gaze meeting mine for a few seconds. It was the first time she had looked at me since we'd arrived.

"I fell in love," she said, spinning around to face Azariah again. "That's what happened to me. That's why I do not return to the water."

"With Michael?" Azariah asked.

"Yes, with Michael. I was distraught when he refused to return to the Orkneys with me. He was everything to me. And he left." She hugged herself as she looked out the window and toward the van. Catching the eye of the man who had walked away from her, she smiled weakly.

"But why did you stay out of the water? Surely you would want to return to your own kind," I questioned.

She sniggered as she looked at me. "Would you ever return to your own kind after the love of this Sachael?" Her gaze switched to Azariah.

I shook my head. I would never find another man like Azariah. If he disappeared from my life, I didn't know what I would do. I doubted I could ever love another as much as I did him.

Melia continued: "Because I had found love with a human once, I hoped there was a chance I would find that same love with another. I knew I would never find it with my own kind. I had no reason to return to the water." Her voice broke, and she sniffed. "It had nothing to offer me anymore."

Michael burst into the room, dropping the two duffel bags onto the floor. He smiled at Melia before kissing her cheek. She immediately brightened, running her fingers down the center of his forehead and along his nose.

Michael snapped at her fingers with his teeth, and she giggled.

"Estelle," Azariah said, demanding my attention. "Would you care to join me on a walk?"

He indicated the door with a wave of his arm, and I didn't hesitate to leave.

As soon as we were outside, he groaned loudly.

"I cannot stay in there with them. There is too much sexual energy. I hope the time we have given them will be put to good use, and the tension will be gone when we return." He reached for my hand and entwined his fingers with mine. "Let us go and look at the Skara Brae, seeing as Michael has brought us here. We can pretend to be ordinary people looking at ruins."

"Tourists," I confirmed as I leaned into his side. "Not people trying to escape from a mad Oceanid."

Azariah grimaced. "What a world I have thrown you into. Do you ever wish you were normal?"

"Normal?"

"Yes. Not a Sachael. Then you would not have to deal with all this."

"I . . . how can you ask me that?" I stopped walking and faced him.

"I just wondered. What if you had never met me? Do you sometimes wish you had never met me?" He didn't look me in the eye as he said this.

"Azariah." I waited for him to lift his gaze. When his bright blue eyes finally met mine, I continued. "I will never regret meeting you. My life may have been quieter without you in it, but to have never met you . . ." I shook my head.

"But all this danger?" He glanced over my shoulder, looking beyond me.

"You mean Orontes?"

He nodded.

"I'm certain Orontes was watching me before you ever saw me. Who knows what he was planning back then? It wasn't the arrival of you in my life that caused Orontes to become obsessed with me; it was my father, all those years ago." I sighed, remembering my first meeting with Orontes. He'd said he'd known my father. "He saw us both doing the submergence ritual. You always warned me that perhaps someone was watching me. I now know that they were."

He tugged on my hand, and we continued walking.

"And I was never normal, was I?" I said. "I just didn't know it."

Azariah smiled, and so did I, as we walked along the sweeping white sands of Skaill bay, heading toward the ruins of Skara Brae. We were both far from normal, but at that moment, walking hand in hand with Azariah, I felt ordinary.

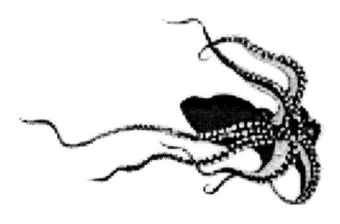

SIX
Claim

Michael was correct in his assumption that Melia would provide us with a feast. Azariah stared at the loaded breakfast plate before him, quietly asking me what things were. He wasn't impressed, though, and didn't eat anything. He only drank the orange juice after inspecting the whole orange carefully.

She never spoke to me. In fact, she hardly glanced at me. Her attention switched between the two men, and she openly flirted with Azariah when Michael wasn't in the room. He paid her no special attention, speaking to her when necessary, but never beginning a conversation. I didn't care about her not speaking to me, but I was uncomfortable with her behavior.

It was only when I was alone with Melia that she turned her attention to me. Michael was busy with the van, checking to make sure it was ready for when we moved on, and Azariah had ventured to the sea to communicate with Chanon.

"Alone at last," she said, as I stood looking out the window, watching Azariah in the distance. "Don't you ever leave his side?"

I turned toward her, aware that her tone was very different to how she spoke when Azariah and Michael were around.

"You two are practically joined at the hip," she continued.

"We don't like being apart," I confirmed, realizing why she'd ignored me until now; she had been waiting for an opportunity to get me alone.

"From what I can see, it's you who won't leave his side. Are you worried about his feelings for you?"

I shook my head, narrowing my gaze at her. I suspected I knew what she'd been waiting to say.

She approached me, her movements fluid and graceful. The sharp smell of citrus surrounded me. Her voice, normally sweet and velvety, turned sharp and bitter. "You're a fool. There's only one thing you can offer him. I can offer him much more." She was next to me, her coldness seeping into my pores.

"Really? You sound like you think you have some claim on him." I turned sideways to her, crossing my arms. The clock on the wall became my focus as it ticked forward ridiculously slowly.

"Naturally. It's how it's meant to be."

I was surprised by her directness. "How it's meant to be? Because you're an Oceanid?"

"Yes." She stood with her shoulders back, her chin held high.

"He sees your kind all the time." I scowled, moving away from her and toward the window. "You're nothing special."

"But Azariah is special, isn't he? I felt it the moment I saw him."

I spun around to face her. Her facade had turned from the serene one that had been fixed in place since our arrival to one of bitter annoyance. "I thought you loved Michael," I said, trying to sway the conversation away from Azariah. "Isn't he the reason you stayed out of the water? You told us you loved him, remember?"

"That was before I met Azariah. Compared to him, Michael is nothing."

I was surprised by her brutal honesty and frowned, tightening my arms around myself. I hadn't warmed to her since we arrived, and now, I had a deep mistrust and simmering hate for her. "So, you don't love Michael now that you've met Azariah? Yet you've lived out of the water because of him. How can you switch your feelings so easily?"

"Azariah and I should be together. It's how it's supposed to be." She moved toward the sideboard, running her hand along the edge of it.

I raised my brow. "You've committed to a life on land. You said you had no desire to go back into the sea."

"But I want Azariah. I would willingly go back into the ocean to be with him." She spun around, her hands on her hips as she scowled at me.

"What about Michael?" I asked.

"What about him?"

"You're deceiving him. He deserves better than this—than you." How could she dismiss him so easily? I'd seen the way she reacted to his arrival. Yes, she'd slapped him, but then she had thrown herself at him. She'd been more than pleased to see him.

Her mouth curled into a sneer.

"And Azariah deserves better than you. You are nothing—a human he has chosen to breed with and nothing more."

I raised my brow again; this time, at her viciousness.

"Do you even know what he is?" she pressed.

It was my turn to smile slyly. She had limited knowledge of all of us. She didn't know Michael was a Sachael, or that I was one. And I certainly wasn't parting with that information.

"It doesn't matter what he is," I said, shrugging and moving away from the window, toward her.

"Then, like I said earlier, you're a fool. He'll leave you when he's impregnated you; he'll return to his world."

How many more times would I hear those words? That Azariah would leave me, that he was only interested in me as a host for his son and heir.

"You know," I started, determined to let Melia know she was way off the mark. "I didn't like the sound of you before I met you. I thought you were a nasty piece of work, treating Michael the way you did all those years ago. It seems my initial perception of you was correct. You are nothing more than a disillusioned Oceanid, one who is so ridiculously out of touch with exactly what is happening here that it is almost laughable."

She frowned but stepped closer. Again, I could feel the coldness emanating from her body.

"I know how to pleasure him properly." She smiled sweetly, sickeningly so. "No human is capable of giving him that experience. A Sachael as strong as him deserves more than a pathetic human. He will never be happy with you."

She smirked, eyeing me from my head to my bare feet, and tutted when she looked back at my face.

"Look at yourself, and then look at me. There is no comparison. I know who he will pick. Once I have seduced him, he will never even look at you again."

Something inside me snapped. Whether it was the smug look she gave me or the situation I'd been forced into, I didn't know. But I straightened up before closing the small gap between us. We were roughly the same height, but because I'd made the move toward her, surprising her with my advance, she took a step back.

"He is mine," I whispered threateningly as I pushed her against the wall. My hand stayed on her chest, keeping her still. "He will never be yours."

Her eyes locked with mine. "You have no claim on him. If I want a man, I always get him. *I* decide whether I keep him or not."

"Really?" I leaned in close, challenging her. "What about Michael? He walked away from you. It was the most sensible thing he ever did."

"He came back."

"For what? This?" I pressed my hand harder on her chest. "To be tossed aside when someone better comes along? You have no idea what love is. No idea at all."

"I want Azariah," she hissed through gritted teeth.

I stepped up to her, nose to nose. "But he has to want you. And he doesn't."

She sneered. "He will."

"I will what?" Azariah stood in the doorway of the room, the jumper he had worn since we left Morag's nowhere to be seen. He was wet, having just returned from the sea, and he frowning, watching the interaction between Melia and myself. I backed away from her.

"Oh, nothing important." Melia smiled as she turned to face him, dismissing our conversation as if it was nothing. She incensed me.

"Tell him," I demanded. "Tell him exactly what you said to me."

Azariah straightened, glancing at me before turning to Melia.

"What have you said to Estelle?" he asked.

"I was only joking with her." Melia twisted her golden hair in her fingers but didn't meet Azariah's piercing stare.

He looked away and came to my side before speaking to her again. "I am still waiting for you to tell me what you were talking about."

Melia was silent. Her eyes wandered his bare chest as she pouted at him. I was sure she fluttered her eyelashes. Azariah stared at her, showing no reaction to her not so subtle flirting attempt.

When she didn't answer his question, he turned to me.

"Estelle, are you okay?"

I was enraged by her defiance. "Yes, I'm fine, but she needs to tell you and Michael the truth," I said, pointing at her.

"Don't you dare bring Michael into this!" Melia screamed at me, her eyes wide and fierce. Azariah immediately stepped between us. He looked concerned as he faced me.

"What has she said?" he asked softly, cupping the side of my face in one of his hands.

"She said she will seduce you."

Azariah pulled me into his arms and chuckled quietly in my ear. "Oh, how little she knows me. And how little she knows you."

"You are nothing, Estelle!" Melia shouted from behind Azariah. "You can't even be with him in the ocean."

Azariah paused for a few seconds, and then released me from his embrace. He turned slowly to face her.

"Estelle gives me more than you can ever imagine," he said calmly and surely. "Her mere existence stirs my heart in a way you will never be able to."

"But I am an Oceanid. Our kinds are meant to be together."

"Is that what you think? I am of the understanding that it is more a pointless union between two species who are incompatible in so many ways."

Her eyebrows drew together. "But you take us as wives."

"Only to satisfy our most basic urges while we seek potential mothers to bear our sons."

"So you admit that you are only with her for the child she will have?" Her voice lifted at her small imagined victory.

Azariah turned to face me and smiled so serenely, I was convinced he had misheard her.

"A child will be a welcome addition to our lives," he said, turning back to Melia. "But you seem to think I am only with Estelle for that reason." He shook his head. "That is not the case. I am with Estelle because I love her."

Melia's mouth fell open, and she lifted her fingers to her parted lips.

"Now," Azariah continued, "I would appreciate you keeping your fantasies to yourself. Michael is very special to me and Estelle, and I am not happy with your obvious dismissal of his feelings. If you continue to disrespect Estelle, then I will have no option but to tell him of your intention to be unfaithful."

"He won't believe you," she snapped at him, immediately recovering her composure.

Azariah smirked. "Are you willing to take that risk? I doubt it. Besides, I will not allow him to be continually treated this way. And he will listen to me."

"I still fail to see what you see in her," Melia mumbled.

"To make things easier, we will leave in the morning." Azariah spoke with authority, confident of the situation. I didn't like it when he spoke to me in such a way, but right now, and to Melia, I was glad he did.

"What about Michael?" Melia asked.

"Are you worried whether I will tell him of your obsession with me, or are you asking whether he will be leaving with us?"

I assumed both were of the same importance to her.

When she didn't reply, Azariah continued. "I strongly suspect he will leave when Estelle and I do. I suggest you enjoy your time with him tonight. I doubt you will ever see him again."

She fled from the room, heading outside.

I looked to Azariah, worried that things were about to go completely crazy. He shook his head before sighing. "We are free to retire to the room Melia kindly offered to us earlier. Let us get away from this madness."

I was glad Azariah had told Melia exactly what he thought of her suggestions, but her furious expression as she fled from the house worried me.

"What do you think she'll say to Michael?" I asked as we headed to the bedroom upstairs.

"Nothing," he replied, letting me walk in front of him up the stairs.

"But you saw her. She wasn't happy."

"All Oceanids react like that. They are fiery. Hot one minute, cold the next. All I have done is ensure Michael has an incredible time tonight. I suspect she will try everything to make him stay."

"Everything?" I stopped my ascent and turned on the stairs to face him.

Azariah grinned, raising his eyebrows before nodding. "Everything."

I stifled a laugh at his expression before rushing up the remaining steps.

"Unfortunately, it means we will get little sleep tonight," Azariah said, "as we are in the room next to theirs."

When I opened the bedroom door, I wasn't sure whether I wanted to smile at the bed before us or kick it repeatedly. Melia would be using hers tonight for a completely different reason than we would be.

Azariah was immediately behind me, wrapping his arms around my waist as he lightly kissed my neck. "I know what you are thinking."

"I doubt it," I replied, twisting in his arms to face him.

"Tell me, then," he breathed as he backed me into the room, pushing the door shut with his foot.

"I hate that Melia is in the next room, and that we will hear her and Michael. Can we spend tonight on the beach?"

The smile that covered his face was all I needed to confirm his answer.

He dipped his head to kiss me, and as his lips covered mine, I relaxed into his hold. My senses became heightened—his scent surrounded me, his touch energized me. I was alive, at one with him, as if this was all that mattered. He slowly moved his lips away, and I opened my eyes to be met by his serious gaze.

"I think a night on the beach would be a lovely idea," he said.

I grinned at him before looking around the room for our duffel bag. As I momentarily glared at the comfy-looking duvet cover, I silently cursed that we would not be here tonight, snug and warm in a large bed. But staying and hearing Melia and Michael having a great time was not something I wished to experience.

I sighed and turned back to Azariah, but as I moved, I caught sight of a doorway leading off from the bedroom.

"A bathroom!" I exclaimed as I moved to the door. "Hot water. Can I have a shower?"

Azariah chuckled at me. "Have a shower, Estelle. I shall sit and wait for you."

I leaned on the doorframe, stretching my arm above my head and posing with a pout. "Care to join me?"

He smirked before throwing himself on the bed. Lying on his back, he narrowed his eyes at me. "That is one of your most appealing ideas, but also one of your most ridiculous."

"Ridiculous? Why?"

"Because neither of us would shower."

My cheeks heated, burning deliciously, and then my whole body decided to join the party. I fanned myself with my hand, pretending to swoon.

"Have your shower, Estelle." A small smirk pulled at his lips. "Take all the time you need."

I huffed at him before stepping into the small bathroom. There were several fluffy towels neatly folded on a wicker chair and an array of scented products lined up on a narrow glass shelf under the mirror. I grabbed the first bottle, flicked the lid and smelled a tangy lemon scent. It reminded me of Melia, and I selected another bottle. This one smelled of lavender, a smell I'd always loved. Holding the bottle under my nose, I breathed in deeply. It reminded me of the bunches of lavender my father used to bring home and display in a small white vase on the sideboard. He used to make small cotton bags full of the seeds so that the smell lingered all year.

Switching the shower on, I intended to be quick. But the hot water didn't help with cooling my overheated body. I flicked the temperature to cold, but nothing changed. Azariah's words were at the forefront of my mind. I giggled, stupidly happy. But then sighed, fed up with the missed opportunities for us to be together in the way I wanted. I hadn't forgotten his refusal of me the other day. And I knew that once we'd slept together, shared our bodies in the most intimate of ways, we'd constantly be looking for ways to be alone, ignoring the seriousness of the situation we were in. Orontes was tracking us, and we needed to be alert enough to stay one step ahead of him.

The mere thought of Orontes sent a shiver through my body, and not a pleasant one. Not for the first time, I struggled to push away the thought of what he would do if he caught up with us. My fear for Azariah and Michael spiraled. Heat spread throughout my body, starting at my chest and radiating outward. I backed into the corner of the shower, leaning against the cold tiles, and clenched my jaw. I had to stop thinking like this. The cool touch of the tiles gradually seeped under my skin, and with the cold water from the shower pouring down on me, I gradually calmed.

I finished washing and switched the shower off. After wrapping a large towel around my body, I entered the bedroom. Azariah was still lying on the bed, flicking through a magazine. The sight of him instantly revived my thumping heart.

"I'm all clean now," I said, wiggling my hips before retrieving a clean top from the duffel bag.

A smile pulled at his lips as he sat up and placed the magazine on the bed.

"This world completely baffles me." He chuckled as he looked at the magazine. "I profess to not knowing what this book is trying to teach its readers. There is not much writing, and the pages are full of photographs of people."

I grinned at his confusion. He was looking at a gossip magazine, featuring candid—and not so flattering—shots of the rich and famous. "Do you want to know? I can explain whatever it is that has you confused."

"No, Estelle. There are some things I think it best not to know." He rubbed the back of his neck. "Life is complicated enough these days without adding to it."

I managed to discreetly pull on some underwear under the towel, but every time I glanced at Azariah, he was watching me, his mouth twitching at the side in silent amusement at my predicament.

"Stop staring at me." I laughed as I turned my back to him before slipping a t-shirt over my head.

"I cannot help it. You mesmerize me. Besides, I have seen many naked women in my world. You have nothing I have not seen before."

I snorted at his comment and turned to face him, the t-shirt languishing about my neck..

His playful expression changed instantly.

"Estelle, you should not tempt me in such a way."

"Remember," I teased. "You've seen it all before." I giggled, slipping my arms into the sleeves before pulling the fabric down over my chest. "Do they strip for you?"

Azariah shook his head, managing a terse smile. "No, of course not. The Oceanids tend to swim free of any clothing when they are in the ocean."

"But they have their fish tails, don't they?"

"Yes, but their tops are not covered."

"What about the men?" Curiosity got the better of me. As soon as I asked my question, I wished I hadn't.

"Their tops are uncovered as well." Azariah grinned at me, knowing exactly what I'd meant. "Estelle, the men have fish tails, just like the females. Everything else is hidden. You will not be shocked, unless, of course, they are aroused. They are very much like us, and humans, when it comes to that part of their anatomy."

"Good," I stated, pulling a jumper over my head. I was sure my face had flushed a deep red.

Azariah slid down the bed.

"Now, are you ready?"

"Just one more thing," I said as I picked up my old top. Carefully, I removed my brooch from the discarded fabric and fastened it securely to my clean jumper. "Now, I'm ready."

Azariah smiled and picked up the duffel bag, slinging it over his shoulder before we quietly left the house.

"Are you not calling Chanon?" I asked as we headed along the beach in the opposite direction to the Skara Brae.

"I called him earlier. I have no reason to speak to him again so soon. I want to be with you, alone, with no one else bothering us."

"That'd be nice," I said. Snatched moments alone with him were my favorite. I just wished they could be for longer.

As we strolled along the golden sand, the evening closed in, another end to a warm summer day. The sound of the waves tumbling ashore was comforting, familiar, the background noise to my everyday life. But the sound was different here to what I heard in Ravenscar. There were rocks and shore platforms at Ravenscar, which meant the waves had a tendency to crash ashore. Here, there was just an endless expanse of sandy beach. It was beautiful, but it wasn't home.

Unfortunately, as Azariah searched for an area he deemed suitable for our evening together, I noticed the familiar bobbing of dark-haired heads out in the curve of the bay.

Chanon and the other Sachaels were in the water, watching us. Even now, we were not alone. I didn't like it, but I knew it was something I needed to get used to.

Azariah indicated a spot on the beach that he'd selected as the perfect place for our evening. As I sank onto the sand, he pulled a blanket from the duffel bag. He swiftly placed it across my shoulders before sitting next to me, curling his arm around my waist.

"This will be a perfect evening for me. Sitting with you on the beach, watching the sun set and the moon rise into the sky."

I leaned against his body, appreciating the removal of his jumper earlier. I hadn't liked the look Melia gave him when she saw his naked torso, but now, it didn't matter.

A flurry of movement, splashes, and shouts alerted both of us to the presence of the Sachaels in the bay. If I hadn't already seen them earlier, then I would certainly have known they were there now.

"They are happy," Azariah reassured me. "They killed the Oceanids earlier this afternoon. They are boasting about who killed the most."

"Really?" I said as I shifted to face him. "They celebrate killing people?"

"They celebrate killing our enemies. Never forget that, Estelle. The Oceanids they have disposed of would have killed any of us and not given it a second thought. They were Orontes's men, part of his army." He folded his hands in his lap and looked thoughtful. "Can I ask you something?"

I nodded, curious about what he wanted to know. "Of course."

"Does it concern you that the army has killed, and that they celebrate it so joyously?"

I nodded. "It doesn't sit comfortably with me. Killing someone shouldn't be celebrated." I pulled my legs up and wrapped my arms around my knees. "I don't like the idea of anyone being killed."

"I can understand that," he said. "But I have killed Oceanids in the past, and I would do so again if your life was in danger. I would not give it a second thought. You seemed intent on killing Pactolus on the beach at Ravenscar. But could you? Could you ever kill someone?"

"Me?"

"If you needed to, do you think you could?"

I shrugged. I'd not given it any real consideration. I had acted instinctively on the beach, when I'd seen Pactolus charge at Azariah with the venom bullet. But the nearest I had ever come to thinking about killing someone was when Orontes had threatened me. I knew I would fight him if he ever tried to force himself on me. Perhaps I could kill him, if I had the means to do so.

"I suppose it depends on the circumstances," I decided. I'd never had any murderous thoughts toward Daniel. Maybe I should have. But I reasoned that it was practically impossible to hate him now that he was dead, murdered by Orontes.

"What circumstances?" Azariah pushed, leaning forward and pulling his legs up to mirror my position.

"Well, if your life was in danger, or Michael's, I think I would try to stop whoever was trying to kill you. If it meant killing them, then that's what I'd do. It's why I attacked Pactolus." I wriggled in the sand, uncomfortable with the topic of conversation.

"I think you are capable of killing. It is the Sachael in you," Azariah said, watching my reaction carefully.

"I don't think so. If I did, it'd only be because people I love were in danger. I'd want to save them."

"You may think that. But I think it is because you are a Sachael."

I narrowed my eyes. "Why does this matter?"

"Because living your life as a Sachael will bring you into contact with others who will want to harm you and those you care about. Unless, of course, you stay in Saicean for the rest of your life, never leaving the safety it offers."

I leaned away from him, pulling my legs even tighter to my body. "I'd feel trapped. And I'll need to visit my mum. I'm not deserting her."

"We shall have to see. My main concern is to keep you safe. That may mean staying in Saicean until Orontes is dealt with. I'm sure my father will not let you leave until it is safe, and he is the man to listen to. It will be his armies that hunt for Orontes; his army that will find him and kill him."

"So he'll keep me in Saicean. That's no better than a prison."

He raised his brow at me before leaning closer. "It means you stay alive."

"No, it doesn't." I jumped to my feet. "It means I'll be a prisoner. It'll be no better than when I was locked up by Orontes."

"You will be safe," he repeated before standing up.

"I want to be safe and free!" I shouted. "No one, not you, not your father, no one will keep me locked up in Saicean. I have a life away from you, remember? I wasn't born the day I met you. I had a life. I had structure to my days. I had my mother."

He stepped toward me, but I backed away, waving him off with my hands.

He sighed and ran his fingers through his hair. "We will have to see what my father says," he said. "But your safety will be his priority, Estelle. You don't argue with him."

I huffed at his words. "I'm not sure I'll like your father when I meet him." I screwed my nose up, once again reminded of the authority Azariah's father seemed to have.

His features hardened. "I ask that you get to know him before you make up your mind about him."

"Do you know what? I'd really like to get along with him. He's your father. But from what you've told me, I think we'll clash . . . a lot. He seems power crazy."

His serious expression met mine, and he shook his head.

"Please, sit down with me. I refuse to argue with you over my father and your safety. Both are of high importance to me."

I circled the sand with my foot. Had he understood anything I'd just said? Did he not see that being prevented from leaving Saicean was no better than being locked up by Orontes?

"You do not want to meet my father," he said softly. "Yet I am anxious to meet your mother when the time is right."

The mention of my mother made me smile, and my mind drifted to the happy, carefree times I'd spent with her before my father's death. All thoughts of Azariah's father disappeared.

"I think she'll like you," I said, recalling how excited and vocal she became when I first told her about the shell he'd left me.

"I am sure I will like her," he said before reaching for my hand. I didn't back away this time. He'd done nothing wrong; all he wanted to do was ensure I was safe. "As soon as it is possible, we will visit her," he said. "I cannot promise when that will be, but it is a promise."

"What about your father? Won't he stop us?" I couldn't help referring back to a man I had no desire to meet.

"If Orontes is dead, then he has no reason to stop us going anywhere. You'll be in no danger when with me. I am a formidable fighter. My father made sure of it." He looked away before shifting closer to my side.

I took a deep breath, my emotions warring against themselves. Part of me wanted to push him further, ask him more, but he always spoke with such seriousness when he mentioned his father. It was the same tone he used when he spoke about my safety. It was as if there was no room to question what he said. And really, how could I argue with him when all he was doing was ensuring I lived?

"Let's sleep," he said. "Another day has passed us by, and we are another day closer to the beauty of the full moon."

I looked to the sky, but the moon was barely visible. Its crescent shape was narrow, signifying a new moon tomorrow. There'd be no moon to see in the sky then. The thought didn't depress me, though; it filled me with joy. It meant that, each evening after, we would gradually see more and more of it. The crescent would grow every night, and we would be heading toward the magic of the next full moon. I paused, realizing what came next—Saicean. Why did I still fear it so much?

Azariah pulled a blanket over our bodies, and, once again, with Azariah by my side, I quickly sank into a peaceful slumber.

I dreamt of full moons, of underwater worlds, and of creatures I had yet to meet.

A terrible screaming noise shattered my peaceful sleep. I woke up startled, my heartbeat racing, nearly exploding with panic as I automatically reached for Azariah. He wasn't next to me.

"Azariah!" I shouted, looking around for him.

"I'm here, Estelle."

He was standing a few steps behind me, facing Melia's house.

I scrambled to my feet, looking around frantically, trying to locate where the scream had come from. "What's all the screaming? What's happening?"

"Melia."

He seemed to think that one word would explain the dreadful noise and the acrid smell filling the air.

He nodded toward the house, his expression firm and fixed, and I followed the direction of his gaze. Melia and Michael were arguing, their voices carrying across the bay on a heated, early morning breeze. Their argument didn't surprise me, but the large burning object next to her house did.

"Is that the van?" I asked, unable to comprehend what I was seeing.

"Yes," Azariah said calmly.

"She set fire to it? Why?"

"She will have hoped that, without the van, Michael wouldn't leave. Pointless really. We can go wherever we want in the sea." A grin flickered across Azariah's face before it quickly disappeared again. "Unfortunately, it means you two will get wet."

"Is it safe?" I asked, glancing to the sea. The early morning sun caught the tips of each wave as it tumbled ashore. It promised nothing but peace and tranquillity to me, but I knew the dangers it also presented. "We traveled across land and in the van because it was safer out of the water. Now we have to go back in?"

"Estelle, do not worry. The army has killed all of the Oceanids Orontes sent after us."

"There may still be a few around. They didn't get Orontes himself. And Chanon said he had taken some of the Oceanids with him." I hated that he dismissed the danger so easily.

"If there are, we will deal with them. There are twelve Sachaels in this army—they will protect us. We will be safe. Anyway, I thought you would like to be back in the water. Do you not miss it?"

I nodded slowly. I did miss it. I missed the sound of the underwater world, the freedom of movement. And Azariah was right. There were twelve strong Sachaels out there to defend us. Surely that would count for something? I would enjoy being in the water, but I didn't think Michael would be as keen. He hadn't developed a strong connection with being in the sea yet. Even though he felt drawn to it, he had only one experience of swimming underwater with Sachaels.

"I have tired of her behavior." Azariah scowled across the beach at Melia. "It is time we left."

He turned to face the ocean and lifted his arms away from his sides, drawing them slowly up above his head. The action was exactly the same as the one he'd completed when he rescued me from The Sect. And, like before, Sachaels began to rise from the surface of the water, walking toward us.

Twelve strong, statuesque Sachaels exited the water. Lit from behind by the early morning sun, they were a formidable sight. Chanon was at the front, leading them ashore.

The shouting and screaming suddenly stopped. In the distance, the fire roared, clashing with the sound of the waves. I glanced toward the burning mass and saw Melia running onto the beach, heading toward us. Michael followed, walking casually, showing no urgency to catch up with her.

"Morning, Azariah," Chanon said.

Azariah didn't respond with a greeting. "It seems the next part of our journey will be in the water. The Oceanid has seen to it that the van is of no further use to us," Azariah explained.

Chanon raised his brow at Azariah's statement and glanced across the beach. He frowned when he caught sight of Melia.

"Do you need me to dispose of her? If her anger is so strong that she feels the need to set fire to things, then perhaps she is too much of a risk to us."

I placed my hand on Azariah's arm, aware of what he had said to me yesterday. I was not to question him when the army was around. I picked my words carefully, ignoring Chanon just as he had done to me before. "She doesn't want Michael to leave. All this is is her way of trying to get him to stay. You can't kill her just because of that."

Chanon narrowed his eyes before turning to me. "I apologize. I had no idea you had struck up a friendship with her."

"She's not my friend," I snapped at him. "I just don't see why she should be killed."

Azariah interrupted our exchange.

"I understand your concern, Chanon, but Estelle is correct. The Oceanid is to be left alone. I anticipate that she will follow us into the sea and try to stay with us. A futile action; they are so much slower than us. But, nevertheless, you must instruct the men not to harm her in any way." He sounded bored, as if her response was not a surprise and perfectly normal.

Chanon nodded.

"I presume I am to travel with Michael again?" Chanon glanced at Michael, watching him approach before turning to Azariah for confirmation.

"Yes. His safety is paramount."

"I will leave him if either your or Estelle's life is threatened. You know you are my main concern, not him."

"Not if there is only a small risk of danger." Azariah pressed his lips together tightly. "You must stay with him. The other Sachaels will assist me."

Chanon sighed, but nodded.

"Do you have the bags with you?" Azariah queried, as he snapped his eyes from Chanon to the other men in the army.

"Yes."

Chanon pulled out two small pieces of fabric from his pocket. When he shook the material, they opened into medium-sized bags. The dark material looked as paper-thin as silk, with a subtle sheen on the surface.

"What's that for?" I asked.

I was sure Chanon grinned at my reaction. It took me by surprise. This was the first time I had witnessed any sign of friendliness from him toward me.

"Your spare clothes. It will keep them dry while we travel underwater," Azariah explained.

"Completely dry?" The material was so thin. How did it work?

"Yes." Azariah chuckled at my astonishment. "It's made out of a similar material to my shorts. Have you never wondered how they dry so quickly when I am out of the water?"

"No, I never really thought about it."

Azariah gathered the blankets and duffel bag and pushed them into the black silky bag.

"Instruct Geleon to carry it, and put Michael's duffel bag in the other one when he gets here.. Estelle and Michael will need them when we return to land."

Chanon nodded before diverting his gaze to Melia, who was striding toward us. "We have a rather irate Oceanid approaching. We need to go."

"You're leaving?" Melia screamed at Azariah. "You're *all* leaving?"

Azariah turned toward her. "I told you yesterday that we would not impose on you any longer. Why are you alarmed by our actual departure, when I told you of our intention last night?"

Her eyes darted to me.

"It's her fault. If she wasn't here, none of this would be happening."

There were tears in her eyes, but I had no sympathy for her, not after the way she'd spoken to me yesterday.

"I assure you, Michael would be leaving with us regardless of Estelle's presence," Azariah said sympathetically.

"I hate you," she spat in my direction, obviously blaming me for everything that was happening.

"It's true," I began. "Michael has to go with Azariah."

"Don't you dare speak to me," Melia snapped.

"Be quiet!" Chanon's growling voice made me jump, and I was even more shocked when he stepped toward Melia, placing himself between her and me. "You do not speak to Estelle like that. She has, this morning, saved your pathetic life."

"She'd never help me," Melia hissed at him.

"She just did. I was willing to snap your neck. She stopped me."

Melia glared at me before turning to Chanon. Unexpectedly, she raised her hand to his face, touching his scars with her fingers. He flinched and grabbed her hand. "Don't touch me," he growled.

"But *you* saved me, not her. Even though you look fierce, I feel you have a strong, passionate heart." I gasped at her sudden switch of emotions, yet again. She was flirting with him. Never had I seen the attraction the Oceanids held for the Sachaels so openly displayed. It was a strange thing to witness, but also incredibly sad. She had no control whatsoever over her feelings.

She stepped closer to Chanon, their bodies touching. "Will you take me as your wife?"

Chanon's hold must have tightened on her wrist, for she grimaced, trying to twist away from his grip.

"I told you not to touch me," he snarled. He maneuvered her to his will, bending her arm and forcing her onto her knees on the sand. He leaned over her, his face next to her ear. "I should have snapped your neck, just as I always do when I come across a vicious, nasty Oceanid. The fact that you are a female is of no concern to me. In a way, I hate your gender even more than the males."

"But . . . but . . ."

"Chanon, stop! Please," I implored.

Michael stood nearby, his bag slung across his shoulder. He was wide-eyed as he viewed their exchange. Azariah sighed, his expression calm. I had no idea how he remained so focused when chaos was breaking out all around him.

"Enough!" Azariah ordered. "We must leave. Chanon, take Michael. There are no further goodbyes to be made."

Chanon let go of Melia, causing her to slump onto the sand. I crouched at her side, wanting to make sure she was okay. She pushed her hair from her face before turning toward me.

"I will track you down, and I will kill you for this," she hissed quietly. Her whispered threat made me step away. Azariah frowned at my reaction.

"Come, Estelle. We must go. Leave her, she is no concern of ours."

I stepped toward him, taking his outstretched hand in mine.

Chanon strode over to the silent Michael and patted his shoulder before they both turned toward the sea. Michael's duffel bag flew through the air toward Geleon, who immediately pushed it into the waterproof bag.

The group of Sachaels formed a protective circle around us, moving as one in our steady advance into the ocean.

"Sanday," Azariah said as he turned to the men. "We are heading to Sanday. It is an island in the far north of the Orkneys. Let us get there as quickly as we can."

I couldn't resist taking one last brief look behind us as the water reached my knees. Melia was still lying on the sand; she hadn't moved. But as we headed into deeper water, her loud, agonized scream rang out across the beach. She had lost us—all of us.

SEVEN
Tension

My journey in the water was as exciting and exhilarating as when we'd traveled to Rackwick Bay. Several seals swam alongside us as we set off, and as we swam along the easterly coast of Scotland, we were joined by a pod of dolphins. Azariah didn't appear to be concerned with their appearance, and participated in playful maneuvers with them, twisting and diving while we traveled—all the time with me on his back.

I really wanted to swim by myself, but there was no way I could keep up with the punishing speed the army set. Azariah still needed to surface every couple of minutes for me to breathe, but as the journey progressed, I no longer needed to squeeze his hands to inform him that I needed air. He guessed the intervals between breaths and rose to the surface regularly. I loved swimming with him. It was a reason to hold him tightly, for our bodies to lay against each other's, and a chance to experience the closeness in private, unseen by other Sachaels. I settled comfortably against his back—my head between his shoulder blades, resting the side of my face against his Sachael mark. Every so often, he would move one of his hands from his chest and place it on my hip, gently rubbing his fingers against the material of my jeans. It was an incredibly simple gesture, but one I knew he did to reassure me. It seemed he was enjoying the proximity of our bodies just as much as I was.

I wondered how Michael was managing. Chanon hadn't seemed impressed with the order to carry him, and he would have to surface more regularly than Azariah did with me. I also worried about how he was coping with what he had witnessed on the beach. Neither Azariah nor I had spoken to him since yesterday evening. Melia's behavior must have shocked and enraged him. He'd dealt with her wild temper before, when he'd refused to return to the Orkneys with her, but I was sure he would never have seen her behave the way she did toward Chanon. I hoped Azariah would take the time to explain it to him. If he didn't, then I would. It wasn't fair to not tell him.

We left the water, paddling toward an empty, sandy sweep of bay. I had never seen such golden sands or turquoise waters. It didn't feel like we were as far north as we were in the Orkneys. It looked more like I imagined a tropical island would. Michael came splashing up behind us, Chanon following close behind him, yanking the bags from Geleon as he walked past him. Geleon slipped back under the water as soon as he was relieved of the baggage.

"Hey," Michael said, grabbing Azariah's shoulder. "What the hell happened back there?"

Azariah stopped walking and slowly turned to face him. He looked pointedly at his shoulder, where Michael's hand remained, before lifting his gaze to his face.

"Let us start a fire to warm ourselves up, and then I shall explain." He nodded at Chanon. "Grab some firewood, and sort some food."

Chanon threw the bags at Azariah, who caught them and grinned. He attempted to spin around and finish walking to shore, but Michael's hand remained firm on his shoulder, holding him still.

"That's not soon enough," Michael snapped. "Tell me now!"

Chanon was immediately at Azariah's side. "Let go," he said—an order, with no room for argument. Michael didn't seem to hear, or if he did, he ignored him.

Michael stared at Chanon. "She offered herself to you, right there in front of me. Why? What? Do you know her?"

Chanon's top lip lifted in a snarl. "No. I'd never seen her before in my life. But if I see her again, I'll kill her. You have no need to worry about my interest in her. Now, I'll tell you again. Let go of Azariah."

Michael suddenly seemed to realize that he was still holding Azariah's shoulder and quickly let go.

"She's an Oceanid," Azariah said, sighing, as if that explained everything. He glanced at me, and then Chanon. "Can you stay with Estelle? Get things organized while I have a chat with Michael?"

Chanon nodded before taking the bags back from Azariah and turning toward me. I looked away, not particularly happy about Azariah's decision. I still had a strange feeling when Chanon was around—he made me anxious, uncomfortable. I knew I'd not had much to do with him, but despite Azariah's reassurance to the contrary, I was sure he didn't like me.

"How are you feeling after your swim?" he asked, wandering alongside me as I strode onto the beach.

"Okay," I said, not really wanting to engage in a conversation with him.

He cocked his head to the side and swung the bags over his opposite shoulder. "You need to get used to it. The swim to Saicean will be hard enough for you."

I raised my brow. "For me? Why?"

"Because you're female," he said. "The weaker sex."

I gaped at him, and then looked away. Sachaels may be the most intense seducers anyone had ever known, but they were seriously out of touch when it came to treating women as equals.

"I'm sure I'll manage," I replied.

I cast my eyes back to Azariah. He had his arm across Michael's shoulders, and they were walking in the gentle swell of the incoming tide. I was glad he was taking the time to explain to him about the Oceanids and their crazy obsession with Sachaels. But I wished Michael would have waited a little longer before demanding answers.

Chanon interrupted my thoughts. "So, Azariah tells me you're from Ravenscar."

I nodded, wetting my salty lips with my tongue.

"Have you lived there since you were born?" He was fully focused on me, his eyes bright and attentive. His face appeared softer, not as hard set as when he'd previously come out of the water.

I nodded again, shooting him an inquisitive look.

"No siblings?"

"No." I frowned. "Why all the questions?"

He smiled—a genuine smile this time, not the usual smirk or the private, hidden amusement he seemed to have when I was around. "Just curious." He pointed to an area of the beach that was sheltered by a high sandy bank. "Over there looks like a decent spot for you to stay."

I walked slowly, enjoying the feel of the sharp sand between my toes. I'd also hoped that Chanon would walk ahead—his stride was a lot longer than mine.

Unfortunately, as I slowed my steps, he matched my pace.

"Not long to go before your next submergence," he said. There was a lightness to his voice that surprised me, and as I turned to look at him, he offered me another smile. I frowned, not knowing how to react to his sudden change toward me. What was going on?

"There's still fourteen days," I replied, knowing exactly how long the wait was.

"Are you looking forward to going to Saicean?"

I scratched my head, confused by his sudden interest in me and my thoughts.

"No," I said.

He stopped walking. I took a few more steps and then stopped. Turning to face him, I decided to be honest.

"I'm scared about what'll greet me when I get there. I'm petrified about being in a world full of males. Azariah keeps telling me how important I am, and that scares me more. I'm not stupid. I know what will be expected of me when I'm there."

He cocked his head to the side, and his frown deepened. "And that is what, exactly?"

"Children." The word fell from my lips as easy as rain falls from the sky. "The possibility that I could have girls—female Sachaels."

Chanon lifted his hand to his brow and rubbed at his hairline. "You don't have to do anything you don't want to do, Estelle. Azariah would never force you to become pregnant." He reached for my hand, but I drew away from him. "Look," he continued, "if anyone tries to force you into a situation you don't want, if anyone tries to harm you, threatens you, or makes demands on you that you're not happy with, come and find me. I'll help you."

I stepped backward, putting more space between us. I couldn't work him out. He'd completely changed character. Gone was the surly, angry-looking Sachael I'd witnessed in the past, and in his place was a concerned and approachable man. Someone who seemed genuinely interested in my well-being. Alarm bells sounded in my head. What was he really after?

"Just don't tell Azariah what I've said. He's incredibly jealous of anyone talking to you, never mind me offering to help you."

"But I thought you two were close. You've known each other for years."

Chanon nodded. "Doesn't mean I always do as he says. Just remember, that's all. I'll look out for you . . . always."

"What are you two talking about?" Azariah was back, an easy smile playing on his lips.

Chanon lifted his head in Azariah's direction before pointing to the area of beach we had originally started to walk toward. "Looks like a decent place to spend the next few nights," he said before strolling away.

I frowned at his departure, somewhat confused, but also intrigued.

"Has Chanon bored you with his talk of all the battles he's been in?"

I forced a smile and nodded. I didn't want to tell Azariah what Chanon had said. If he was genuine, then his offer of friendship would indeed be welcome when I got to Saicean. I loved Azariah, but I knew life with him wouldn't always be easy. Chanon's words played on my mind. He said he'd look out for me. In what way? He said he'd help me if I needed help. How?

I sighed heavily and leaned against Azariah as we followed Chanon across the beach.

"Are you tired?" he asked, placing his arm around my shoulders.

"Just a bit. A lot's happened over the last few days. I think it's catching up with me."

"Well, we will be staying here for a while. Hopefully you will be able to relax a little. You can also sleep now, if you want."

"I'll try to stay awake, otherwise I won't sleep tonight," I said. I glanced back over my shoulder. Michael was sitting on the sand at the edge of the waves, focused on the horizon, not moving. "Is he okay?" I asked.

Azariah followed my gaze. "Yes. He understands Melia's behavior now. He does not like what happened and is now questioning whether any of her emotions were real. She was his first lover, and the first woman he ever loved. She has, although unintentionally, broken his heart twice."

"Poor Michael," I said. "It's so unfair."

"He will be fine. He asked for some time to himself. I suggest we tread carefully around him for the rest of the day." He offered me a smile, and then lifted his gaze to Chanon. "I see he is already sorting the fire."

The bags were on the sand, and, a few feet away, Chanon leaned over a small pyramid of twigs. He jumped to his feet as we approached and headed off along the beach searching for driftwood and dry seaweed.

Azariah and I positioned ourselves next to the bags, and I promptly dried my hair and changed my top. I slipped out of my jeans, cursing the wetness of the material as it clung to my legs. Azariah watched the entire time I was changing, grinning. He found my predicament entertaining. But there was also another set of eyes watching me. A focus that quickly flew away whenever I turned his way—Chanon. His sudden interest confused me; it seemed to have come from nowhere. And I wasn't totally convinced he was genuine. Somewhere at the back of my mind alarm bells were ringing. I needed to listen to them.

Michael was quiet for the rest of the day, just as Azariah predicted. He often left us and took walks along the beach. He paddled in the gentle, tumbling waves but frequently stopped and stared at the horizon. Azariah always stared after him, concern covering his features.

As the evening drew in, we cooked the fish Chanon had again caught for us. Azariah took charge, leaning over the fire and removing the sticks with the impaled fish from the flames when he deemed them ready. He offered the cooked fish to Michael and me.

It was only as Michael finished eating his fourth fish that he turned to look at first me, then Azariah with a confused, bewildered expression.

"You have a question?" Azariah asked.

"Well, in a way, yes, but not concerning female Oceanids. I think I've done all the thinking I can where Melia's concerned. It's about male Oceanids, specifically Orontes."

I shuddered when he mentioned his name. Azariah wrapped his hand around mine—a silent reassurance.

"Go on," Azariah encouraged, turning back to Michael.

"Does the attraction work the other way? I mean, Estelle is a Sachael, not a land one, but not a full one, either—she's sort of in between. But I never did understand why Orontes acted the way he did with her."

"I think it is possible," Azariah said, pulling me tightly against his side.

"I'm positive about it," I added. "And you're right. I'm not even a full Sachael yet. What the heck would he have been like if I'd completed my submergences in Saicean?" I shuddered again. Visions of Orontes filled my head—his tall, muscular body standing over me, his threatening words, his intimidating behavior. His sly smile when he thought he'd managed to wheedle his way into my affections. And the kiss. The one time I'd not fought with him, the one time I'd willingly kissed him. I lifted my fingers to my mouth and traced the outline of my lips before lowering my gaze to the sand and hugging myself. Guilt—I recognized the feeling.

"Can we change the subject?" I asked, my voice shaky. "I really don't want to think about Orontes and my time with The Sect. They're not exactly pleasant memories."

Azariah lifted one of his hands to cup the side of my face. His azure eyes burned through me with their intensity. "I have already promised that when you are safe, I will hunt him down with the strongest, fastest army I can gather, and I will kill him."

"Kill or be killed," I muttered. I knew how it felt to want someone dead. Perceptions could shift depending on the circumstances. And sometimes, it was necessary to protect what was important.

"Exactly," Azariah stated solemnly. "That is exactly how you should be thinking."

"Spoken like a true Sachael," Michael agreed.

It was a serious moment; a time when Michael and I understood just how important our lives had become. No matter how much we tried to think we were human, there was something, someone to remind us differently. We were similar in so many ways, our worlds united in our behaviors. Both Sachaels and humans fought for what they believed to be right. How many wars had raged on land over the years? How many battles had been fought between Sachaels and their enemies? On land, the laws were complex, designed to protect the innocent, serve a justice that had been set down for centuries, but at the end of the day, wasn't it all about survival of the fittest, or the most intelligent? I shook my head, my mind buzzing with my raging thoughts.

I sighed heavily, leaning against Azariah.

"Are you still tired?" he asked.

I nodded, even though I suspected he already knew my answer.

"Would you like me to help you sleep?"

"Work a bit of your Sachael magic?" I queried, wriggling my nose and grinning.

"Magic?" Michael exclaimed. "What magic?"

Azariah chuckled as he lay on the sand, pulling me to his side.

"Sachaels have the ability to calm people. You will have it to some degree, even though you are a land Sachael."

Michael frowned. "I remember Lilith telling me she felt calm when I was near her. And when I met Estelle, I felt something—a calmness, tranquility. When I left her to find your shell, I was on edge. I presumed I was worried about getting caught. But it was probably because I was away from Estelle, huh? I must have gotten used to her calming vibes." He laughed as he finished speaking. Azariah grinned at his explanation.

"And you!" Michael shouted excitedly, wagging his finger at Azariah. "That first night after we left my mum's. I was in the van, and you two were on the beach. I told you I had the best night's sleep ever. I assumed it was because we were free, but it was you. Wasn't it?"

"I see my ability did get you at least some rest that night."

"Will I be able to calm people the way you do when I've done my submergences?" Michael's words were rushed, his excitement bubbling over.

"Yes, the ability is born within you. With each submergence, it will become stronger."

"This is amazing," Michael enthused, and I chuckled softly. At least he'd found something to be excited about, a silver lining in all this chaos.

"Shhh . . ." Azariah encouraged. "Let Estelle sleep. It is late, and we need to rest. It has been a busy day."

Azariah placed the blanket over us before wrapping his arms around me. As his lips pressed a kiss to my forehead, my eyelids became heavy. He was already working his Sachael magic.

I was soon fast asleep.

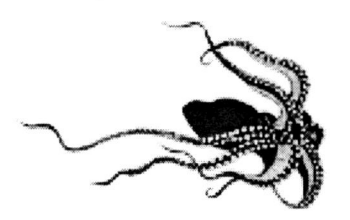

EIGHT
Unease

We stayed on the beach at Sanday for four days before moving to another. Four days later, we moved again. Life was simple, but not easy. None of us had forgotten why we couldn't settle or stay anywhere for long. Tempers were building. Annoyances were becoming arguments; disagreements became rumbling storms of anger threatening to explode. Every time we moved, it brought us that much closer to the full moon, but also that much closer to devolving into a battle of wills.

We'd been on this beach on Fetlar for three days. It was an island in the Shetlands, even further north than the

Orkneys, and it was the same island where two of Michael's friends from University lived. He kept suggesting we go and visit them, but Azariah was having none of it.

The weather had been kind to us since we settled here, but today, there was a strong wind blowing across the bay. Michael wasn't his usual cheerful self, the situation having caused him and Azariah to argue at length last night. Today, he took every opportunity to complain.

"We need to move from here, go and stay with Sam and Cleo," he said to me, as Azariah walked across the beach to speak to Chanon. He contacted Chanon every morning and every evening in the same way. Chanon hadn't come out of the water since the day of our arrival, and I only saw the heads of the other Sachaels bobbing in the water. No one disturbed us; it was just Michael, Azariah, and me.

"I don't think it would be wise to stay here any longer either, but you know what he's like." I nodded in Azariah's direction, seeing him place the palms of his hands flat on the water before sinking slowly below the surface. "He didn't enjoy staying with Melia. Neither did I."

"If his reason for not going is because he thinks Sam and Cleo are Oceanids, then he's wrong. They were never hot-headed like Melia. They were normal." His hands were tucked in the pockets of his jeans, and he kicked at the sand.

"So you keep saying, but what if you're wrong? The female he can cope with, and so can I, to a point. But Sam is male. Male Oceanids hate Sachaels. What reception do you think he'll give Azariah if he is, in fact, an Oceanid? You as well, when he knows the truth? And me? What will his reaction be to me?" I wished Michael could understand why Azariah didn't want to stay with them. I felt caught in the middle of their argument, both of them refusing to see the other's point of view. They were very much alike in that way—stubborn.

"If they are Oceanids, and it is as bad as you think, then we can always leave. We can go somewhere else. I don't know about you, but I need a comfy bed, even if it's just for one night. And some food other than fish. And a shower. I stink." He chuckled, and I couldn't help but laugh. He had a point. The sand was comfortable for one night, but eleven nights in a row was too much. I didn't fancy another evening spent on the hard, unforgiving sand any more than he did.

Michael stared in the general direction of Azariah, watching him rise from under the water. "What does it feel like?" he asked. "Doing the submergences?"

"It just feels like ducking under the water, but afterward, it's amazing," I said, lost in my memories of the last submergence I did with Azariah. "I always feel renewed, stronger, as if I could face anything."

"Do you think I'll feel like that after my first one?"

I shrugged. "I'm not sure, but I should think so. It's quite strong."

My eyes locked with Azariah's as he walked toward us.

"Azariah?" Michael called. "I can't stay here any longer." He stood tall, as if ready for another disagreement, the previous topic clearly forgotten. I sighed.

"Why not?"

"I need a few home comforts and a decent meal. Surely you must be missing the luxuries you have in Saicean?"

"I do not need luxuries in my life." He turned to me as he took my hand. "I have all I need right here."

"Michael has a point," I stated, understanding both of their concerns. "We've been here for three days. Surely it would make sense to move somewhere else? We do need to keep moving."

Azariah frowned. "You want to leave?"

I scratched the side of my head. "It's not that I want to leave; it's more I think we should."

Azariah sighed. "So it shall be. I will tell Chanon of our plan to move." He turned to head back to the sea.

"Hey, wait!" Michael exclaimed, stepping up to Azariah. "I'm not going in the water today. We travel over land this time. It's too wild out there for me."

Azariah stopped in his tracks, turning to scowl at Michael. "You will come to no harm. Chanon will be with you."

Michael shook his head. "No. Not today."

"You are a Sachael," Azariah snapped, moving to stand in front of him. The tone of his voice deepened, and his lips curled. "You should not show fear about traveling in the swell of the sea."

"I'm not a proper Sachael, though, am I?" Michael said, glaring at Azariah. "I'm a land Sachael. I haven't submerged yet. I don't even know what I need to do when I submerge. I love the ocean as much as you, but I have no desire to be dragged through it today by Chanon. It's not far to Sam and Cleo's. I'll walk."

"I cannot leave you by yourself."

"Then you'll have to come with me, won't you?" His lips twitched as he raised an eyebrow.

Azariah's posture became stiff, his muscles rigid. Another argument was brewing.

Azariah pinched the bridge of his nose and closed his eyes. He sighed heavily.

"Okay," he said, rubbing the back of his neck. "Where exactly do they live?"

"Next to the beach at Tresta. It's on the other side of the island," Michael said, grinning at his small victory.

"I will tell Chanon where we are heading," Azariah said through gritted teeth. "You may as well pack the bags. You will be carrying them."

I suppressed a laugh at the look on Michael's face. He mumbled something under his breath, glaring at Azariah as he watched him stroll calmly back toward the sea.

"Cheer up," I teased, gathering the blankets from the sand and shaking them. "At least we're moving away from here. You can have some decent food, and a shower."

While I was looking forward to a cozy bed and something other than fish and crabs for sustenance, I was also dreading the possibility that we were about to face two more Oceanids. The only experiences I'd had of Oceanids were Orontes, Pactolus, and Melia. I would hardly put any of them on my list of people I wanted to spend time with. One of them had wanted to go off into the sea with Azariah, another wanted to go into the sea with me, and the other had hated me because of my attraction to Sachaels. Perhaps it was as Azariah said—Oceanids were a breed best left alone.

Michael took the blankets from me before stuffing them into one of the bags.

"Does Cleo look like Melia?" I asked. The way Azariah had explained Oceanids had piqued my curiosity. Where they all as stunning as Melia?

Michael turned in my direction, but his gaze was somewhere else.

"She has blonde hair," he stated, snapping out of his trance. "But she always wore it short. I never gave her appearance much attention."

"And Sam, what's he like?" He was my main concern, if indeed they were Oceanids. Not only because of the way he would potentially act toward me, but how he would react to Azariah.

"He was a good friend. Serious, but with a wild side. He had a ridiculous mohawk when we were at University." His familiar grin reappeared, and I nodded at his descriptions of them. They were the two people I'd seen in the other photos back at Melia's

"And they've been together all this time?"

"They've known each other since they were children. I think their relationship is strong. Not like Melia and me."

"Are you ready?" Azariah called as he returned. His face was hard-set; no hint of amusement pulled at his features as he waited for Michael to fasten the duffel bags.

"Stop glaring at me like I'm your enemy," Michael grumbled, catching sight of Azariah's expression.

Azariah's turned his full glare on Michael then. "If you were my enemy, I would have killed you a long time ago."

"Azariah," I gasped. How could he say such a thing?

"Good job I'm related to you then, *Uncle*, and am not your enemy," Michael said as he slung the duffel bags over his shoulders.

I shook my head at their interaction. They squabbled like children. They were acting like they'd known each other for years, not just a few weeks.

"Their names convince me of their origin," Azariah said quietly as he came and stood beside me.

"Cleo and Sam?" I didn't see anything unusual in their names.

"Michael told me their full names are Cleodora and Scamander. Scamander is a typical Oceanid name. Cleodora, not so much, but still highly unusual for people who claim to have Scottish heritage, do you not agree?" He continued to watch Michael, who was waiting for us to move.

"They do sound a bit Oceanid-ish," I replied, grinning at Michael, who huffed.

Azariah waved his arm in an exaggerated circle, silently instructing Michael to lead the way.

"You're too hard on him at times," I whispered as he took my hand in his and we followed Michael's lead.

"No, I am not. He should have traveled in the sea today. The army will see him as weak, and that is not a good thing for any Sachael."

"But, as he said, he's not yet done a submergence. He loves the water, you know that, but he doesn't have a passion for the ocean in the way you do. And, to be honest, I wouldn't have wanted to travel in the sea today, either—it looks wild." I gazed at the churning water. "I rescued you from a stormy sea once, remember?"

"Yes, I remember—how could I forget?" He squeezed my hand. "But the sea is nowhere near as angry as it was that night. It is this strange movement of air causing the waves to look fierce. Under the surface, it is relatively calm."

As if to verify his point, a strong breeze blew from the direction of the sea and across the sand dunes. We didn't get much further before it started raining. Azariah smiled as his hair brushed across his forehead.

"I find the elements on land most interesting, but also enchanting."

"The wind, or the rain?" I asked, surprised by his statement.

"Both."

I didn't share his enthusiasm for either and hunched my shoulders as the rain started to fall even heavier. "Don't you have anything like them in Saicean?"

"No. We have no . . . wind, no rain." Azariah looked to the sky above as he walked, and grinned as the rain hit his face.

"What about the sun?"

"No sun."

"Really? Isn't it cold, then? And dark?" I glanced around at the landscape we were walking through. The island wasn't as hilly as Hoy, but there was a lack of trees and houses, just as there had been there. The wind was also a lot stronger here, and it blew bitterly cold.

Azariah grinned at my curiosity. He lifted my hand and placed it on his shoulder.

"Feel how warm my skin is. We don't feel the cold. Our bodies adjust to whatever the temperature is. Have you never wondered why you didn't get cold in the sea when you did your submergences?"

"I never really thought about it."

He released my hand. "A normal person would be shivering after being in the water for any length of time." Azariah spoke quickly, his pace matching his words. I trotted to keep up with him.

"Tractor!" Michael shouted from up ahead.

I pulled Azariah onto the grass verge and waited with him for the rumbling vehicle to pass along the narrow road.

"You look ridiculous without a top on," I said to Azariah, having noticed the quizzical look the driver of the tractor gave him.

Azariah shrugged. "As I said, I am warm. I do not feel the cold. But what about your submergences?" He picked up on what we'd been discussing before.

"Well, maybe because my father didn't feel the cold, I presumed it was normal. But why did he not feel it? Surely, if he were a land Sachael, he would have. You said once seven submergences have been missed, the Sachael has none of his normal abilities." I was puzzled by Azariah's obvious excitement about the subject and focused on Michael instead, who strode ahead of us, seemingly as desperate to get out of the rain and wind as I was.

"For some reason, the ability to not feel the cold of the sea is with us when we are born and never leaves us," Azariah said. "I only found this out recently."

"How?" I pushed my wet hair behind my ears and tried to stop my teeth from chattering. It was all well and good talking about not getting cold in the sea, but on land, for me and Michael, it was an entirely different matter. Maybe we should have made this part of our journey in the sea—we'd be warmer.

"Michael," he stated quietly, nodding in his direction. "When we arrived at his mother's, I missed that he was not shivering when he got out of the water. He should have been if he was human. I cannot believe I did not pick up on that. I told Chanon to keep an eye out for any sign of the cold affecting him when we left Melia's. He was fine when we arrived on the island. He has not submerged, not once in his life, but he does not feel the cold of the ocean."

"I never even thought about it," I said.

Azariah grinned. He'd always reveled in finding out new things, in experiencing events on land for the first time. But it was intriguing to see his natural curiosity leading him to discover more about his own kind, and their land existence.

I was struggling with the crazy weather that was bombarding us. My bare feet stung each time they pressed against the gravel road, and my hands were losing any feeling they'd had. I'd given up trying to stop my teeth chattering and hugged myself, rubbing my hands up and down my arms as we continued our hasty walk to get to Sam and Cleo's.

"You asked if we have light in Saicean," Azariah reminded me as he pulled my shaking body against his warm one. "Yes, we do. The seven moons provide us with light. We never have the darkness of a night."

"It never gets dark?" I was surprised. I'd always imagined Saicean as a dark place to live.

"No."

"Is that why you always like staying on the beach at night? You like the dark?" I snuggled into his heated flesh, welcoming his arm as he placed it around my shoulder.

"No. That is only one of the reasons." He turned to me and ran his fingers through my soaking wet hair. "It is because I want to spend the night with you under a starlit sky. It is perfect."

"Such a charmer," I said as I smiled at him.

"Oh, come on you two," Michael moaned. He was walking backwards, watching our interaction. "The faster we walk, the sooner we get there."

"I see he is as eager to visit Sam and Cleo as he was to visit Melia," Azariah commented as Michael spun around and walked at a faster pace than before.

"Really? I think it's because it's freezing out here. He wants to get inside, out of the rain and away from the wind."

Azariah nodded. "Maybe, but I am most anxious about what we are walking into this time. I do not think I will have much patience with Cleo if she behaves the same way as Melia. And you must tell me if she upsets you."

"I will. Surely they can't all be as bad as Melia. Although, I'm not so sure how I'll cope in Saicean. All those Oceanid women fawning over you." I placed my arm around his waist, curling my fingers under the waistband of his shorts.

Azariah chuckled and placed his arm around my waist.

"You have no reason to worry. They will leave me alone when they see you are with me. I am more concerned about the behavior of the Sachaels when they see you."

"Why?" Now what didn't I know? I tilted my head to look at Azariah. "I thought it was only the Oceanids who have an attraction to us?"

Azariah smiled.

"You spoke as one of us, Estelle."

"What?"

"You said you thought it was only the Oceanids who have an attraction to us. Us. You classed yourself as a Sachael. It is the first time I have heard you say it."

I grinned at his enthusiasm over my word choice as he proceeded to answer my initial question.

"Oceanids are attracted to us, but your appearance will cause quite a stir amongst the Sachaels. Many of them will want your attention. Think about it, Estelle. You are the same as them—they will be curious. And they will definitely be attracted to you." He focused on the road ahead, which had a gentle incline and led to the sea. "The men in my army are talking about you. They shut their minds to me when I am in the water, but Chanon has mentioned their discussions."

"Chanon? Does he see me that way?" I hadn't seen much of him recently, but the quick talk we'd had last week still played in my mind.

"He is not allowed to think such things," Azariah replied. "He would be dishonoring the woman I have chosen. If he had any feelings toward you, he would not be able to continue with his position as second-in-command. Therefore, he forbids himself to think that way. I know he has reprimanded the other men for some of their talk as well. It is best I do not know what they are saying."

I frowned. "Best for whom?"

"For them, Estelle. I would have to kill them if I knew of their words."

I narrowed my eyes, looking blindly ahead. I hated it when he spoke this way.

He must have sensed my unease, as his arm pulled me closer.

"You have nothing to worry about," he whispered. "We are very honorable."

I huffed at him. I knew he was honorable, but I doubted all Sachaels were.

"Stop trying to make me feel better," I protested. "As long as you are with me, I know I'll be okay. And you'll have no need to kill anyone."

"Come on!" Michael shouted, spinning around to face us. Once again, he walked backward as he continued talking. "We're nearly there."

The road before us led down a gentle slope, heading toward the sea. Green fields sprawled out on either side of the road, but there was still no sign of any houses.

"Jeepers, I'm soaked," Michael grumbled. "It'll be a miracle if I don't get pneumonia. I need that shower more than ever—you too, Estelle. Look at you. Are your teeth chattering?" He laughed when I nodded my response. "I need a decent shower, and a shave."

I turned to Azariah as Michael turned back to face the way he was going. "Are you going to shave?"

"Do you think I need to?" He rubbed his jaw.

I remembered seeing him in the water several times with Chanon, both of them shaving each other's stubble with the knives they carried. I was alarmed at first, seeing the metal blades catching the sunlight. It was only when Michael told me what they were doing that I had watched with fascination as they carefully assisted each other.

Today, Azariah's face showed a dark stubble. I lifted my hand to the side of his face, stroking the rough surface running along his jaw.

"I like your stubble. It's how I picture you when I dream."

"Then I will not shave for a few more days, although I warn you now. I am beginning to look like my father."

"He has a beard?"

Azariah nodded.

"Maybe you should shave then." I grinned as I responded, and Azariah laughed.

We continued to trudge along the road, avoiding the dips at the side that had quickly filled with puddles. For the last five minutes of the walk, the rain stopped, but we were all thoroughly soaked. My teeth eventually gave up chattering, but the cold had seeped into my bones—I didn't think I'd ever get warm again. I clung to Azariah, welcoming the heat he generated as we made our advance on the stone cottage.

Michael strode on ahead of us as we approached the building that was set out over two floors. I sighed heavily, seeing the similarity to Melia's house. It did nothing to ease my worry.

"Sam, Cleo!" Michael called as he knocked on the door.

A blond male opened the door, and Michael held his arms out to his side. "Afternoon, Sam. Bet you didn't expect me turning up on your doorstep."

Sam's face flushed red. "Michael? What the hell?" A huge grin covered his face as he held his arms out and stepped toward Michael. They hugged, slapping each other's backs.

"No Cleo?" Michael asked as he released Sam.

"She's out swimming, gone to fetch our dinner. She'll not be long."

"He is an Oceanid," Azariah whispered to me.

"How do you know?" I whispered back.

"I told you before. I can tell. It is instinctual."

Michael broke our hushed conversation by clearing his throat. I looked over to where he stood. Sam was next to him, his brow deeply furrowed. His legs were planted wide apart, and his hands rested on his hips. His face was still red, but he held his chin high, defiant.

"Sam, this is Azariah, and Estelle. Friends of mine," Michael said.

Sam's eyes widened when he caught my eye, but his stance stiffened as Azariah moved forward to shake his hand. He didn't offer his hand in return.

Azariah pulled his hand back and fixed Sam with a hard stare, the tension between them palpable.

"Woah, woah, woah," Michael said, stepping between them and waving his hands at both of them. "What's all this?"

Neither of them answered.

"Az? Sam?" He looked at both of them in turn.

"He is a Sachael," Sam growled. "I will not have him anywhere near my house."

Azariah straightened but stood his ground. I placed my hand on his arm, willing him to calm.

"Az is all right," Michael said, patting Sam on his shoulder. "He's a good man."

"Good? Sachaels are not to be trusted. They are vicious and uncouth, and have no sense of right or wrong."

Azariah raised his brow and sighed heavily.

"How many more Oceanids do you know, Michael?" he said. "Are all your 'friends' the same?"

"What do you mean? I've told you, Sam's not an Oceanid."

Azariah raised his brow even more. "Really? How does he know I am a Sachael then? Our existence is not extensively known."

"Sam," Michael said, cocking his head to the side. "Is that how you know he's a Sachael? Are you an Oceanid?"

Sam drew in a deep breath before nodding at Michael.

"Oh, for crying out loud." Michael tipped his head to look at the sky, and then burst out laughing. A response none of us expected.

Azariah pushed his shoulders back, tensing even more. Sam matched his gesture. I saw nothing funny about the situation.

"So Cleo's an Oceanid as well?" Michael asked, his laughter fading.

Sam nodded.

"All this time, you two, Melia. Why didn't you tell me when we were all at Uni together? I feel like I missed out on a great opportunity to tease you all."

"I have no argument with you," Sam said, not sharing Michael's amusement at the situation. "But I am concerned about the company you keep."

"Az and Estelle are great," Michael said, sobering instantly. "He saved my life, and Estelle's. Honestly, Sam, you have nothing to worry about." He shrugged his shoulders and held his hands out to the side. "What do you expect him to do?"

"I have come across his kind before. I have seen how they treat us."

"You, as in Oceanids?"

Sam nodded before crossing his arms and stepping closer to Michael.

"I am no threat," Azariah said, his shoulders relaxing. "But one of your own kind is a threat to Michael. He brought us here so we could relax for a few days before leaving. I will not allow Michael to be caught."

I eyed Azariah warily. He was telling half-truths, but I understood his reasoning. Sam may let us stay if he thought Michael was in danger. And it wasn't a lie. Michael was being hunted, just like Azariah, and me.

"My own kind?" Sam inclined his head. "Trying to catch Michael? Why?"

"It's true," I said. "You were at University with Pactolus, Michael told me. It seems Michael has upset Pactolus's father." I chose not to mention Orontes by name; the less Sam knew, the better. "He wants to find him. It's best that he doesn't."

Michael nodded, catching on to what we were doing.

"I rescued him once from Pactolus's father," Azariah added. "And I intend to keep him safe from now on." He sighed and took a step forward. "Sam, none of us are a danger, a threat, or even interested in your existence as an Oceanid. I see beyond that, and ask, as Michael's friend, if we can stay for a few days. Both Estelle and Michael are in need of a shower, and a few home comforts. I understand if you do not want me in your home, but can you please let them stay?"

"And where will you be?" Sam asked.

Azariah shrugged. "I can stay on the beach, or in the sea."

"I don't think that's your best idea," Michael mumbled.

"Not at all," I added, grabbing his arm. "There's no way I'm letting you stay out here by yourself. I'll stay with you. Michael can stay in the house."

Sam frowned at me. "You'd stay out here, with him, by yourself?"

"Yes. Why wouldn't I?"

He sighed heavily and eyed each of us cautiously. We must have looked quite a sight. We were all soaked thanks to the torrential rain; Azariah was only in his shorts, but Michael and I were in wet, darkened clothes.

"How long have you been traveling without a proper place to stay?" Sam asked.

"A few weeks," Michael replied. A drop of rain dripped from his nose, as if accentuating the point. "You going to make us stand out here all day?"

Sam groaned. "Look, I'm not too happy about this, but . . . well . . . you can all stay in the house. I can't leave you outside in this weather. But I warn you,"—he looked straight at Azariah—"one look, action, or word that upsets Cleo, and you're out. Understand?"

Azariah nodded. "I do. And thank you. I promise not to give you any reason to make me leave."

Michael placed his hand on Sam's shoulder. "Thanks. Even though Az won't say it, I think he's as desperate for a comfy bed as I am."

Sam nodded, but his jade-green eyes were on me. He watched me with an interest I found a little creepy.

"What are you?" Sam said quietly.

I presumed he was talking to me, seeing as I was the focus of his attention. What did I say? Did I lie?

"Me?" I feigned surprise, and lifted my hand to my chest.

"Yes."

I shrugged my shoulders and turned to Azariah. "I'm with Azariah."

He lifted his chin and frowned. "Human?"

I bit my lip and nodded.

I hated lying, but there was no way I was going to admit to Sam that I was a Sachael.

"All these questions," Michael said. "Can we go inside and chat? Please?" He placed his arm over Sam's shoulders and turned him away from us. As they entered the house, Michael looked back and shot a deep stare at both me and Azariah. "We have a lot of catching up to do," he said, patting Sam's shoulder. "But first, I want to know everything that's happened with you and Cleo."

"She'll be home soon."

Azariah and I wandered to the open doorway.

"Crazy Oceanids," Azariah muttered. "Now, do you believe me?"

"I think he's worried," I said. "I don't think he hates you. He's just . . . concerned about you. I wonder what he thinks you'll do."

Azariah shook his head. "I understand the hate his kind have for Sachaels, but that is usually through fear of their women falling for us. From what Michael told us, Sam and Cleo are inseparable."

"But maybe that's what he fears."

"Maybe."

Sam waited just inside the doorway. His eyes lingered on me as I passed him, and I felt the intense coldness emanating from him. If Azariah hadn't already told me he was an Oceanid, I would've guessed from the icy chill surrounding him. We stood in the hall with Michael, like soldiers in an army waiting for instructions on what was next.

"You look like you could all do with a hot bath and a change of clothes," Sam said, closing the door him.

"Me first; I stink," Michael complained.

"Help yourself," Sam said. "The bathroom's through there."

Sam indicated with a nod of his head to a door at the end of the small hall.

"Thank you for allowing us to stay," Azariah said, as Michael disappeared into the bathroom.

Sam pursed his lips, and then nodded. "Michael's a friend, and if he trusts you, then I will try to as well. I'm sorry for my reaction when you turned up. I didn't expect anyone, never mind a Sachael. We rarely get visitors. The occasional tourist passes through, but that's all."

"It's a beautiful place to live," I told him, dipping my head to the window in the living room. "The beaches are amazing. Not so much the weather."

Sam smiled as he led us into the kitchen. "The beaches are one of the reasons why we came here. It's also a good distance from the Atlantic."

Azariah momentarily frowned at Sam's words, but his look quickly disappeared.

"Have you just arrived on the island?" Sam asked.

"We arrived a few days ago," Azariah said, forced enthusiasm in his reply. "We only stop for three or four days in one place. Michael was most insistent we visit his friends before we left Fetlar."

Sam laughed as he flicked the kettle on. "Yeah, he always was a pushy kid. He used to drive me mad. Cleo was the one who always took his side. Speaking of Cleo, she should be back by now." He stared out the window, frowning at the sparkling water beyond.

"Where's she gone?" I asked.

"Into the next bay. Don't worry, she never goes far. She's a strong swimmer." A small smile hung on his lips as he mentioned her prowess in the water. His pride for her was evident.

I took that as a good sign. Maybe this pair of Oceanids was different after all.

"Would you like a drink?" Sam offered.

Azariah waited for me to answer first. I shook my head slightly to clear my thoughts and turned my attention to the question.

"I'll have some milk please, straight from the fridge," I replied.

"Same here," Azariah added.

"Anything to eat?" Sam asked as he opened the fridge door and grabbed the milk carton. "I can heat some soup for you. Cleo made it last night."

"Maybe later," Azariah said as he leaned on the doorframe.

"Well, make sure you get yours before Mr. Greedy. Michael will eat all of it if he gets the chance. He always had a huge appetite."

"That has not changed," Azariah said, and I saw the traces of a smile grace his lips. It was the first since we had arrived.

"Go and sit down; take a seat in the living room. You may as well make yourself comfortable, although I think we may bore you when Cleo returns and we catch up on all the gossip with Michael."

"Not at all," Azariah said, as Sam showed us into the room we had passed when we first came inside. "I would like to hear your stories."

"Cleo has the most amazing memory," he said as he returned to the kitchen, shouting his response. "I'm sure she will have plenty of tales to tell you regarding Michael. How long have you known him?"

"A while," Azariah responded, as he wandered over to the window and dipped his head to look at the scene outside.

"He seems okay," I said softly as I joined him. The sea was a mix of grey and glistening, reflected light whenever the sun made a brief appearance. The crests of the waves danced like diamonds each time they were bathed in in the sun's rays.

Azariah nodded. "Yes. He does. Crazy or not, he appears to be a decent man."

His focus was out the window as his eyes scanned the bay.

"Are they out there?" I asked, peering through the glass and looking for the familiar bobbing heads.

"Yes."

"Do they mind?" I said, resting my hands on the window sill. "I mean, all they do is follow us."

"It is their duty to do so. Sachaels are loyal and committed to their task," Azariah said as placed his head next to mine.

A cough made me spin around. Sam was in the room, and he smiled as he placed two glasses of milk on the table. He came and stood behind us.

"It's a stunning view, isn't it?"

"Very much so," Azariah agreed. "I think if I lived here, I would spend all my time looking at the sea."

"You mean the time when you are not actually in the ocean?"

Azariah turned to Sam, smiling at his comment. "That is exactly what I mean."

Sam nodded before turning back to the window, his features drawing tight with concern.

"She should be back by now."

"You are worried?" Azariah said.

Sam sighed. "She is never usually this long. I can't help but worry."

"Would you like me to ask my men to search for her?"

"Your men?" Sam exclaimed. "You mean you're not alone?"

"I have an army in the bay," Azariah offered as reassurance. "I am sure they will quickly find her. They can help." He straightened up and took one step toward the door, but Sam cut him off.

Clutching the edge of the doorframe as if to hold himself up, Sam shook his head. His face was ashen, eyes wide and overly bright.

"Michael!" he shouted, turning into the hall. "Michael, I need your help."

Azariah frowned as Sam banged on the bathroom door.

"Quickly. Cleo hasn't returned. I need you to help me find her."

"Sam," Azariah called. "I can help. I will get my men—" Once again, he stepped toward the door.

"We don't need you."

"We can help," I offered, hoping he'd listen to me. If he was as worried as he appeared, then surely the more people who searched for her, the better. If she was in the sea, the Sachaels were the best people to find her. I didn't hold back like Azariah, and strode to the doorway, waiting for Sam's response.

He ignored me.

"Michael," he called again. "Hurry up!"

"Sam, this is ridiculous," I said. He paced the hallway, his hands curling into tight fists as he continually shook his head.

Michael opened the bathroom door, water dripping down his body. He had a towel wrapped loosely around his hips.

"What's all the noise?" he said, squinting at Sam, who was already at the front door, pulling it open.

"Put some clothes on quickly. We need to find Cleo."

"Okay, just hang on a minute," Michael called as he backed into the bathroom.

Azariah's hand rested on my shoulder and I turned my head to look at him. He huffed impatiently and shook his head. He was just as puzzled as me by Sam's reaction.

"Why is he willing to let Michael help, but not us," he muttered quietly.

"Maybe it's because he knows him," I said. "He wants people he can trust to search for her."

Sam waited by the door, and it wasn't long before Michael rushed from the bathroom, frantically rubbing his hair with the towel that had been around his waist a few minutes ago. Thankfully, he'd managed to put his jeans on before running past us.

Both Azariah and I wandered back to the window and watched them sprint onto the beach.

"This is madness," Azariah grumbled. "I could have helped them."

"I know." It was weird, strange how Sam had completely changed in front of us. He had looked petrified when Azariah mentioned the army.

"Oceanids. They are the strangest people I have ever come across. Sam's behavior only proves that further. Hopefully, we will find out more when Cleo returns. Or maybe the madness has just started, and we have lots more to come." He smirked before pulling me into his arms. I returned his hold, resting my head against his shoulder.

The main door of the house crashed open, and we both froze.

"Sam, Sam!" It was a woman's voice. "Sam, where are you?"

The owner of the voice appeared in the doorway of the living room. She was wet and naked, her belly softly round—pregnant. As soon as she saw us, she hastily grabbed the towel Michael had thrown to the floor as he'd rushed out. She wrapped it securely around her body and backed into the hallway. She looked around, blinking fast, her eyes flicking into every visible corner.

"Who . . . who are you?" she gasped. "Why are you in my house? And where's Sam?"

I stepped toward her.

"I'm Estelle. This is Azariah. And I presume you are Cleo?"

"What have you done with Sam? Where is he?" Her voice quivered as she addressed Azariah. He remained quiet, still, watching her. "He was here when I left," she said. "He should be here now."

I approached her slowly. She was wet and shaking with either fear or cold. Her gaze kept flicking to Azariah. She appeared ready to flee the building if he moved.

"He went with Michael to look for you," I explained.

"Michael?" She backed into the hall, seemingly on edge with my presence as much as Azariah's.

"Yes. He's a friend of yours, right?" I said, halting my advance. "He's also a friend of ours. That's why we're here."

"So Sam is with Michael. They're okay?" Her lips were trembling and she blinked rapidly, pulling the towel even tighter around herself.

I nodded. "They were concerned for you. Sam expected you back a while ago. Then, when Azariah mentioned he could help, Sam took off."

"But he's a Sachael," she hissed, as if I was unaware of the fact.

"I know." I kept my voice calm and my stance as unthreatening as possible. My hands were at my side and I leaned away from her, trying to give her the space she so obviously felt she needed.

"You say you are friends of Michael's. For how long?" she asked.

Azariah spoke up. "A while," he said, repeating his earlier response.

Cleo's gaze shot to Azariah, and she refused to look away.

I didn't understand why she was so terrified of him. Her reaction was the complete opposite of what we'd expected. She should have been flirting with him, pushing me aside so she could be with him. This was not the standard reaction for an Oceanid to show toward a Sachael.

"Stay over there. Keep away from me," she continued, pointing a shaking finger at him.

"Cleo, I am no threat to you," Azariah said, low and calm, his hands held up in a placating gesture. "Why would I be?"

"I've told you. You are a Sachael."

The front door slammed again, and the raised voices of Sam and Michael followed.

"Cleo." Sam's voice. "Thank god, you're all right."

"Sam . . ."

She flung her arms around him as he reached her and began sobbing against his shoulder.

"They've returned," she stated. "I'm so scared. I . . . I . . ."

"Shhh, I know." Sam held her in his arms.

Michael leaned against the doorframe, looking bewildered by his friends exchange. I couldn't stand it any longer. Something wasn't right. I glanced at Azariah, seeing he was as confused as me.

"Sam, Cleo," I said, "will one of you please tell us what's going on?"

NINE
Friends

Sam continued comforting Cleo, guiding her across the room and ignoring Michael as they passed him in the doorway. Sam sank onto the sofa, pulled her next to him, and reassured her with whispered, soothing words as she buried her head on his shoulder.

"You're safe now," he told her.

"But I'm not safe, am I?" She moved her head from his shoulder. "They're out there. There's already one in our house. Why? Why is he here?"

"Shhh, it's okay. Azariah is a friend of Michael's. So is Estelle. They mean us no harm."

"Please," I asked. "Why are you scared of us?"

Sam sighed heavily, looking at Cleo in question. She nodded her permission before looking away, refusing to meet our eyes. Sam turned to me and Azariah.

"Many years ago, Cleo and I moved here, deciding we would be safer on land than in the sea."

I caught Azariah's frown. I was unsure why they would make such a decision; perhaps he was too.

"We chose to live here, away from Mercivium and the rest of our kind." His hand rubbed Cleo's back as he told us their story.

"Mercivium?" I queried. Azariah had never mentioned it.

"It is in the Atlantic," Azariah stated. "Like Saicean."

"But why did you move away?" I queried, moving nearer to them.

"It wasn't safe," Cleo replied, gaining control over her voice. "The Sachaels live there."

"We moved to get away from the Sachaels who rule the waters of the Atlantic," Sam clarified. "The way they behave, the way they treat female Oceanids, that is what made us move away. It's why Cleo was scared, and why I panicked when she hadn't returned as expected. When you told me of your men in the bay, I had to find her. She always comes that way, and I knew the sight of them would terrify her."

I sat down on a chair opposite the sofa they were on and nodded, encouraging him to continue.

"I swam to the next bay when I saw them," Cleo said. "Luckily, they didn't come after me."

"They would not come after you. They have no reason to bother you," Azariah stated, his brows drawn together in confusion.

"That's not what always happens," Sam said. He looked intently at Cleo, smoothing her curly blonde hair from her face. "You are safe now," he whispered. "You both are." His hand rested on her belly. He sighed loudly before turning again to Azariah. "Look, everyone is okay; Cleo is back. Let's just leave this for now."

"Agreed," Michael said, springing away from the doorframe he'd been resting on.

"I do not agree," Azariah snapped.

"Not now." Sam was on his feet, standing tall as he faced Azariah. "I told you the conditions for your stay here. You start throwing your weight around even one tiny bit, and you leave." He shook his head and stared at Azariah intently. "I know Michael trusts you, but we have only just met you. And you have an army of Sachaels in the bay where we live. They are the reason both Cleo and I moved here—to get away from that very thing. Maybe when we get to know you and Estelle, we will tell you our full story. But not now."

The way he included my name made me wonder if he'd linked me with Azariah because I was with him, or because he sensed I was a Sachael. Had he seen straight through my earlier lie?

"The full story," Azariah snapped. "I want the full story, now."

"I won't warn you again," Sam shouted, pointing his finger at him. "Back down, or leave."

"Azariah, not now," I pleaded. I jumped up from the chair when I noticed his scales beginning to rise. I placed my hand on his shoulder, hoping to calm him. This was not what we needed. "Sam has told us he needs to trust us before he'll say any more. We have to earn that trust, and respect his decision."

Azariah turned to me, his face one of complete exasperation.

"Please," I silently mouthed and stepped in front of him. "Please, calm down."

I offered him a small smile, and placed my hand on the side of his face. He closed his eyes and took a deep breath. The scales on his back and arms gradually flattened, and he placed his hand over mine. When he opened his eyes again, he nodded. I dipped my head and rubbed his cheek with my fingers.

He looked past me toward Sam. "I will earn your trust," he said.

Michael chose that moment to break the awkwardness and sprang onto the sofa, next to Cleo.

"Cleodora, where's my big hug?" he said. "And look at you." He gestured toward her belly, hidden under the towel. "It seems congratulations are in order."

I took a deep breath of my own and released it slowly. Azariah had dropped his head and was looking at the floor.

Sam backed away, smiling as he caught the conversation between Cleo and Michael.

"I've missed you," she sobbed, clinging to Michael as he wrapped his arms around her. "So, so much. And then you go and allow a Sachael into my home. What were you thinking?" She gave him a watery smile and a half-hearted smack on the arm, but her eyes still darted warily between Azariah and me.

"Don't worry about Az, he's just a big softy underneath that tough exterior," Michael said, completely ignoring Azariah's pointed snort in response.

Michael twisted in Cleo's hold, extending his hand to Sam. "Congratulations, mate. When's it due?"

"Four months' time." Sam smiled proudly, his gaze fixed on Cleo.

Cleo clung more tightly to Michael. It seemed she wasn't willing to let go.

Azariah was frowning now, seemingly confused by their friendly interactions. There seemed to be so much more to say, and I knew he wanted the earlier conversation to be continued.

I reached for his hand, aware he was still perplexed. He turned to me, and then pulled me into a hug. It seemed our visit would once again prove to be a complex arrangement.

"So typical of Oceanids," he whispered. "Half-riddles and strange behavior."

I smiled, relieved to hear that the angry edge to his voice had completely disappeared. He appeared calm and in control of the situation once more, but was he?

Azariah closed his eyes and sighed heavily. "I need to speak to my men. Please excuse me."

He headed straight for the door, not bothering to look back. My initial reaction was to follow him, but I stayed where I was.

At Azariah's departure, the calmness that always surrounded me disappeared. I moved to the window to watch him, aware of Sam staring at me. I ignored his unblinking gaze; I wasn't willing to talk to him about my origins any more than he was willing to tell Azariah and me about his and Cleo's choice to stay out of the water.

The rain looked like it would return. The grey clouds hung over the water with a threatening edge and matched Azariah's posture as he strode to the beach, his shoulders hunched, his stride slow and heavy. I wanted to tell him everything would be all right, but I was as confused as he was.

With the air heavy and silent, I turned back to the friends in the room.

"Congratulations," I offered, nodding toward Cleo's belly, trying to distract myself from her initial worrying reaction.

"It's brilliant news," Michael enthused. "Can I be an honorary uncle?"

"You?" Cleo swatted him playfully. "You're the biggest kid I've ever met."

I glanced out the window again and watched Azariah sink under the surface of the water. When he hadn't resurfaced within several minutes, I broke my gaze and headed out of the house.

"I'm going to the beach," I said as I left the room, not glancing backward at the three united friends who were deep in conversation. I didn't like it when I couldn't see Azariah. It made me nervous. Orontes was still out there somewhere. Even though the army was in the bay, keeping watch, my intrinsic fear overruled the situation. My heart beat loudly, increasing in speed as I rushed toward the water.

As I scanned the sea, Azariah broke the surface further along the bay. I stopped walking and watched him, assessing his mood. He strode slowly to a small area of rocks and sat, staring out to the sea. I decided to make my way over to him, all the while trying to think of what to say to break him from his melancholy mood. Had he spoken to Chanon? Had he made any sense of what Sam said?

I sat next to him, taking his hand in mine, but remained quiet, giving him time to think.

The words he eventually said surprised me.

"I am sorry," he said quietly, looking at his sandy feet.

"For what?" I rubbed my fingers over the back of his hand. "What do you have to apologize for?"

He shook his head slowly. "I should not have left you with them."

"You reacted to a situation completely out of your control," I said, trying to reassure him.

"Even so, it was wrong. I will apologize to Sam and Cleo for my behavior. They will hardly want me to stay here if I appear to be hot-headed and unreasonable."

He huffed dramatically. "I am beyond frustrated at the events happening around us. The sooner we can go to Saicean the better. I cannot cope with this for much longer."

It was my turn to apologize. He was only on land to keep me safe until our next submergence. And I could tell he hated it. "I'm sorry."

"Just as you said I have no need to apologize, neither do you, Estelle."

He released my hand and gently pulled me against him as we stared out at the bay.

"Why was Cleo frightened of coming ashore here?" he puzzled. "Because my men are in the bay? It makes no sense."

"Maybe she was scared she would feel an attraction to one of them, seeing as she quite obviously ignored her attraction to you." I nudged him with my elbow, but he didn't respond to my teasing.

He scowled at the water.

"I'm joking," I said, shifting my position to face him. "She's obviously very much in love with Sam, and he with her."

He was quiet for a while, staring into my eyes as if reading my deepest thoughts. He smiled before cupping my cheek with his hand.

"They are like us then. I know I will never love another woman as much as I love you. I am not interested in anyone else."

I smiled and turned my face to kiss his hand.

"Only three more days until the full moon, Estelle. Three days," he said, slowly standing and holding his hand out to me. "Come, walk with me. We need to go back." He tipped his head back and surveyed the clouds above. "I sense there is a storm coming."

I glanced out at the bay, concerned for the Sachaels in the water.

"Will they be okay out there?"

"They will move to deeper waters to avoid the ferocity of the waves. Do not worry. They will still be able to protect us. No Oceanid would come this close to land when there is a storm. They are even more incapable of weathering a storm in the shallows."

"I wasn't thinking about our protection. I was worried for their safety." I took his hand and let him pull me to my feet.

Azariah smiled at me. "You astound me at times. Your concern is never for yourself. It is always for others."

"I don't want them to get hurt while helping us," I explained.

"Estelle, they are an army. It is their duty to protect us. I have told you that many times. If it means they injure themselves, or if they have to put themselves in danger for us, then they will do it."

We linked hands as we walked back to Sam and Cleo's.

"I am looking forward to doing my submergence with you," Azariah said, changing the subject as he swung our joined hands back and forth between us. "I remember last time." His voice was soft, deep with meaning and heavy with passion. My eyes widened at his unspoken promise. I too remembered the last time we completed the submergence together, along with what had nearly happened beforehand. So much had happened since then.

"It is a pity that Michael and the other Sachaels will be with us," he added.

His words were a reminder that we would not be alone when we did our submergence. I felt deflated; I wanted it to just be us two.

On seeing the pout which inevitably formed on my lips, Azariah grinned, stopping our walk and dipping his head to kiss me softly on the mouth.

"But perhaps we can swim further around the island afterward. We can test your speed and find some privacy," he whispered as he rubbed his cheek against mine.

My breath caught in my throat. I was sure Azariah would be aware of my heart beat as it began to race.

"Are you sure you can control yourself for the next three days?" he asked. The lilt in his voice hinted toward a joke, but I sensed the hesitancy in his voice.

"Can you?" I asked, turning to place several soft kisses against his cheek.

"Estelle," he murmured. "You tempt me so much."

I kissed his shoulder, intending on moving to his chest, but his firm hands moved my head, forcing my lips to meet his. His kiss was soft at first, growing with intensity as we both gave in to our emotions. I felt alive, elated. As his tongue swept over mine, I suppressed a groan, letting my body mold against his as he pulled me closer.

As our kiss finished, I stared into his pale blue, hypnotizing eyes.

"Three days," I reminded him, my voice sounding as husky as his. "And I shall count every one of them."

"As I shall count the nights."

He sighed wistfully before we continued our walk back to Sam and Cleo's.

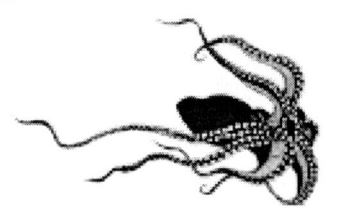

TEN
Full Moon

The following days at Sam and Cleo's were spent reflecting upon the events that had unfolded since Azariah and I had left Ravenscar.

Each morning, Azariah strolled to the beach, entering the water to speak to Chanon. Every evening, we sat together in the small living room and listened to Michael, Sam, and Cleo as they told entertaining stories concerning their lives at University. Pactolus and Melia were also mentioned; it seemed they were quite a group when together. I couldn't help but feel my time at University was a wasted opportunity for me to have found close friends. Soon after arriving in York, I'd met Daniel, and he had made sure I never had the chance to meet anyone else.

Finally, on the night of the third day, a full moon crept into the evening sky, throwing its magnificent glow across the beach. Tonight, Michael would complete his first submergence, and I would complete the one I'd missed, returning my Sachael abilities to me.

"Can you give me a few moments to myself?" I asked Azariah as he stepped toward our bedroom door.

He frowned. "Are you okay?"

"Yes. I just . . ." I shrugged my shoulders. "I want some time to remember my father. These nights were our nights. I know it's silly, but I need to have a few moments to talk to him. Full moon evenings were special to him and me, and their meaning is even more so now that I know the reasons behind them."

Azariah nodded. "I understand. I will wait downstairs. Take as long as you need."

The door closed as he left. I sighed heavily, sitting on the edge of the bed. I wondered what my father would think of all of this. I recalled his excited, yet serious mood on these nights. And I silently thanked him for ensuring I had never missed a submergence while in his care. If he'd ignored everything about my birthright, never shown me the submergence ritual, then I'd not be where I was now. I was sure he'd like Azariah, but what would he think about me traveling to Saicean with him? He had left his Sachael world. Would he agree with me going to one?

"Michael! Are you coming?" Azariah was downstairs, his shout drifting up through the floor beneath me. It was time.

Exhaling a deep breath, I headed out of the room and down the stairs. Azariah was standing in the hallway, near the front door, waiting to head to the beach. When he saw me, he shot me a knowing smile. "Are you ready?"

I nodded.

"Michael!" he shouted again, just as the man in question strode from the living room, closely followed by Cleo.

"Why is he going with you?" she asked. "You usually only go to the beach with Estelle."

"Tonight, Michael is coming with us," Azariah replied, not offering anything further.

He was cranky and anxious to be in the water. He had his own submergence to complete tonight. One which would ensure he kept his full Sachael abilities. The Sachaels in the bay would also need to complete the ritual, because they weren't in Saicean.

"Come, Estelle. It is Michael's decision as to whether he follows or not." Azariah took my hand as we stepped outside. "Perhaps he is content to stay on land and mix with Oceanids for the rest of his life," he stage-whispered to me, glancing back at the open door.

"I thought you liked Sam and Cleo?" I questioned his tone.

"They are nice, but they are still Oceanids." His pace was faster than normal tonight. His urgency to get in the water was very obvious.

"And . . . ?" I said, having to trot to keep up with him.

"And I do not like placing so much trust in them. We must always remember they are Michael's friends, not ours. How far would they go to help us if we were in trouble?"

I paused before answering, momentarily struck by the sight of the full moon over the sea. It was beautiful, and lit the white sandy beach like a glittering carpet of diamonds.

"I think they'd want to help us," I said, in answer to him. "You speak as if they wouldn't."

"I am not sure they would."

"You base your theories on what you've learned in Saicean. Has your time with me not yet made you realize that your life has been sheltered, that your father may not have told you the truth?" I stopped walking and braced myself for the pull of Azariah's hand as he continued his determined stride across the beach. I hated that he dismissed Cleo and Sam so easily. They'd shown us nothing but kindness since our somewhat frightening arrival. Why was he still so prejudice about Oceanids?

My shoulder jarred as I expected and Azariah spun around to face me, not releasing my hand. A deep scowl etched across his features.

"My father would never lie to me," he said.

I picked my words carefully. "I didn't say he had. But maybe he hasn't told you everything, either."

"My father can be a difficult man, but I believe he has told me everything. Perhaps, in the past, he had been told wrong."

His serious expression halted me from voicing any further thoughts on Kaimi.

Something moving in the sea caught my attention, and Azariah followed my gaze.

"The guards are already doing their rituals," he explained. "They do them early so they are renewed and physically strong by the time we do ours. There is no point in waiting until later to complete such an important event," he said solemnly.

I'd always considered my submergence ritual as a bit of fun, a memory I kept alive for my father. The way Azariah spoke made me realize it was incredibly important, perhaps even a matter of life and death for a Sachael.

I cleared my throat and placed my hand in his. "Let's go. I've been looking forward to this for what seems like years."

He smiled. "You joke with me on one of the most important nights of our lives, and yet I still love you more than life itself. You truly are the most precious and wondrous woman in the world."

My cheeks warmed. Why did he always do this to me? I should be used to his romantic words by now.

"I see you have no response to my declaration of love," Azariah said, as we resumed our walk along the beach.

"Oh, I have plenty I could say, but I prefer to let my actions speak for themselves," I teased. I was prepared to run into the sea and swim into deeper water, hoping Azariah would follow me, but stopped when I saw Michael jogging toward us.

"Come on then, Uncle," he shouted as he approached. "Show me what I need to do." He placed his arm across Azariah's shoulders, and I stifled a giggle at Azariah's annoyed expression.

"I would prefer it if you did not call me 'Uncle.' It makes me feel old."

I turned away, grinning wildly at Azariah's comment.

"Okay," Michael agreed, removing his arm from Azariah. He bounced on the souls of his feet, looking first at me, and then at Azariah. "Well, what are we waiting for? What do I do?"

"Firstly, I will call Chanon," Azariah said. "He can protect Estelle while I am in the water with you."

"I'm sure I can manage to look after myself for a few minutes," I mumbled. I didn't want Chanon sitting with me; I was concerned about what he'd say. What doubts would he put in my mind this time?

"I am calling Chanon. I do not wish to take any chances with your safety when you are so near to completing your final land submergence. He will be with you whether you want him here or not."

I resisted the urge to respond. I was capable of looking after myself, but I understood his concern, even if I did think it was slightly over-the-top. This was the head-strong, dominant side of him showing itself yet again. I let it pass, not wanting to argue with him tonight.

As Azariah walked to the edge of the water, continuing further into the gentle swell of the waves, Michael came to my side.

"Is he always this grouchy when there's a full moon?"

"He wasn't last time." I grinned, recalling our last submergence together, and then quickly sobered. I wasn't with him the last time he did a submergence. I was locked up. The vision in my memory from was two submergences ago. "I didn't see him, though. Well, not properly. I only spoke to him in my dream, and that was completely different," I mumbled quietly.

"Hmmm . . . he was seducing you, wasn't he?" I was sure Michael was teasing me, but I wasn't willing to listen.

"Michael, please don't bring that up again."

"Chill, Estelle. I'm only joking." He turned toward the sea.

"Here they come." He nodded toward Azariah and Chanon as they rose from the water. "They look like twins."

I frowned. Apart from their clothing, I was unable to see any resemblance between them. Chanon walked slowly, his eyes darting around the beach, constantly alert. But Azariah was relaxed when Chanon was with him—his whole demeanor changed. His shoulders didn't appear as tense, and he certainly wasn't frowning at the moment.

As they walked toward us, I concentrated on Chanon. I took in his appearance as he walked toward us. He was almost as tall as Azariah, but he was broader, more muscular. His long, dark hair was tied back from his face; he obviously didn't grow it to hide his scars. He stared at me while listening to whatever Azariah was saying to him.

"There is no need for you to come out of the water and babysit me," I protested, as Chanon came to stand by my side.

"But it is what Azariah wants," Chanon replied, as if I was crazy for trying to prevent him from staying with me.

"And what he wants, he always gets," I mumbled. "I feel like a child," I snapped at them.

Chanon bent to whisper in my ear. "That's because you are behaving like one. Be grateful he cares so much he doesn't want to leave you alone on the beach. What would happen if Orontes suddenly appeared? Anyone would think you wanted to be dragged into the ocean by him."

"What?" I shot him an icy stare as he backed away.

"Chanon, what have you said to Estelle?" Azariah ordered.

"Nothing she shouldn't know. I was merely reminding her of her vulnerability."

"Estelle?" Azariah questioned. "Is he telling the truth?"

I glanced at Chanon, who had the decency to look away.

"Yes," I confirmed. "He was reminding me of why he's looking after me while you are with Michael."

Azariah seemed satisfied by my explanation. Stepping toward me, he gently lifted my chin with his fingers.

"I will not be long, and then we will complete our submergences together. Alone." His lips met mine briefly, leaving me wanting more. All thoughts of Chanon left my head.

"Don't be too long," I said.

"I shall be as quick as possible. But you know how important this is. Michael must learn what to do. We will not be here on the next full moon."

My heart sank. He'd reminded me we would be leaving for Saicean in the next few days. We needed to find somewhere safe for Michael, and then there was nothing to stop our departure.

"Michael," he called. "Come with me. This will not take long, but you must remember everything. If you forget any of what you do, you cannot complete the ritual at the next full moon. If that happens, you will lose any Sachael abilities bestowed on you after this first submergence. You'll stay a land Sachael."

"So you'll definitely not be with me on the next full moon?" There was an edge of panic in Michael's voice.

"No. You know I am eager to take Estelle to Saicean, where she will be safe. I may not be with you, but some of the others will be. I promised you I would make sure you were safe before we left, but we will not be with you after that. If you do forget, you could ask the men with you, but it would be best if you knew. Geleon is the strongest Sachael after Chanon. When Estelle and I leave, I shall appoint him as your main guard. He is incredibly trustworthy and will be honored to assist you."

Michael looked worriedly at Azariah.

"Do any of them know I'm related to you?" he said quietly, shifting his gaze to Chanon.

"Only Chanon. The others would be naturally curious if they knew, though, just as they are about Estelle."

Azariah strode toward the water, and Michael followed. I stared after them, eagerly awaiting my turn.

"He's not completely correct, you know," Chanon said quietly. "The men are more than curious about you."

I turned my attention away from the water, eyeing the man beside me warily. "And what about you?"

He shrugged his shoulders before sitting on the sand.

"You could at least have the decency to answer me," I snapped. "I lied for you earlier."

"You had no need to do so." He didn't look at me as he replied.

"If Azariah had heard what you said to me—"

"He wouldn't have been happy. Nothing more, Estelle."

I didn't respond, choosing instead to watch Azariah and Michael continue to walk into the ocean. I wanted to be the one with Azariah, not Michael. I had a desperate need to be in the water—to complete my awaiting submergence. The pull was strong tonight, even stronger than normal. But I needed to wait. And, unfortunately, that meant waiting with Chanon.

"Why do you hate me so much?" I said, glancing at the man sitting a few meters away from me on the sand.

"Hate you?" His face tipped toward mine, and he shook his head.

I didn't understand why he appeared shocked. Every time he'd come out of the water to talk to Azariah, he'd practically dismissed me. And I hadn't missed the snide comments or filthy stares. There was only one time he'd offered any support, and when I thought back to that conversation now, I viewed it as a little creepy.

"Is it because I've come into Azariah's life, and you want him to yourself?" I said, trying to guess what the issue was. "Is it because I spend time with him? Have I taken your best friend from you?"

He laughed, planting his arms behind him as he leaned backward. "Estelle, I do not hate you. And I do not want Azariah for myself." He smirked as he continued. "I am his guard. It's a very honored position to have."

"He trusts you with his life."

"I know. And you should as well." He turned away and cast his ever roaming gaze across the sea. He was alert even when sitting on the beach.

"But I don't know you. You've never given me a chance to get to know you," I said.

"You don't need to know me to trust me." He glanced quickly up at me before resuming his inspection of the sea.

I followed his gaze, looking across the water at Azariah. He was instructing Michael on how to do the submergence ritual. They were standing with the water level at their chests. Michael ducked under the surface before coming back up and looking to Azariah. They were saying the mantra together, and I whispered it to myself.

"I claim the truth of my existence under the full lunar phase, and submerge within these jeweled waters to keep me safe from harm."

I was unable to tear my gaze away. Azariah looked striking in the moonlight. It was a direct contrast to how Michael appeared, spluttering and coughing every time he completed a dip under the water.

Chanon stood beside me.

"You have to go back to Saicean with him," he stated flatly.

"I know, but I don't want to." I turned to face him. A steely look masked his face.

"You have to. Orontes can't touch you in Saicean. You need to complete your submergences there. You need to complete your transition to a full Sachael."

"I know this. You don't need to tell me." I sighed, my vision drifting back to Azariah.

"Then you should have no doubt in your mind about it. I sense that you wish to delay it as long as you can."

I shrugged. "I don't see why this has anything to do with you. It's between Azariah and me."

Chanon didn't reply straight away. When he did, he ignored my comment. "You need to leave immediately. I know you're fond of Michael, but you need to be safe. You'll need to leave him behind."

"I know. But we have to find him a safe place before we leave. We can't let Orontes find him."

"The longer you stay on land, the more chance Orontes has of finding you." His voice rose, and he shifted his position so he stood in front of me. "Do you think he'll let you escape so easily next time? Do you think he will wait to put any of his plans into action? The moment he finds you, he'll drag you away with him."

I narrowed my eyes at him. I hated the reminder of Orontes's intentions. Even his name sent icy shivers up my spine. The hairs on my arms lifted and goosebumps broke out across my flesh. But it wasn't my safety I was most concerned about—it was the others'. The fear of what he would do to Azariah and Michael was uppermost in my thoughts.

"Well," Chanon said, sounding disinterested and bored. He looked back to Sam and Cleo's house before continuing. "I suppose there's one good thing if he grabs you—you'll not drown, after tonight's submergence. Although, if you miss the next full moon when he's hiding you somewhere in the ocean . . ."

"Stop trying to frighten me," I said through gritted teeth.

He grabbed my shoulder and shook me. "I'm making you aware of the dangers. Do you think Orontes will let you complete your submergence?"

I pushed his hand off and backed away from him. "If he knows I'll drown without it, then yes, I think he will." I was as confident as I could be that Orontes didn't want me dead. He had other things in mind for me. Another shiver rippled along my spine.

Chanon's eyes hardened. "You'll be giving him information he could use against us."

"What?" I narrowed my eyes, confused.

"Do you think he knows everything about Sachaels?" Chanon's brows rose as he questioned me, leaning closer, too close.

I stepped back again. "No, I don't think he does."

"So you would willingly let him know that we need to submerge under the land full moon if we are not in Saciean, otherwise we will drown?"

I shook my head, fighting with the images Chanon was painting all too vividly. "It won't come to that."

"But if you don't go to Saicean, that is what you are risking. Would you willingly drown, to keep our secret safe?"

"Chanon, please. Stop it." I closed my eyes and shook my head. I didn't want to hear this. I didn't want to spend my time thinking about the vile, unpleasant possibilities of capture by Orontes.

"Your decision to return to Saicean should be your priority. I have stressed my concerns to Azariah. You should both leave straight after you have completed your submergence."

"And what about Michael?"

"He will be safe. Geleon will be with him, as well as four other men." He glanced at Michael and Azariah in the water. "But the decision isn't mine or yours to make. It's Azariah's. You need to go to Saicean with him. Don't try to change his mind. This is one decision he has to make without your interference."

"I never interfere," I protested.

"But you do. Azariah would never have come here and stayed with Oceanids if you hadn't pushed the point. He'll ignore Michael's requests if he disagrees with him, but not yours."

"Well, he's not always right."

Chanon grinned before laughing quietly. "No, he's not." He instantly sobered, and his forehead creased. "Look, Estelle, I have something to tell you, something I've been waiting to say—"

"He's waiting for you," Michael shouted as he approached.

I continued looking at Chanon, waiting for him to continue whatever he'd been about to reveal.

He shook his head, his brows pinched together. "It doesn't matter. It's not important." He immediately straightened and addressed Michael instead, our conversation seemingly forgotten. "How do you feel?" he asked, stepping toward him and placing his hand on his shoulder.

"Amazing. I feel energized, stronger. It's weird."

Chanon smiled at Michael, but any further conversation between them went unheard as I turned my attention to the sea and the man who waited for me. He stood watching me, the water circling his thighs. The moment our eyes locked, calmness washed over me. Not caring that Chanon and Michael were next to me, I removed my jeans and my jumper before heading into the sea. As I approached him, he took my hand in his, and we walked silently into deeper water. When the water was around our waists, he stopped.

"Why did you not take your top off?" he asked. "You normally do when you submerge."

"That's because I usually have something on beneath it. Tonight, as I am sure you have noticed, I only have this t-shirt."

Azariah's mouth twitched as he stared at my chest. My t-shirt was wet and clinging to me. I was sure he could see the prominent outline of my breasts.

"When I complete my submergences in Saicean, I am usually naked," he said, a cheeky grin pulling at one corner of his mouth. "We all are."

"Naked?"

"It feels more natural, uninhibited and at one with the water."

"Is this a plan to get me out of my clothes so you can have your wicked way with me?" I whispered as I closed the small gap between us.

"Would you complain if it was?" Azariah's hands rested on my hips under the water before pulling me against him.

"Never," I breathed, just before our lips met.

His hands gripped me tightly as he kissed me. Mine slipped along his arms, meandering between our bodies to feel the taut muscles of his stomach.

"We are surrounded by others," he spoke against my lips, "and, as much as I would like us to be naked, I think we should wait until we swim into the next bay."

He leaned backward, watching me. "When I am with you, I focus completely on you and often forget we are not alone. If the others were not here, then I would most certainly be undressing you at this very moment." He smirked a little, lightly kissing my lips before trailing his finger along my neck and then lower, pulling the center of my t-shirt's neckline down with his movement. "Although, this top you are wearing doesn't hide much."

I followed his gaze as it lingered on the wet fabric covering my breasts.

"You told me you'd seen lots of naked women in Saicean."

"I have." His eyes traveled back to my face. "But none of them are as beautiful as you." Resting his forehead against mine, he spoke quietly. "Say it with me, Estelle. Let us speak the mantra together."

I nodded, closing my eyes as we began the ritual.

"I claim the truth of my existence under the full lunar phase, and submerge within these jeweled waters to keep me safe from harm."

We sank simultaneously beneath the surface of the sea. A few moments later, we lifted the top of our bodies from the water before starting to speak the mantra again. This time, I kept my eyes open and locked on Azariah. He smiled as he spoke the words with me. Again, we sank below the surface, repeating the ritual until all seven submergences were complete.

When we surfaced after the last repetition, Azariah grinned, moving his fingertips behind my ears. His touch was a purposeful caress, like a thousand tiny fairy kisses speckling my over sensitive skin. It was proof that my gills had immediately recovered. They should be fully functional, and I would be able to breathe underwater again. I sucked in a deep breath, feeling the air fill my lungs.

"I can breathe again," I said.

Azariah frowned.

"Ever since I missed my last submergence, my chest has been tight—not anymore." I inhaled another lungful of air before blowing it out.

Azariah chuckled. "It seems you are as good as new. Shall we swim into the next bay?"

"So you can have your wicked way with me?" A smile played on my lips, and I kissed him on his nose.

He immediately became serious. "I promised you we would get away from all these prying eyes. We can be alone."

I examined his face, seeing the intensity of his gaze willing me to understand. I lifted my chin, a last defiant gesture to everything thrown at us since we met, and nodded my agreement.

I had tried to understand what had made him single me out the way he did. What had attracted him to me? Why had I been so special? But the answer was obvious now. I was a female Sachael.

"What are you thinking?" His smooth voice broke my wandering mind, his fingers twisting a stray wet strand of hair from my face.

"How much I love you," I responded, so sure of my feelings for him, but not ready to let him into my deepest thoughts—not yet.

He smiled. "Come, Estelle, we will swim into the next bay. I will inform my men to stay here and not disturb us."

Taking a small step away from me, he sprang backward into the water. I laughed at his action before following him, diving into the water in the exact spot he'd disappeared.

As soon as I was under the surface, his hand took mine. I looked toward him through the clear waters of the sea, and he pointed in the direction he wanted us to go. I nodded my agreement, letting go of his hand as I kicked my legs hard to propel me forward. I grinned as I recognized that my speed had returned, and, with it, my ability to breathe underwater. My throat didn't burn, and there wasn't any pain behind my ears. The submergence ritual had instantly renewed my Sachael abilities.

Azariah's hands grabbed my ankles, immediately reminding me of the first time he swam with me. My reaction that night had been one of fear, a desperate need to get away. How wrong I'd been.

I glanced behind to see Azariah pulling himself up my legs while we both swam. I grinned at his action and swam faster. Within seconds, Azariah was above me. He wrapped his arms around my waist and spun me to face him. It was a strange sensation, swimming on my back while underwater, but with Azariah holding me, my whole body relaxed. I let him guide me through the water, curling my arms around his neck as I pulled myself closer against his body. He traveled slowly, nowhere near as fast as he usually did, and I hoped he was enjoying our closeness as much as I was.

When he stopped swimming, we slowly sank onto the sandy bed of the ocean floor. The shallow water covered both of us as he hovered above me. His hand cupped my cheek, and I kissed it, my own fingers reaching to his face as I returned the gesture. Azariah twisted in the water, breaking the surface with me so that we were both standing. The night air brushed against our skin, and the water lapped at our waists. His hands rested lightly on the bottom of my t-shirt, but within seconds, the wet fabric was lifted upward, and I raised my arms above my head to enable the easy removal of my top.

"You are even more beautiful than I imagined. A true vision," he whispered as he observed my practical nakedness. He pulled my body protectively against his. His hands trailed up my sides, nudging the sides of my breasts in their journey. There was no urgency in his touch; just a languid ease in the way his fingertips grazed my skin.

"Your skin is so soft," he murmured before his lips covered mine and his body pressed against me. I twisted my fingers through his hair before moving my hand across his back. My naked breasts pressed against his chest, warm skin against skin. I'd never instigated this type of behavior; I was always the one who responded. Not this time. I wanted him. We'd waited long enough, curbing our most basic desires until the time was right. There was no need to wait any longer. He was as much mine as I was his, and tonight, it would happen.

He'd mentioned us undressing, and I was eager to help him with the removal of his clothes. I reached for the buttons on his shorts, expecting him to stop me, to tell me that we needed to control ourselves, but he didn't.

His lips moved along my neck, kissing upward to behind my ear. I moaned loudly, unable to curb the strength of my building desire.

"I want you," I murmured breathily. "I want you so much."

"I need to warn you," he said, each word a breath against my skin. "My kind are intense lovers. The Oceanids I have shared myself with were used to a Sachael's behavior. You, however, are not an Oceanid."

He was worried, but there was no need to be. My response was simple. "No, I'm not an Oceanid. I'm a Sachael. Has it never crossed your mind that I might also be an intense lover? That I could be just like you?"

"Estelle," he whispered as he pulled me into the breaking waves with him. He lay beside me in the water, watching me. I skimmed my hand across his chest before trailing it downward, slipping under the waist of his shorts. Familiar small bumps appeared across his torso, and I sighed, knowing it was his reaction to me—only me. His hand rested on my stomach, his fingers circling my belly button before moving to the edge of my underwear. I sighed again, this time in anticipation, as his fingers slid under the fabric.

A rush of water flew into the air behind Azariah.

"Azariah! What are you doing?" It was Chanon, glaring at Azariah, his voice urgent, angry even.

Azariah jumped to his feet, dragging me with him before shielding my body with his own. He growled at Chanon. "How dare you approach me at this moment?"

"You cannot do this. Not here, and definitely not now." Chanon's jaw was tense, the vein in his neck clearly visible as he challenged Azariah.

"What? You question my motives with Estelle? Have you forgotten to whom you speak?"

The sharp scales on Azariah's back scratched my breasts as I stood behind him.

"I am fully aware of who I am speaking to. But your love for Estelle has blinded you to all sense and reason. You know the consequence of what you were about to do. Does she?" Angry eyes flashed at me before returning to Azariah.

"What?" Azariah snapped. "Explain yourself."

Chanon sighed and closed his eyes. When he opened them, they were softer and his jaw wasn't as tense looking as before. "It's the night of a full moon."

Azariah's shoulders slumped, and the scales on his back immediately flattened. He was silent, as was Chanon.

I stayed behind Azariah, hiding my body.

"Azariah?" I asked, quiet, almost scared to speak. What was going on?

Azariah's voice was calm as he spoke to Chanon. "Leave us."

Chanon straightened, not willing to walk away. "Azariah! Did you not hear me? Your passion has made you lose sight of reality. If you carry on—"

"I know what will happen if I carry on. I am not a fool. Your warning has been heard. Now leave us."

"Please, do not do something you will both regret."

"Chanon, I will not warn you again. I am ordering you to leave us alone. Go!"

Chanon looked at me before hesitantly moving backward. It was as if he wanted to say something, but didn't. He turned his back on us both and dived into the water.

Azariah didn't move; he was frozen in place, looking at the beach around his feet. He didn't speak either, so, when I could bear it no longer, I did. "Has he gone?"

Azariah turned slowly and pulled me against his chest. "Yes."

I welcomed his embrace, but as I looked at his face, his eyes were still focused on the beach.

"Estelle, I cannot express how sorry I am that I let my emotions run away with me. If we . . ." He shook his head. "You would have become pregnant."

"Stop it," I demanded, breaking free from his arms. "Just stop it."

I was sick of him constantly carrying the responsibility for both of us. "I was as much to blame as you."

"But I should never have forgotten. I cannot believe I was so careless, and I nearly. . . . It is not something we should consider at the moment."

"This is why we should never have left it so long. You should have listened to me when we first arrived in the Orkneys."

"I wish I had let you seduce me. We would not be so ready with our actions now, if we had given in to our desires then."

"Want to bet?" I grinned, knowing we would have been just as bad, if not worse.

Azariah sighed. "You tease me, yet again."

He turned to me, his eyes catching the reflection of the moon as it lit the water's surface. "Let me find your top, and then we shall head back to Sam and Cleo's. I shall sleep in the chair in our room tonight. If I am on the bed with you, I fear I will not be able to control myself, now that I have seen your true beauty."

He kissed my forehead before reaching for my t-shirt floating in the water.

"Here," he stated. "It does not hide much, but it is better than nothing. May I ask that you go straight to our room when we get back? I have seen the way Sam looks at you, and I would prefer it if he did not see you like this."

"Of course," I replied, all too aware of Sam's interest.

"Estelle," Azariah said. "I feel I have let you down tonight. I promised we would have our time together and look what happened."

"It doesn't matter," I responded, reaching to kiss his lips. "It will happen. And it will happen soon."

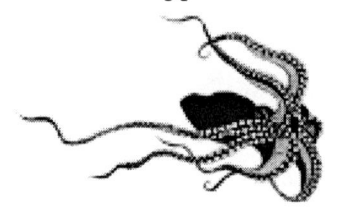

ELEVEN
Second Shell

Every time I turned over in my sleep, I glanced at Azariah's slumped form in the corner of the room. He had fallen asleep in the chair, but not before moving it as far from the bed as possible. He'd also made me cover up before I climbed into bed. Tonight, I slept in a vest top and cotton pajama bottoms that Cleo had leant me.

I still couldn't believe we had come so close to letting our emotions run away with us. Chanon had acted responsibly in stopping us, but it also made me feel increasingly uneasy. He must have been watching us, must have followed us when we swam away from the others.

When asleep, I floated through dreams that were calm, happy, and carefree. I was always with Azariah—in the field in Rackwick Bay, on the beach at Melia's, or in the water with him. We were wrapped in each other's arms, enjoying our close proximity.

The rumbling of the ocean increased, filling my head with a loud roar. The sparkling, still waters erupted into a squally sea. Restless waves were tipped with dark edges, and I backed away from their ugly fierceness.

"Stay away from him." A voice said. "You should leave him."

I gasped, peering into the dark peaks and troughs of the waves.

"Leave who?" I questioned, unsure as to whether or not I was imagining this. Was I dreaming? Or was this real? Something about this was so familiar.

"You must leave Azariah," the voice continued.

I wasn't dreaming. Someone was speaking to me.

"Why? Why do you want me to leave him?"

"I am worried he is using you." One particular wave rose in height, dwarfing the others around it. When it crashed to the waiting depths below, I found myself tumbling in the underwater currents.

"He's not using me," I shouted, desperate for this person to hear me above the noise. "What makes you think he is?"

"He cannot help himself." I was being thrown around in the water and tried to grab on to anything that would stop my uncontrolled movements.

"Why? Has he done this before?"

"No, never. But you should still stay away from him."

"I can't," I insisted.

There was another loud roar as more waves crashed on top of me, and I struggled to answer as I groped in the murky depths of an ocean I couldn't see.

"Why not?"

"Because I love him." My words were the truth. If this man visiting me in my dream had hoped his words would turn me away from Azariah, he had sorely misjudged me. "Who are you?"

"Someone who cares a great deal for you."

"Who?"

There was no response.

My head broke the surface of the water, and I took a deep lungful of air, free from the suffocating darkness that had surrounded me moments before.

"Who are you?" I repeated.

Again, no response.

He had gone.

"Estelle, Estelle, wake up." Azariah was shaking me.

I opened my eyes and immediately grabbed his arms. I held him tightly, afraid he may disappear.

"You were having a bad dream," Azariah whispered.

"Someone spoke to me in my dreams," I blurted out. "He wanted me to leave you. He warned me to stay away." I clung even tighter to him.

"What? Who spoke to you?"

"A man."

"But there is no one in the room apart from me." He ran his fingers through my hair and rocked me in his arms. "You were thrashing around and mumbling. It was just a bad dream. That is all."

"It wasn't a dream. He was definitely talking to me." I pushed away from Azariah, trying to think of an explanation.

"Estelle, look, there is no one here but me." He switched the bedside light on and glanced around the room before returning his gaze to me.

"He was talking to me," I insisted.

Azariah frowned. "Are you sure?"

"Yes." I nodded. Why didn't he believe me? It had happened before, when he used to speak to me in my dreams. Then, I realized.

"He was a Sachael," I said, confident with my statement.

"But why? And how? How has he made the connection to you?" Azariah's frown remained.

I shrugged. "I don't know."

"Have you picked anything up from the beach? Did you bring anything back tonight?"

"No. I have the necklace." My hand rose to cover the single pearl lying at the base of my neck. "And the two shells you left for me at Ravenscar."

Azariah's eyes widened.

"The ones Michael picked up," I clarified.

"Two shells?"

"Yes," I repeated, pointing to them on the bedside table.

Azariah followed my gaze. "I only left you one."

I reached for the shells, handing them to Azariah.

"This is the one I left." He held the spotted conch shell in his right hand. I took it from him as he studied the other shell Michael had brought back for me. "This is an Atlantic Dog-whelk, nothing special, and very common. You would find one on the beach out there. Are you sure you did not pick this up?"

"I've already told you. It was one of the ones you left at Ravenscar on the Mermaid Table. Michael brought it back. I presumed you had left both of them."

He shook his head. "Not this one. It would seem that the Sachael who spoke to you tonight left this when I left mine. There is only one Sachael who knew what I was doing when I placed this shell on the rock for you at Ravenscar, and he is close enough to speak to you tonight."

"Who? And why did he leave a shell for me?"

He didn't answer me. He jumped from the bed, thrusting the shell into his pocket. His back was already sharp with the formation of tiny spikes. Clenching and unclenching his fists at his sides, he paced back and forth across the room.

"Calm down," I said.

"I shall kill him if he thinks this is what he can do." Azariah's tone was short. I didn't need to see his face to know he was furious.

"Who?" I asked again.

"Did you not recognize his voice?" He stopped pacing and fixed his eyes on me.

I shook my head, unable to place my nocturnal visitor. But even if I had recognized the voice, I was too distracted by Azariah's reaction to identify it.

I had only seen Azariah this angry once before—the day I was taken from him on the beach at Ravenscar.

"Who is it?" I asked, fearing his response.

"Chanon," he growled.

"Chanon? Why is he warning me to stay away from you?" I pulled the sheet tight around me.

"I have no idea. I was prepared to forget his interruption last night. He had good reasons, but there is no reason for this. I do not want or need his explanation. He will have to go. I have had enough of his constant interference."

"Azariah, please, calm down," I begged, shifting to the bottom of the bed and reaching for his hand. He shook me off.

"No, Estelle." His voice rose. "I should kill him for the way he has interfered. He should never have left you a shell. He has no right to contact you."

"You can't kill him. He's your guard, your companion— your friend."

"Not anymore. He has stepped too far this time. I will not have any guard trying to seduce you."

"He didn't try to seduce me. He warned me—"

"To stay away from me. He wants you to himself."

"He never said that."

"Not yet. He will be waiting until you do as he says, and then he will make his move." He hadn't moved since turning to face me, but now, he looked to the door.

"But I don't see him like that."

Azariah wasn't listening. And really, who was I to judge? I didn't know Chanon as well as Azariah. A few argumentative discussions were all we'd shared, whereas Azariah had known him a lot longer.

Azariah shook his head. "He obviously has intentions toward you. I cannot allow it."

He marched to the door, opening it with such force I was surprised it wasn't pulled from its frame. Jumping from the bed, I intended to follow him as he headed downstairs. I stopped when Sam and Cleo's bedroom door opened.

"What's all the shouting for?" Sam asked, his gaze following Azariah as he rushed down the stairs. "Where's he going?"

"To the beach. He's not happy." I didn't want to spend time talking to Sam. I glanced past him toward the stairs, showing my intent to follow Azariah.

Sam stepped forward, blocking my way.

"Cleo is petrified."

"She has no need to be," I said, not wanting Cleo scared by Azariah's loud behavior.

"An angry Sachael is a good enough reason for her to be afraid," he said.

I ignored Sam, too concerned with Azariah and what he was about to do.

The walls shook as the door downstairs slammed shut.

"I have to follow him." I moved toward Sam, but his outstretched arm stopped me.

"I want to know what's going on," he insisted.

"Let me pass, Sam. I have to follow Azariah."

"Why?"

"Sam, let me through. Now!"

The other bedroom door opened, and Michael stood there, rubbing his eyes. As Sam turned toward him, I ducked under his arm, running past Michael and down the stairs. Ignoring their shouts, I ran out of the house and on to the beach.

It was early morning, and even though the sun hadn't fully peeked above the horizon, there was enough light to see the outline of two people ahead.

Azariah and Chanon were in the water, the waves crashing against their ankles. Without any hesitation, I rushed toward them. Azariah's back still showed his angry risen scales. I expected to see Chanon with the same reaction. Instead, he stood completely still, his hands by his sides, his head down.

"You dared to interrupt us last night, and now I discover you are talking to Estelle in her dreams. I should kill you for your actions!" Azariah yelled at him. "I trusted you with my life, with Estelle's, and this is how you repay me. Go back to Saicean, and take the army with you."

Chanon lifted his gaze to Azariah. "I understand your anger, and I know how this must look, but please, do not leave yourself and Estelle unprotected."

"I do not want you here. I am capable of looking after Estelle. I want you to go."

"I can't. It's too dangerous." Chanon didn't back away from him. "Azariah, please, I beg you to reconsider your decision. It is madness to leave yourself unprotected like this."

"I do not want you here. You are disrespecting me and Estelle. Your interference is beyond your duty."

"I promise I will not interfere anymore. Please, I need to stay."

"Why? So you can seduce Estelle?"

"Seduce Estelle?" He stepped backward. "No, I have never tried to do that. This is a misunderstanding."

"I am ordering you to go to Saicean. Take the rest of the army with you."

"Azariah, please," Chanon begged. The scales on Azariah's back were still raised, and even though Chanon's face was in shadow, I could hear the anguish in his voice.

"Are you disobeying my orders?"

Chanon shook his head, but as I approached, he lifted his chin. Was he angry with me, or upset? I stared at him, unable to look away as he slowly turned his back on Azariah and walked into the sea. Such was his loyalty that the moment Azariah ordered him to leave, he had no choice but to obey.

As Chanon sank under the surface of the water, I turned my attention to Azariah. He stared at the place Chanon had disappeared. The sharp scales on his back were flattening, returning his skin to normal.

"Azariah!" I called as I stepped toward him.

He turned quickly, looking surprised to see me. But as I reached him, he returned his gaze to the sea stretching out in front of us.

"He has gone. I ordered him to go," he said.

"I heard."

I wrapped my arm around his waist. Why had Chanon felt the need to interfere?

"Have they all gone?" I asked, seeing no sign of movement in the bay.

He nodded, his focus not shifting from the water. "I had no choice."

I followed his gaze. There were no heads bobbing up to inspect what was happening on land. It was as Azariah said. They had all gone.

"Do you know what is strange about this?" Azariah questioned. "You needed to complete your missed submergence last night so we could go to Saicean. Now you have done the ritual, I am in no rush to take you there. I selfishly want you to myself. I am not ready to share you with anyone."

"Share me?" My relief over him not wanting to immediately go to Saicean was instantly replaced with another worry—one that had been playing at the back of my mind. I would be traveling to a place that was predominantly male. While I had no doubt Azariah would ensure I was treated properly, I still didn't like the idea of being the only female

Sachael there. The nightmare I'd had when he first asked me to return to Saicean with him still weighed heavily on my mind.

"Your arrival in Saicean will cause great interest and speculation," Azariah said, his voice lighter, but proud. "Everyone will want to meet you. I fear my father will monopolize your time. It will not be just you and me."

I moved in front of him, holding each side of his head in my hands, forcing him to look at me. "All this time, you've told me it's the only safe place for me. Now, you start to question whether we should go."

"I never said we shouldn't go. It is the safest place for you, therefore we need to go—but maybe we can have a few days alone first."

"So you're still set on us going?" For a few moments, my heart had soared with the possibility of him changing his mind. But staying on land for any length of time had never been an option for him.

He nodded. "When we go to Saicean, I will be at your side. My father may demand your time, others may want to see you, and it will be difficult, but you have to be there. You are the most important Sachael in the world. You are the only female in existence. You are not only my future, you are every other Sachael's future as well."

I screwed my nose up.

"Children, Estelle. There is the possibility you could give birth to a girl."

"But—"

"Have you never considered it? That any child of ours could be a girl?"

I nodded. It was something I had considered—the pressure I may be put under to conceive. It had always been a thought dancing around the back of my mind. Although, with Azariah and the ridiculously prim and proper way he behaved, the actual necessity of having sex with him in order to produce a child was something I only dreamt about.

"We'd have to make love first," I said. "And you are resistant to my advances."

He laughed, pulling me against his chest. "Oh, Estelle, whenever I am serious, you lighten my mood; when I am angry, you calm me."

I smiled against his skin. "Do you want to stay on the beach for a while, walk through the arches and caves over there?" I pointed to the area, hoping he would agree.

"No, let us go and sit on the dunes instead." He glanced in the opposite direction. "I would like to watch the ocean. We have to be careful now that I have sent them away. We need to move from here soon. It does not make sense to stay in one place for too long."

"What about Michael? You've sent the army away, and he's happy here. He's with friends. I don't think he'll want to leave."

"If he is unwilling to come with us and find somewhere safe to stay, then we will go straight to Saicean. As much as I want to keep you to myself, I am also aware of the danger we face by staying away. If Michael has no interest in leaving his friends, he can stay here. He knows the ritual, and we can return for him in time for his seventh submergence. But I would much prefer it if he moved away. He would be best moving to a busy city, somewhere he can hide easily. He only needs to return to the coast once a month to do his submergence. Without Geleon and the other members of the army guarding him, he has no need to stay near the coast permanently. We can take him whereever he decides, but then we leave him."

"But if Orontes finds him, he'll kill him."

Azariah nodded. "Of that, I am aware. We can only help him so much. Ultimately, he has to make the decision. I can only hope he makes the right one. You are my priority, not him."

As we settled on top of the dunes, watching the sun rise, Azariah sighed heavily.

"I shall miss this place when we leave. There are many things I have come to like about living on land."

"Such as?"

"The darkness of the nights. The warmth of the sun. And the strange feeling of the breeze on my skin, even the rain."

I grinned, surprised by his admittance.

"I like the sound of the birds singing in the mornings," he continued. "You always stir in your sleep when they start their songs." He grinned before kissing me. "Oh, Estelle. If only we were in the water now, not last night. I would finish what we so wonderfully started. I hardly slept last night. I was unable to take my eyes off you."

I cocked my head. "What?"

"I watched you all night. I know it sounds strange, but—"

"No, not that bit. The other."

"Which bit?" Azariah grinned, enjoying the tease.

I widened my eyes. "You made it sound like we could, you know . . ."

"Estelle, I have no idea what you are trying to say." His smile spread further across his face.

"Stop teasing me." I couldn't decide whether to laugh or pout.

Bright blue eyes stared straight at me. "Then tell me exactly what you want to know."

"You said that if we were in the water now, you would finish what we started. Does that mean what I think it does, and if so, how?"

"How?" Azariah's serious expression faded, and he smirked.

"Stop it." I giggled.

He pulled me across his body, lying back on the sand before kissing me.

"You know exactly what I mean," he whispered.

"But it was a full moon last night, doesn't that mean you can still get me pregnant?"

He shook his head. "The sun is rising. We have been watching it for the last few minutes. When the sun rises, all the powers the full moon bestows on me disappear. Your gills began to hurt the moment the sun rose on the night after your missed submergence, did they not?

"Yes, but I'm not interested in my gills." I quickly pushed the subject aside. "Are you saying that when the sun rises, you lose your fertility? You'll not get me pregnant?"

He nodded, slowly, narrowing his eyes. "Estelle, you promised you would help me wait until we were in Saicean. We are not there yet."

I pouted, slowly walking my fingers across his chest. "I've never wanted to wait, though."

His hand covered mine, stopping its wandering trail.

"I made you a promise." His gaze held mine, sincere, unwavering.

I dipped my head, nuzzling his neck. "Break it then."

"Estelle . . ."

"Break your promise. I don't care."

I slipped my hand from his fingers and pushed myself up. Sitting astride him, I rotated my hips.

"It's not as if you don't want to," I said quietly, adding another slow rotation. "Your body certainly does."

Azariah grinned. "Of course it does. You know how much I want you."

I leaned over him and placed a chaste kiss on his lips.

"Then prove it," I whispered, my mouth hovering over his.

He groaned loudly and closed his eyes. I took the opportunity to kiss him again.

When he opened his eyes, I gasped at their intensity. He brought his hands to either side of my face and held me still.

"Your eyes are the purest blue I have ever seen," he said, his voice low, thick with unspoken desire. "They dance with the waves of the ocean and the mischief of the child that still stirs within you." He slipped his hands into my hair and ran his fingers through its untamed length. "And your hair is the darkest chestnut I have ever seen, but I love the way the sunlight catches the natural streaks of red that run through it."

I closed my eyes, letting his words caress me.

"But most of all, I love you. Are you sure about this?" he said. "I do not want to rush you."

"Rush me?" I smiled at his concern. "You are joking, right?"

A wide grin pulled at Azariah's mouth before he pushed me to the side and sprang to his feet. He grabbed me, his eager hands lifting me from the sand and throwing me over his shoulder. I screamed with joy at his playful action, giggling as his hands slipped up my legs and rested on my thighs.

Instead of heading in the direction of the house, though, he headed further away, deeper into the sand dunes. I nearly squealed with excitement when I realized his intention. There'd be no comfy bed for our first time together, we would be on the beach as the sun bathed us in its early morning glow.

"Where are you taking me, Mr. Sachael?" I giggled.

"Somewhere private. Somewhere we will not be disturbed."

His hands tightened on my thighs, and I shrieked again when one squeezed my bottom. He didn't carry me far, just further into the dunes. Finding the privacy he wanted, he lowered me onto the sand.

"This is perfect," he stated, standing over me and looking in every direction. He'd placed me in a circular dip in the sands. Grasses sprang up in random tufts of greenery around us. It was a hidden spot, well away from everything. I propped myself up on my elbows, taking the opportunity to observe him. And, when he turned his attention away from perusing the landscape, his eyes met mine.

"Come here," I said, curling my finger at him.

"There will be no going back after this, Estelle. I will never leave you alone."

"What more could I ask for?"

He stepped to my feet before sinking onto the sand to lie beside me. I shifted my position, leaning over him to kiss his shoulder. I familiarized myself with the taste of his skin. Always salty, always warm. He lay on the sand, stretching his body before resting his hand on my thigh. As my lips moved across his shoulder and onto his neck, he exhaled a long breath, and his hand curled around my leg, pulling it across his body. I followed his silent instructions, straddling his hips as I continued ghosting my lips across his neck. His eyes were shut, and he breathed steadily; deep, relaxing breaths.

"Remember last night?" I murmured against his skin. "What happened before Chanon interrupted? I certainly wasn't wearing this many clothes."

Azariah's eyes opened as I pushed my upper body away from his and lifted my vest top over my head, throwing it onto the sand.

His eyes widened for a few seconds, and then the corners of his mouth lifted in a smile.

"You still have too many clothes on if you want me to make love to you," Azariah stated, his fingers already untying the ribbon on the front of my pajamas. After the tiny bow was released, his hands caressed my stomach before moving to my hips. He gradually pushed the cotton material down my legs, twisting me onto my back when our position wouldn't allow for any further removal of them.

It was a few seconds before they also flew across the sand to join my top.

"That's better," he said, sitting next to me, observing my practical nakedness.

His eyes scanned my whole body, a tender smile playing on his lips as he followed the path his fingertips teasingly traced on my skin. My senses heightened, and my mind blocked everything apart from Azariah. Each touch was like a tiny electric shock, each of his slow, rhythmic breaths a reminder of the man beside me. I gasped as his finger touched my nipple, and groaned when his mouth covered the exact same spot.

Pushing my shoulders into the sand, I lifted my chest higher, wanting more, needing more. He licked, sucked, and scraped his teeth across the nipple before switching to the other, lavishing it with the exact same care and attention. I sighed wantonly as his mouth meandered along the center of my body and his tongue dipped into my belly button. All I could think of was how I wanted him to go lower, to have his tongue on another part of my body, the part desperate for his touch.

As his nose slid back and forth across the top of my underwear, his fingers hooked into each side of them. I wriggled, squirming with eagerness to have him remove my final scrap of clothing. He chuckled, his warm breath tickling me as his hands swiftly grasped and removed the flimsy barrier.

"Stay still," he murmured.

I lay completely exposed to him, but reveled in the early morning air blowing across my skin. My body flooded with warmth as he gazed at me, and I struggled to lie still. I wanted to reach for him, to touch and explore his whole body. A serious expression crossed his face, and he narrowed his eyes, slowly scanning every part of me. His gaze was hypnotic, addictive, and never ending. Seconds led into minutes, and, as each tick of time passed by, I became eager for his attention.

"Please," I whispered. A heartfelt plea for him to do more, to take away the aching need within me.

"What do you want, Estelle?" he asked, his attention back on my face.

"You. I want you. Please."

He trailed one hand down the center of my body, his pace a slow torture, but stopped his journey when his fingers pushed against the spot desperate for his touch.

I wanted to scream his name, yet also whisper it tenderly; I wanted him to know no other man had ever made me feel so alive, so wanted, and so safe.

I moaned loudly, pressing the back of my head into the soft sand as his fingers pressed and slid against me. Within moments, the heat of his mouth covered the place where his fingers had been. The sensation was overpowering, and yet I wanted more. My hands flew to his head and I grasped at his hair, tugging it and pulling his face further against me. It was as if my mind couldn't work out what I wanted most. My body knew—my body had known for a long time. It wanted Azariah in every perceivable way.

Taking a deep breath, knowing I was about to end this exquisite torture, I gripped his shoulders.

"On your back," I demanded, trying to move him to the side of me.

He lifted his head, grinning wickedly at me. I saw the intense longing in his eyes, the sapphire blue of his iris clear and bright. It was a wonder I didn't beg him to rip his shorts off and take me immediately. A soft kiss was placed on my stomach before he followed my instruction.

"What are you going to do to me, Estelle?" he asked. The earlier seriousness in his voice had disappeared. It had been replaced with sultry, breathy desire.

"Everything," I responded, not breaking the eye contact we had established. "Everything you could possibly want me to do." I crawled over his body, settling across his hips.

Wetting my lips, I leaned over his chest to kiss him. Our previous kisses had been slow and sensual; this was the complete opposite. The passion between us increased. Our heightened emotions fought to be released as we urgently sought each other's mouths. Teeth clashed against teeth, and tongues fought for dominance as we moaned and gasped at our renewed need for each other.

I grinned into our kiss as I recalled a conversation I'd once had with him. When we'd first come to the Orkneys, he'd mentioned he had a scar, one Orontes had inflicted on him. He'd told me where it was as he patted his left hip. I knew what I wanted to kiss next, but there was a problem. His lower body was still covered.

"Do you ever take these shorts off?" I murmured close to his ear.

"Yes."

"I've never seen you without them."

"The night of the storm, when I stayed at your house, I removed them. I remember that night fondly. It was the first night you spent wrapped in my arms."

I remembered it as the night I'd saved his life, and also the night he'd told me he had killed someone.

"I was a fool trying to shut myself away from you," I said.

"You had your reasons, and if you had remained shut away from me, I think I would have crawled into your bed to join you at some point during the night."

I raised my eyebrows at his admittance.

"That was the first night I witnessed the way your skin reacted," I recalled.

"Only to you. Just as it is doing now."

The small, rounded bumps were scattered across his chest and stomach. I shifted lower until I was sitting astride his knees.

"I think they need to come off again, don't you?" I grinned wickedly at him.

I ran my hands along the side of his shorts, frowning at something in his pocket.

"My knife," he reminded me.

I pulled it out of his pocket, keeping it encased in its protective cover, and placed it on the sand above our heads. He didn't need it now.

Returning to his body, I slipped my hands under the waistband of his shorts before lingering on the top button.

He drew in a long breath, releasing it with a shudder, and then froze beneath me as I popped open the buttons. I concentrated, determined to look at his scar before I became distracted with anything else, but it was difficult.

I tugged on the sides of his shorts, surprised at how easily they began to slip down his legs. Forcing myself to ignore the most prominent part of his body, I focused on the area where I would find his scar. When his shorts were pulled to his knees, I saw the full damage Orontes had caused.

"Azariah," I gasped, seeing the three deep welts running from the side of his hip across the front of his leg. After all this time, they were still dark red. Whatever Orontes had attacked him with hadn't allowed the scars to fade.

"I think you'll agree that Chanon came off worse," he joked quietly.

"These are worse scars, though, deeper than his."

"But hidden away. Not in full view, like Chanon's."

"Do they hurt?"

"No, not now."

I couldn't stop myself from kissing the point on his hip where the scars began, and I slowly kissed the length of the first scar before repeating the action with both of the others.

His hand rested on my shoulder while I kissed him. Placing one last kiss just above his knee, I gazed up at him.

He smiled, cupping my chin in his hand. "I am sure they will be practically invisible soon, now you have kissed them."

I grinned at his comment before contemplating my next move. Azariah watched me intently, his eyes never leaving mine. I was acutely aware of his nakedness, as well as my own. But as I slid further across his body, intending to kiss the most prominent part of him, he must have sensed my intention. He moved quickly, pulling my body level with his.

"Not now," he whispered. "I can hardly contain my need to make love to you."

My pout must have amused him, as he traced his finger over my lips. "These would feel too amazing on me at the moment." He paused, looking deeply into my eyes. "Now, I believe we have something else to finish, something you distracted me from earlier."

I frowned at him, but hardly had time to focus before he flipped me onto my back. He was immediately on top of me, his strong, muscular body crushing mine into the sand. If there was any doubt in my mind about whether he wanted me as much as I did him, it fled before the evidence of his hardness pressed against me.

His lips ghosted across my body, taking the same path as they had earlier, and I was unable to prevent a soft, rumbling vibrating against my throat.

"You are purring, Estelle," he commented as he slid his hand between my legs.

I didn't respond; I couldn't. His fingers were already causing my body to shiver with renewed anticipation. I could feel the tension building in my body, the throbbing of a deep ache within me. It was too much. I was briefly aware of Azariah's fingers moving within me, hitting a spot I never knew existed, and I was lost. I closed my eyes as I moaned, managing to gasp his name while my body shook with intense warmth.

Bliss. I had never experienced anything like this in my entire life. Every nerve in my body exploded; every fiber of my existence reacted. I lay motionless as my mind tripped with the euphoria of what had happened.

When I eventually opened my eyes, I was greeted by Azariah gazing at me.

"Thank you," he whispered.

I smiled at him lazily.

"What for?"

"For letting me see how beautiful you are. Seeing you like that was the most beautiful thing I have ever seen."

I closed my eyes again, smiling as my muscles tingled, the ache within me calmly thudding—waiting, wanting more.

"Are you ready for me?" he asked.

I nodded, unsure whether I was capable of making any controlled sound myself.

He shifted his body completely over mine. I was aware of his weight upon me once again, but loved the feeling of him being there. His knees gently nudged my legs, and I responded by opening to him completely. I felt his hardness again, only this time, it pressed against a part of me which was more than ready to welcome him.

"Please," I breathed heavily.

My request was immediately granted as he slid into me. I gasped, my hands gripping his waist as he stilled. He rested his forehead on mine before kissing me. This kiss was strong, passionate, and consuming. I flexed my hips as he kissed me, wanting him to move, needing him to take away the sweet fire simmering within me.

He needed no further encouragement and began to move, slowly at first, pushing deep within me. I groaned shamelessly, gripping his ass, pulling him hard against me as his movements began to increase in pace. We fit together so perfectly, so completely.

His kisses moved across my face, down my neck, and along my collarbone as he continued to thrust into me. Without warning, he suddenly knelt, grabbed my hips, and pulled me against him, all while keeping our connection. I stretched my arms out behind my head, arching my back as his mouth descended on one of my nipples. His hold shifted as he slipped his arms under me and gripped the back of my shoulders, guiding my movements to match his.

The ache within me grew on each of his subsequent thrusts. He had maneuvered me to exactly the right position. I whimpered, beginning to lose the ability to think straight. I wanted to call his name, whisper words of love to him, but I couldn't find my voice.

As if sensing my impending release, Azariah increased his pace, thrusting harder, pulling me to meet him on every single stroke.

He groaned my name before a deep rumbling noise vibrated in his chest.

He was growling—again.

I was lost. The sound triggered my orgasm. My body danced with the most intense and wonderful release. I reacted instinctively, thrusting my hips wildly against Azariah's. Every nerve exploded within me, every muscle twisted and turned, celebrating the most amazing sensation in the world—in my life.

All I could see was Azariah, his beautiful face watching me come undone as I surrendered to him completely. He hissed under his breath before letting the most wonderful growl burst from his lips as his own release shook him. His gaze remained fixed on me as his rhythm became irregular and his hips jerked. His whole body quivered.

He had said I was beautiful, but looking at him now, I failed to see how anyone could look more amazing than he did. His eyes danced with passion, his features soft against his strong jaw, and his skin glistened with a fine sheen of perspiration.

Eventually, he stilled. His hands still held me against him, keeping our connection.

"Thank you," I whispered, feeling overwhelmed by what we had just shared. Had I known it was going to be like this, I would have insisted he made love to me earlier. I sighed as

I reflected on all the missed opportunities we'd had when we could have given in.

"Estelle," he breathed huskily, still recovering from his exertion. "You have no need to ever thank me. It is I who should be thanking you, yet again. I will forever remember how it felt to be connected to you so intimately, and so completely."

He released my shoulders, letting me relax onto the sand. He followed, carefully lying on top of me. I grinned as he continued to flex his hips against mine, prolonging the intimacy. As he caressed my face, he dipped his head to kiss me. We shared slow, long, intimate kisses, ones that sealed our love in so many ways.

Eventually, as our intimate connection was lost, he rolled to my side. "I have never, ever experienced anything like that," he admitted. I turned to face him, letting him tenderly brush my hair from my face. We gazed at each other, not speaking for a long time, just content with staring—too wrapped up in the afterglow of what we had done, and what we would undoubtedly do again.

The early morning sun had risen in the sky just enough to peek over the edge of the sand dune. The golden rays lit both of our bodies, warming us as we basked in their glow and our afterglow.

"I know I have told you many times before, but I have to tell you again," he said. "I love you, Estelle. I think I always have. I knew there was someone in the world just for me. I didn't care whether they were a human or an Oceanid. But

I never dreamt it would be another Sachael. I wanted true love. A love that would defy the odds; a love that would last forever. With you, I have found that love."

I kissed him, unable to respond verbally. Tears swam across my eyes, threatening to escape, but I didn't want to cry, not now. I didn't feel I deserved such comments—not from him, a man who was not only the most stunning man I had ever met, but a man with the most beautiful heart I'd ever known as well. I pushed my doubts aside, not willing to dwell on my insecurities. We had finally come together, shared our love for each other in the most physical way possible. I didn't want anything to spoil our moment.

I suspected Azariah understood why I was quiet, what I was battling within, and he gave me time to contemplate, circling his hand lazily on my hip.

Eventually, he spoke. "I hope you are not intending to have a full night's sleep ever again," he whispered jokingly. "Because I will not allow it."

"Not allow it?" I managed a small smirk at his choice of words.

He grinned before laughing. All his former worry had washed away. This light-hearted mood was something I hoped would remain. It was a side of him he kept well hidden.

I stroked the side of his face, deep in thought, thinking about everything we had gone through since meeting. I had never believed in true love, in instant love, but with Azariah, I'd experienced both.

"Is something wrong, Estelle?" A familiar frown filled my vision.

I shook my head. "No, I've just realized how completely and utterly I love you."

Azariah huffed playfully. "I have always known how much I love you, and how much you love me. There has never been any doubt."

As he kissed me again, I could do nothing but moan my approval.

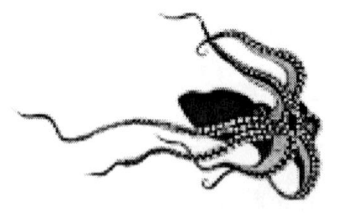

TWELVE
Trust

The rest of our day was spent together, away from the others. We wandered along the beach, exploring the nearby labyrinth of arches and caves. We laughed and joked. Neither of us wanted to go back to the house—we wanted to remain in our own bubble, and returning would undoubtedly burst it. Azariah was incredibly tactile, either holding my hand or pulling me against his body as we strolled through the arches. And he practically pounced on me when we were deep inside the caves, pushing me against one of the walls. The privacy once again led to us letting our instincts take over. Our lovemaking was frantic, more eager than earlier. It was as Azariah had said. He couldn't leave me alone. What he hadn't bargained for was my passion. I couldn't leave him alone, either.

When the sky became overcast, we returned to the shelter of the house.

"Let us see what chaos we are returning to," Azariah said, as we strolled hand in hand through the gentle surf of the waves.

"Hmmm," I responded, as unsure as he was about what would greet us after this morning's rushed exit.

Azariah sighed. "We need to inform Michael of our decision to leave."

"We're definitely leaving?" I stopped walking.

"We need to go to Saicean," Azaria responded. He stopped as well, and turned to face me. "We will see where he wants to go and get him as near as possible to his destination. And then we will leave for Saicean."

I took a deep breath, not liking the definite plan he had organized for us all.

"The last time you mentioned Saicean, you weren't so eager to return," I reminded him. "You wanted to keep me to yourself."

Azariah smiled. "But you are mine. There is no doubt of it now." He stepped toward me, closing the small gap. He lifted my chin with his fingertips, and his dancing eyes caught mine in their gaze.

"I know you have your doubts about going. I understand them; really, I do. But you need to become a full Sachael. It is where you belong. I will kill any man, be he Oceanid, Sachael, or human, who tries to steal you from me."

"There'll be no need," I said, pursing my lips and looking down at my feet.

"There might be."

His soft lips kissed the top of my head as he tightened his arms around me.

"Do not worry, Estelle. It is merely another adventure to take. And I will be with you as you take it."

I lifted my head from his chest and looked at him. Chanon's words echoed in my head. He'd told me not to fight Azariah about my journey to Saicean. He'd told me it was the only safe place for me to be. I sighed inwardly. I had to go. I didn't want to constantly be on the run, moving every couple of days from one beach to another, not when there was an alternative. And life in Saicean offered me a wonderful future. It would be one with Azariah. We would be together, safe. Life could move on, not stay still or hang in the balance as it was now. Azariah would relax—I was looking forward to seeing him without his constant frown of worry and confusion.

"Okay," I said, taking a deep breath.

"Okay?"

"I'll go to Saicean, but only after Michael is sorted. I'm not prepared to leave him in any danger."

"Estelle, he will always be in danger. Until he travels to the safety of Saicean, he will, unfortunately, be at risk of being discovered. He cannot stay in the same place for long. Staying here would be a mistake. He needs to move, and keep moving."

I looked at the house in the distance. It was the perfect example of a welcoming home. The comforts of a large bed, hot food, and his friends all within it. I sighed again.

"But we can't force him to leave," I said. "It has to be his decision."

"It does," Azariah nodded. "And I think he will come with us."

He looked toward the house before taking my hand in his. We left the freshness of the tumbling waves and headed across the sand. When we arrived at the house, it was surprisingly quiet. Usually, Cleo was singing, or Michael's laughter was booming out. Not today.

Azariah held the door open for me, and I smiled at his gesture before we entered the hallway. We were greeted by Michael, who was sitting on the bottom of the stairs. He lifted his head from his book, narrowing his eyes at us. "You decided to come back. What changed your mind?"

Not waiting for an answer, he slammed the book on the floor and headed into the kitchen.

"Michael?" I called, surprised by his reaction.

"Leave him," Azariah suggested, as he turned into the living room. But I wasn't prepared to ignore the way he had reacted. I followed Michael into the kitchen, but was greeted with his back. He stared at the clock on the wall.

"You're back, then?" he repeated dryly.

I frowned. "Is something wrong?"

"You tell me."

I had no idea what had angered him so much. His sarcasm was usually left for when he was joking about something. This wasn't his usual temperament.

"Michael, have I done something?"

He spun to face me. His eyes were narrowed, face red. I was taken aback.

"I presumed you'd gone!" he shouted as he pointed toward the door. "And then I worried that Orontes had gotten you both."

"We were—"

"I presumed you'd been caught. That Azariah was dead, and Orontes had dragged you off into the sea. I've been worried sick all day. And then you turn up, all smiles and happy faces, and wonder why I'm angry?" His nostrils were flaring, and his hands were fists.

I shook my head. "I never gave our absence any thought. I'm sorry if—"

"Sorry?" His stance shifted, and he planted his feet firmly apart before folding his arms across his chest. "Believe me, Estelle, 'sorry' is nowhere near enough for what I've been through today."

I looked away from him, uncomfortable in his cold, unflinching stare. I didn't know what to say. Part of me thought he was overreacting, but part of me also understood.

"Where have you been?" he asked, his voice calming slightly. "I searched the beach, you weren't there."

I was about to respond, but Azariah strode into the room. "We walked through the arches," he said from behind me. "But let us talk about something else." There was an edge to Azariah's voice, the one I didn't hear very often. The one I didn't like. He looked straight at Michael. "While we were away for the day, you talked to Sam and Cleo."

"I thought you'd been caught by Orontes. I needed them to help me," Michael mumbled.

"Help you? You told them everything!" Azariah roared. "Absolutely everything. Have you any idea of the danger you have put Estelle in?"

Michael frowned, matching my expression as I looked at each of them in turn, silently questioning them both.

"You know I would never put Estelle in any danger. She's in no danger from Sam, or Cleo," Michael said, pushing past Azariah as he headed out of the kitchen.

Azariah snarled at him as he passed.

"What's going on?" I questioned, still concerned about the anger emanating from Azariah.

"When you followed Michael in here, I went into the other room to apologize for my angry reaction this morning. But before I could say anything, they started questioning me. Michael has told them everything. They know he was part of The Sect, what The Sect is, and how they operate. They know about Orontes and your imprisonment. He also told them he is a Sachael."

"And me?"

"They know."

I was surprised and shocked that Michael had parted with all our secrets. I could only believe that he really did think we had gone, and he told Sam and Cleo everything in the hope they would help him.

Azariah closed his eyes, looking as though he was fighting the rage within him. "Let us go and see what they have to say. If they know our secrets, I think they can at least tell us theirs. I am still anxious to know their story, and why they fear the Atlantic Ocean so much."

As we entered the room, three sets of eyes fell on me. I didn't react; I didn't want them to see me any differently to how they had before they knew I was a Sachael. They were all seated. Azariah and I remained standing.

"I'm sorry, Michael," I said, focusing on him and ignoring the curious stares from Cleo and Sam. "We never gave our absence much thought. The last thing we'd wanted to do was worry you."

"Well, you did." He crossed his arms across his chest, refusing to look at me.

I sighed heavily. He was one of the most stubborn men I'd ever met. I turned to face Azariah, who was glaring at Michael.

"You need to tell him," he said. "Tell him of our plans."

"Plans?" Michael frowned.

I nodded. "You need to make a decision."

"About what?"

"We're leaving tomorrow morning. Are you coming with us?" I asked.

"Why tomorrow?" He turned to Azariah. "Is it because I've spoken to Sam and Cleo? There's no need to go; they're not a risk to us."

"That is not the reason. We need to move somewhere else," Azariah responded. "We cannot stay in one place for long. I have sent Chanon and the army back to Saicean."

"What? Why?" Michael jumped to his feet and stepped forward. Cleo clung to Sam.

"Certain things have happened," Azariah said, straightening to his full height. "Things which are of no concern to you. I do not need them here any longer."

"Just forget about yourself for one minute," Michael said, his eyes firmly fixed on Azariah. "What about Estelle, and me? There's no one to protect any of us now."

"I am not thinking about myself. I assure you, Estelle is my priority." Azariah narrowed his eyes. I wondered if he was having second thoughts about his earlier rash decision.

"So, you've sent the people away who were protecting her?" Michael shook his head and scratched the back of his head. "It's the most ridiculous decision you've ever made."

Azariah glared at Michael.

"Michael," I said, hoping my intervention would help. "It was a decision Azariah *had* to make."

"I can't believe you've sent them away." He sank onto the settee, running his hands across his face. Cleo moved next to him.

"I'm glad they've gone," she uttered, placing her hand on his shoulder.

Sam stood, a shield for his wife and his friend. It was as if a dividing line had been drawn through the room; Azariah and me on one side, the three friends on the other.

Sam looked at me, his gaze still one of intense curiosity. "You still haven't told us why Azariah was shouting this morning. It caused a lot of upset."

"I was angry," Azariah said, his gaze locked on Sam. "And I apologize. I had no intention of upsetting anyone, least of all Cleo. But things had happened that, unfortunately, resulted in me losing my temper."

"So, it had nothing to do with any of us?" Sam insisted, moving to sit beside Cleo.

"No," Azariah shook his head. "Why would it?" He addressed both Sam and Cleo with his question.

Cleo closed her eyes, taking a deep breath. When she opened them, she looked straight at Azariah.

"I have seen your kind before when they are angry. You may think I overreacted, but I have seen things, things that will haunt me for the rest of my life. Your anger brought it all back."

Azariah pulled a chair out from under the table before sitting on it and facing Cleo. He bent forward and held his hand out to her. "I want to know why you are scared, and what has happened to make you both live out of the water."

She took a deep breath and placed her hand in Azariah's. He wrapped his fingers around it and waited.

I swallowed nervously, aware of Cleo composing herself before she began to talk. I was also aware that Azariah was potentially calming her. I knew how much stronger his ability was through touch.

"I didn't have any fear of Sachaels until I was fifteen. I had already met Sam, and we were planning to be together when the time was right." She looked to Sam, who offered her a tight smile. "I was swimming with my friend, Xanthe. We were chasing the fish, doing nothing wrong, when we were suddenly surrounded by four Sachaels." She closed her eyes.

"Go on," Azariah encouraged, his voice soft, quiet.

When Cleo opened her eyes, a solitary tear ran down her cheek. "One of the Sachaels took a great interest in Xanthe. She wasn't interested in him, but he wouldn't leave her alone. We started swimming home, but they followed us. When we swam faster, they easily kept up with us. It eventually became a chase, and Xanthe and I became separated. My mertail was damaged, but somehow—and I still don't know how—I managed to escape. I hid behind a crop of rocks. The Sachaels didn't bother looking for me. They had already caught Xanthe."

Azariah didn't speak as Cleo paused again. She took several deep breaths before continuing.

"They raped her."

Azariah hissed and released Cleo's hand as he leaned back in the chair. I stepped behind him and rested my hands on his shoulders. Now was not the time for him to lose his temper, even if it was in reaction to what he was hearing.

"The one who had taken an initial interest in Xanthe dragged her away after the attack. I never saw her again."

Sam pulled Cleo into a tight hug before adding his own comments. "The guards at the entrance to Saicean don't just stop enemies from entering," he said. "They stop Oceanids from leaving. Have you any idea how many of our women are kept there against their will?"

"How do you know this?" Azariah asked. His voice was quiet and controlled, but I sensed the anger and upset within him.

Sam continued to explain as Cleo quietly sobbed. "Cleo and I couldn't leave the ocean until we were eighteen; we weren't allowed. Cleo lived in fear for three years. She never ventured from our home; she was a complete wreck. It was only when we came to land that she began to live without distress. But while we waited to be allowed to live on land, an Oceanid escaped from Saicean. She told us of the nightmare many of our women endure. Azariah, many of the Oceanids are unhappy, and they want to leave. They are married to the Sachaels against their will, frightened of what will happen to them if they refuse their husbands sexually. Some of the females snatched from us were not even women—they were girls!"

"The Oceanids I have seen are happy," Azariah snapped. "Lots come willingly; they want to live in Saicean."

"But not all of them," Sam insisted. "Surely, if there is only a handful that do not want to be there, who are forced to be with your kind, then they should be allowed to leave."

"Of course," Azariah responded quickly.

"That's not what happens, though. In the three years between Xanthe being taken and us coming to land, six of our females went missing. All of them were young."

Azariah rose from his chair. "This cannot be happening. It is not acceptable and would be dealt with most severely. We have no need to force anyone to be with us. Your kind has an attraction to us—you want to be with us."

"Azariah." It was my turn to snap. "Cleo hasn't reacted to you or Michael that way, and Sam hasn't to me. Maybe this attraction isn't as widespread as you think it is."

He turned to Cleo, his eyes searching hers. "Cleo, did you feel anything for the men who chased you and Xanthe? Was there any attraction to any of them?"

"None. I only felt fear for those men, and I'm sure Xanthe did as well. She fought them, Azariah, she really did. She was battered when they dragged her away. Her fins and mertail were badly damaged; she had tried desperately to escape."

"I do not understand this," Azariah said, shaking his head. "All Oceanids have an attraction to Sachaels. But you do not."

"I can feel it," Sam stated, "an attraction to Estelle. So there must be some truth to it. I didn't understand it at first, but as soon as Michael told us she was a Sachael, it made sense. It's a feeling that makes me want to be with her. It's purely physical. But I can ignore it."

Azariah shook his head. His eyes narrowed, and his brow furrowed. "That is not how it normally is. The attraction is always overpowering."

"Like Melia?" I queried.

"Exactly like Melia. I have never known of an Oceanid resisting us."

"You mean you have never had an Oceanid resist *you*." My words were said as I thought them. I never intended to speak them out loud.

"Exactly. They follow me around in Saicean." He sighed heavily, running his hands through his hair, looking exasperated. "Do you have names?"

"Names?" Sam asked.

"The men who took Xanthe."

"The Oceanid that fled Saicean said she had spoken to Xanthe, but always when her husband wasn't there. Apparently, he was a man to be feared."

"His name," Azariah growled.

"Ixion," Cleo mumbled. "The Oceanid who escaped called him Ixion. He has a large scar that—"

"Runs diagonally across his back?" Azariah finished her sentence.

Cleo nodded.

"You know him?" I gasped. "You know who did this?"

"He is in my father's top army." He turned to look out the window across the bay. "I have never liked him. He is known for his ferocious attitude."

"You think it's the same Sachael?"

"Yes." His gaze didn't falter as his eyes remained fixed on the horizon. "It is not a common name, and he is the only Sachael I know of who has such a scar. No woman would ever be a match for him."

I moved to his side. He didn't speak, but I could see his chest rising and falling heavily.

"Azariah?"

He ignored me.

"Azariah?" I repeated. He still didn't respond, just continued to stare out the window.

"Take him upstairs," Michael said. "Calm him down."

I nodded, knowing Michael understood Azariah's reaction. He'd listened to him talk freely about what an amazing place Saicean was, how everyone was happy there. This information destroyed that. Unfortunately, all it did for me was increase my fear. I still didn't want to go to Saicean.

I took Azariah's hand.

"And, Estelle," Michael said, as I began to steer a silent, dazed Azariah across the room. "If you insist on leaving in the morning, then I'll come with you. I have to, don't I?"

"No," I said quietly. "You can stay here if you want, but it would be best if you left and found somewhere safe, away from the sea.."

Michael nodded. "I'll come with you then."

He turned to hug Cleo and Sam. I smiled at their closeness; it was heartwarming to see such friendship and trust. I had every confidence, as did Michael, that our secrets were safe with them.

Azariah appeared to have gone into some form of shock. He didn't talk; he didn't even appear to register that I was taking him upstairs to our room. Even when I guided him onto the bed, all he did was close his eyes.

"Azariah, are you okay?" I whispered, softly kissing his cheek before I settled next to him.

"No," he whispered, as he blindly reached for my hand. "I am not."

I shifted closer to him, but he turned his head away.

His silence made me feel uneasy. In all the time I'd known him, he had never refused to speak to me. Everything he knew had been turned upside down. He'd found out Oceanid females were caught and dragged to Saicean for the Sachaels' sexual thrills. They weren't there because they wanted to be; they were there because they couldn't leave. No wonder the females always flocked to him. They saw the goodness in him; a Sachael who would never treat them as the others did. He was a kind man, one who would save them from their miserable lives.

"What Cleo has told us is horrendous—" I started.

"Horrendous!" he shouted, at last turning to look at me. His eyes were bright, vivid blue, sparkling with unshed tears. I placed my hand on the side of his face, understanding his anger and distress. "It is more than horrendous," he growled. "I intend to have Ixion dealt with as soon as I return to Saicean, but first, I will find out who his accomplices were in that unforgivable attack on Xanthe. I will also ensure she is escorted safely back to her home."

"I know. I know you will." There wasn't any doubt in my mind that he would try to put this right. He may not be able to take Xanthe's memories from her, rid her of what had happened all those years ago, but he could at least save her from her forced existence in Saicean.

He closed his eyes, turning his face into my hand before kissing it.

"You are an honorable man," I said.

"I am just me," he said, helpless, at a loss for words. He pulled me against him and laid backward on the bed.

"What else is there I do not know?"

"I don't know," I whispered.

His fingers traced the side of my face.

"I want to make it right for them," he mumbled.

"I know you do."

"Xanthe has to be able to leave if she wants to. And so do the others." His voice was barely a whisper as he spoke.

"Shhh . . ." I shifted my position, holding him close. "When we get to Saicean, we'll sort this out. We'll do something about this. I will stand beside you and argue as strongly as you about punishing Ixion and the other men."

Azariah sniffed, his eyes glistening with tears so close to spilling over.

"I am sorry, Estelle. We have had a wonderful day. It was the best day of my life, and now it ends with a horrendous disclosure."

"There will be other days."

I wriggled further up the bed, letting him rest his head on my shoulder.

"Just stay here all night," I said, pulling him against my side.

Tonight, it was my turn to comfort him. There would be more wonderful days with Azariah, many nights spent in his arms. But now, as we lay together on the bed, he needed comforting. I had never seen him like this. Cleo's story—the reason she was scared of him and the army—was horrific. It made her initial reaction to our arrival completely understandable.

I continued to whisper words of reassurance to Azariah, telling him what we could do to prevent this happening again. And, as the evening wore on, and the mumbles of the others talking and moving downstairs gradually faded, Azariah fell asleep.

With a racing mind, and equally racing heart, I silently faced my ultimate fear. Hearing Cleo's story earlier had confirmed my fears about the men in Saicean. What if I was treated the same way as Xanthe? What if Azariah couldn't control what happened? But if I stayed on land, I would be constantly running from Orontes. Azariah's life would be in danger as well as mine.

My tears trailed down my cheeks as I silently cried. My fear was spiraling out of control. This morning, everything had seemed so much brighter, promising, and carefree. But now, with my full moon ritual complete, there was nothing to stop our departure to Saicean—only Michael. And Azariah had already said we would only stay on land long enough to ensure his safety as best we could. I'd be traveling to Saicean within the next few days.

And it wasn't what I wanted.

THIRTEEN

Betrayed

During the night, Azariah woke me several times. He wanted to forget the horrors Cleo had shared with us. He wanted to reassure me he wasn't the same. Tender comforting kisses gradually became searching urgent ones. We lost ourselves in each other again, but not before Azariah asked me if he could make love to me. He seemed set to prove he was different; he wouldn't force himself on me, make me do anything I didn't want to do. He needn't have worried. I doubted I would ever refuse him—not when he made my whole body react the way it did.

The early morning sun slid through the crack in the curtains, and I rubbed my eyes, yawning. Stretching, my muscles ached delightfully, and a lazy smile crept across my face.

I recalled Azariah's moans of pleasure and grinned when I remembered the way he'd pleasured me, how we'd enjoyed each other's bodies. I felt like I was the most loved woman in the world; loved by Azariah.

He was a demanding lover, yet selfless with his actions, ensuring my satisfaction before his own. I'd tried to stay quiet, but the blissful torture had overpowered my body so many times I gave up trying. And he wasn't particularly quiet either.

I grinned again, thinking how quiet he'd be this morning when confronting Sam, Cleo, and Michael. They must have heard us. My cheeks heated; I'd have to face them as well. I threw the duvet over my head, embarrassed, but still unable to tear the ridiculous grin from my face. Was it going to be like this every night?

As I turned over to face him, an empty space greeted me. Frowning, I shifted to look at the clock on the bedside table. It was early, like yesterday. The sun had just risen. His knife lay next to the clock, exactly where I'd placed it when undressing him last night.

A sudden dread came over me. He was unprotected without it. He would be in the water by himself—the Sachael army had gone.

"Shit," I mumbled, jumping from the bed. My clothes were scattered across the floor, and I dressed as quickly as possible. I grabbed his knife before rushing down the stairs and heading straight for the door.

"Estelle?" Michael called from the living room. "Where are you going?"

"The beach," I responded. "Azariah forgot his knife."

"Slow down, I'll come with you."

I continued running, and scanned the beach, looking for any sign of him. When I didn't see him, I stared at the sea. My spine tingled, and a shiver ran through me. There was a light breeze blowing across the bay, but nothing that should have caused such a reaction from my body.

"Shit," I muttered again. Something wasn't right.

"We're unprotected now." Michael's voice took on an urgency I hadn't heard before as he caught up to me, matching his stride to my own. "If something's happened to him, what the hell are we meant to do?"

"He'll be fine. I'd just be happier knowing he has his knife with him, that's all." I tried to sound positive, not worried. "He usually swims with the army in the morning and chats with Chanon," I said, recalling the way I'd seen him throw himself out of the water as he played around. But I couldn't see him now.

"At least the water's calm today," Michael stated.

"What?" I asked impatiently, walking faster. I focused on the sand, looking for fresh footprints. When the skin on my back tightened, I slowed my pace. Something definitely wasn't right.

"Cleo and Sam told me it was calm in the sea today. They were out there before the sun came up. Now the army is gone, Cleo feels safe enough to go in the water. You know I'm annoyed with Azariah for getting rid of the army, but you should have seen the look on Cleo's face when she came back. She was like a different person—all smiles and laughter. It's why I was up so early. They were hardly quiet. I'm surprised you didn't hear them."

"Good. Great," I mumbled, not really listening to him. I felt an underlying fear, one I hadn't experienced since I was on the beach in Ravenscar, when I'd sensed someone watching me. That same feeling flooded my senses now, driving my unease.

Michael walked beside me, his constant chatter infuriating me. I wished he'd stayed at the house.

"There," he said, seeing fresh footprints in the sand. My eyes followed the path.

"He's gone through the arches," I stated, following the trail myself. I had only gone a few paces when loud voices disturbed the morning. First shouting, and then cheering.

My pace quickened before turning into a determined run on the soft sand. I hadn't gone far when Michael grabbed my arm.

"Estelle, wait," Michael whispered urgently.

A tremendous roar was followed by a flurry of splashing. I knew that roar. I'd heard it before. It was Azariah.

I opened my mouth to scream his name, but a firm hand covered it. Michael spun me to face him; the knife I'd been carrying flew from my hand and onto the sand. He pushed me against the rock side of the cliff, and the back of my head hit the rough surface. Michael pushed himself against me, trapping me between his body and the cliff face. He pressed his hand even firmer over my mouth. I grimaced at the throbbing in the back of my head before lashing out at him, scratching his cheek. I wanted to scream, but couldn't. Was he betraying me? After all this time, was this when he handed me over to Orontes? Had all this been an elaborate set up? My stomach heaved and I wriggled, desperately trying to free myself. Tears of annoyance and anger flooded my eyes. I'd trusted him. Azariah had trusted him. And now this!

"Shhh," Michael whispered.

I mumbled against his hand, and lifted my knee, trying to kick him where it hurt, but he had pinned me to the side of the cliff with his side.

"Stop it," he hissed.

I lashed out at him again, and mumbled as loud as I could against his hand, telling him exactly what I thought of him.

"Stop it, Estelle. I'm not trying to hurt you, but you need to stay quiet."

I squirmed anyway, not listening.

He shook his head. "Stop it. Don't you know who's through there?"

I shook my head. I didn't care who it was. I needed to help Azariah.

"It's them. The Sect. I'm praying they haven't seen us, but if you make any noise at all, they'll definitely know we're here."

Filled with remorse, I nodded frantically, letting him know I understood. He tentatively removed his hand from my mouth.

"The Sect?" I whimpered. "They've caught Azariah?"

"I think so," he replied. "I caught sight of Lilith—she's wearing her cape." He dabbed at his cheek with his fingers, wincing when he touched the deep scratch I had made in his cheek.

"Sorry," I offered. "I thought . . . no, it doesn't matter."

He frowned at me. "That's twice now you've attacked me. Try not to make it three times." There was no humor in his voice.

"Is Orontes there?" I asked, ignoring his comment.

Michael shrugged. "I didn't see him."

A female voice, empty, drained of any emotion, spoke out. I remembered the cold edge to that voice. She had only spoken to me once—when I was caught at Ravenscar.

Lilith.

"Well done, Orontes. That's another one we do not need to concern ourselves with."

I swallowed nervously, my eyes widening in fear. Orontes was here, and he had caught a Sachael.

"Azariah," I murmured. My head spun. Had Orontes killed him?

Michael gripped my hands tightly, moving both of us nearer to the archway. "Careful, don't let them see us," he instructed.

We both peeked out from behind the rocks, keeping our bodies hidden.

Orontes walked from the water, looking as fearless as ever. His hair hung in wet lengths across his shoulders, and he was completely naked. I hardly registered the menacing sight, though, as my vision fell on the person he dragged across the sand.

Azariah.

Orontes had his arm wrapped around Azariah's neck. Azariah kept trying to walk, but every time he tried to stand, his legs gave way beneath him. His skin had taken on a grey coloring, his flesh peeling in places, and there was blood. A trickle of bright red blood trailed from his neck.

Michael pulled me back so we were completely hidden again.

Anger threatened to overpower me. I wanted to scream at Orontes, run from my hiding place, and, if I'd had one, attack him with one of his own venom bullets.

"Where are your bullets?" I whispered, my fear obvious in my shaky voice.

"Back at the house. Where's the one you had?"

I'd completely forgotten about the bullet I'd picked up from the beach at Ravenscar. "I think I've lost it," I muttered.

"What?" Michael hissed.

"I've lost it. And I've got no idea where."

Michael's grasp on my shoulder tightened. I couldn't decipher whether it was in response to me losing the bullet, or in fear of me doing something stupid.

"What have they done to him?" I asked, my voice a low whisper.

"The venom. I'm pretty sure Orontes has injected him with the venom. Looks like he got him in the neck."

My heart was crushed, my world tumbling out of control. This couldn't be happening. Not now. I wanted to cry but refused to let the tears form. This was not the time to break down. I needed to be strong.

"I'll hand myself over in exchange for him," I said. "They can't kill him."

"Don't be stupid," Michael hissed at me. "That's exactly what he wants. He'll drag you out into the ocean, kill me, and still kill Azariah."

I grimaced. Michael was right. If I offered myself in return for Azariah's safety, we would all perish. I wasn't just risking my life—I would be signing Michael and Azariah's fate. Orontes would probably kill Sam and Cleo as well, if he thought they had helped us.

Sam and Cleo—they were in the water this morning, and now Azariah had been caught. Was there a link? I silently promised Azariah that if they'd had anything to do with his capture, I would ensure, somehow, that they never went in the water again. Cleo didn't fear female Sachaels at the moment. Pregnant or not, she certainly would by the time I'd finished with her.

"Sam and Cleo," I muttered. "Have they betrayed us?"

"What? You think they told them where we were? Don't be stupid, they'd never do that."

I huffed at him before risking another look through the arch. I didn't know what to think.

"She did well!" Orontes shouted as he pushed Azariah face down into the sand at Lilith's feet. My stomach churned at the sound of his voice. It was too familiar, too near. I practically whimpered at the pathetic sight of Azariah sprawled on the sand. He was a strong man, proud. He should never be treated this way.

"Where is she?" Lilith questioned.

I grabbed Michael's arm. "Who are they talking about?"

His eyes widened. "Melia. Look, she's in the water."

"Melia," I whispered, angry with myself for not thinking of her sooner. She knew Orontes—Michael had said he'd caught them chatting when they'd stayed at the house a few years ago. Her last words to me were that she would kill me. I practically snarled as I recalled how I'd stopped Chanon from killing her. He'd had the right idea all along.

We should have never come here. We weren't safe, we never had been, and we had been careless and stupid to stay here for so long. Melia knew where Sam and Cleo lived. She'd betrayed us.

Lilith's emotionless voice echoed through the arches. "Melia told us of the location. But you were the one who watched and waited for the right time. Do not underestimate how important your skills were in hunting this one, Orontes."

She sneered at Azariah as he remained crouched on the sand. Orontes grabbed his hair and pulled his head back. The strength of his grip caused Azariah to rise to his knees.

Lilith leaned forward and stroked the side of Azariah's face.

"Such a handsome one. It almost troubles me to have him killed." She lifted his chin, gripping it between her fingers. "But you cause so much heartache. Do you actually have a soul, or a heart?"

I swallowed hard, fighting the overpowering urge to run out and help him.

"You killed my son!" she shouted, anger and hatred spitting from her mouth. "Therefore, you must die. A life for a life."

Michael squeezed me tighter, making sure I stayed where I was. My arms screamed against his hold. I had to do something.

"Kill him," she ordered.

"I want him alive," Orontes snapped. "He is of no danger to any of us at the moment. As long as I keep him in this state, balancing the dose of venom I give him, he will never escape."

"I said kill him!" She forcefully pushed Azariah's face away, and he fell onto the sand.

"I will not."

My blood pounded in my head. Had I heard correctly? Orontes was saving Azariah's life?

"I don't want him dead. I want the girl."

"You still insist on your ridiculous theory," Lilith hissed.

"I know it's true."

"You are talking of the impossible. Has the seawater shrunk your brain?"

Orontes stepped forward, ignoring the crumpled figure of Azariah. "She *is* a Sachael. It is possible. I know it is, and I will prove it to you."

Lilith stared at Orontes, not speaking. Her decision came after a few moments of deliberation. "Very well, I will humor you . . . for now. You may take him; do what you want with him. As long as he doesn't escape, I don't care. But you will kill him eventually."

Orontes nodded. "When I have the girl, I will kill him. You have my word. I intend to take him to the Arcuato Ruins. We will not be bothered by anyone there, until she comes to find him."

"If you will not be bothered by anyone, how do you expect her to find you?"

"She will." Orontes glanced toward where we were hiding. We both ducked behind the rock.

"Did he see us?" Michael whispered.

I was positive he had. He knew we were here, or rather, I was. He'd sensed me. He always said he knew when I was near.

"She will come for him. She will come to the Arcuato Ruins," he said loudly. I had no doubt his words were meant for me to hear. He was telling me where to find him. "She will prove to me once and for all what she is when she swims to rescue him. That's where I want to see her—not on land, but in the water, where there is no doubt of her Sachael abilities."

Angered by Orontes's words, I carefully peered around the rock again. He lied so easily to Lilith. He didn't want to prove to Lilith I was a Sachael. He wanted me in the water so he could grab me and swim away with me—the water was the best place for our confrontation. Whereas I was glad that he didn't make any attempt to catch me now, I knew I'd have to face him in the future.

Lilith smirked. She looked satisfied with Orontes's promise.

"Go," she told him. "Go and test your theory. I hope, this time, you don't let her slip through your fingers so easily."

"I will not make the same mistake again. I trust no one."

"Not even me?"

Orontes stepped up to Lilith and kissed her passionately.

"Not even you," he snarled as he backed away from her.

His tall frame bent toward Azariah and pulled him from the sand before settling him over his shoulder. He called Melia's name as he walked toward the sea.

Glancing away from the sight of Azariah hanging limp and unresponsive, I focused on Melia, standing in the swell of the incoming waves. Only her top half was visible, but just like Orontes, she was naked. My mouth turned into a tight sneer as she laughed. I promised that after I'd rescued Azariah, I would find her and kill her for betraying us.

"Estelle." Michael's quiet voice interrupted my angry thoughts, but my gaze was once again fixed on Azariah. I could hardly believe that the man being carried into the sea, looking near enough dead, was the same man who'd had me in a quivering state of ecstasy last night. It seemed so long ago now. I swallowed hard, straightening, fighting the urge to sink to the sand and cry.

Michael held me tightly as Lilith began to walk away from the caves. She was followed by the two men who had stood with her throughout her interchange with Orontes.

I watched over Michael's shoulder, seeing Melia, Orontes, and Azariah slowly disappearing under the water.

Gone.

Azariah was gone, and there was nothing I could have done to prevent it.

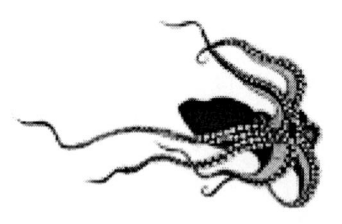

FOURTEEN
Chanon

The journey back to the house from the beach seemed like weeks ago. The wails from Cleo as she heard about Azariah's capture still set my heart thumping wildly. But her reaction had me resolute in my plans. I was determined to get Michael safe, and then I would travel to Saicean. I had to speak to Azariah's father. He was in charge of the armies—he would be a well-educated man concerning the oceans. Surely he would know where the Arcuato Ruins were.

We'd packed as soon as we arrived back at the house. We said our goodbyes, debating over where Michael should go. It wasn't until Sam mentioned the Faroe Islands that a glimmer of hope lit our way. Apparently, the Faroe Islands were surrounded by Selkies, and Selkies were natural enemies of the Oceanids, but allies of Sachaels.

With our journey mapped out before us, Michael and I walked all morning, traveling over grassy, uneven terrain. We wanted to avoid the coastal paths and roads, aware of the potential danger of being spotted by members of The Sect.

When we eventually arrived at the ferry port of Hamars Ness, tired and weary, we'd already missed the lunchtime sailing to Yell, and had to wait for the mid-afternoon ferry to take us on the half-hour journey across the water. I wished the army of Sachaels was here to take us to the Faroe Islands; traveling with them would have made this quicker, and ultimately safer.

We arrived on the island of Yell as the skies began to take on their evening tint. I was tired and needed to rest. I hadn't slept much last night, and while I wouldn't have changed what kept me awake, I recognized the heaviness in my legs and the aches in my body.

Thankfully, the next part of our journey consisted of travel by bus, and we could rest while in transit. The small bus was practically empty. An old woman sat near the front, gossiping to the driver. Another elderly woman clicked knitting needles together as she twisted yarn around them. Leaving Michael to sort the payment, I shuffled to the back, not wanting to be near either of the local women. The sound of the engine and the gentle undulating of the bus as it traveled through Yell made me feel drowsy, but I was distantly aware of Michael's chattering. It was only when he nudged me that I realized I'd fallen asleep.

"Estelle, wake up," Michael said softly. "Let's get off at the next stop and find somewhere to spend the night. You're exhausted."

"No, I'm all right. We need to stay on the bus. We have to get to the Faroes as quickly as possible."

"We'll not get there tonight. This bus doesn't take us all the way to Lerwick. I think we'd be best getting off and spending the night on a beach somewhere. Maybe you can call Chanon."

I raised my brow at his suggestion.

"Well, it's all well and good getting to the Faroes, but you still need to get to Saicean. How are you going to do that? Do you know where it is?"

I shook my head. Honestly, I'd not given it any thought. How stupid of me, not to even think about it.

Michael patted my shoulder. "Let me have a word with the driver, see if he'll stop for us. We've passed a couple of nice secluded beaches."

I nodded. Even though I wanted to continue traveling, he was right. We had to rest.

Once off the bus, I leaned on Michael as we strolled in the direction of the beach. No vehicles passed as we walked slowly along the road. The Shetlands were as quiet as the Orkneys. It was the perfect place to hide. Michael pointed into the distance, toward a sandy beach—a place to spend the night.

As we walked along the trail to the beach, I couldn't help but compare it to the one at Ravenscar. It was a sharp incline downward, with brambles and nettles growing prolifically on either side of the bare-earthed path.

The line of driftwood indicated that the sea didn't cover the uppermost part of the beach when the tide was in, and Michael found a sheltered area against the cliff face for us to spend the night. No one from the top of the cliff would see us. Unfortunately, it was difficult to stay hidden from anyone out at sea, no matter what we did.

"Do you think Orontes will find us?" Michael asked as he plonked the duffel bags on the sand.

"No," I replied confidently. "I think he'll be keeping a close eye on Azariah."

"But he may have others looking for us—other Oceanids." Michael eyed the sea with a narrowed gaze.

I shrugged. "I'm not so sure. Orontes has told us what he wants to happen. I think he's waiting for me to rescue Azariah. It wouldn't surprise me if he's told them all to leave us alone."

"You can't be sure about it, though, can you?"

"No. I'm not sure about anything Orontes does or says." I sighed, concentrating on the shoreline, not on what lay beyond it. The waves tumbled onto the beach, but their action was slow, clumsy, and heavy. The air was still; there was no breeze. It was quiet—too quiet. It felt wrong to be on the beach at night without Azariah. I missed him so much. It was like part of me had been taken away.

Michael fidgeted beside me, bringing me out of my thoughts. It was just him and me—again.

"We'll be on our way to the Faroes tomorrow," I said, turning to face him. "So as long as we get through tonight—and unless he gets on the same ferry as us, which I doubt—then we'll be safe."

"I hope you're right. I really do." Michael sighed as he glanced at the sea again.

An easy silence developed between us as we both watched the surface of the water. The glistening reflection of the evening sun was a beautiful sight, although I didn't think it was as stunning as yesterday's morning sun. I continued staring into the distance, my eyes fixed on the horizon.

"You need to try to call Chanon," Michael suggested, trailing his fingers through the sand.

"I'd rather not," I replied.

"Why not? He's Azariah's top guard; I thought they were friends. And anyway, who else do you know?"

"No one," I replied. Chanon was the only guard I'd spoken to. The only one that had spoken to me. There wasn't anyone else. Chanon was our only hope.

"I don't know how to contact him," I said, my mind racing.

"Just do what Azariah did." Michael nodded toward the sea. "You always watched him when he went into the sea to call him."

"But I don't know what he said, how he managed to talk to him."

Michael tapped his forehead. "Telepathy, remember?"

I shook my head. "I need to be a full Sachael to do that. I have to complete my seven submergences in Saicean."

Michael's shoulders dropped.

"But I suppose I can try," I said. "I have no idea what he said or did when he was under the water, but I'll give it a go. I have to."

I'd observed Azariah call him numerous times. He always walked into the sea, and then sank below the surface for a few minutes. When he reappeared from under the waves, Chanon was always approaching. Like Michael, I presumed Azariah spoke to Chanon telepathically while underwater.

"Why did Azariah send him away? You never did tell me," Michael questioned.

I paused before answering, unsure whether to tell Michael the depth of Chanon's betrayal. But there was really no reason not to tell him.

"He contacted me in my dreams—warned me to stay away from Azariah," I said.

"Really? No wonder he was mad." Michael turned to face me, wide-eyed, waiting for me to continue.

"Azariah thought Chanon was interested in me romantically, and that, if I finished things with Azariah, Chanon would step up and claim me."

Michael shook his head. "Don't you ever think they're all a bit primitive? You know, the way they make claims on females. 'I am the stronger species,' and all that?"

I smiled, laughing a little at his impression of Azariah. But then, I was filled with sadness. It was too much of a reminder of what had been stolen from me. How could I sit on a beach and laugh when his life was in danger? It was wrong.

I jumped to my feet and walked toward the sea.

I didn't think I'd be able to call Chanon, but if I did contact him, what would I say? How would I tell him what had happened?

I glanced back at Michael. He was on his feet now, watching me as I reached the edge of the waves. The water had always welcomed me before, relaxed me. But tonight, I wanted to turn away, flee its never ending restlessness. Each touch of a wave made my stomach roll and flutter. Nausea threatened. But I pushed forward, one step in front of another, gradually walking into deeper water. When the water was level with my hips, I concentrated on the sound of the waves behind me. Regular whispers of comfort returned as I heard the words: "*Welcome, welcome, welcome . . .*"

I sank below the surface.

I kept my eyes open, alert and fearful. If I had misjudged Orontes, if he had left Azariah and was searching for me, I was an easy target for him now. My heart began to beat faster, my fear building rapidly. My hand drifted to my chest as I placed it over my wildly thumping heart. This was ridiculous; I couldn't let my fear overpower me this way. I had to speak to Chanon, and the only way I could try to do that was by being in the sea.

My hand drifted to my neck and the pearl of my necklace. I remembered the sight of Azariah's limp, lifeless body thrown across Orontes's shoulder.

I had to do this.

I closed my eyes, concentrating.

Chanon. Chanon. Can you hear me? It's Estelle. I need your help. Azariah has been caught by Orontes. I need you.

I kept my eyes closed, hoping he would respond, that I would hear something, anything—but his answer never came. I stayed where I was for a few minutes before opening my eyes and focusing on the water in front of me.

Nothing.

Standing, I left the sound of the rushing water behind. I was being ridiculous. Even if he'd heard me, he wouldn't be able to get here immediately. I somehow managed a smile as I wandered across the sand to Michael. Azariah had constantly told me how fast Sachaels swam, and I had always questioned him. My doubt had always amused him. But now, I was disappointed that Chanon wasn't here, that he hadn't gotten to us fast enough.

"He didn't come, then?" Michael asked.

"No." The disappointment in my voice mirrored his.

"You can always try again later. Perhaps it's some strange thing they do when the moon's out. You know how attached they are to it."

I smiled at Michael's easy assessment of things. I didn't dampen his enthusiasm by telling him I had seen Azariah call Chanon during the day as well as in the evening and morning. I was sure Michael had also seen him do it. Maybe he didn't remember.

"I'll try again later," I promised.

"I'll go and collect some wood then. We can light a fire to keep us warm tonight."

I didn't look at Michael as he wandered off; my eyes were fixed on the horizon, watching the sea, yet again. Any ripple of water made my heart leap with excitement, but it was always followed by disappointment when the ripple turned out to be nothing but seaweed or a curious seal bobbing its head above the surface.

Michael's attempts at lighting the fire were far less impressive than the way Azariah and Chanon lit them. He produced a lighter from the side of one of the duffel bags and lit the kindling. Nevertheless, the small fire provided us with warmth as the summer evening descended. We had nothing to cook, but that didn't bother me; I was still running on nervous energy. I nibbled on one of the sandwiches Cleo had hastily prepared for us before we left, not really interested in eating. My stomach was too tied up in knots, and Michael didn't complain when I told him to eat my share of the food.

The sun gradually sank toward the horizon, leaving the romantic evening light of "simmer dim" and the moon high in the sky above us. Only two nights after a full moon, it still lit the beach in a soft glow. I would hate to be on a beach during a new moon now, so exposed in complete darkness. I was relieved that when it last happened, I was with Azariah. He had no fear of the dark, just a strange curiosity about it. His absence was felt even stronger now that the sun had set. I was too used to sleeping in his arms, feeling his heat surround me as we lay together. I missed his deep breathing as he slept, and the noises he used to make when he dreamt. I sighed heavily. Would I ever have the opportunity to experience that closeness with him again?

Without explaining to Michael what I was doing, I headed for the sea. I had to contact Chanon.

As before, I wandered into the water until it lapped against my thighs. Only this time, I had no fear, no underlying panic threatening to break free. I felt calm and relaxed as the undulating water welcomed me. Instead of sinking below the water straight away, I placed my hands on the surface, copying what Azariah had done. Again, I called Chanon, asking for his help as I dipped below the surface, and again, he didn't appear or speak to me.

I gazed out at the darkening water. Would he ever hear me? Could he hear me? Was I wasting my time? I turned around, ready to return to the roaring fire. As I took a few steps forward, Michael suddenly jumped to his feet, shouting my name and indicating wildly with his hands, pointing at me.

I froze, understanding Michael's frantic gestures as I became aware of someone behind me. If this was Orontes, then I had no chance of escape, he would drag me away without a second thought. I breathed deeply, all my dreams crashing around me. This was it; this was what my life was to become—Orontes's unwilling and broken partner. I prepared to accept what I was sure would happen.

"Estelle?" A familiar voice came from behind me.

I spun around.

Standing in the chest-high water several meters from me was Chanon. His hair was loose, flat against his face, not neatly tied back, and his gaze held mine.

"Chanon!" I shouted, trying to rush toward him. The resistance of the water slowed my movements, but the distance was covered quicker than I expected as he moved toward me too.

When we reached each other, I flung myself onto him, sobbing loudly.

He'd come. Everything would be okay.

He wrapped his arms around me, hugging me to his bare chest. He didn't speak as I continued crying, but as I gradually calmed, I became aware of his comforting hold that had no right to be there. I sniffed loudly, moving away as I remembered his interference and Azariah's anger at his intrusion.

"Where's Azariah?" he asked, looking directly into my eyes. It was as though he could see straight into my soul—something Azariah had always managed to do. Now, Chanon was doing exactly the same. It unnerved me even more. He had no right to look at me so intensely.

The surface of the water churned behind him, and my eyes widened in terror. Was this Orontes?

"Don't worry," he said, inclining his head to the side. A small smirk covered his face before he lifted his arms into the air. Twelve Sachaels began to rise from the water.

"I come with an army," Chanon stated. "On Kaimi's orders."

"Kaimi sent you?"

He nodded. "Azariah tried to contact me this morning. It was obvious he was in trouble. Then he went quiet. I can't hear him anymore. As soon as I told Kaimi I had lost contact with him, he ordered me to return with this army. I traveled to Tresta to speak to you, but you weren't there. I ventured from the water to call on Scamander and Cleodora, but unfortunately, my arrival somewhat scared them. They told me you'd left in a hurry and were traveling to Lerwick. I have swum along the coast looking for you all day. Now I've found you and Michael, but not Azariah. Where is he, Estelle?"

I breathed deeply.

"Estelle, please, what has happened?" His voice was gentle, more placid than I had ever heard before. But his tone was serious, and his expression hinted at nothing but concern.

"Orontes," I blurted. "He took him. We were betrayed."

Chanon tilted his head back and roared loudly into the night air. I had no doubt his back would be covered in sharp-pointed scales. Fearful of his sudden anger, I stepped away. I had no idea if I would be blamed for Azariah's capture. Female Sachael or not, would I be punished?

He slowly turned his attention back to me. Eyes of the deepest blue held me in their gaze. I couldn't turn away.

"I couldn't stop them. Orontes—" I began, but he interrupted me.

"I know of Orontes."

"You . . . you have to take me to Saicean."

Sighing deeply, he frowned at me before shaking his head.

I felt my panic rising. I couldn't let him refuse my request so easily.

"You have to take me to Saicean. If you don't, then I will find it myself!" I shouted, my anger growing along with my desperation.

"Impossible," he sighed, shaking his head even more.

"I have to save Azariah." I threw the words at him. "If you won't help me, then I will find a Sachael who will." I turned to the twelve men behind Chanon. They appeared strong; surely one of them would agree. "Which one of you will take me to Saicean?"

They remained quiet, watching me.

"I can travel there. I've completed my missed submergence." I looked to each of them in turn. "Please, one of you."

Chanon's hand rested on my arm. "I never said I wouldn't take you."

"You shook your head. You said it was impossible."

"I was shaking my head in disbelief. And I meant that you are impossible. Not that traveling to Saicean was impossible."

He stepped closer. I looked away, avoiding his penetrating stare this time.

"How can I refuse a request from you?" He spoke quietly, his tone encouraging me to look up at him.

"So, you treat me differently because I'm a female Sachael, then?" I hated the moments their primitive ideals chose to surface. Azariah was the same way. It was infuriating.

Chanon surprised me by grinning. "No, Estelle. Listen, there's something I need to tell you." He glanced at the other men, suddenly serious. "The reason I've been so protective of you. The reason I spoke to you in your dreams . . ." His voice trailed away to a whisper.

I backed away from him again.

"Estelle—"

"Is that why you've come now? You'll drag me back to Saicean, or another of the worlds, and expect me to forget about Azariah?"

Chanon's seriousness disappeared, and he smiled.

"Estelle, will you please be quiet for one minute?" He reached for me with his hand, but I shied away from him, flinching. "I do not have any romantic interest in you. You are Azariah's mate, and I would never dishonor either of you by even thinking of you in such a way. All I have ever done is try to make you see how dangerous this life is, how carefully you need to think about your future." He looked away for a second and sighed again. "Azariah is used to the life he lives. You are not."

"But I need to be with him."

He closed his eyes and ran his fingers through his hair, tucking the long strands behind his ears. "You should have run in the opposite direction when he told you what he was, what he did."

I frowned at his statement.

"This could all have been prevented if you'd turned away. You'd not have been caught by The Sect, and Azariah would be back in Saicean—safe. You'd be safe as well."

"And we'd both be broken-hearted." I shook my head. "I'd never have chosen that path. And I'm a Sachael; my father was as well. I refuse to turn my back on what I am."

Chanon didn't respond. He looked up the beach, no doubt seeing Michael, and sighed again. "Very well. I will take you to Saicean."

I stared at him as conflicting thoughts ran through my mind. Could I trust him to take me to Saicean and not somewhere else? Was he telling the truth? I suspected he was under orders from Azariah's father to find Azariah, and, if nothing else, that order should ensure my safe arrival in Saicean. I doubted anyone would want to disobey the man in charge of the armies.

"Estelle?"

I nodded. "You promise that's where you'll take me?"

"Of course. I appreciate my interference at times may have given you and Azariah the wrong idea. But please believe me when I say that I was concerned for you and the mess surrounding all this." He stretched his arms out to his sides. "I would risk my life for Azariah, and, as Azariah's mate, I will also do it for you. Trust me, Estelle, please. There are still many things you do not know. Eventually, you will find the truth, but for now, you need to trust me. I will take you back to Saicean, and I will ensure that Azariah is rescued and returned to you. Let me take you to the place you should have gone as soon as you completed your last submergence."

His words sounded genuine, and they made sense. I definitely should have gone to Saciean with Azariah the morning after the full moon.

"I knew something like this would happen," Chanon said, once again pushing his hair away from his face, "but I thought it would be you that Orontes took, not Azariah."

"Melia betrayed us," I said.

"I should have killed her when I saw her," he said through gritted teeth.

"I wish I'd let you."

Chanon smirked at my response. "Seems you are more a Sachael than I thought. You need to keep thinking that way."

I managed a small smile at his comment. I shouldn't have smiled, it was wrong when thinking of killing someone, but Melia was the exception to the rule. I would never forgive her for her betrayal, and if anything happened to Azariah . . .

I bit my lip, halting another burst of tears. I looked toward the twelve Sachaels, an army sent to find Azariah. Their wide shoulders were softly outlined against the fading sun, but I could still make out some of their features. Alert and curious eyes returned my gaze, and I recognized Geleon as he smiled. None of the others acknowledged me.

Chanon sighed. "We need to ensure Michael is safe, and then I'll take you to Kaimi. I have no idea how he will react to your arrival."

"He needs to listen to me."

Chanon smirked at my reaction.

I began to head to the beach, the resistance of the water pushing against my legs on each stride.

"All you need to know is that I will be right beside you," Chanon said, walking next to me as if to accentuate his point. "Kaimi is intimidating when you first meet him." He paused, shooting me a sideways glance, and then chuckled. "Actually, Kaimi is intimidating whenever you meet with him."

"I have more important things to worry about than an old man."

"Ruler," Chanon corrected me. "And he's not that old."

"Ruler?" I stopped short, turning to face him fully. "Isn't he just the man who controls the armies?"

Chanon raised his brows and grinned. "Oh, he's slightly more than that. He's our king. Did Azariah not tell you?" I shook my head. It wasn't often I was lost for words, but at that moment, I was struck dumb. Azariah's father was . . . that meant that Azariah . . .

My hands flew to cover my mouth as I gasped. "Azariah's a *prince*?"

Chanon's lips twitched as if he was holding back his laughter. "He'd hate to be called that, but technically, yes, that would be his title."

"And you, who are you exactly? Another prince? He said you were his second-in-command."

Chanon burst out laughing, but as he calmed, he explained. "I'm not a prince. I'm his personal guard. I've known him all my life. We grew up together."

I jerked my head back. "This is unbelievable. Why didn't he ever tell me?"

Chanon shrugged beside me. "He'll have had his reasons. I used to be able to guess his actions and why he did things, but since he met you . . ." He left the sentence hanging. I assumed that meant Azariah had changed since he met me. I remembered what he was like when I first met him, how evasive he'd been of my questions about his life in Saciean. It seemed he had even more secrets than I realized. What else didn't I know?

I took a deep breath and released it slowly, trying to calm my already racing heart. Kaimi. He wasn't just Azariah's father, he was also the king. And I would have to face him.

"Where do we take Michael?" Chanon nodded toward the man in question. "He needs to go somewhere safe."

Michael was still standing by the fire, fidgeting, leaning to first one side, then the other, drawing his feet back and forth in the sand.

"We need to get him to the Faroe Islands," I stated, confident of Sam's earlier suggestion.

"The Faroes? Why there?"

"You don't know?"

He shook his head. "Know what?"

"About the Selkies," I prompted.

"Seals? They're everywhere around here." He raised his hand, gesturing to the water around us.

"Not seals, Selkies. The seals that shed their skins. Apparently, Sachaels have a special relationship with them, going back hundreds of years. I don't know the exact story, but the Selkies protect Sachaels."

Chanon laughed loudly, making me jump. "Seriously?"

I nodded, grinning at his glee.

"Well," Chanon mused, nodding toward the beach to invite me to start walking, "you know something that even we were not aware of. How did you come across this information?"

"Sam told me."

"Scamander? The Oceanid you stayed with?"

I nodded. "Perhaps if you still had an Elder in Saicean, you'd know. If he hadn't been sent to another land, then surely this sort of information would have been passed down?"

Chanon shrugged. "Maybe, maybe not."

Michael eyed Chanon warily as we approached. "What was all that about? No wonder Azariah sent you away."

Chanon glared at Michael. "Azariah was wrong," he said.

"Really? Because you two certainly looked *friendly* just now." Michael didn't back down from Chanon's intimidating stare, and it was Chanon who looked away first.

"You need to go to the Faroe Islands," he said, glancing across the sand at the duffel bags.

Michael looked anxiously at me while Chanon continued informing him of the plan.

"I have to take Estelle to Saicean. We're all leaving immediately. Have you got everything you need?" Chanon asked him.

Michael nodded, grasping for the bag containing his clothes. He rummaged in the pockets before pulling out one of the bags we'd used when traveling underwater.

"There's only one," Michael mumbled. "Where's the other?" He continued rummaging through the side pockets of the duffel bags.

"You only need one," I said. "The whole duffel bag will fit in it."

"What about your clothes, Estelle?" Chanon asked.

"I'm fine. As long as I have my brooch and my necklace, I'll manage." I reasoned I would be able to change into other clothes when I arrived in Saicean. Michael wouldn't have that privilege. He'd be living rough for several more months.

Chanon noticed my hand twiddling with my necklace. "He had that pearl for years. He found it in the Indian Ocean; we traveled there after his eighteenth birthday. He wanted to keep it until he found someone he fell in love with."

I smiled at Chanon. I already knew where Azariah had gotten the pearl from and why he'd kept it, but hearing it from Chanon made it feel incredibly special.

"I'm ready," Michael declared, standing with the water-proof bag slung over his shoulder.

Chanon nodded before looking to the sea. "I'll go and tell the men what's happening. Six of them will escort you to the Faroe Islands, and six of them will return to Saicean with Estelle and me. I'll leave you to say your goodbyes."

As he walked confidently back to the water, I turned to Michael.

"I hate goodbyes. They're too final."

"But this isn't final, is it?" He took my hands in his, and his gaze met mine. A small smile pulled at the corner of his mouth, but his lips twitched with nervousness.

"As soon as we've saved Azariah, we'll come and find you." I released his hands and pulled him into a hug.

"You'd better." He chuckled as he held me tightly. "I don't want to be stranded on an island with only seals for company."

I laughed. Only Michael would joke about something so serious. Pulling away from him, I made sure I caught his eye. "Don't fall out with them. They might save your life one day."

Michael grinned before releasing me and linking his arm with mine. We followed Chanon to the edge of the waves.

Six Sachaels stood there, waiting for us. One stepped forward and took the bag from Michael as Geleon moved next to him.

"You'll be traveling with Geleon," Chanon said. "I doubt your journey will be as smooth as it was when I transported you, but he is the strongest out of the six." He turned from Michael to Geleon. "Go, waste no more time. Get him to safety."

Geleon placed his hand on Michael's shoulder and practically forced him into the water.

"Until next time," I called, as they edged into deeper water.

Geleon dipped under the water, and Michael suddenly disappeared. A few seconds later, he surfaced on Geleon's back, a considerable distance away. He managed a shaky wave before sinking under the water again.

He was on his way. He would be safe.

"Are you ready?" Chanon was beside me.

I nodded nervously.

"Keep hold of my hand. If you get tired, I can carry you. Just let me know."

Again, I nodded.

Chanon grinned. "Let's go and meet your future father-in-law."

This was it, I was about to swim to the deepest part of the Atlantic Ocean, heading to a place I'd never wanted to go to—Saicean.

FIFTEEN
Saicean

"Ready?" Chanon asked the remaining six Sachaels. They immediately fell into position; two in front of us, two behind, and one on each side.

We strode into the water. Even though I was internally questioning my journey and what awaited me when I arrived in Saicean, I couldn't doubt my decision to go there. Azariah would die if Orontes didn't see me at the Arcuato Ruins. Kaimi would know where they were, and we would rescue him.

It was as if the water understood my rambling internal discussion. It welcomed me this time, wrapping its invisible hands around me and ushering me into its never ending depths.

As the water slowly crept up my thighs, Chanon turned to me. "Usually, this would take around three hours, but with you, it'll take longer."

"I'm fast," I told him, managing a smile.

"Not as fast as us. Not yet." His smile matched mine. "Keep hold of my hand," he said, reaching for mine. "Remember, I'll carry you if you get tired. All you have to do is squeeze my hand to give me the signal."

We slowly sank below the surface, and I kept my eyes open, watching the others around me. Our slow pace into the water immediately changed as we all became hidden from the land above. Like a car suddenly swung into acceleration, we were off. We traveled fast; it was an exhilarating feeling. I'd forgotten the buzz that came from swimming so fast, so freely. I'd missed it.

As always, the underwater depths were dark, but not consumed by the blackness that should have been there. My vision adjusted, guiding me through the water.

Our pace remained constant, the swirls of the currents around us caressing my limbs, smoothing my transition through the water. We swam straight, never changing direction. I occasionally caught sight of something shooting past us, but we swam so quickly I didn't have time to focus.

After half an hour of swimming, my legs ached, and I became aware of my growling stomach. I'd hardly eaten all day; my energy levels were dipping.

Aware of my tiredness, perhaps feeling the drag of my hand, Chanon pulled me next to him. He swam below me, positioning me against his back. Grabbing my hands, he pulled them under his arms and across his chest. He held me firmly—just like Azariah did when he traveled with me. Once I was settled, we sped up. With no need to surface for me to breathe, we traveled at the true speed of a Sachael. Unable to focus on anything, becoming dizzy when I tried, I rested my head in the dip of Chanon's shoulders, settling comfortably against his Sachael mark. My mind began to drift, tiredness lulling me to sleep. I dreamt of Azariah and everything we had experienced together. The times we'd laughed, cried, and celebrated that we were the same—Sachaels. The nights spent wrapped in each other's arms, his warm embrace, his loving words and actions. I missed him so much.

I became aware of Chanon tightening his grip on my hands, and I lifted my head. We were moving at a slower pace, weaving amongst a sea of brightly colored dots of light. They were everywhere. Thinking I was still dreaming, I closed my eyes and then opened them again, expecting not to see the lights anymore. But they were still there, hundreds of them lighting the water with a stunning firework display. One of the lights came nearer, and I watched in fascination as it glided past Chanon. It was a tiny jellyfish. They were all jellyfish. The sight was magnificent.

Chanon must have slowed just to show me the stunning creatures, because we shot through the water again. Chanon's relentless pace continued, and I eventually fell back asleep. I only woke when Chanon slowed again, and then completely stopped. As he straightened up in the water, I slipped from his back, surprised to find my feet resting on solid rock. He took my hand before looking at me. The striking blue of his eyes wasn't there; instead, they glistened white, exactly as Azariah's had on the night we swam together. Chanon pointed to his eyes, and then mine. I nodded, wanting him to know I understood the change. He grinned before turning away and looking to the other Sachaels standing with us. With one hand still holding my arm, he pointed in the direction of our feet, but when I looked at where he indicated, my blood ran cold. We weren't standing on a platform of rock, but a thin ledge with a dark chasm beneath us. I backed away from the ledge, but Chanon's grip on my arm remained tight. I shook my head, blinking rapidly at him as I wriggled in his hold. I didn't want to go into the dark, foreboding blackness beneath me. Chanon raised his brow before nodding at two of the Sachaels. They immediately propelled themselves forward, off the ledge and into the waters below.

Chanon stepped forward, pulling my hand as he moved, and nodded his head toward the area the Sachaels had gone. He wasn't giving me a choice. This was part of our journey to Saicean. I gulped down an imaginary breath of air before cautiously shuffling forward. My gaze switched between Chanon's amused expression and the intense darkness of the chasm below us.

A high-pitched long whistle suddenly replaced the soft rumble of the ocean, and I snapped my hand away from Chanon's, covering both my ears. I looked to him for reassurance, but the smiling expression he had shown a few moments ago had vanished. He looked fierce, almost angry. I panicked and tried to push him away, but he reached for me, grabbing the top of my arms. The horrendous, ear-splitting whistle altered to an even greater uncomfortable cry, but I was unable to cover my ears now that Chanon had hold of me. His brow was deeply furrowed, and the spikes on his back were fully extended. All my trust in him disappeared. Had this all been an elaborate trap to get me alone? Had he fooled the other Sachaels as well, or were they in on the whole thing?

I attempted to turn away, prepared to swim as fast as I could to get away from him, but even as the plan was forming in my mind, I knew how pointless it was. He still stood in front of me, his hands uncomfortably tight on my arms. I struggled in his hold, trying to loosen his grip. He ignored my attempts to escape, and his head whipped to the side before he jerked me from the ledge and into the chasm. I was immediately pulled under his body, dragged along with him as he swam. His movements were jolted as he darted from one side of the chasm to the other. He changed direction rapidly as we continued heading deeper. I screamed when he suddenly twisted my body, jerking me sideways before pushing me into a deep crack in the sheer rock face. He followed, shielding me from the waters we had swum through. The horrendous noise continued, but it had altered into a fast clicking sound, still uncomfortable in my ears.

With Chanon blocking my escape into the chasm, I leaned against the wall of the crevice, attempting to control my building panic. I wished I could talk to him. I'd be telling him exactly what I thought of his promise that I could trust him. I hit him in the back, ignoring the sting of the spikes, and hoped the blow would have some effect, even if it only let him know how angry I was. But he ignored my pathetic attack, hardly moving as I hit him again. His shoulders lifted and then dropped before he half turned his head to look at me. The frown on his face didn't match what I'd expected, and as he turned away, facing the yawning chasm, I caught glimpses of the other Sachaels as they whizzed past our hiding place, heading upward.

I remained still, my heart thumping loudly. What was happening? I thought he'd dragged me here to hide me, live out his intentions, keep me from ever seeing Azariah again. This behavior didn't follow that of a potential kidnapper, though. He was more focused on what was happening outside of our hiding place, not me. He stared upward, following the path the six Sachaels had traveled. I desperately wanted to talk to him, but couldn't.

We stayed where we were for several minutes. I didn't attack him again, choosing instead to try and stay calm, hoping that I'd misunderstood what had just happened. There was no sign of anyone or anything, but Chanon kept nodding. I presumed he was talking telepathically to the other Sachaels.

His shoulders relaxed, his back flattening at the exact moment the horrendous squeals and whistles stopped. As the ocean noises returned to their familiar rush and calming regularity, Chanon moved forward. A large, fish-like creature drifted in front of him, and I instinctively backed further into the crevice.

Only when the fish disappeared did Chanon twist around to fully face me. As his eyes met mine, he closed them before mouthing the word, "Sorry."

His hand came to my face, and he attempted to pull me toward him. I didn't move. I backed away and pointed to the chasm behind him.

"Enemies," he mouthed, and, with a fierce scowl, pulled his finger across the front of his throat. Whatever it was had been killed.

I nodded my understanding, limited as it was. He turned and pointed to his back while moving to the edge of the crevice. I paused, not willing to immediately continue my journey. The doubts had crept in. But as he raised a brow at me and flashed me an encouraging smile, I realized that this was all part of life in the ocean. It was what he'd warned me about. Chanon had saved me from something that attacked us, not tried to whisk me away. A lump developed in my throat as I thought about my attack on him.

"Sorry," I mouthed, stepping toward him.

He grinned and pointed to his back once again. With no hesitation this time, I grabbed his shoulders. His hands rested over mine before he sprang from the ledge and followed the journey the dead fish had made.

He continued swimming, always heading deeper.

When he eventually slowed, I narrowed my eyes, focusing on the dark area of water we were swimming toward. As we approached, four Sachaels swooped before us, stopping Chanon's advance. They let the other six Sachaels swim forward, but not us. These Sachaels were huge. They wore the customary black shorts, but they also wore a deep belt with numerous knives and loops of rope attached to it. A deep red band was wrapped around each of their biceps. Their eyes showed no sign of a pupil—they were like Chanon's, white. Their lips were slightly parted; it was as if they were growling at us. Chanon remained where he was, suspended in the water with me holding onto his shoulders. After a few moments of staring, first at Chanon, then at me, they nodded before moving apart, allowing us to swim toward the darkness beyond.

Chanon released his hold on me, and I slipped from his back but grabbed his hand. We swam into the darkness. I'd always been able to see underwater, no matter how dark it was—even in the dark chasm, I'd had good vision—but here, I couldn't see anything, not even my hand holding tightly to Chanon's. I'd never experienced such a suffocating darkness while underwater. Chanon kept urging me forward, dragging me when my instincts were screaming at me to swim back, and after a few minutes of traveling, the darkness began to disperse. First Chanon's hand, and then his body became visible. When I saw his face, his gaze was on me, and he inclined his head, indicating for me to look ahead. Following his instruction, I saw what we were heading toward—light. My eyes widened in understanding. Was this the cave Azariah had told me about? The one he swam through to enter Saicean? Were we here?

The light became brighter as we swam toward it. I found a burst of speed, and Chanon let go of my hand, swimming beside me as we headed upward.

My head broke the surface, and I burst out laughing with relief.

We had arrived. I was in Saicean.

Chanon's head appeared next to mine before he smiled. "Welcome to Saicean, Estelle."

My laughter gradually faded, replaced by stunned silence. I turned slowly in the water, taking in this new world.

Greens of every shade filled the land, but interspersed among them were patches of vivid reds, vibrant pinks, bright yellows, and deep purples.

"It's beautiful," I gasped. "The colors . . ."

"Recognize anything?" he asked. His intense, questioning eyes watched me.

I looked around, trying to see anything familiar. I shook my head. "I've never been here. Why would I recognize anything?"

"Your father's paintings?" Chanon queried.

"How do you know he painted?"

"Azariah told me. He couldn't believe the pictures at your house. The paintings were one of the things that convinced him your father was a Sachael. The colors here are pretty extraordinary. He said he captured them perfectly." Another wide smile graced his lips.

I nodded, grinning at his explanation. "I can see the colors, but I don't specifically recognize any of the things he painted. My favorite picture had several waterfalls falling from a high cliff face."

Chanon frowned. "Maybe he wasn't from Saicean. Maybe he was from one of the other worlds."

He started swimming toward the land at the edge of the lake. "Come on, we can't stay in here all night."

I followed him, slowly gliding toward the shore. The lake in Saicean was larger than I'd imagined, and the tree-covered land sloped away into the distance all around it. In fact, the whole of Saicean was larger than I'd imagined. It wasn't a little city; it was a sprawling landscape. I walked out of the lake with Chanon at my side. My legs were wobbly, achy, but I refused to sit down. I breathed deeply.

"What's that smell?" I asked, frowning and sniffing again. "I recognize it."

"It could be the—"

"Lavender," I said as I placed the strong, sweet and herby smell. "You grow lavender?"

Chanon's lips twitched, and he nodded. "It grows quite prolifically in certain areas. We have several fields of them dotted throughout Saicean."

I drew in a deep sniff. At least something was familiar. I looked around for any random clumps of the purple flower but couldn't see any near us. I continued looking at the other spots of colors as they sprang out from the darkness of the greens. "Why is everything so bright?" I puzzled.

"It's the moons." Chanon lifted his gaze to the space above us and nodded. "They make everything glow."

I stared above me. There were no clouds; only the moons Azariah had told me about. All seven were at different phases of their cycle, shimmering against a dark blue background. They varied in size, and none of them were at their full stage tonight. Night. How did anyone in Saicean know it was nighttime? Azariah had said the different moons constantly lit the world with their subdued glow. Was this daytime?

I was suddenly aware of the complete silence. There was no one around, but the quietness was more than merely a lack of people, it was an eerie silence—one that signified no movement at all. I remembered the fascination Azariah had had with the wind as it blew across his face and ruffled his hair. He loved waking up to hear the birds sing and had commented several times about the constant buzz of the insects. Even the sound of the waves breaking on the beach had made him smile. I hadn't understood why such small things made him happy. Maybe this was the reason.

Saicean was a still world. Almost stagnant, without the forces of nature fluttering around.

"Where is everyone?" I asked.

"Asleep," Chanon answered, smirking at my question. "There's no darkness in Saicean, but our nights are marked by the phases of the moons. They're only full at night, and there is a full moon every four days. So, in a way, our clock mirrors the circadian rhythm you knew on land."

I stared at the moons again. "They're beautiful."

"I like the reflections they make in the water. Seven reflections for seven moons."

I forced my gaze from the moons to look at the water before me. It was completely still. Even the ripples we had created had dispersed. Nothing disturbed the surface, and the reflections of the moons were as crystal clear as the actual ones above us.

"If you didn't protect Azariah, would you ever leave?" I asked, turning to Chanon.

"Unfortunately. We do have to leave for certain things." He didn't turn to face me, but instead, continued to look across the lake.

I sighed, once again reminded of the cold hard fact of why they needed to travel to land.

"Have you any children?" I asked. He was the same age as Azariah: twenty-five. He should have fathered a child when he was twenty-one.

"Why are you asking?"

"Just curious."

I wanted to push for further details, but his frown and the way he focused on the ground made me decide against it.

"Will Kaimi be awake?" I asked, completely changing the subject.

"Eager to meet him?" His expression lightened.

"Yes, and no. I'm dreading his reaction to my arrival, and the reason for it."

"I think he'll be surprised and somewhat shocked by your arrival. And he will be angered and dismayed by Azariah's capture by Orontes. I suggest you meet him with an open mind."

"I'm ready to face him," I stated confidently.

Chanon grinned but immediately turned serious as he glanced toward the path leading away from the lake. He stood straight and moved next to me. "It seems Kaimi's guards are already aware of our arrival."

I followed the direction of his gaze and felt the heat of his hand as he rested it on the small of my back. Four men approached us. They were dressed in the same dark shorts I was used to seeing, but all of them wore deep black bands twisted with gold thread around their biceps.

"Chanon, what's the meaning of this Oceanid being brought here at this late hour?" one of the men barked at him.

"She's not an Oceanid," he replied through gritted teeth.

The guard who questioned Chanon, the largest one, smirked. "You have to drag her back at night so she can't see your face?" he snorted, seeking approval for his taunt by glancing at the other men. "No woman would ever want you. Your face would frighten them off."

The hairs on the back of my neck rose, and I struggled to stay quiet at this man's cruel insult.

"You should keep your face covered, save us all from having to look at you. Or perhaps I should lend you my wife. I could order her not to look at your disgusting face."

I snapped. "Why are you speaking to him like this? It's cruel and unnecessary."

Chanon reached for my arm as I stepped closer to the guard who had insulted him. "Estelle, no."

The man growled at me before looking at Chanon. "You need to control her mouth, or I will do it for her." His eyes caught mine before his gaze traveled my body. He licked his lips, his eyes lingering on my wet t-shirt, but his expression changed as his gaze lowered. He seemed confused by my jeans. His composure was quickly recovered as he stared at me, though, narrowing his eyes. "I would take great pleasure in keeping this one quiet."

I huffed at his threat. I refused to be intimidated. There were more important things to deal with. I shrugged Chanon's hand off my arm.

"I want to see Kaimi," I said. My tone left no room for argument.

"'I want to see Kaimi,'" the man mimicked.

"If you won't take me to him, I'll go myself."

I took a step in the direction I had seen them come from.

"Oh no, you won't." My path was immediately blocked by all four guards.

The large one spoke again. "Kaimi won't be happy with you, Chanon. He sent you to find Azariah, and you've returned with this stranger. The entrance guards alerted him of your return. He wants to speak to you. Your reasons better be good." He paused before grinning at me. "I will keep her entertained while you explain your failure."

My dislike for this huge man turned to disgust.

"She will come with me," Chanon growled, the spikes on his back rising. "I have brought her to see Kaimi. She has already been claimed by Azariah."

"The human?" Another of the guards gasped.

"The female Sachael," Chanon corrected him.

The main guard widened his eyes, but once again quickly recovered. "Then you will both come with me." He turned to lead the way as the others walked behind us. Chanon held my hand as we followed him, and I was more than happy for his support when I lifted my gaze to look at where we were going. The guard in front of us had a long scar running diagonally from his shoulder to his waist.

"Ixion," I mumbled under my breath. The Sachael who had raped Xanthe, and then forced her to return here with him. My disgust for him deepened.

"Hurry up!" he snapped. "You don't want to keep Kaimi waiting. He's in a bad enough mood as it is."

I took a deep breath, trying to steady my nerves.

I was in Saicean. I had met Ixion. Next, I would meet Kaimi.

SIXTEEN
Unexpected Greetings

I stared at Ixion's back, taking in the detail of his scar. It was nothing like the ones Azariah had on his leg, and it certainly wasn't as bad as the ones on Chanon's face. Both their scars were red and raised, still angry-looking even after all these years. Ixion's scar was a straight line—one that couldn't have been inflicted by the same method as Azariah's and Chanon's. It was too neat. I wondered who had caused it, and why they'd attacked him.

Ixion caught me staring at him, and a smirk covered his mouth before he turned away.

Chanon's hand tightened around mine, and I glanced at him. He looked forward, frowning. I couldn't decide whether he was worried or just concentrating. Determined not to let my nerves take a hold, I let my gaze wander and inspected the area we were being led through. Greenery surrounded us. Tall plants towered above us, and smaller wide-leafed ones brushed my legs as we hurried along the narrow track. I recognized some of the plants: ferns, hostas, and bamboo. As I glanced past Ixion, following the track ahead, trying to see where we were going, a smattering of bright color caught my attention. It was one of the plants my father had painted. Bright yellow flowers covered the ground on either side of the track, and as we turned a corner, I was greeted with more intense color. Giant exotic-looking plants—wide leaved, with vivid pinks and deep reds—surrounded us as we kept walking. This was the world I had seen in my father's paintings.

I wanted to pick the flowers; take them to my mother, and see her reaction when she compared them to the flowers in my father's paintings. Maybe I could take some home for her.

"Where exactly are we going?" I asked Chanon.

"The Hall," he replied. "You can't see it from the lake."

"Quiet," Ixion ordered, stopping and turning to face us. "I've already offered to keep her mouth shut if she can't. Azariah's mate or not, I'll still silence her. Teach her a lesson or two."

"Over my dead body," Chanon hissed.

"That can be arranged," Ixion snarled, stepping in front of me, too close, invading my personal space. Chanon immediately pushed himself between us, facing Ixion.

"Back off, Ixion. I will fight to the death to protect her. She is not, and never will be, yours."

"Accidents happen," Ixion growled, pushing him aside and grabbing my chin in his calloused fingers. The other three guards grabbed Chanon and pulled him further away. He twisted and turned, but with his arms held tightly in their grasp, their strength overpowered him.

"Leave him alone!" I shouted, trying to pry Ixion's fingers from my chin. He gripped me tighter, pushing my head backward. I was forced to stretch onto my toes.

"I think she may be worth the entertainment. You know how easily I get bored." He sneered. "I don't think I'll get bored with this one."

The rough fingers of his other hand grabbed the front of my jeans.

"Don't touch me!" I yelled, my hands lashing at his face.

One of the men holding Chanon rushed behind me and pulled my arms behind my back.

"I swear it, Ixion!" Chanon shouted. "I will kill you if you carry on."

His words went ignored as Ixion yanked me against his body.

"I want to see what's got the prodigal son so excited. Her body is certainly appealing, and she's warm, not like the cold-fleshed Oceanids." He sniggered, moving his face nearer to mine. I refused to flinch, to make any gesture of weakness. And when he licked my face from my chin, up across my cheek, I fought the disgust and fear pulsing through my body. I resisted the instinct to whimper. But when his insistent fingers popped the top button on my jeans, I knew I had to act. Fast.

I'd been threatened this way before, by Daniel. And I knew there was one area of male anatomy which was always an easy target for a woman. With my hands still pinned behind my back, my front pulled flush to Ixion, I raised my knee—quick and hard.

He released me, doubling over, grimacing.

"You touch me again, and I'll scream so loud Kaimi will hear me!" I shouted.

Staggering forward, recovering far faster than he had any right to do, he pulled his knife from its sheath. Another wave of fear washed over me; my knees threatened to crumple beneath me, and I swallowed hard.

"Kill me, and you sign away your own life," I threatened, sounding far more confident than I was.

"I'm not going to kill you," Ixion smirked. "I'm going to teach you a lesson. Hold her still," he said to the man holding me. "Let me see if I can draw on her face so she matches Chanon."

I struggled against the arms that held me, but I wasn't strong enough to gain any freedom of movement. This was exactly the welcome I had feared. I'd always been told I'd be safe in Saicean. I wasn't. Azariah had been wrong.

Chanon was incensed by Ixion's threat. He shouted and swore at him, struggling frantically to free himself from the two guards holding him back. "Ixion. I swear—"

"Shut up. When I've dealt with her, I'll deal with you."

"What is the meaning of this?" A loud, booming voice interrupted. Three further guards appeared from somewhere along the path. These men wore red bands around their arms—the same as the entrance guards.

"Markos," Ixion stated, immediately replacing his knife in its protective covering. My arms were released.

The guard who had appeared continued. "You were told to bring Chanon to the Hall. Why are you terrorizing this Oceanid, and . . . Ixion!" the man barked. "Why is Chanon restrained by Pentheus and Silenus?" He turned to the men still holding Chanon. "Release him at once. Kaimi is waiting."

Chanon turned to the men who held him, his eyes dark and sinister. "Your days are numbered," he growled at them.

When he looked at Markos, his expression was softer, calm.

"Markos, please escort Estelle and myself to the Hall. It seems Kaimi's guards are not to be trusted with Azariah's mate."

Markos's eyes widened. "You are the female Sachael? The woman who is to be our future queen?"

"I . . ." I didn't know what to say. Is that how the men here viewed me? As either a future queen or a piece of meat to be abused and used for entertainment? I'd never known such conflicting opinions.

"It will be my pleasure to take you to Kaimi," he stated.

Ixion stepped toward him. "You need to watch your back as well, Markos. Any friend of *this one* is no friend of mine." He pushed past him. "I will lead the way," he snarled.

I grabbed Chanon's hand as we continued our walk, clinging to him for support—both physical and emotional. He was familiar. And it seemed he'd been right all along; he was the only one I could trust. Ixion stomped forward, not bothering to look behind. Markos slipped next to me, on the other side to Chanon, and the men who had arrived with him walked behind us. Ixion's three accomplices trailed behind.

As the path twisted through the tall trees, it became wider, and within a hundred meters or so, a sheer, smooth rock face appeared ahead of us. A wide, gated entrance was cut into the rock. Two pillars were carved into either side of the gateway, the greenery of training plants hanging randomly over the top of the structure. Not only did metal gates bar our entrance, but so did two guards, wearing red bands around their arms—identical to Markos's. They each held a long spear, which they pointed toward us as we approached.

"Move!" Ixion barked at them.

They didn't react to his instruction and remained where they were, spears held threateningly at Ixion.

"Your games do not amuse me," Ixion snapped. "Move your spears and let me enter. I am Kaimi's head guard, and you have no authority over me."

"I apologize," Markos stated, moving forward. "They are following my orders from Kaimi. I told them not to let anyone enter until I discovered what the shouting was. We cannot be too careful these days." He nodded at the guards holding the spears, and they pulled them away, leaving a gap for us to pass through.

Ixion strode forward, leading us into a long passageway. I expected it to be dark, but the walls held small fire-lit torches every couple of meters. The primitive lights cast elongated shadows throughout the passageway as we headed deeper into the rock face. I gasped when the winding corridor suddenly opened into a wide chamber. This space was brighter, due to the numerous torches high up on the walls. The lower walls were covered in detailed, colorful shell mosaics. I viewed my surroundings quickly, trying to make out the numerous designs. It was busy, colorful, but I recognized sea creatures, phalluses, lots of moons, and stars with seven points.

No one spoke as we crossed this room; all I heard was my breathing and the dull thud of bare feet on the hard ground. Other long passages led away from this chamber. I counted four running off in different directions. They all appeared similar to the one we'd walked through to get here.

Ixion stopped in front of a set of arched double doors, once again guarded by Sachaels with red bands. As they moved aside, I was able to see the detail on the doors. One held a painting of a naked woman, and the other a naked man. Their hands met at the top of the doors, creating a perfect archway to pass beneath.

"In," Ixion snapped at Chanon and me as he pushed both doors open.

The strong, pungent smell of lavender flooded my nostrils as we entered the room. My head spun, and I tightened my hold on Chanon, waiting for the dizziness to pass. I'd always liked the smell of lavender, but this was too much—it caught in the back of my throat, burning and making my eyes water. The only thing that prevented me from being sick was my awe at my surroundings. I had been surprised by the shell mosaics in the corridor, but nothing had prepared me for this room. Before me was a huge, circular hall. It wasn't lit by fire torches on its high walls; it was naturally lit from above. There were several pillars around the circumference of the room, holding up an ornate blue cupola. The dome itself was different shades of blue. It looked like glass. Hundreds of pieces arranged in segments to create a wave pattern. At the center of the design was a large white circle.

"It's impressive, isn't it?" Chanon whispered from my side.

I nodded before covering my mouth and nose with my free hand, filtering the sharp sting of the lavender as I continued to look around.

The walls were covered in murals, but not shells; the colors were rich, the paintings detailed. One part of the wall showed stars and planets, another an underwater scene with fish and corals. In the floor itself was another mosaic of a star with seven points—made from shells again—but this was smooth and highly polished. It sparkled in the light flooding through the dome in the ceiling. As I continued taking in the detail of the room, I noted three steps leading up to two elaborately carved chairs, one significantly grander than the other. They were the only chairs in the room, and anyone who sat in them would be quite a bit higher than anyone else in the room.

"Stand there," Ixion ordered, manhandling me into the correct position. I didn't miss the way his hand brushed the side of my breast. I glared at him, but he just smirked; he knew what he'd done. Markos and two of the guards who'd originally arrived and put a stop to Ixion's vile behavior remained at the doors.

Chanon bowed as a door to the left of us opened. My attention instantly switched to the figure who stormed into the room. He wore a black waistcoat, embroidered with an intricate gold design, and he wore the same black shorts as all the other Sachaels, but these were also threaded with gold at the sides. There were bands around the top of his arms, although his were not material like the others I'd seen—his were metal. Gold. I surmised that the angry, wild-haired and bearded man striding toward us was Kaimi.

"Chanon, what is the meaning of this?" he shouted. "I send you to find Azariah, and you return with an Oceanid." His focus was on Chanon, not me.

"I'm not an Oceanid," I said. I refused to let Kaimi intimidate me.

"Be quiet," Ixion barked. "You only speak to Kaimi when he speaks to you."

Kaimi's eyes widened as he stopped his advance and stared at me. He didn't look at me with greedy eyes, or undress me with his gaze as Ixion had done. He just stared. It was impossible to guess what he was thinking.

"She is not an Oceanid," Chanon said. "She is a Sachael; Azariah's mate. Kaimi, please allow me to introduce Estelle."

"Estelle," Kaimi repeated, his voice low. "So, this is the woman he has obsessed over for months."

He strode toward me. I remained where I was, rooted to the spot, not taking my eyes off him.

He stopped a few feet away before frowning. "How should I greet you, Estelle? Do you expect a king to bow to you?"

His question caught me completely unaware. Chanon had bowed to him as soon as he entered the room, but I hadn't noticed what Ixion or the other guards did. Presuming it was expected for me to also greet him in such a way, I took a small step forward, ready to curtsey. As soon as I moved, Ixion growled. He grasped the back of my neck roughly and forced my head down far lower than necessary, causing me to bow to Kaimi. I didn't want his calloused, dirty fingers touching me and as soon as he released me, I flew at him, slapping him across the face.

"I told you not to touch me, you disgusting, cruel excuse for a man!"

Chanon was immediately behind me, grabbing me around the waist and trapping my arms as he pulled me away from Ixion.

"No, Chanon, put me down." I wriggled in his hold, pushing at his arms, trying to loosen his grip.

I didn't see Ixion's hand as it flew through the air, but I felt the sting as it made contact with my face. My weight was thrown sideways, and both Chanon and I fell to the floor.

"You do not speak to me like that!" Ixion roared.

Chanon sprang to his feet, standing between Ixion and me. "I'm running out of warnings, Ixion. This needs to be settled, one on one. I challenge you to a fight to the death." The scales on his back rose as he challenged Ixion.

Ixion laughed. "Why are you so protective of her? I thought she was Azariah's mate, not yours."

"Do you not accept my challenge?" Chanon was bent over in a crouching position, ready to attack.

Kaimi, silent while this was happening, suddenly sprang to life. "Chanon, Ixion, enough. I will not have you two fighting. It is not necessary for us to fight amongst ourselves."

Chanon didn't move straight away, but when he did, it was to help me from the floor. When he lifted his hand to my cheek, I winced. "He's cut you, Estelle," he whispered. "Broken the skin."

There was blood on Chanon's fingers. It didn't surprise me; I could still feel the sharp sting from Ixion's hand, but I was determined not to let him or Kaimi see me cry.

"Why?" Kaimi addressed me, a deep frown so like Azariah's gracing his forehead. "Why has Ixion upset you so much?"

Ixion began to speak, but Kaimi shot him a look that silenced him.

"I've met people who know him," I explained, inclining my head toward Ixion. "They told me what he did to Xanthe. And from the way he behaved with me down at the lake, I suspect he would have done the same to me."

Ixion glared at me. If I had been near him, I was sure he would have attempted to hit me again.

"Xanthe?" Kaimi queried, switching his attention to Ixion. "Isn't she your pretty young wife?"

Ixion nodded; his whole demeanor had altered. Gone was his arrogant, bullish attitude, and in its place was a man who refused to meet Kaimi's eye. He looked at the floor.

"Continue, Estelle. I presume you have more to say." Kaimi wandered further toward Ixion, his steps slow and purposeful. "What did he do to Xanthe, and what was he going to do to you?"

I concentrated on Xanthe's attack, knowing hers was far more serious than mine. "He and several others assaulted Xanthe in the ocean. They raped her, and then he dragged her back here."

Kaimi stood silently behind Ixion but inclined his head at Markos, who moved to stand beside him.

"Did you force yourself on a young maiden?" Kaimi said, close to Ixion's ear. "Did you and your friends want some 'fun'?" He practically spat the word at him.

Ixion didn't answer. He must have heard the threatening tone in Kaimi's voice.

"I asked you a question, Ixion. You answer me." Kaimi grabbed Ixion's hair and pulled his head back. Even though I suspected Ixion was far stronger than Kaimi, he made no effort to wriggle free. "Did you rape her?"

"No."

"Liar!" I shouted. I wouldn't listen to his lies. Cleo had been petrified of Azariah because of what she had witnessed. That kind of reaction wasn't forced or faked. It came from personal experience. "She was fifteen. You and the others scared her to death, and then raped her."

Kaimi nodded at Markos before placing his mouth next to Ixion's ear. "I'll ask you again. Did you rape her?"

Ixion bent his legs, sinking to his knees. "You've seen how beautiful she is."

Kaimi snarled loudly and walked away from him, heading to me. "So, Ixion, you assume that because you like a woman, you have the right to take her, to force yourself on her?" He didn't bother to turn and face Ixion; his gaze was fixed on me. "Estelle tells me that Xanthe was fifteen. A girl. A child even!" Kaimi bellowed. "And what about Estelle? You threaten my son's mate with the same vile treatment?"

"No." Ixion shook his head, not lifting his gaze from the floor.

Kaimi stood so close to me our shoulders were touching. In complete contrast to the anger he directed at Ixion, he spoke softly to me.

"What shall we do with him, Estelle?" Kaimi said.

"You're asking me?" I had no idea what punishments were on offer. I knew nothing about life in Saicean.

"Yes, I'm asking you."

"I . . . I don't know." My nerves suddenly failed me. What was I expected to say?

"Are you confident that the person who told you this was telling the truth?" Kaimi asked, moving in front of me.

"Yes," I answered. I'd seen the terror in Cleo's face. I had no doubt.

Kaimi shook his head slowly. "And look what he has done to your face." His fingertips touched the top of my cheek. Eyes so similar to Azariah's bored into mine. The brightness of pale blue danced in them—mischief, anger, and something else. "And what do you think he would have done to you?"

I frowned. If I admitted the truth, told him what I'd suspected Ixion would do, then I was sure his punishment would be severe. But as I glanced at Ixion, he sneered at me, and with that one look, I decided to offer his fate to Kaimi.

"I would have been treated the same. His intentions were clear," I said.

Kaimi nodded. "So, I ask you again, Estelle. What do we do with him?"

Ixion growled, and I realized at that exact moment that I would never be safe in Saicean while he was around. Was this my choice? Live in fear, or get rid of the man who would undoubtedly seek some sort of revenge for what had happened. I looked Kaimi straight in the eye and lifted my chin, confident with my answer. "I don't care what happens to him," I said. "The decision is yours."

"That's all I needed to hear." He smiled at me before nodding once again at Markos. Patting my shoulder, he turned and walked toward the steps where the chairs were.

"Kaimi, please, I beg you," Ixion shouted across the room. "I am your head guard. I have served you well. Twenty years I have lived only to protect you. Twenty years! Does that mean nothing? Just because she has turned up, and—"

"She?" Kaimi roared, spinning to face him again. "She is the most important person you will ever meet. She is the future of Saicean, and yet you have threatened to rape her. You have beaten her, here, in front of me. I have her blood on my fingers to prove it!"

"I . . . I . . ."

"Kill him." Kaimi's orders were spoken calmly; no hint of regret in his tone as he stared at Ixion. Markos stepped forward, pulling his knife from his belt. Part of me wanted to call out and make him stop, but another part of me was glad Ixion was being punished and paying for his loathsome behavior with his life.

Chanon pulled me to him, forcing my head against his chest. The room was silent apart from a muffled gurgling and the dull thud of what I presumed was Ixion's body falling to the floor. I breathed heavily, immediately wishing I'd held my breath instead. The sickly smell of lavender didn't disguise the metallic smell of blood, and I swallowed the bile gathering in my throat.

When Chanon released me from his tight hold, I peeked around his arm, seeing the sight that would confirm my suspicions. Ixion was dead, lying in a pool of his own blood. Crimson liquid still pulsed from the cut across his throat.

"Clean this mess up," Kaimi barked as he sat heavily on the steps. Markos immediately grabbed Ixion's limp body and dragged him out of the Hall. Seconds later, two other men came in to clean the floor.

I took another deep breath, forcing myself not to dwell on what had just happened. I was glad he was dead. He couldn't hurt anyone anymore. But even still, what I had witnessed shocked me. I knew it shouldn't have—Azariah had warned me how ruthless Sachaels could be when dealing with an enemy—but Kaimi had been so cold toward a man who had served him for twenty years. He'd ordered his death as if it was nothing.

"Come here, Estelle," Kaimi said softly as he beckoned me forward. He signaled to the step beside him, and I cautiously sat where he indicated.

"I apologize. That was a most unpleasant thing for you to witness before we have gotten to know each other." He sighed before looking to Chanon, who remained in the center of the Hall. "Chanon, I suspect that, because you have brought Estelle here and not Azariah, something has happened to him." His voice was barely a whisper. It was as if he suspected the worst. "I need to know if he is dead."

"No, he's not dead," I said, instinctively wanting to reach for Kaimi's hands which were clasped together tightly on his knee. I didn't, though, and kept my own folded carefully in my lap.

Kaimi turned to me and smiled. "He is alive?"

I nodded. "Yes, but he's been caught by an Oceanid."

"Orontes," Chanon interrupted.

"Orontes?" Kaimi's posture stiffened, and I noticed the vein in the side of his neck pulse. His shoulders tensed, and his eyes hardened, becoming unfocused.

"He's taken him to the Arcuato Ruins," I said. "Do you know where they are?"

Kaimi snapped from his trance and faced me, shaking his head. "I don't, but Azariah is a strong man now, not the boy he was the last time he faced Orontes. He will be able to fight him and escape. He will find his way home."

"No, you don't understand." I did reach for his hands this time, and clasped them in mine. I didn't see the leader of Saicean next to me, only Azariah's father. A man who loved his son. "Orontes has drugged him. He's poisoned him with venom."

"Venom?" His frown returned.

"Yes. The venom of the Blue Ringed Octopus. One dose is lethal to humans, but a Sachael needs two shots of it. Orontes somehow managed to overpower Azariah and inject him with it. He'll be unable to do anything. The venom will have taken away his sight, and he will have no strength in any of his limbs." I tightened my hands around his. "If Orontes doesn't get what he wants, he will kill him."

"And what does he want? I shall give him whatever he desires for the safe return of my son." Kaimi sat straight but didn't pull his hands away from mine.

I didn't respond. I knew what Orontes wanted. Would Kaimi use me as a pawn for Azariah's safe return? I had no idea what he would do. I didn't know him.

"Tell him," Chanon instructed softly. "Tell him what Orontes wants."

"Estelle?" Kaimi's eyes silently pleaded for the information that would save his son.

"He wants me," I told him.

"He knows of you, that you are a Sachael?" Kaimi pulled his hands away from mine and ran them through his hair.

"He suspects I am a Sachael. That's why he wants me."

"The attraction," Kaimi stated before standing. "Has he been close enough to you to feel the pull the Oceanids have to our kind?"

I nodded, deciding now was not the time to question his broad statement of the attraction between Oceanids and Sachaels.

Kaimi stroked his beard as he wandered toward Chanon, but he then turned back to speak to me. "When did he manage to get near you? I cannot imagine Azariah would have allowed it."

How much did Kaimi know? How much had Azariah told him? Regardless, he needed to know the truth.

"When he caught me," I said quietly, unsure of his reaction.

"He what?" Kaimi roared.

"I thought you knew. You sent your army with Azariah to rescue me."

"Yes, yes I did. But obviously the full details were not passed on to me." He glanced at Chanon, but Chanon didn't flinch. "I was told you were taken prisoner by people on land, not that you were caught by an Oceanid. And Orontes of all people. How dare he!"

Chanon spoke up. "We need to figure out how to get Azariah from Orontes without offering Estelle to him."

"I agree." Kaimi rubbed his forehead, as if trying to smooth the furrow away. "When did Orontes catch him?"

"This morning," I responded.

"Yesterday morning." Chanon corrected me. "I've heard nothing since I lost contact with him."

Chanon stood alone, shoulders high, proud, refusing to show any weakness to Kaimi, but I saw the miserable, defeated man he really was, saddened by the news he'd brought Kaimi. I couldn't bear to see him so dejected. None of this was his fault.

"Chanon, are you okay?" I asked. He turned to face me, his gaze unfocused, but as I stood, prepared to offer him support, his eyes locked with mine. He was broken. Both physically and mentally. And I'd doubted him. I felt so guilty—all he'd ever tried to do was help.

"What is the meaning of this?" Kaimi demanded.

I turned and frowned at Kaimi.

His face was red, his eyes penetrating. "I see the way you look at each other."

"What? It's not—"

"You, Chanon, should not be thinking of Estelle that way. She is too important to be joined with a guard. Only I or my sons are of a high enough position to be with her."

The hair on the back of my neck stood up. I was sure that if I were a full Sachael, the scales on my back and arms would have risen, and Kaimi would truly see how angry I could be.

"I don't believe this," I started. "All Chanon has ever done is protect me." I stepped toward Kaimi, ignoring the shocked stare he gave me. "And another thing. Don't you *ever* think you can decide who I belong to. I choose who I want to be with, not you."

"All your words mean nothing." He glowered at me. "You will stay here with me, but you, Chanon, will be banished from Saicean. Let us see how you manage alone in the oceans."

Kaimi snapped his fingers, nodding at the guards who stood by the doors. "Take him away. Brand him, and then inform the guards at the entrance of his fate."

The seriousness of the situation hit me. Despite everything that had happened, Chanon was the only person I trusted. If he was ripped away from me, then I had no one. My greatest fear would become reality.

"No!" I shouted. "No, you can't do this, please, no . . ." I rushed to Kaimi, grabbing his arm. "Kaimi, please . . ."

He shook his arm free, and I slowly sank to the floor, my exhaustion careening through my body and colliding with my fear. My shoulders shook with each shallow breath. I couldn't watch as they dragged Chanon away. My sobs grew louder.

Why was he silent? Why didn't he fight? I needed him!

Kaimi's guards advanced toward Chanon.

"You're making a huge mistake," Chanon said as the guards took hold of his arms. He didn't struggle like he had when Ixion's oafs grabbed him.

"I don't think so," Kaimi growled. "You've let me down. You've deceived Azariah. And now this!" His gaze bore down on me as I knelt in a crumpled heap on the floor.

"I never touched her," Chanon said, but his voice was not as strong as before. "I never once had interest in her the way you're implying."

"Then what it is? I know you, Chanon. You don't look at other women the way you look at Estelle. I can see it in your eyes. The attraction, the lust."

"No, it's neither. It's because . . ." He closed his eyes and looked at the floor.

"Because?" Kaimi ducked his head, his arms outstretched, encouraging Chanon to explain.

Chanon lifted his head, and his gaze met mine. "I'm sorry, Estelle. I should have told you."

I frowned. What should he have told me? Had I got it wrong? Was Kaimi right?

"I'm your brother." His eyes held mine for several seconds before he turned to Kaimi. "I'm Estelle's brother."

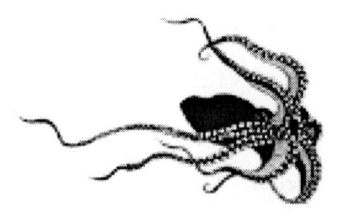

SEVENTEEN
Siblings

Silence.

It was as if time had stopped.

"My brother?" I questioned. "I don't have a brother."

"You seriously expect me to believe that you are related to Estelle?" Kaimi strolled over to Chanon.

Chanon nodded. "I know it sounds unbelievable, but it's true."

Kaimi glanced at each of the guards holding Chanon and dismissed them: "Leave him."

Chanon rubbed the red marks on his arms where the guards had held him as the men retreated to their original posts, and then looked to the floor.

"So, Chanon," Kaimi said. "I think both Estelle and I would like proof of your claim. Do you have any?"

Chanon nodded. "Your brooch," he said, focusing on me. "I have one exactly like it."

"Show me," I demanded, immediately on my feet and walking to where he stood.

He crouched down and released a twisted leather strap from around his ankle. As he stood back up, he presented me with an oblong piece of jewelry. I didn't need to compare it to mine. The black pearl and the enamel work were exactly the same.

"My brooch was all I had with me when I was found outside Saicean," he said. "I crafted it so I could wear it on my ankle."

"My father made mine especially for me," I said, staring in disbelief at the matching items. "He made it in celebration of my birth."

Chanon nodded. "It seems he made two."

Kaimi held his hand out for Chanon's brooch, and then looked to me. "Yours, Estelle."

I quickly unpinned mine from my t-shirt before handing it to him. I didn't look at Kaimi; I kept my gaze on Chanon. He was my brother? A brother I didn't even know I had. I narrowed my eyes and tried to make out any similarities between us, or between him and my parents. Why hadn't my mum said anything? All these years, and she'd never mentioned it.

Chanon didn't look at Kaimi, either. He was focused on me, his eyes unblinking and his brow furrowed. "I have suspected I was your brother since the first night Azariah swam with you."

"But how?" He'd known about me since that night, since all this started. So why hadn't he said anything?

"I went ashore when you were in the water completing your submergence ritual. I looked through your things on the beach and saw your brooch. I was searching for anything that could harm Azariah. I had no idea what his intention was that night; he was so obsessed with you. I needed to be sure you were a safe female for him to have selected."

I didn't know whether to laugh or cry. Me, safe enough for Azariah to have selected?

Kaimi cleared his throat. "That still doesn't explain why you thought you were related—just the brooches? It's not a lot to go on."

I wasn't convinced by what he'd said either.

"My mother's never mentioned a brother," I said. "Surely she would have said something." I was struggling to understand why she'd never told me, if what Chanon suspected was true.

Chanon shrugged. "Would she? I mean, I've thought long and hard about my discovery that night. I'm three years older than you. I could have been whisked away as soon as I was born. I was found outside Saicean, remember?"

"You weren't even a day old," Kaimi added before handing our brooches back to both of us. "Such a small little thing. I remember when the guards brought you in." His gaze rested on Chanon before he turned away and wandered to the steps. He slumped down on them and sighed heavily.

Chanon stepped up next to me. "Perhaps our mother never mentioned it because it would have given you the information that she and Dad tried so hard to keep from you."

"What information?"

"That you're a Sachael."

I pinched the top of my nose, concentrating as much as I could. This was all so unbelievable. When I looked up, both Chanon and Kaimi were watching me. "My father made sure I did my submergences at every full moon," I said. "That's hardly the action of a man who wanted to hide that he was a Sachael, or that I was."

"Isn't it?" Chanon took my hand in his. "Estelle, you had no idea what you were. Even when you met Azariah, you didn't suspect you were any different from all the other humans that live on land. You may have done your submergences, but you knew nothing about Sachaels. You didn't know we existed."

"But she never said anything." I ran my fingers through my hair and gazed at Chanon, unfocused. I wanted to believe that he was my brother, I really did. He'd be a welcome friend in this strange and unfamiliar world. Our brooches were indeed identical, but I couldn't understand why my mother had kept this from me, particularly after my father died.

"I came to the conclusion, that Dad brought me here because he felt it was his duty. But he loved our mother so much he went back to her. How old was Dad when you were born?"

I quickly did the math in my head. "Twenty-four."

"That's a bit old for a Sachael to travel to land for the first time, isn't it?"

I narrowed my eyes, concentrating.

"I'm twenty-five, Estelle. Three years older than you. Dad would have been twenty-one when I was born—the age we travel to land."

Again, silence flooded the room.

"There's only one person who can answer this," Chanon said, squeezing my hand. "Your . . . our mother."

I nodded, trance-like. Everything Chanon said made sense. It was yet another secret, one that my mother had kept. And it wasn't the first. She'd kept others as well. She knew about Sachael's. She knew what I was, and yet she'd never told me. What was one more secret to her?

Kaimi sighed and scratched his head. "However crazy this seems, I think Chanon is possibly correct. I have had men that leave us. They fall in love with the human woman they have seduced. It's rare, but it does happen. What was your father's name?"

"Aaron," I said, hoping that Kaimi knew of him. Was this the moment I found out where my father was from? Would I finally discover what had happened to him? Was there even a glimmer of hope that he was here, that he'd returned?

Kaimi shook his head. "The name is not familiar to me. I have never known a Sachael of that name here. He must have come from one of the other worlds."

"Perhaps the Elder would know him," I suggested, momentarily hopeful, but then I remembered. "You don't have one here, do you?" Azariah had told me that Saicean's Elder was living in another land. He'd been banished years ago, not by Kaimi, but by his grandfather. Or was it great grandfather? I couldn't remember exactly.

Kaimi surprised me by chuckling. He sounded just like Azariah. My chest constricted at the reminder of why I was here and what we were meant to be doing.

"You know a fair bit about us," Kaimi said, "but not enough about me. I do not need an Elder telling me what I can and can't do. I know there has never been a Sachael called Aaron living in Saicean." He paused, looking at Chanon, and then me. His frown returned as he stood. "But I am curious as to how you came to exist."

"So am I." I fought a yawn that pulled at the back of my throat, but Chanon must have caught it.

"Kaimi," he said. "Estelle needs to rest. She hasn't slept properly since yesterday."

"Of course, of course. I should have realized." Kaimi patted my arm before smiling. "Show her to Azariah's rooms. If he were here, she would be there with him." He smiled even more. "It makes perfect sense for you to settle yourself there. Chanon, you must stay with her. No other man is to approach her, understand?"

Chanon nodded.

"And don't worry," Kaimi said, his eyes bright and clear. "I won't banish you, not after your explanation. We'll find out the truth, eventually. Your actions so far are forgivable because of what you thought your relationship was with Estelle. But I warn you now, Chanon. If we find out that Estelle is not your sister, then you back off. Immediately."

"I understand."

Kaimi nodded before turning away. "I will send one of the girls to tend to her cheek, and also provide suitable items of clothing. I have no idea why a woman is dressed in men's clothes." He tutted and shook his head.

Chanon caught my eye and grinned at me, obviously amused by Kaimi's comment, but I was concentrating on Kaimi. "Where are you going?" I asked, panic-stricken as he strode toward the door he initially came through. "We need to rescue Azariah."

"I assure you, I will be devising a plan while you sleep."

How could someone make a sentence sound so condescending? Did he think I wanted to rest? I wanted Azariah back, and I would give up sleeping for the rest of my life if it meant he would be safe and in my arms.

"Do you think you can guard her properly, Chanon?" Kaimi said. "Don't let her get caught by the Oceanids the way you let Azariah be snatched from us."

I took a long breath, preparing to respond to Kaimi, but he'd already gone.

Chanon hooked one arm behind my legs and swung me into his arms.

"Hey, I can walk." I pushed on Chanon's chest—it felt strange to be held by anyone other than Azariah—but he held me firm.

"You're exhausted, Estelle. I didn't just say it to Kaimi for the sake of it. You really do need to rest."

"But—" My words faltered as I looked up at Chanon's face. I momentarily caught sight of a small dimple in his right cheek—it was exactly like my father's.

"No more arguing," Chanon said. "Not today. Promise me?"

I relaxed into his hold. It was secure and comforting, and even though there was still a lot of explaining to do, I believed he was my brother. "Okay." I closed my eyes and kept quiet as Chanon headed for the same door Kaimi had disappeared through. Suddenly feeling incredibly weak, I rested my head on his shoulder, grateful he was carrying me.

The passageway Chanon carried me along was narrower than the one we were in earlier. There were many small burning lamps on the walls, and the murals were stunning. These ones contained significantly more gold. I smirked, surmising that we were in the living area of Kaimi's home. This was also where Azariah lived, I realized; rooms and passageways full of bright colors and busy designs. The opulent richness of everything matched Kaimi and his attitude, but it didn't fit Azariah.

"Here we are," Chanon stated, pushing a single door open. I gasped as Chanon carried me into the room. This wasn't just a room; it was a suite—three rooms running into one spacious, open-planned space. It wasn't colorful like everywhere else. Everything was white or natural stone, apart from a small pot of lavender flowers in a vase on the table. Chanon placed me on the large bed before stepping back.

"It's so plain and uncluttered," I said, trying to take everything in.

"Yes, it's a bit different in here, isn't it?" He looked around the room and smiled. "It seems weird to be in here when he isn't." He inclined his head toward the table and four chairs, and the overstuffed bookcase. "That's where we plan things—jokes, attacks, rescuing you."

I widened my eyes.

"It's peaceful in here," Chanon said. "Azariah never did conform to his father's ideas. As soon as he was given this space, he covered everything up."

I nodded. "It's beautiful. It's just so, so . . ."

"So Azariah," Chanon stated. "Did you honestly think he would have a room decorated like the passageways or Kaimi's Hall?"

"Kaimi's Hall?"

Chanon nodded. "That's its official name."

I grinned. "His throne room."

Chanon chuckled as he walked to the end of the bed. "There's clean water through there." He nodded toward a closed door. "If you need warm water to bathe, I suggest you let me alert Kaimi to your request. Hot water is a luxury here."

A quiet knock on the door stopped our conversation. A woman had arrived with clothes and a bowl of water to bathe my cheek. Chanon shooed her away and proceeded to hang the garments up before sitting on the bed next to me.

"I'm sorry about earlier," he said as he dipped the cloth in the bowl.

"Which bit?"

"Well, all of it. But mainly the confrontation with Ixion when we first arrived. I wasn't prepared. I should never have allowed him to grab you. I was so pleased to have gotten you here safely that I forgot the dangers within. If I had been alert, I would have killed his side-kicks before they grabbed me. If Markos hadn't come along when he did . . ."

"But he did."

He dabbed my cheek with the cloth, and I winced at the contact.

"Markos is a guard you can trust, Estelle. I've known him all my life. He is an honorable man. Never forget that. He will protect you against anyone." His eyes narrowed in concentration as he continued cleaning my cut. "His position as an entrance guard means he should never have questioned Ixion. But he did. He reacts instinctively, and is rarely wrong."

"I'm glad he was there today."

"So am I."

He finished bathing my cheek, the cold water numbing it. My attention turned to the long, flowing dresses Kaimi had sent. They hung from hooks in the wall.

"I can't wear any of those dresses. I'll look like a bride," I said, eying the white material.

"All the Oceanids wear them," Chanon answered, as he disappeared into the bathroom with the bowl containing the red-stained water.

I huffed. "Well, I'm not an Oceanid, am I? I'll stay in my jeans and t-shirt."

"They need washing, then," he shouted at me. "If you intend to keep wearing them, they'll soon rot. And, they can't be comfortable, they don't dry as quickly as our shorts."

The damp denim wasn't comfortable, and I begrudgingly agreed to let him wash them while I slept. He stepped back into the bathroom, leaving me to get undressed.

Too tired to pay attention to the dresses Kaimi sent, I slipped into the first short one I came across before calling Chanon back. After picking up my jeans and t-shirt, he disappeared into the bathroom once again.

Laying on the softness of Azariah's bed, I focused on the sound of Chanon's rhythmic scrubbing of my clothes.

"Are you asleep?" he called.

"I am," I replied, smiling at the easy way we'd settled into our newfound relationship. It was strange how readily I'd accepted him. I frowned as I tried to work out my reaction. I'd always been wary of meeting new people, and history proved I'd not always been the best judge of character. But with Chanon, all my earlier fears about his intentions had disappeared the instant I realized we might actually be related. He was the big brother I'd never had, and I felt confident that, from now on, he was the one person I could trust.

The scrubbing stopped, and a few seconds later, he leaned against the bathroom door, drying his hands on a towel. "You need to sleep. Seriously, Estelle, I don't know how you've managed to stay awake as long as you have."

"I'd stay awake longer if I needed to, if it meant Azariah would be safe." Again, my chest tightened as I mentioned his name.

"I know you would. We all would." He looked away, his shoulders lifting and then dropping. I wasn't the only one who was struggling with Azariah's capture. "But you need to sleep."

I smiled weakly at him. "Are you staying with me?"

I didn't want him to leave. I was in a strange, unfamiliar world, and didn't know anyone.

"I'm not going anywhere. Kaimi ordered me to stay, remember? And even if he hadn't, I would still be here for you. I promised you that a long time ago, didn't I?"

On the beach, when we'd left Melia. He had promised to look out for me. I'd not forgotten, and neither had he. "Thank you."

"I'll doze over there." He pointed to a chair in the corner of the room.

I sighed, remembering when Azariah had slept in the chair at Sam and Cleo's.

"Are you okay?" Chanon asked.

I nodded, closing my eyes, trying to block the memories. They would keep me awake, and Chanon was right—I needed to sleep.

His kissed my forehead before moving across the room.

"Do you want me to help you sleep?" he asked.

"Please." It didn't bother me that I would be calmed by Chanon. I knew whenever I let Azariah work his calming magic on me, I slept really well.

"Sleep, Estelle." His soothing words drifted into my head.

"And you," I muttered, already feeling the first waves of pending sleep pulse through my body. I was ready to welcome them, so I could forget all the horrors of the day. In my dreams, I could imagine being back with Azariah.

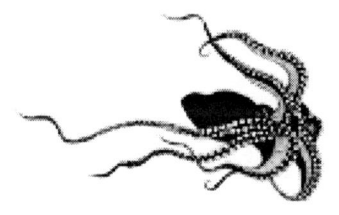

EIGHTEEN
Retribution

"*Estelle . . .*"

Azariah was with me, holding my hand. He reassured me of his love as we walked along a twisting path in Saicean.

"*Estelle . . .*"

We were heading to the lake to do a submergence together. He turned to face me, smiling, before leaning forward to kiss me.

"Estelle. Estelle . . ."

The whisper became urgent.

"Kaimi has ordered you to come see him. You need to wake up."

"What?" I opened my eyes immediately, sitting up. Where was I? An unfamiliar bed, a strange room. I rubbed my eyes before focusing on the person standing at the side of the bed. Chanon.

"You've slept for a long time," he said. "A full day."

"What? No! You should have woken me." I should have been awake, helping with the plan to rescue Azariah. I swung my legs over the side of the bed and looked around the room, trying to locate my jeans.

"I wanted you to sleep—you were exhausted. I left you as long as I could." He was calm, watching me with an amused expression, whereas I was jittery.

"Where are my jeans?"

Chanon disappeared into the bathroom, emerging a few moments later with the dark denim material. "Here, they're not completely dry, though."

I reached for my jeans and attempted to pull them on quickly. I cringed at the lingering dampness of the material as it clung to my legs, hindering my ability to hurry.

"We need to see what Kaimi has planned. I hope he's sorted everything," I muttered.

Chanon grinned as I struggled to fasten my zipper.

"What?" I asked, scowling at him.

"Your clothes. Kaimi will not approve." He laughed, shaking his head at my continued groans of exasperation as I dressed.

As soon as my jeans were on, I strode to the door.

"Hang on," Chanon said. He trotted into the bathroom before returning with my t-shirt.

"Put this on. It covers you up a bit more." He thrust the t-shirt into my hand, and I sighed as I pulled it over the flimsy short dress.

I opened the door to the brightly colored passageway, narrowing my eyes against the glare.

"My brooch?" I asked, feeling for the familiar item on my top. "Where's my brooch?"

"I gave it to the woman who made the ankle braid for mine. You'll have it back soon. I think your ankle will be a safer place to wear it. You'll not need to keep removing it and placing it on different items of clothing then. It will always be with you—just like mine."

"Thank you," I offered, suddenly feeling emotional. He was looking out for me and caring for me in the way I imagined big brothers did. How much easier would life have been on land, with my mother, if he had been there? He would have taken charge, and taken care of me. Maybe he would have prevented me from making so many mistakes.

He smiled before indicating with a nod of his head that we should carry on to the hall. "Let's go and see what he wants."

"I hope it's to tell us he knows where Azariah is. Do you think they've found him already? Is he here?" Hope surged through me, and I didn't listen to Chanon's answer as I ran to the door ahead.

I flung it open, rushing a few steps into the room. My eyes scanned the space quickly, checking for Azariah.

Chanon was behind me and placed both his hands on the top of my arms. "Estelle, he's not here. You would have been the first and only person he would have wanted to see."

Kaimi was standing next to a table with six guards surrounding it. He looked up at my rather noisy and brisk entrance and raised a brow at my appearance.

Swallowing hard, I gathered my thoughts before speaking. "Have you found him? Do you know where the ruins are?" I asked.

Kaimi frowned at my legs. "I see you insist on wearing your old clothes. Do I have to burn them to make you wear the ones Ianira provided you with?"

"They're white. I don't want to look like a bride," I said.

His brows rose, and then he grinned.

"I see she takes after you." He looked to Chanon. "Your obstinacy was always an issue for me when you were young."

Both of them looked at me, and I waited, unsure of how I was supposed to respond. Finally, Kaimi looked away.

"We have a plan of attack," Kaimi said, rubbing his forehead with his fingers. "But I need to talk to Chanon. He's the most experienced fighter I have, since you ordered Ixion's death."

"Me?" I was astonished he was blaming me for his death. "You were the one who ordered for him to be killed."

"I would have saved him if you'd told me to, locked him up for the rest of his life. Ultimately, the decision was yours."

He crossed the room toward me. "Your opinion matters, and you will need to get used to making decisions. You will be the future Queen of Saicean." He placed his hand flat against my damaged cheek. "Azariah has chosen well. If he had not selected you as his, and I had seen you on the beach instead, I would most definitely have left you a shell. It would have been a pleasure and a challenge to seduce you."

I backed away. Unable to stop my true disgust from showing, I screwed my nose up. "You're old enough to be my father."

He grinned, looking amused by my reaction and comment. "But I'm not your father, am I?"

A woman's voice stopped my cutting reply. "Kaimi, stop teasing her."

Turning to where the voice came from, I saw a blonde woman walking toward us. She was dressed in a floor-skimming, flowing white dress that was threaded with twists of gold, and her long hair was tied into a beautiful plaited arrangement on top of her head.

"Ianira," Kaimi beamed. "Come and meet Estelle."

She stood in front of me and took my hands in hers. Her touch was cold; it reminded me of Orontes and his cold fingers, and the times he'd trailed them down my back. I forced myself not to shiver. I didn't want to insult her.

"Definitely a Sachael. You're too warm to be an Oceanid. And your hair; it's a deep mahogany—so beautiful." Her smile was genuine and welcome.

"Estelle certainly makes a change from all the blondes that surround me." Kaimi chuckled, looking amused by Ianira's comment. "Estelle, this is Ianira, my wife. The most beautiful woman in the world."

Kaimi's declaration surprised me somewhat. I never expected him to speak in such an open way. He was proving to be a more complex character than I'd given him credit for. He gently held Ianira's arm before kissing her cheek. "I have plans to make. Please, excuse me." He turned to Chanon. "Chanon, come and give me your opinion."

They both strode to the table, which was covered in rolls of paper.

"Are you rested, Estelle?" Ianira asked, guiding me to the steps I'd sat on with Kaimi when I first arrived.

"I think so," I said. "I'm not sure how I slept at all. I'm really worried about Azariah."

"I understand. If something is bothering you, you can always come to me. You can tell me anything, just between us girls." We sat down, and Ianira moved close, shooting a sideways glance at Kaimi. "I don't share everything with Kaimi. Sometimes, his obstinacy is a blessing in disguise."

I managed a brief smile. "I just want Azariah safe. I miss him so much." My fingers drifted to the pearl of my necklace. It was all I had to connect him to me. Ianira's gaze followed my hand.

"He saved that pearl for someone special." She smiled wistfully. "I miss him as well. We all do. I know how much Azariah loves you, and Kaimi will make sure he returns safely.

He's doing everything he can. He's our son, and we want him back just as much as you."

I nodded. She wasn't Azariah's birth mother, but she was the woman who had brought him up since the day he was born. She'd raised him and his brothers. My heart ached for her.

"I'm sorry about Elpis," I said, recalling his young, jovial face.

She dipped her head. "Thank you. It was hard on all of us to lose him, but his death shook Azariah. He was incredibly fond of his brother. I understand he brought him to meet you. It proves how much he loves you, how much he wants you to be a part of his life."

"But if he hadn't come to land to meet me, he would still be alive."

"You must not think that. Elpis was betrayed by his guard. If he had stayed to protect him, as he should have done, then Elpis would be here now. If he had not done so that day, then I assume he would have done it at a later time. He was weak, and should never have been assigned as Elpis's personal guard." She looked down at her hands and sighed heavily.

"Who chose him?" I asked. "Who chose him as his personal guard?"

"Kaimi."

My eyes widened.

"He was the son of Kaimi's old head guard. He trusted him. We all did." She sighed again. "I can't bear to lose another son, neither can Kaimi. It will destroy him if he loses Azariah."

Taking her hands in mine, I tried to offer her some comfort. We both loved Azariah, but in completely different ways.

"But none of that matters!" Kaimi shouted, throwing his hands in the air. The rolls of paper flew to the floor. "We can have hundreds of plans on the best way to rescue him, but until the scouts I have sent out return with its location, we have no way of knowing where to organize an attack."

Chanon stood next to Kaimi; he hadn't backed away from his outburst like the other men had.

Kaimi turned to us, gesturing for us to join him. "Estelle, Ianira, please come here."

We both complied, walking to where he stood.

"Ianira, I know I have already asked you, but please, think hard. Have you any idea where the Arcuato Ruins are?" Kaimi's tone was serious, begging her to have the information he needed.

"I'm sorry, Kaimi. I have no idea where they are. I came to be your wife when I was seventeen, remember? I was not privy to such information at that young age."

He sighed heavily, turning to Chanon. "If we cannot find this place, then I fear we may never see him again. If Orontes keeps him drugged and he remains weak, he will never be able to escape, and he will miss the next full moon."

I closed my eyes as my heart screamed. Not only was there danger in Orontes giving him too much venom and killing him, but if we didn't find him before the next full moon on land, he would drown. I felt helpless, just as I had when Azariah first went missing. Since his capture, I'd spent my time planning how to get Michael safe and concentrating on getting to Saicean. I'd relied on Kaimi leading his army to the ruins and rescuing Azariah. Never once did I think he wouldn't know where it was. But it made sense. Kaimi wasn't an Oceanid.

"Hebrus," I muttered. Chanon, Ianira, and Kaimi turned to me as one. "Hebrus will know where the ruins are. He has to."

"I refuse to speak to that man." Kaimi waved his hand in the air as if shooing away an annoying bug.

"Kaimi, please," I said. "He'll definitely know—he's the King of the Oceanids. You must contact him."

"No." His word was firm, and I suspected it was his final answer. But I wouldn't let it rest. This was an opportunity, perhaps the only one we had.

"Please," I repeated. "Surely any differences can be put aside if it means Azariah can be found."

"His whole family is a disgrace," Kaimi retorted angrily.

"But—"

"Enough!" Kaimi roared. "You have no idea how he dishonored me. I will never speak to him."

Everyone was quiet, apart from Ianira. "Not even when your refusal to do so will most certainly mean that our son will die?" She spoke quietly, but everyone heard her words.

Kaimi spun to face the guards. "Out. All of you. Out!"

As the men quickly shuffled to the door, Chanon came and stood by my side. Either he knew Kaimi hadn't meant for him to go or he was seriously pushing his luck. Kaimi scowled at him.

"I stay with Estelle," Chanon said.

Kaimi sighed heavily before turning to Ianira. "You know what he did, what his daughter did. I cannot allow myself to go begging to him. I can't."

"But if he can tell us where the ruins are, we can bring Azariah home," I reasoned. "Please, Kaimi, speak to Hebrus."

"I can't." He shook his head. "I will never ask an Oceanid for help."

"You asked me." Ianira snapped.

"That's different." Kaimi looked pleadingly at his wife, silently asking her to understand.

"Is it? I'm an Oceanid—the race you have ridiculed and hated all your life."

I stepped back as Ianira prodded Kaimi with her finger.

"That's not true," Kaimi said quietly, all his earlier anger gone.

"In all my years of being your wife, I have stood by your decisions. I've seen you choose a way of life which leads to heartache and hate between your kind and the humans. But your decision to live this way is destroying the very thing you try to protect—the Sachaels. Your refusal to approach Hebrus and ask for his help will cost you the life of your son." She jabbed him with her finger again, and he raised his hand to hold hers still. She shook his hand away, but continued talking. "Can you remember when Azariah was with Camarina? You and Hebrus were overjoyed at the union. You had high hopes for the future of our kinds existing in harmony—it was the happiest I have ever seen you."

"He refused her. She should have tried harder," Kaimi sneered.

"Camarina was Hebrus's daughter?" I couldn't stop myself from interrupting.

"Yes," Chanon whispered from my side. "Hebrus and Kaimi thought it a perfect match."

"Love is a two-way feeling," I said, turning to Kaimi. "From what I understand, neither Camarina nor Azariah felt that way for each other."

"She should have seduced him with her body and sexual skills," Kaimi hissed. "If she'd pleased him that way, he would have been happy to have her as his wife."

I huffed at his ridiculous, chauvinistic comment. "So this is what you and Hebrus fell out about? Azariah and Camarina not wanting to be with each other?"

"It was slightly more than that," Ianira replied. "Wasn't it, Kaimi?"

"I have no need to relive our conversation. As far as I am concerned, I will not speak to Hebrus ever again. He hates me as much as I hate him." He raised his hands in the air. "He hates all of us. I actually think he would be glad Azariah is caught. He probably planned it."

"I'm confident Orontes is doing this by himself," I said, "and not under orders from Hebrus."

"How do you know?" Kaimi's teeth were gritted. "You don't. None of us do. But I'll tell you one thing, this is

Hebrus's fault, and I will ensure every one of the Oceanids responsible for my son's capture is killed."

Ianira sighed and turned away from Kaimi.

"How is this Hebrus's fault?" I asked.

"He has turned the Oceanids against us. Just because I told him what I thought of his daughter, that she should have tried harder to seduce Azariah. He should have forced her to stay here, not let her return home. He accused me and all Sachaels of being brutal and cruel."

With no understanding of why he sounded hurt by Hebrus's accusations, I rolled my eyes. Everything Hebrus had said was the truth.

Kaimi must have seen my action, because he stepped up to me. "Do you agree with him?" He glared at me, his piercing blue eyes locked on mine.

"Sachaels are cruel," I said. "You seduce innocent woman. You take newborn babies from their mothers as soon as they are born, and then you disappear from the woman's life. She loses the man she loves and her newborn child."

Kaimi's face turned red, and I backed away when the scales on his arms began to rise.

"You have no understanding of Sachaels," he growled.

I wouldn't back down, though, not even when he was angry enough for his skin to react the way it had. "So, what I have said is a lie?"

Kaimi didn't respond.

"You know I speak the truth," I continued. "How do you think I would feel if Azariah did that to me when, at this moment in time, I am willing to risk my life for his?"

Kaimi's scales flattened, his skin returning to normal, but I continued directing my torrent of anger at him. "The behavior of the Sachaels and their heartless treatment of women is the reason The Sect is killing your kind. The reason you have made enemies of the Oceanids is because of the way your men abduct the Oceanid women and drag them here to be their wives. There is no wonder the male Oceanids are attacking the Sachaels—they hate what you do to their women."

"You have no proof of any of this."

"Ixion!" I shouted at him.

"That was one man, not all of us. I repeat—you have no proof."

"I do. I was caught by The Sect. There are human and Oceanid men in it. You have managed to make enemies both in and out of the water."

Kaimi huffed before walking away. Ianira followed him, placing her hand on his shoulder when she reached him.

"If you won't speak to Hebrus, then I will," I shouted at him. "I will do anything to ensure Azariah returns safely, even if I have to go and meet Hebrus myself."

"You'll have no contact with the Oceanids," Chanon told me. "They're too volatile at the moment. We were attacked when we swam here. Did you not see the Oceanid floating into the abyss?"

I recalled the dead creature I'd seen when Chanon and I were hiding in the side of the rock face.

"That was an Oceanid? They're huge. I thought it was a fish."

"Their tails are the largest part of their bodies. I think they attacked us because of you. Your appearance in the water must have shocked them. A female in the water at that depth, who obviously isn't an Oceanid, would be something they have never seen before."

Kaimi turned to face me, unaware of the conversation I'd shared with Chanon. "You would meet with him? You are prepared to meet with Hebrus?"

"Yes." I nodded my instant response. There was no question. If that's what it took to bring Azariah home, then I would do it without a second thought.

"No," Chanon snapped. "I will not allow Estelle to travel to Mercivium. It's too risky."

Kaimi held his hand up, silencing Chanon with his gesture. "I agree. I do not want to risk losing Estelle as well as my son. He will need to come here."

"But Hebrus will not speak with a Sachael. Not now. He's too proud.," Ianira said.

"I have to speak to him," I stated. "He will be able to find Azariah for us. He needs to know what his people are doing. I know he may not like what you are and what you do, but surely, if he is a man of any honor, he'll want peace; he'll not want his people treating your kind like this."

"That is true, but the problem will be in getting him to come here." Kaimi scowled in concentration as he returned to studying the maps.

I began to laugh quietly as the answer dawned in my mind. I couldn't believe I was about to propose the very thing I'd feared—being put on display and gawked at. Azariah had told me repeatedly that I would be the cause of much curiosity and interest. It was time to use that to our advantage. "Me. We use me. Hebrus would come to meet a female Sachael. His curiosity will overpower any mistrust of your kind."

Kaimi didn't move for a few seconds, and then he threw his arms in the air, beaming. "You are right. Of course. He would definitely come to see you. He'll be too intrigued; he'll want to see you with his own eyes."

Kaimi paced toward me. "We need him to get the message that there is a female Sachael in Saicean, and that she wishes to meet him," Kaimi mused, running his fingers through his beard. "I fear he will not trust the words of a Sachael with this information."

"Is Xanthe still here?" I asked, realizing she would have no reason to stay here now she was free from Ixion. "Perhaps she can tell Hebrus about me."

Kaimi spun to face me.

"Yes, she's still here. Chanon, go and fetch her. She needs to meet Estelle if she is to give the message to Hebrus. Find three guards whom you trust to escort Xanthe to Mercivium."

"Go," I told him when he hesitated, glancing between Kaimi and me, clearly torn. "The sooner she sees me, the sooner Hebrus will be here."

Chanon bowed to Kaimi before leaving the room.

"I am impressed, Estelle," Kaimi spoke genuinely. "I hope Hebrus is as well. But you need to look presentable in order to meet him. I insist you change out of those clothes before he gets here."

I sighed. "As long as it's not white." I glanced at Ianira. "I'm sorry, and I certainly don't mean to offend you, but the Oceanids wear white. I'm not an Oceanid. And that's exactly what we need to prove to Hebrus. Dress me in any color you want, as long as it's not white."

Ianira nodded, and then smiled at me. "No offense taken, Estelle. You are completely right with your reasoning."

Kaimi chuckled, and then turned to Ianira. "Please go and find something suitable for Estelle to wear for when she meets Hebrus. Something to show off her figure. Let Hebrus see how much of a female she is."

I groaned under my breath. I didn't mind wearing a dress—my damp jeans and top were extremely uncomfortable—but I didn't like Kaimi's reasoning. I wasn't a doll. I had no desire to be dressed up and paraded in front of anyone, even if I had been the one to propose it.

He shouted for his guards to return to the room. Then, with short, sharp orders he sent two of them to inform the entrance guards to expect Hebrus and potentially several other

Oceanids. Kaimi seemed well aware that if Hebrus came, he would come with his own personal army for protection.

I watched him intently as he gave the orders to his guards. He was dismissive in the way he spoke to them, but his tone ensured they did exactly what he said. If he hadn't been the ruler of Saicean, I guessed he would have made an excellent guard himself. He stood tall, even when surrounded by men larger than himself. I doubted he'd ever felt intimidated in his whole life. I recalled the things Azariah had told me about him. Kaimi was strong, opinionated, and, at times, ruthless. I also remembered how Azariah had argued with him when he first came to visit me on land—when none of us suspected I was a Sachael. I could easily imagine Kaimi's anger at Azariah's decision. When did the turning point occur? When did Azariah tell his father I was a Sachael? Was it when I was caught, or was it before then?

I sighed heavily, my mind miles away, lost in memories.

When the doors to the hall opened again, only Chanon entered. I had expected to see Xanthe with him, but she wasn't there. I frowned as Chanon bowed at Kaimi.

"Kaimi, I bring Xanthe to you as requested."

Kaimi walked away from the guards, moving between myself and the door. "Well, bring her in then."

I moved to the side, managing to see the doors as Xanthe rushed into the room. She ran forward and sank to her knees in front of Kaimi.

"Please, I beg you. Do not hurt me. I have done nothing wrong." Her voice was quiet, broken with sobs as she spoke.

Kaimi's shoulders rose and fell as he sighed.

I immediately broke into a hurried stride, crossing the room to stand beside him.

"Please," I said quietly, so only he heard me. "Can I speak to her?"

Kaimi patted my arm and nodded before stepping back and away.

I bent down next to her, wrapping my arm around her shoulder. She wore a simple white dress, one which gapped open as she crouched on the floor. "You have done nothing wrong. Kaimi will not hurt you."

Xanthe turned to face me, her cheeks smeared with tears. Her complexion was pale, her eyes heavy with fear. But I still saw her beauty.

"Shush," I whispered, wiping her tears with my fingertips. "No one will hurt you ever again."

"But Ixion. He will be furious I have been brought before his leader. He will not wait for me to explain anything." Her voice quivered as her eyes searched my face.

"Ixion is dead!" Kaimi snapped from behind me. "Estelle ordered his execution."

"D . . . dead?"

"Yes," I hurriedly replied. I needed Kaimi to stay out of this and keep quiet. I tipped my head up and frowned at him, putting my finger to my lips. I hoped he understood my signal.

"I arrived in Saicean in the early hours of yesterday," I explained. "Before I came here, I stayed with Scamander and Cleodora. I believe they are friends of yours."

"Cleodora is alive?"

"Yes. She is very much alive. She told me of your attack, and how you were brought to Saicean against your will."

Xanthe nodded.

"Unfortunately, I was greeted by Ixion on my arrival. I didn't take kindly to his presence, knowing what I did."

Xanthe managed a cautious smile.

"When Kaimi discovered what he'd done, he wanted him punished. It seems I ultimately held the decision on whether to save him or not. I didn't."

Xanthe flung her arms around me, crying with what I hoped was relief.

"Oh, how can I ever thank you? You have no idea what my life was like with him. The fear, the abuse, the beatings."

"I can well imagine," I replied, remembering his strength and the way he'd spoken to me.

"She speaks of nothing but lies." One of Kaimi's guards stepped toward us, his hand poised over the knife that hung in a diagonal sheath across his upper body. "Ixion was a great man."

"Pentheus?" Xanthe cried.

I immediately stood, facing him as he approached. He was one of the men who had restrained Chanon when we arrived in Saicean—one of Ixion's "gang."

Chanon stepped forward, ready to defend me from any attack. Xanthe cowered behind me.

"How does Xanthe know your name?" I asked.

He sneered at me. "Why should I tell you?"

"Tell her," Kaimi barked from the side of the room. I glanced at him. He was leaning forward, poised and composed, listening to the interchange between us all. "And don't you dare draw your weapon."

"Tell me," I ordered.

"I was with Ixion when he found her. She was pathetic. Crying rape when she really wanted it."

"You were with Ixion?"

He nodded. "We hunted together."

"Hunted?" What did he mean? Was he hunting for food, or something else? Then it dawned on me. They were looking for a girl, perhaps any girl. Cleo and Xanthe were in the wrong place at the wrong time.

Xanthe's hands gripped my ankle.

Pentheus smirked at me. "She was eager for all of us. Four of the strongest and best guards in Saicean. No woman would refuse us. Ixion has shared her with us ever since."

He had just sealed his fate.

"Kill him," I ordered.

As soon as I spoke, two of the guards stepped behind Pentheus and held him. Kaimi nodded at Chanon. With no hesitation, he pulled his knife from his pocket. I froze. I didn't know whether it was in shock from what was about to happen, or that Chanon was the one about to do it.

Once in front of Pentheus, Chanon placed the metal blade against his throat.

"I told you yesterday I'd kill you," he snarled at him.

The knife flashed across his throat and blood spurted forward.

I turned away. I couldn't watch. Neither could Xanthe. She clung to my thighs, sobbing. A loud gurgling filled the room, quickly replaced by a shuddering gasp. I wished I could block my hearing.

"Don't tease, Chanon!" Kaimi shouted. "Finish him off properly."

More shuffling—then silence. A few seconds later, Chanon was by my side.

"He's dead," he informed me.

I turned toward him, not looking in the direction of the body. I'd seen too much death recently as it was. Chanon's chest was covered in droplets of blood, his hand bright red. I shuddered at the evidence of Pentheus's death.

"Take him away!" Kaimi shouted. His gaze followed the removal of the body, and once it was out of the room, he strode over to me. "That's two of my best fighters you have slaughtered. How many others do you intend on killing?"

"There were four men who raped Xanthe. I want the names of the other two," I said confidently.

Kaimi raised his eyebrows but didn't reply.

"Who were the others?" I asked Xanthe. "You have nothing to fear from them; they will be dealt with in the same way as Pentheus and Ixion. And you are free to return to Mercivium."

"Free?" Her wide, bright emerald eyes suddenly came alive.

"Yes."

"But how? Why? Why are you giving orders?"

I smiled at her. "Have you ever met or seen Azariah, Kaimi's son?"

She nodded quickly. "I've seen him a few times, when he walked in the gardens. He was always surrounded by the most beautiful Oceanids."

"He is mine," I told her, unable to stop the twitch of my lips as I recalled the word Azariah had written in the sand at Ravenscar. It had incensed Orontes. "But I am not an Oceanid. I am a Sachael, just like him."

"But . . . but they don't exist. You can't be."

"I am." I took her hands in mine. "Feel how much warmer I am than you. Look at the color of my eyes—blue. My hair is naturally dark. My skin isn't as pale as yours. I am a Sachael."

Xanthe stared into my eyes before touching my hair and face. "You are a miracle."

"Not quite. But there is a lot of mystery surrounding my existence." I paused, waiting to tell her what I needed her to do. "I need you to help me."

"Anything, I'll do anything to help you. You have saved me from a life of torture."

"I want you to go to Mercivium and go straight to Hebrus. Tell him you've met me, and that I'm a female Sachael."

"He'll not believe me."

"You have to convince him. He must come to see me. Tell him I'm the one who gave you your freedom. Tell him I want things to change here, and I'll do everything I can for it to happen. But most importantly of all, you must tell him I'm a female Sachael, and I request a meeting with him, here, in Saicean. He'll be expected to come immediately."

Xanthe nodded, still staring at me.

"Good. Chanon's selected three guards who'll escort you home. I'd like you to see them first. I don't want you to be scared of them."

Chanon strode to the doors. Three guards walked forward into the room. Xanthe's eyes widened as she caught sight of one of the guards.

"Don't you want to travel with him?" I asked, picking up on her discomfort.

"I . . . I know him." She blushed a deep red.

"And?"

Kaimi straightened, possibly preparing himself for the death of another of his guards.

"I am Castor," the young guard stated. "I am a friend of Xanthe's." His eyes met with hers. I immediately recognized the look he gave her. I had seen it many times in Azariah's eyes. They were in love.

I turned back to Xanthe. "You must go straight to Mercivium to give Hebrus my message. Once you've done that, you're free to do whatever you want. If you choose to return with Castor, if that is your wish, then you are free to do so. But if you wish to stay in Mercivium with your own kind, you can."

"Really?" She squealed excitedly. A smile covered her face for the first time since she'd arrived in the room.

I nodded, returning her smile.

"Oh, thank you. You have no idea how much this means to me."

She turned to Castor, who couldn't look away from her. He was young, about the same age as Xanthe, not twenty or so years older like Ixion.

"I'm ready to leave," Xanthe stated.

"Just one more thing before you go," I said. "Names. Give me the names of the other guards who attacked you."

"Taras and Diomedes."

"I'll deal with them," I promised her.

"But,"—her hand grasped my arm—"I have friends who are also living in fear. Their lives are no better than mine is . . . was."

"How many?" Her words didn't surprise me, but they obviously did Kaimi. He coughed loudly as he paced the room.

"There are three others I know of," she confirmed.

"Tell Castor their names. Kaimi will speak to them. Perhaps when the Sachaels with them know what's happened to Ixion and the others, they'll behave."

"Thank you."

"You've no need to keep thanking me, Xanthe." A sudden idea hit me—something I'd never considered until that moment. "What do you do during the day here? Do you work?"

"Yes. I work in the gardens between here and the lake. I pollinate the flowers and tend to the seedlings in the warm houses."

"If you choose to come back, I'd like you to look after me. I've got no idea how things work here, but I'll need someone to help me if I'm staying. Would you be willing to do that?"

"Yes, yes, of course I would."

"Good." I hugged her tightly. "You must come and see me if you return."

"I will."

She glanced toward Kaimi, who waved her away with his hand. Without looking back, she practically skipped toward the guards, smiling widely at Castor, who took her hand in his. They quickly left the hall.

"Well, Estelle," Kaimi said, his hands on his hips. "You seem to see yourself as someone who can give orders."

I froze. "I—"

"Hush. I am not angry with you, although I should be. I am actually very impressed with how you handled what was, I admit, a very frightened Oceanid."

"She was petrified."

"She said there are others here like her, Oceanids who are not happy with the Sachaels they are with. That will be dealt with. I also know of the guards whose names she mentioned." He focused on the remaining guards in the room. "One of you go and fetch Taras, and one of you go and find Diomedes. Bring them to me, but do not alert them of their fate. After this, I expect you to tell the others of what has happened here. Spread the word that this type of behavior will not be tolerated. It has to stop."

The guards gradually dispersed, leaving two guarding the doorway.

"I am somewhat relieved that Taras and Diomedes are not part of my select guards. They are experienced Sachaels, though, and should know better than to behave in the way Xanthe said they did."

"What will you do with them?"

Kaimi lifted a brow and inclined his head. "Kill them, of course. Have you not already told Xanthe it is their fate? That you would find them and deal with them in the same way you dealt with Ixion and Pentheus?"

I nodded, aware that I had said those exact words.

"If you did not mean it, then you should not have promised it to Xanthe. I have no choice but to follow up on your words. Two more Sachaels will be executed." Kaimi smirked. "You have the blood of four Sachaels on your hands within only a few days of arriving here."

I turned away. I'd had enough. I didn't need or care to see the other two Sachaels killed. Kaimi seemed to enjoy the actual act. I, however, didn't.

"Chanon, will you come with me?" I asked. "I need to rest before Hebrus gets here."

Chanon turned to Kaimi for confirmation.

"Go," Kaimi waved us away.

As we reached the door to exit the hall, Kaimi called across the room: "Remember to make sure you look pretty for Hebrus."

Chanon's arm circled my waist, stopping me from heading back to tell Kaimi exactly what I thought of his suggestion.

"Leave it, Estelle. Learn to pick your battles with Kaimi. Not everything he says is worth fighting against."

"I just . . . just . . ."

"I know. But I honestly think you've more than pushed your luck today. Let's get you to Azariah's room, and we can talk properly."

He steered me along the passageways, away from Kaimi. The further we walked, the calmer I became. My priority was to speak to Hebrus. And I needed to think carefully about what I would say to him when he arrived.

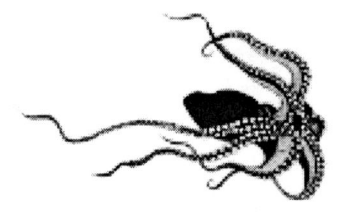

NINETEEN
Information

As soon as I entered Azariah's room, I noticed the gown. Hanging on a wooden hanger against the wall, it was impossible to ignore. Chanon disappeared into the bathroom and proceeded to scrub his hands and chest—removing Pentheus's blood.

When he wandered back into the main room, he grinned at the dress. "I see Ianira's selected a gown she deems appropriate for you to wear when you meet Hebrus. It's beautiful."

He picked the dress from the hook and held it against himself.

I laughed. "I don't think red's your color."

"I think it suits me." Chanon twirled with the dress. "I wonder why she selected a red gown for you," he said, placing it back on the hanger.

"It's not white. That's all I can say." I sat heavily on the bed. The events that had happened in the hall were replaying through my mind. I had no understanding of the world I'd arrived in. I'd never wanted to come here, and even if Azariah had been at my side, I would have struggled. At least Chanon was with me. He knew how everything worked. I took a deep breath, trying to clear my head.

"Will you tell me more about life here?" I asked.

Chanon plonked himself in the chair he'd slept in last night. "Such as?"

"What people do, how everything works. Who decides who does what?"

Chanon grinned, hunching forward. "It's simple really. There are seven factors of hierarchy here."

"Seven, I should have guessed." I rolled my eyes at the repetition of the number.

"I'll concentrate on the factors, leave the guards until later."

"Factors, not factions?"

Chanon grinned and nodded. "Factors. The first factor is Leaders. It includes Kaimi, his wife, his sons, and their wives. It also includes Kaimi's brother and his family."

"His brother?" I couldn't recall Azariah ever mentioning an uncle. "Kaimi has a brother?"

Chanon nodded again. "Pelias. Kaimi doesn't get on with him. If he had his way, I think he'd send him to live with the Nomen."

"Nomen?"

"The seventh factor—the lowest. Sachaels who contribute nothing to the way Saicean operates. They are unskilled, uneducated, and a drain on our resources."

I frowned at Chanon's explanation as he continued talking.

"Kaimi wears two gold bands—one on each arm." He rubbed at the top of his own arms. "You've seen him. He never takes them off."

"Never?"

He shook his head. "All the other members of his family wear one gold band—usually on the right arm."

"Azariah doesn't," I said.

"I know, and it leads to constant arguments between Kaimi and him. Azariah spends a lot of time away from Saicean. He leaves the gold at home when out in the ocean. It would attract too much attention. And everyone here knows who he is, so he sees no need to wear it." He sighed, glancing away. "It was his way of constantly reminding Kaimi how much he disliked what was expected of him."

I understood. I only had to close my eyes to imagine the arguments he would have had with his father. Both of them locking horns, both of them obstinate and opinionated when they felt they were right.

"So, who are the second factor?" I asked, not wanting to linger on the side of Azariah I had seen and struggled with on occasion.

"The Elders. And, as you quite rightly mentioned to Kaimi earlier, Saicean doesn't have any."

"The one you did have was banished years ago, and now lives in the Mediterranean."

Chanon grinned. "You are well informed, aren't you?"

I nodded, feeling smug with my knowledge, even though it was limited.

"But did you know that the Elders are not allowed to take an Oceanid wife? They travel to land when they turn twenty-one and return with their son when he's born. Then, they are never allowed to go to land again."

"That's unfair."

"The Elder's life is a privileged one; one which orders him to make such a sacrifice. Did Azariah mention what his main responsibility is?"

I shook my head. I had no recollection of him telling me.

"He keeps a record of every seduction of a land female. It's to prevent a cluster of pregnancies in one area. It's not an easy job. He often tells the men where they can and can't go to find a land female, depending on his handwritten records. The Elder is also viewed as our most intelligent man. He has a wealth of knowledge passed down to him from his father." Chanon yawned and rubbed his eyes, but I wanted him to continue.

"The third factor?" I said.

"You want to know all this now?" His hand attempted to hide another yawn.

"Please. I'll let you sleep once you've told me about all the factors." I yawned myself, an involuntary action.

"The third factor is the Guards. There are seven levels of guards."

I snorted as he mentioned the magic number yet again.

Chanon ignored my reaction.

"I'm not going into all their levels today. I'll save that for another time." His grin turned into another yawn before continuing. "Factor four is the Intelligents. They are our cleverest men—teachers, doctors, inventors. Factor five is the Adstators."

"The what?"

Chanon chuckled. "The Adstators; the people that look after the leaders and their families. They cook, clean, entertain, dress, and bathe them."

"So, servants." I screwed my nose up, not liking the idea of someone dressing or bathing me. I wasn't sure about the entertaining part either.

"The Crofters are the sixth factor. They are the men who farm our land. "

I nodded. "And then there is the Nomen factor."

"Exactly. They do nothing, as I said."

"Nothing at all?"

Chanon sighed. "One day, I'll take you to see where they live. You'll see the difference. Maybe then you'll understand."

I shrugged my shoulders. It would take time for me to understand everything, and I was well aware that I would potentially never like or agree with certain things. But this was to be my home now. I needed to learn what I could about it so that I could adapt, survive.

A knock at the door disturbed our conversation.

"Ahhh . . . food." Chanon sprang to his feet before opening the door.

I sat up when a delicious smell drifted my way. Chanon carried a large wooden tray laden with food to the table. Pulling out a chair, he indicated with a wave of his hand for me to sit down. "Kaimi has provided you with quite a feast."

"You need to help me eat this. There's no way I can eat it all."

I scanned the array of fruits and nuts, and a steaming bowl of soup.

Chanon pointed to the bowl. "It's a healthy broth that only Saulos, Kaimi's head cook, knows how to make. It's full of prawns."

I picked the wooden spoon from the tray and dipped it into the steaming stew before tentatively bringing it to my mouth. The heat made my lips tingle, and the aroma was mouthwatering. I licked my lips in anticipation.

"Eat it," Chanon encouraged.

I slipped the spoon into my mouth and closed my eyes as the velvety liquid coated my tongue and slid down my throat. It was delicious.

"Try one of the prawns. They're Kaimi's favorite."

I tried to scoop a prawn up onto the spoon, but it was so large I needed to hold it in my fingers. As I bit into the prawn, the richest and juiciest flavor burst into my mouth. I moaned in pleasure at the taste. Chanon laughed before grabbing an apple and a handful of nuts from the tray. I continued to eat the soup, savoring every mouthful as Chanon paced the room.

"I still can't believe you told Kaimi to shut up," he said.

"I didn't," I sputtered as I continued eating. I hadn't appreciated how hungry I was and had unashamedly stuffed far too much food into my mouth.

"You did. You put your finger to your lips, instructing him to be quiet. I was surprised he didn't erupt in anger." He leaned against the wall as he bit into the apple. "I've never seen such a look cross his face as the one that did at that moment." He chewed the apple while talking to me. "He was shocked by your action. But do you know what he did when you turned away?"

"No." I shook my head. "I didn't pay him much attention; I was worried about Xanthe, not Kaimi."

"He smiled. He never took his eyes off you. And he smiled. I have never, ever, seen him do that before. His mannerisms and actions were completely out of character."

"That's because I'm a female Sachael. He has no idea how to deal with me."

"Maybe. I think it was because you stood up to him. No Sachael would dare do what you did. The risk of having their throat slit by one of the guards would be too much of a risk."

"You mean, he could have killed me?" I placed the spoon down, shocked.

"I think if you were a male Sachael, of any factor, then yes, you would be dead."

"I had no idea. Why did no one tell me?" I mumbled. "See, this is why I need to know how things work here. I could have unwittingly done something really bad, without even realizing."

"I doubt it. In Kaimi's eyes, I don't think you'll ever do any wrong." He stepped away from the wall and swiped another handful of nuts. "And, if you had upset him today, he would have needed to kill me first. I was ready to defend you. I kept my eyes on the guards. Sometimes, Kaimi gives a tiny nod of his head in their direction; it's as if he silently converses with them."

"He did that to Markos just before Ixion was killed."

"Yes, I noticed." Chanon paused. "He'll never kill you, though. You are his son's mate, and a female Sachael. And you seem pretty headstrong." He sat back in the chair and placed his hands behind his head. "When I first saw you, when I suspected we could somehow be related, I thought you were a bit, well . . . weak." He laughed when he caught my expression.

"I was never weak," I shrieked, laughing with him, enjoying his teasing.

Chanon laughed even more. "I'm relieved you're not as fragile as you first appeared. Ordering the death of Sachaels and intending to kill the biggest Oceanid I have ever seen are definitely signs of a strong and fierce woman."

I grinned before eating more of the soup. Chanon's words filled me with hope that there was a future for me in Saicean. Chanon would look after me. That's what big brothers did.

By evening, there was still no news about Hebrus's visit, and I began to worry that he might never come. I was restless, struggling to focus on anything. And as I lay in bed, the full force of this whole horrendous situation hit me. Azariah could die. Then what?

I shuddered. I didn't want to think that way. I had to concentrate on the positive, not the negative. Hebrus would come, he would know where the ruins were, he would lead us there, and we would find Azariah alive and bring him home. I would help him recover, and together, we would make plans to leave Saicean and find Michael.

I'd never looked at life through rose-tinted glasses, never believed in thinking the impossible, but now I worried that I was. I huffed, frustrated with my inability to even believe in my positive thinking. But no matter what I did, I couldn't forget that there were two very real, very dangerous people stopping my happy ending. Orontes, and Kaimi.

"Are you okay?" Chanon was awake, probably disturbed by my sighs and restlessness.

"I can't sleep. I'm worried about Azariah. When will Hebrus get here?"

Chanon was across the room and sitting on the side of my bed in an instant.

"Hebrus will come. You must believe that. He is a very honorable man."

"People keep saying that, but where is he?"

As Chanon took my hands in his, I noticed mine were shaking.

"Estelle, Mercivium is a fair distance away. It will take Xanthe several hours to get there. She then has to talk to Hebrus and persuade him to come here. But he will come. He won't believe there is a female Sachael in Saicean, and he will insist on seeing you with his own eyes. Honestly, it is too much of a temptation for him to ignore. He will be here, just not as fast as you want." He put his finger to my lips to silence my response. "And as soon as he knows what's happened to Azariah, he will want to help."

"But didn't you say Kaimi and Hebrus fell out because of Camarina and Azariah? If that's the case, he'll hate Azariah as well."

Chanon shook his head. "No, his argument was always with Kaimi and his attitude toward his daughter. Hebrus got on very well with Azariah." He half smiled, and then looked away. "Anyway, enough of this." He stood and gestured for me to get up as well. "Put your jeans and t-shirt on, we need to complete a submergence. It's the full moon of Canopus tonight, and you need to submerge. Your first one in your transition to a full Sachael."

I widened my eyes. I'd forgotten about the submergences I needed to do here. There was so much going on!

"Will everyone be there?" I asked, surmising that the lake would be a very busy place if all the Sachaels did their submergences at the same time.

"Everyone?"

"All the other Sachaels."

"Oh, I see. No, they'll not be there." Chanon stretched his hands above his head and yawned. "While you slept, I received a message from Kaimi that you and I were to submerge under Canopus. I expected that you would, but not me."

I frowned at him as I reached for my jeans hanging on the back of the chair. "Why not?"

"Canopus is the moon the Elders would usually submerge under. I am particularly honored to be granted the opportunity to submerge with you tonight."

"But why?" He wasn't making himself clear.

"The only time Sachaels are allowed to submerge under Canopus is when they need to complete a submergence under each moon to become a full Sachael. You have to do this. As part of your transition to a full Sachael." He sat on the edge of the table and tapped his fingers on the wooden edge.

"So, what do you normally do?"

"I submerge under three moons, like the rest of the guards. Three times a month—under Rigel, Capella, and Spica. Only the guards submerge three times, all the other factors are given one moon. As long as they submerge under it every month, they keep their Sachael abilities. The Nomen submerge under Procyon. It is the smallest, weakest moon, but it's enough."

I screwed my face up at the mention of the Nomen. Not because of what they were, but because of the way they were treated.

"Estelle, if you saw the Nomen, you would change your opinion about them."

"Why? Do they look different to other Sachaels? Do they have three heads or something equally shocking?" I pulled up the zipper on my jeans and stepped toward him.

Chanon ignored my sarcasm. "On your land, I suspect they would be the people who didn't fit in with society through either bad health or low intelligence."

I tilted my head to the side. "Really? But that's wrong. They need to be helped, not persecuted. You do realize that our mother would be classed as a Nomen under that criteria?"

Chanon frowned at me. "Why?"

"She isn't well." I pulled a chair out from under the table and sank onto it. "She's suffered with depression ever since our father died. She isn't capable of looking after herself when she gets ill."

"So, who is looking after her now?" He stopped the random tapping of his fingers.

"She's in a care home." I said, suddenly thrown into a swirl of guilt about having left her. I missed her, more than I thought I ever would. I'd lost track of when I last saw her, but it was months now, not weeks. It was before Orontes caught me. I sighed and closed my eyes.

Chanon didn't speak for a few seconds, but when he did his voice was soft, tentative. He placed his hand on my shoulder and leaned forward.

"I'd like the chance to be able to get to know her. I know Kaimi's not totally convinced that we're related, but I am. The more I get to know you, the more things make sense. I can't really explain it. I just know. It's strange, I've lived for twenty-five years not knowing who I was, or where I belonged."

"You are the son of a Nomen," I said, hoping he may see them in a different light if he made the comparison to our mother.

He remained serious. "I fear that if Kaimi had his way, he would kill them all. He barely manages to tolerate them as it is."

I shook my head. I didn't agree with the way they were treated, and I doubted I would even after I'd seen them. Maybe I could change Kaimi's opinion about them. I didn't voice my thought to Chanon, though; I kept quiet, reserving judgment until I had seen what they were like—just in case.

"So, which moon will I submerge under when I've completed all seven?" I said, rising from the chair and turning the conversation back to the submergences

Chanon immediately responded, jumping off the table as he did so: "Sirius. I have no doubt that Kaimi will insist you submerge under Sirius with him and Azariah."

I sighed heavily. That would only happen if Azariah returned. We'd gone full circle.

"I'd better freshen up," I said as I headed into the bathroom. The urge to cry had suddenly come over me.

"Estelle," Chanon called just before I closed the door. "We will find Azariah. He will return to Saicean. He will be back in your arms."

"I hope so. I really do." I closed the door and leaned against it, waiting for my tears to come. They didn't. I couldn't cry anymore.

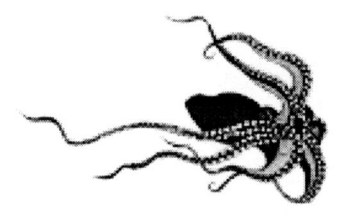

TWENTY
Waiting

"So, which is moon we are submerging under?" I said as we stepped outside. I stopped, stunned once again by the beauty before me. Everything was covered by a green shimmer. The leaves on the plants were bright, not dark, jewel-like and emerald, almost glowing. Every surface, every part of this world was glowing.

"Canopus," Chanon replied, smiling and nudging my shoulder as he nodded at the moons above us.

I glanced upward, seeing the brightest and largest moon in the sky. It dwarfed the others, and shone with a green haze.

"It's beautiful," I said, unable to take my eyes off it as Chanon led me to the lake.

"Wait until you see the others." Chanon grinned. "My favorite is Capella. She brightens the world even more. The yellow of the flowers is like the sun on land when she is full." He pointed to a thin crescent in the sky above us. Capella was only just visible, but I could still see its glow.

"A yellow moon?" I asked, picking up on his thinking. "I think it's really sweet, by the way, how you view all the moons as female."

Chanon shrugged his shoulders. "I've always thought of the moons as female, all of us do." His gaze drifted off into the distance, and I walked silently beside him. I had only ever done my submergence by myself, with my father, or Azariah. I recalled Azariah saying he did his submergences in Saicean while naked, that everyone did, and I glanced nervously over at Chanon. He didn't seem like he was preparing to remove his shorts, but we all had different ways of preparing for the ritual. I had no idea what Chanon's was, and so kept quiet, leaving him to concentrate.

As soon as my feet touched the water, a warmth radiated throughout my body. Each and every time I made the connection, I came alive in a way that only the water could make me. My body relaxed, my mind cleared. I kept walking into the welcoming water. I was home.

When it was up to my chest, I stopped. Chanon was next to me, looking around, his eyes darting to the shore in first one place, and then another. I became aware of the complete silence. It was a strange, unnerving quietness and reminded me once again of Azariah's love for the constant noise and movement of air on land. I glanced at Chanon, who immediately dipped his head toward me.

"Are you ready?" he asked, standing a few feet away, facing me.

"Well, it would have been easier to take our clothes off when out of the water," I said, as I prepared to lift my top over my head.

"Stop! Estelle, why are you taking your clothes off?"

"Azariah told me it's what you do when you do your submergences in Saicean."

Chanon grinned. "And you believed him?"

"He . . . shit." I had fallen for Azariah's teasing words.

"You two gave me endless problems that night." A smiled tugged at the corner of his mouth.

"I'm sorry," I said, managing a grin even though I was embarrassed Chanon had seen more of me that night than I ever intended, and that I had been prepared to strip in front of him a few seconds ago.

That night seemed so far in the past, when it had only been four days. It felt like Azariah had been gone for months.

"I miss him so much, Chanon. I'm scared we may not see him again."

"We will. You must believe he is still alive." He paused, swallowing loudly. "We all miss him."

I was lost without him. I deliberated over the coming days and the possibility of seeing Orontes again. I had no desire to be anywhere near him, but I wasn't frightened of anything he could do to me. My worry was for Azariah, for what Orontes may have done and would do to him.

"Come on, Estelle," Chanon said, lifting his chin. "Let's complete the ritual."

I looked to the moon above us. It was on the night of a full moon that I'd first met Azariah and my life changed. It reminded me of what we had discovered, and how much we still had to experience together.

"Estelle, are you ready?"

"I'm ready," I stated. And I was. This submergence was the first of seven that would make me stronger and faster in the water.

I was more than ready to embrace its powers.

Once Chanon and I had completed our submergences, we returned to Azariah's room. Chanon insisted I sleep, yet again, promising me he would do the same.

When we awoke, a tray of food was positioned on the table at the side of the room. I questioned Chanon on the things we were eating. It surprised me to learn that I was eating shark and lionfish. Apparently, the lionfish were considered something of a delicacy.

A loud knock on the door had Chanon jumping to his feet. He left his half-finished meal and went to investigate. Only opening the door for a small gap, he peeked outside, then quickly opened it fully and bowed. I immediately stood, surmising that Kaimi was the person outside.

"May I come in?" I was right, it was Kaimi.

Chanon stepped back, allowing the space for him to enter.

"Ahhh, Estelle." Kaimi smiled at me, and I immediately curtseyed. He stepped toward me, looking at the food on the table. "I interrupted your meal."

"It's fine," I said. "We'd nearly finished."

He raised his brow. "Good, because you and I are going for a walk." He adjusted the cloak that hung in a curtain of red down his back.

"You need to see Saicean, not just these four walls. You must be bored; Chanon's not the most talkative of men." He cast Chanon a friendly smirk.

"We have a lot to talk about," I replied. "A lot of catching up to do."

Kaimi nodded, pondering my words. "And he shall be here when you come back." He walked past me and studied the dresses that were hanging up, still on their hangers on the wall, and then turned to face me. "I see you still have not changed out of those clothes."

"I needed to wear them when I did my submergence last night. I don't want to ruin the dresses."

Kaimi's eyes widened, and then he nodded. "I shall have the Oceanids make you something suitable for your submergences. . . . Then will you destroy what you are wearing?"

I nodded. "Yes, and I'll wear the red dress when I meet Hebrus."

"Good, good." Another smile graced his face.

"Have you heard anything yet?" I asked. "Is he on his way?"

He shook his head and looked away. "I've heard nothing."

"But he will come?"

Kaimi puffed his chest out. "Yes. He will come."

I glanced at Chanon, who had remained near the door since Kaimi entered. He wasn't watching Kaimi; he was glancing into the corridor outside.

"Come, Estelle," Kaimi said. "Let me show you what a wonderful place Saicean is." He held his hand out to me, waiting for me to move. It wasn't a request, it was an order.

"Chanon, be here when we return," he said as we passed him.

"Yes, Kaimi."

When the door closed behind us, Kaimi placed his hand on the small of my back, guiding me through the maze of corridors and into the open space of Saicean.

"Chanon tells me you are eager to see how the factors live. How everything works here."

I nodded half-heartedly, not in the least bit enthusiastic about my impending tour.

"Where would you like to start? Shall we wander to the lake, and walk around it? It will give us a good view of each sector as we pass through."

"This really isn't necessary," I protested.

"Of course it is. And what better way for you to see it than with me?"

I glanced at his face, trying to decipher whether he was serious or not. I deduced from the hard, set line of his mouth, partly hidden behind his whiskers, that he was.

He walked forward, and I trotted to catch up with his large strides as he headed through the gardens to the lake. As he passed a few Oceanids tending to plants, he greeted them with "Good morning," resulting in a duo of giggles in response. He walked a few steps past them before turning and shooting them a mischievous grin. Catching me watching him, he smiled, and then carried on walking.

As he approached the lake, he spun to face me.

"Come along. We have lots to see." He gestured with a wave of his arm for me to catch up.

We took a turn to the right, following the lakeside path as it twisted along the water's edge. Silence surrounded us. It was different to being on land. Here, no insects flew in the air; there was no breeze, no sound of running water. The lake didn't even ripple. Looking to the moons, I puzzled at their existence. My logical mind argued that Saicean could exist, an air bubble trapped deep in the ocean, but the moons? I had no idea why they were in the dark blue void above, or how they got there.

"Why don't the moons make the water move?" I asked, thinking of the way the moon affected the tides on land.

"Make it move? In what way?" Kaimi swished his cloak as he walked.

"Depending on where the moon is in the sky, it affects the edge of the ocean. The moon pulls the ocean toward it—a gravitational pull. High tide, low tide. The phase of the moon dictates the difference between the two extremes."

"Are you talking of the moon in the sky above land?"

I nodded.

"Ah, but there is only one moon above land. Here, we have seven."

"That should make it pull the edge of the water even more," I reasoned.

"What, this tiny lake? I don't think so."

I turned to the lake. It wasn't small. It would easily take a good hour to walk around the shore.

Kaimi waved his arm in the direction of the water. "And have you ever considered that the positions of our moons may mean they cancel each other's gravitational pull? That is, if these moons have such a thing."

I frowned, thinking through what he said.

"I tend to view them as lights which illuminate our world," he explained. "Although Procyon's glow is hardly enough to light anything."

"Procyon. Which factor submerges under that moon?" Chanon had told me, but I struggled to recall all the factors and the different moons they submerged under.

"The Nomen." Kaimi practically growled the word.

Right. The Nomen.

"So, you give the weakest moon to the Sachaels who need the most strength. It's not right."

"Why? You think my guards, the men who protect our land, should submerge under it?" He turned to face me. He wasn't quite as tall as Azariah, but his pose was intimidating. With arms folded, he glared at me.

"Well . . . no."

"Then do not question it." His sharp tone halted any response I might have made. I stared at the ground, quiet. Why had he insisted I take this tour with him? If it was to try and make me forget about Azariah, he was mistaken. This was something Azariah and I should have done together. All Kaimi was doing was reminding me that he wasn't here to do so. He continued his walk, twirling his cape like I imagined villains did in the books my father read to me when I was young. I still hadn't figured out whether Kaimi fit that role or not.

He took a few steps and then stopped, waiting for me. I didn't look up. I was contemplating whether or not to go back to Azariah's room. Azariah could show me around when he returned. Doubt crept through my thoughts again, and I chewed my lip, desperately wanting Hebrus to arrive. He was the only one who could help. He was the one person we were waiting for, and I hated that we had no control over when that would be . . . if at all. I dropped my shoulders and moved my foot back and forth across the sand on the path. This should all be happening with Azariah at my side, not Kaimi.

Gentle fingers lifted my chin, and I found myself gazing into Kaimi's eyes. He sighed. "I apologize. I had no intention of upsetting you."

"I'm not . . ."

"You are."

A tear trickled down my cheek. Yesterday's apparent lack of tears was being made up for today. There were still plenty willing to escape.

"Oh, Estelle . . ."

Kaimi wrapped his arms around me, and I was pulled against his solid body. For some reason, his gesture triggered a full sniffling crying session. Large hands smoothed my hair as he spoke quietly to me. "You've had a traumatic time. Such bravery and spirit. You are strong, Estelle, but never forget we are all frightened children within. There are times when all the love in the world is not enough to protect us from ourselves."

A loud sob escaped me, and my tears wet his chest as he hugged me.

"Chanon told me your father drowned many years ago. And I know I will never replace him, but . . . well, I would be honored if you would view me as a father figure. Someone you could talk to if you needed advice. A friendly ear to listen to your concerns. I am not a monster, although some of my men may disagree." He chuckled softly. "I'd like to keep it that way. So, if you ever need to see me about anything, please do not hesitate to find me, but ensure we are away from listening ears."

I sniffed loudly, stepping back from his hold. Could I ever view Kaimi as a father figure? I doubted it. "Thank you. But I'm not sure I could come to you with any problems between Azariah and me. It wouldn't seem right," I said, wiping my tears away with the back of my hand.

Kaimi chuckled again, a sound that reminded me so much of Azariah's infectious laugh. "I am the perfect person to talk to if you have problems with Azariah. I understand him more than he understands himself." He studied me as he talked, his eyes unblinking, his focus completely on me. "He is stubborn, and it causes most of his problems. He wears his heart on the outside of his body, unlike you."

I frowned at his comment. "Unlike me?"

"Yes. You keep your heart locked up, and you are full of secrets. Azariah has none. He is a . . . what is the phrase? Ah, an open book. He is an open book." Kaimi's mischievous grin twitched his whiskers. I kept my expression neutral, but looked away. Azariah wasn't an open book. He had kept things from me, important things, things like Kaimi being the King of Saicean. It was hardly something he'd just forgot—no, he had purposely led me astray, told me half-truths. It seemed his father didn't see that side of him.

"Come, we have lots to see," Kaimi said, brushing his hand up and down the top of my arm. "But, please remember, my offer is open ended. If you ever need to speak to me, regarding anything—not just Azariah—I will be here for you."

"Thanks," I offered again, although I suspected that if I had anything to ask, I would speak to Chanon first. I'd only known him a short time, but we were already close. I knew I could talk to him about anything. It would take a while before I felt the same with Kaimi.

"So, what do you think of Saicean?" Kaimi asked, puffing his chest out and looking at the path in front of us. "Are you impressed?" His eyes twinkled mischievously as he stepped forward, leading the way yet again.

"I've not seen much of it yet. When Azariah described it, he never mentioned how big it was. I imagined somewhere smaller," I said, following him along the narrow path.

"Smaller? If it were any smaller, we would not fit all the people in."

"How many live here?" I asked, matching his stride as I caught up with him.

"I have exact figures in my books. But, as far as I can remember, there are just over five hundred, including the Oceanid women." He stroked his beard before tapping his chin. "There are approximately a hundred and fifty serving members of the army. That number includes hunters, guards, and messengers. We have twenty-three Intelligents, though thirteen are living on land at various phases of their time away from us. The Intelligents spend seven years away, living on land. They find jobs, and research anything that would be of use to us here. They bring back items we need."

"Such as?" I stopped myself from snorting at the use of the number seven. It was crazy how many things revolved around it.

"Seeds, books, fabrics, metals, and sometimes jewels. Our doctors spend time learning medicine. Some take exams, some come back and ask to return immediately because they are involved in research or something which will be of benefit to us. I am quite strict with them though. Sometimes, the Intelligents get wild ideas about what we can do here." He indicated for me to walk ahead of him with a sweep of his arm toward a narrow part of the path. "Their life on land makes them forget we are restricted. I need them to stay here to look after us when we are sick, and their knowledge needs to be passed on to others. The teachers, the ones who instruct the youngsters, very rarely go to land. They see their job as nurturing and educating future generations. I insist they stay. It's the ones who have a thirst for knowledge, an ability to stretch themselves in a foreign land and bring the benefits back to us, that I allow to go."

"Do they always come back?" I was curious about the Sachaels that left here. They would have a sudden freedom to do whatever they wanted when on land, whereas everyone else sounded as trapped as I would be, awaiting Kaimi's permission to leave. It seemed I wasn't the only one who didn't want to stay here forever.

"Not always. It is a risk with the Intelligents. They fall in love with the job they find, or begin relationships with human females. Seven years is a long time to be in a relationship and just end it. I understand, but I don't like losing them."

"Surely they don't all have relationships," I said, pushing my hair away from my face. "Some of them must remain single."

Kaimi raised his brow. "We are sexual men, Estelle. I am sure Azariah has shown you the love of a Sachael. It is intense, is it not?"

I turned away, sure my heated cheeks gave Kaimi the answer he was looking for.

"We need women in our lives. So of course they all have relationships. I would be horrified if they remained single. It does them no good."

Thankfully, Kaimi continued walking, striding across a small stream which trickled silently into the lake. He turned around and held his arm out, waiting for me to take his hand as I crossed the stream. I brightened at the small gesture, warmed by seeing the chivalrous side of him. He immediately reminded me of Azariah.

"I think it will be easier to explain each section of Saicean as we get to it. Right now, we are entering one of the sectors the guards live in. They live in various sections around Saicean. For instance, there is a barrier of guards on either side of the royal gardens. Those areas house the guards that protect me and my family—my top men. Their families are allowed to live with them as well. There are about . . ."—he started counting a whispered breath of numbers—"twenty-six guards, plus their families."

"When you say 'families,' what do you mean?"

"Their Oceanid wives, and their children. Of course, not all guards have wives." He chattered freely as we walked. He didn't seem to be hiding information. In fact, he seemed proud of the world we were walking through.

I stopped walking as his statement sank in. He'd said children, not child. "Don't they only have one son?"

"Some have a few sons," he said, walking ahead.

"But I thought you were only allowed to go to land once—on your twenty-first birthday."

He stopped, paused, and then turned before closing the gap between us. "Estelle, I can go as often as I like. I presume you exclude royalty from your statement?"

I nodded.

"That is the case for most of the men, but these men, the royal protectors, are granted the opportunity to travel to land as a reward. If they do something to please me, then I will let them father another son. They are the guards I have the most to do with, so they are the most rewarded. Haemon has six sons. I think he is aiming for seven."

I was prepared to argue with Kaimi, tell him how cruel it was, disagree with the reward he gave them. But his cheeky grin appeared as he mentioned Haemon and his desire for a seventh son. However much I hated the way they existed, I understood it.

"But most of the other guards only have the one son?"

"Yes."

Our conversation was interrupted as a group of four young boys ran to us.

"Kaimi, Kaimi!" they shouted, surrounding him and pulling on his cloak.

"Now then, you little pests, what is this excitement for?" He ruffled the hair of the boy nearest to him. "Shouldn't you be in school, Zotikos?"

"Dad said I could stay at home today."

"Did he now?" Kaimi chuckled.

The smallest boy, perhaps only four years old, insistently tugged Kaimi's cloak. "Who is your pretty lady?"

"My pretty lady?" Kaimi scooped the boy up in his arms. "She is not my pretty lady. She is Azariah's," he stage-whispered in the boy's ear.

The boy turned to Kaimi, cupped his hands between his mouth and Kaimi's ear, and whispered something to him. Whereas I'd heard Kaimi's whisper, I didn't hear what the boy replied.

"Yes." Kaimi laughed. "Yes, that would be a very nice idea."

"My mum likes weddings," the boy shouted excitedly.

"Everyone likes weddings."

The small boy caught my gaze. "Will you marry Azariah?"

Every set of eyes focused on me, waited for me to say something. It didn't matter that Kaimi was the only adult, the boys' stares were just as intense. Thankfully, Kaimi saved me.

"You can't ask a lady outright if she is going to marry someone. She has to be asked. What if she told you she would marry Azariah, and then he never asked her?"

Kaimi laughed again, placing the small boy on the ground.

"Now scram, the lot of you. I have grown-up things to discuss with the pretty lady."

They dutifully skipped away, excitable voices disappearing into the trees and bushes. Kaimi took my hand before nodding forward. I took his gesture to mean that the tour was to continue. "I apologize for their enthusiasm and impertinent questions regarding your love life."

"It's okay. I liked seeing them. It never truly crossed my mind that there would be children here."

"Really?" Kaimi seemed amused.

I nodded, then frowned. How stupid of me not to envision them whenever I thought of Saicean. For some reason, it made Saicean more acceptable.

"Do you know all the children?" I asked.

"Most of them," he said, wafting his hand at a low branch that threatened to hit him in his face. "But I will admit to not remembering the names of all the guards' sons, though I definitely know the ones of those who serve me directly."

"So, how many children are in Saicean?"

Kaimi smiled. "There are roughly a hundred under the age of sixteen—a healthy number. And there are thirty-six in training—those are the ones between the ages of seventeen and twenty-one."

"Will they become guards?"

"Not necessarily. It depends what factor their father belongs to. The son is expected to follow in the same factor as his father. But if they show special skills in fighting, or something impresses the teachers, they do have the opportunity to join the army at a level suitable to their talent." Kaimi's eyes sparkled as he spoke. "The messengers are usually found this way."

"Messengers?"

"The fastest Sachaels. Speed is a gift. If you are an incredibly fast Sachael, you will become a messenger regardless of your father's factor. They live in the same sectors as the royal guards—a privileged life. I need them near. Their job is to alert other worlds to anything of any importance. And sometimes, they need to leave immediately."

I hadn't wanted to take this walk with Kaimi, but I was certainly learning a lot.

"We have crossed into the next sector. This is where the Adstrators live. There are ten of them at the moment. They are the people who care for us. They cook, clean, and entertain."

I scratched the side of my jaw, trying to work out how that was possible. "Ten men cook for the whole of Saicean?"

Kaimi laughed again. "No, Estelle. They work for *us*, for the royalty and their families. This is the only sector which welcomes unmarried Oceanid women. As well as the ten men, there are over twenty Oceanids. The sector can be increased or reduced, depending on how many of us there are. We are small at the moment. The brutal murder of my sons has depleted the royal household somewhat." He sniffed and rubbed his nose with his hand, keeping his eyes trained on the ground. The signs of his excitement had suddenly gone. He drew in a deep breath. "We only need ten men at the moment."

I nodded, silent, trying to think of something to say that could reverse his change of mood without glossing over the sadness of what he had just mentioned.

"What happens if the royal household increases in size?" I asked.

Kaimi lifted his head and smiled. "We bring more men in from the lower level of Crofters. We'll enter their sector after another for the guards." He set off walking at a faster pace than before, as if eager to leave the conversation behind us.

"So the guards live between all the sectors, not just on either side of the royal gardens?"

"Yes, although not between the Crofters and the land they farm. There is no need to have anything between them and their crops—well, except the lavender."

"I smelled the lavender as soon as I arrived," I said, lifting my nose as I was reminded of the scent. It was everywhere, constantly suspended in the air. I had become used to its potent fragrance.

"It's the one plant we grow prolifically here. It's also used in our cooking and medicines. It's a wonderfully diverse plant."

I nodded, knowing of its many medicinal benefits, but not much about its use in cooking.

As we approached the next guard factor, a group of nine men with blue bands around their arms walked into the lake. They carried nets and talked excitedly.

"Ah, I see the hunters are heading out." Kaimi nodded at them as they spotted him and dipped their heads. "Bring something nice for us to eat," he called. "We've not had a Sunfish for a long time. See if you can catch one. If not, tasty Halibut would be nice."

"A Sunfish?" I had never heard the name before.

"It's a big fish. Solitary in its movements. It's something of a delicacy." Kaimi rubbed his stomach. "You should try one."

"They swim down here? This deep?"

Kaimi chuckled. "Estelle, our hunters do not hunt in the depths we live in. They head through the chasm and into the open ocean. There would be nothing but spiky, bony fish for us to eat if they hunted this deep."

The hunters disappeared under the water, causing ripples which gradually met the shoreline. Kaimi indicated for me to walk ahead of him as the path narrowed and tree branches hung low over the water. When the path opened up again, I stopped. Before me was a blanket of lavender. The flowering purple plant ran from the edge of the water right up the sloping ground, until it reached the rock face on the edge of Saicean. I couldn't understand why I hadn't seen it when I first arrived, but maybe the canopy of trees had hidden it from my view.

"How many of these areas are there?" I asked.

"Three," Kaimi responded. "It's quite a sight, isn't it?"

"It's beautiful."

Kaimi's hand rested on my back, urging me forward.

"This is where the Crofters live. There are fewer trees here, so the ground isn't sheltered like the rest of Saicean. Our crops need as much light as possible."

I stared at the houses dotted on the sloping landscape. From here, I could see them properly, not just limited peeks of them as I'd previously seen. They were made of wood, like small log cabins—very small log cabins, with no windows. The roofs were flat, and covered in large leaves or planks of wood.

"Can you see the different types of homes?" Kaimi asked.

Narrowing my eyes, I struggled to see any distinct difference between them.

"There are a few homes I allow to raise fires. I like to limit what we send up there." He pointed upward. "One cooking home for every—"

"Let me guess, every seven homes?"

"No, for every ten."

I laughed, and Kaimi joined in, resting his arm across my shoulders. "I'd hate for us to be that predictable."

"How many crofter homes are there?"

"Currently, we have forty-three. The number will increase if our numbers do. They'll be moved from the other side of Saicean."

"There are two areas with Crofters?"

"Yes—the other area deals with different things. Whereas the crofters here make homes for everyone, and their wives cook, the others make our weapons, and utensils. Their Oceanid wives make our clothes."

I widened my eyes.

"You appear shocked. Can I ask why?"

"It's so well organized. I don't know what I was expecting, but it's thought out really well."

"I like to keep things organized. It's not always been this way. But, when I came to rule, I made sure every Sachael understood which factor he belonged to, and what my expectations were of him." He shook his head and huffed. "The lines were somewhat vague when my father ruled. He was not the most organized of rulers."

Another sector of guard's homes was next on my tour. We passed through practically unnoticed, but anyone who saw Kaimi showed their respect, dipping their heads if they were Sachael's, curtsying if they were Oceanids.

I couldn't hide my surprise at what I was seeing. Saicean was a well organized world. The men looked after each other, and all the ones I'd seen so far today seemed cheerful and happy. I relaxed as Kaimi chatted and began to survey this new, beautiful world with a growing fondness.

But I was stunned at what greeted me next.

"The Nomen," Kaimi announced dismissively.

The land before me was muddy, not lush and green. There were only a few trees dotted around the barren ground. The homes were nothing but ramshackle huts—not built to the same standard as the others I'd seen. I stopped walking, taking in the pitiful state of the land before me.

"We leave them to look after themselves," Kaimi said.

"They don't get any help at all?"

"No. They're a drain on our land. I see no reason for us to give them anything when they don't give anything back. Every other Sachael has his place in Saicean—providing, cooking, hunting, building, something, anything. These idiots do nothing. They are lucky I tolerate them as I do."

A man poked his head out from behind one of the wooden constructions—I couldn't call them homes; they looked like sheds.

I smiled at him, offering a friendly face. His toothy grin showed in return, the brightness in direct contrast to his dirty face.

"You. Come here!" Kaimi had also seen him.

The man disappeared from view, and I stepped away from Kaimi as he placed his hand over his pocket.

"I said, come here. Show yourself, or I shall come in there and find you."

There were a few moments of silence, a wait I dared to not breathe through.

The man crept from his hiding place before limping toward us. His left leg offered limited support and was bandaged with filthy rags. I was shocked by his appearance. He wasn't dressed like the other Sachaels. In fact, the dirty cloth wrapped around his lower body was hanging loose. It didn't cover what it was intended for and left nothing to the imagination. I concentrated on his face, and not on the involuntary flashes he was giving.

"Filth!" Kaimi roared at him. "How dare you approach me looking like that?" He drew his knife from his pocket. The man cowered, shielding his head as he sank to the floor. The branch supporting him fell away.

"No." I grabbed Kaimi's arm. "You can't kill him. You asked him to come to us. He's doing what you said."

"Get up!" Kaimi shouted, ignoring my feeble attempt to pull him away. "Get up. Get up!"

"Kaimi, please," I begged.

"Please, spare me, sir," the man begged, crawling to Kaimi's feet.

The disturbance alerted others. Other Nomen crept cautiously toward us. They were unarmed, shuffling forward, eyes on the man who remained on the ground. They were dressed in a similar state of rags, although many of them wore nothing at all. From where I stood, I caught sight of a woman running from one of the more decent-looking huts and across into the guard area. An Oceanid, here, with the Nomen?

"He's done nothing wrong," I insisted, relaxing my hold on Kaimi's arm. I hoped I was appealing to Kaimi's compassionate side. I knew he had one—I'd seen it earlier with the children.

He slipped his knife back into his pocket and huffed at the man still at his feet.

"Leave him be!" A loud, clear voice shouted.

Both Kaimi and I looked toward where the voice came from. Strolling from the hut I'd seen the Oceanid sneak from was a tall man. His hair was unkempt, curly and long, and he had a small beard under his chin that was woven into two plaits. He was dressed like the Sachaels I was used to seeing. He wasn't dirty like the others, and walked proudly toward us, never taking his eyes off Kaimi. It wasn't his clothes that drew my attention, though, it was his body. With a wide chest and taut muscles, he looked like any other Sachael. But there was one significant difference. He had no hands. Both his arms stopped just below his elbows.

I was sure Kaimi growled.

"To what do we owe the honor of your visit?" The man asked, bowing to Kaimi before glancing at me. I smiled at him, instantly warming to his demeanor and friendly approach. He was a handsome man. I guessed he was about my age.

"Gennadios." Kaimi scowled as he said his name.

The man cocked his head to the side. A ringed piercing in one of his eyebrows caught the glow from one of the moons, and a smile graced his lips as he waited for Kaimi's answer.

"You need to control these men," Kaimi sneered. "Or I shall take great pleasure in killing all of you."

"Even me?"

Kaimi lifted his chin, looking him straight in the eyes. "Even you."

Gennadios raised his brows before a slight smirk pulled at the corner of his mouth. He turned to look at me. "Is our great leader showing you around his land?"

"Yes. He was most insistent I see all of Saicean."

Gennadios laughed, the numerous hooped earrings he wore jangling against each other, and shot Kaimi an incredulous glance. "I should think he would want to rush past this part of Saciean. No point in upsetting anyone with the freaks, is there, Kaimi?"

Kaimi scowled, but didn't reply.

I was confused, but also intrigued by the way they interacted. Gennadios seemed to taunt Kaimi; he had no fear of him.

"I won't keep warning you, Gennadios. I only just tolerate you. Do not push your luck, or you may find yourself a permanent resident in the prison."

Gennadios grinned before bowing to Kaimi again. "As you wish, oh great leader. Always as you wish."

Taking my hand, Kaimi steered me away from Gennadios and the other Nomen.

"What . . . who . . . what was that about? Why is he dressed differently from the others? You knew his name."

"I told you earlier, I know the names of all the Sachaels here. That includes the Nomen."

"Is Gennadios their leader?"

Kaimi stopped. Turning to me, he took a deep breath. "No, he is not their leader. I am the only leader in Saicean. Gennadios likes to control the Nomen, as he has no place of worth anywhere else. You saw him—he cannot hunt without arms. He can't even swim."

I couldn't resist a glance back at them, and was surprised by what I saw. The man who had been at Kaimi's feet was standing, blowing me a kiss. Other Nomen waved, and as I focused on Gennadios, he smiled.

"Come back soon!" he shouted, which only made Kaimi drag me away quicker.

"He seems nice. You shouldn't punish him because he's disabled."

"Really? Maybe I should have left him in the ocean to die, rather than let him live in Saicean." He glanced at Gennadios, as did I. "I'm not punishing him, Estelle. I saved him."

He set off at an alarming pace. Something had changed, altered his demeanor.

"Ah, normality," he announced as we passed through another sector for the guards. The second set of Crofters was next, and then another section of guards.

"The Intelligents," Kaimi stated, gesturing to the land at the side. "I told you about them earlier. No need to repeat myself."

His stride had definitely lengthened and quickened. I struggled to keep up with him.

"More guards," he said, not pausing as we passed through their area. "The last three now. This area is where the schools are, where Zotikos should be. Next are the training grounds where the seventeen to twenty-one year olds spend most of their time. They learn to fight here, but much of their training takes place outside of Saicean, in the water. This is their training site on land, where they can spar with each other if the need arises. It's monitored at all times."

We fell into a contemplative silence as we passed through the last guard sector.

"Have you enjoyed your tour?" Kaimi asked finally.

"It's been interesting," I said. It was the truth. I'd discovered a lot, and I was curious about Gennadios. Something seemed weird about Kaimi's scathing words and abrupt departure. Why did he save him from the ocean if he hated him so much?

As we walked through the gradual sloping gardens and up to the entrance to the royal rooms, my head would not clear of the imagery of the Nomen. Their appearances had shocked me, as had their helplessness and the conditions they lived in.

"You are very quiet," Kaimi announced as we reached Azariah's room.

"I'm thinking," I responded, not turning to look at him.

"Well, I shall leave you to your thoughts then." He knocked lightly on the door before opening it for me. "Here she is. Safe, and returned in one piece. Now, I must find Ianira. I need to talk to her."

"Thank you," I said, appreciating the time he'd spent with me.

"Anytime, Estelle. And remember what I said." He leaned forward and planted a kiss on my forehead. "I'm here, if you need to talk."

He nodded at Chanon, and then left. The door closed quietly behind him.

Chanon shot me an inquisitive look as he sat down into a chair at the table, an open book before him. "Learn anything?" he asked.

"Lots," I replied, wandering over to him and glancing at what he was reading. "Who's Gennadios?"

"You met him then?" Chanon closed the book and twisted in his chair to face me.

"Yes. It was weird. Kaimi really doesn't like him, but he seemed okay."

Chanon chuckled. "Kaimi hates him. I think it's because he sees him as a weak man, incapable of doing anything. He doesn't like to see any Sachael as weak, and that is, unfortunately, how he sees Gennadios."

"What about you?" Did my brother have the same bigoted view about him?

"I get on with him okay, so does Azariah."

I breathed a sigh of relief. Neither Chanon nor Azariah viewed him any differently to others.

A smile graced Chanon's face. "Azariah and I used to swim with him when we were younger, but Kaimi put a stop to it. Apparently, it wasn't fitting for a future ruler to be seen swimming with him. He was a good swimmer too. He had a really fast maneuver that he did, basically used his head as a battering ram. Got me in the stomach once. It really hurt."

I giggled at Chanon's story.

"He's a nice man, but Kaimi only sees what he wants to. And even though Azariah's swims with him were stopped, he still regularly visits him."

"So Azariah goes to see the Nomen?"

Chanon shook his head and screwed his nose up. "No, he doesn't visit the Nomen. He goes to see Gennadios."

My giggles turned to silence. So, the Nomen in general were still seen as outcasts, worthless, but not Gennadios. I wondered why.

"Did you see anything else?" Chanon asked as he disappeared into the bathroom. The sound of running water followed a few seconds later. The sweet, pungent smell of lavender drifted my way. He was filling the tub for me.

"Lots," I repeated, still mulling over Gennadios and Kaimi's strange interaction.

He popped his head around the door. "Well, have a soak and relax. I'm sure Kaimi gave you plenty to think about."

I nodded. The tour around Saicean had been an eye-opener for many reasons. Kaimi had left me with lots of unanswered questions, more curiosity, and a distinctly good impression on how well this world was organized. Unfortunately, the unanswered questions were the ones I always concentrated on.

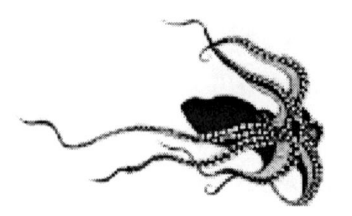

TWENTY - ONE
Visitors

My following days were spent with Chanon. I continued to learn more about Saicean and the people within it. He told me of the large area the Sachaels covered when traveling to land—England wasn't the only country they visited. Scotland, Ireland, France, The Netherlands, Spain, and even the eastern coast of America were all frequented.

I wasn't eating in my room with Chanon anymore in the evening, either. Instead, I was summoned to eat with Kaimi and Ianira. Meal times were spent with Kaimi telling me of the many battles his army had won, and how proud he was of his people. I nodded in what I imagined to be the right places, spoke when I was invited to speak, but I never offered my opinions. Not now. I felt I'd overstepped my position when I first arrived in Saicean. I wanted to fit in, not stand out, and I surmised that the best way to do that was to keep as quiet as possible. I often had no appetite, and pushed food around my plate while I listened to the others chatter around me. I was becoming increasingly worried about Azariah.

Every time there was a knock at the door of Azariah's room, my heartbeat quickened, and I became alert, hopeful that there was some news. There never was.

I submerged again, with my brother by my side, on the full moon of Rigel, and again, four days later, when Arcturus was at its complete fullness. Chanon always asked me if I felt any different, any stronger after my submergences. I could only offer him a smile and nod where I thought I should, uncommitted with my response. The truth was that I had no idea if the submergences were making me feel any different. All I felt was fear, a rising panic that threatened to consume me if I let it. I was used to the sound of my heart pumping loudly now, it was the background to my everyday life. Even when I sat in Kaimi's Hall, listening to the musicians as they played their instruments, I could still hear the constant drum of my heart. It ached, heavy with the loss of the other heart that made it spring alive. I was pining, lost in a strange world and without Azariah.

I'd stepped back in time, to a world where men ruled by force and fear. I'd witnessed Kaimi fly into a rage when two of his guards started a fight in his Hall. I'd seen Oceanids flee from view when Chanon and I walked to the lake to complete my submergences. And I still remembered the fear in Xanthe's eyes when she was brought before Kaimi.

And all the time I worried, stressed over the safe return of Azariah, I planned. I had to organize my future, and I had to face the unwanted possibility that Azariah may not return. I hoped that he would be back with me, and soon, but I also had to plan in case it never happened. I wasn't prepared to stay here, not without Azariah.

I needed to complete my rituals, submerge under the remaining four full moons I had yet to see. I would then be a full Sachael. And that was when I'd leave. I was still working on exactly how I would do it, but when the time came, I would not let anyone stop me. This quiet, morose, and feeble female Sachael would roar like never before. No one, not even Kaimi, would stop me from leaving.

"Kaimi has asked for our presence in the Hall." Chanon stood before me, concern settling in his eyes like it did every time he looked at me.

He gestured toward the red dress still hanging against the wall.

I turned slowly, not trusting, not believing that the moment had finally come.

"Does that mean . . . ?" My words failed as I waited for him to answer.

He grinned and nodded. "Yes, it means that Hebrus is here."

I jumped up from my chair and threw myself at Chanon. Laughter that I thought would never return escaped as he turned in a circle with me. Tears of happiness pricked at my eyes before running onto his shoulder.

"You need to get dressed, quickly. Let's not keep him waiting," he said as he lowered me onto my feet.

I rushed to the dress and grabbed it before heading into the bathroom to change.

"Call me if you need any help!" Chanon shouted.

I shut the door and leaned against it, breathing hard and fast. This was it. Hebrus was here. Now, all I had to do was persuade him to help us save Azariah.

I looked down at the dress I held and ran my fingers over the softness of the fabric—it was like silk. Gold threads were twisted through the dark red material. The dress was gorgeous. There were no mirrors in Saicean, and I couldn't check my reflection. So as I opened the door back to the bedroom, I stood still, waiting for Chanon to approve, or not.

"Estelle . . ." His mouth dropped open. "You look beautiful."

I smiled. Chanon's opinion mattered. I hoped Hebrus agreed with him.

"Here," he said, gesturing for me to walk toward him. He pulled the band out of my high ponytail and rearranged my loose curls. "That's better."

I let him fuss, even though I wasn't used to it. He pushed the ornate, gold-embroidered shoulder straps further away from my neck and smoothed the fabric of the skirt with his hands. "Stand tall, Estelle," he said. "Do not let Hebrus or Kaimi intimidate you. But most of all, just be yourself. Be the woman you were when you first arrived here—the one fighting for what she believed in. Don't be the weak, nodding, broken person you've let yourself become over the past week. Find the true Estelle; find your fighting spirit. It's the person I want to see, and it's the one Hebrus needs to see."

I nodded, taking a shuddering breath. I knew he'd noticed; I knew they'd all noticed. But he was right. I had to snap out of my current state and believe, just believe, that this was the start of Azariah returning. Things would work. They had to.

As we headed into the corridor, I struggled to focus on where I was going, the garish colors of the walls disoriented me. The flames on the candles burned like always, but as I passed, they danced higher, brighter, as if sensing my mood. My hands itched, needing something to do. I fiddled with my hair, twirling it in my fingers several times.

"I'm so nervous," I said.

Chanon took my hand and offered a smile. "You'll be fine. Just remember what I said. Be yourself."

Any hope that Hebrus and Kaimi may have forgiven each other, or even mellowed in the four years since their fall out, was dashed when loud shouting came from the hall.

Chanon raised one brow as he turned to me. "Wait here. Let me announce you."

He pushed the door open, and the shouting immediately stopped as he spoke. "Kaimi, Estelle is ready to meet your guest."

"I didn't come as a guest of Kaimi's."

I presumed the deep, booming voice belonged to Hebrus.

"I came to meet a female Sachael. Xanthe was most insistent I come to see her. If this is another of your tricks, Kaimi, I will be seriously angered by your actions."

I swallowed, nervously taking a deep breath before entering the hall.

There were four guards standing behind Kaimi—their black bands twisted with gold signified that they were his personal guards. A huge man, far taller than Kaimi, stood next to him. He wore a red length of fabric wrapped around his lower body and twisted across one shoulder. I momentarily contemplated if that was why Ianira had sent a red dress for me to wear. He was surrounded by another eight men, dressed similarly, but in black robes. All of them, apart from the tall man, turned to face me when I entered the room—their eyes lingered far longer than was necessary.

Kaimi held his hand out to me, beckoning me to him. His smile was the widest I had ever seen. His round cheeks were puffed with color; he looked like he was going to burst.

As I walked toward him, I felt the gazes of the other men in the room. It was as if time stopped, like in a movie, a fairy tale entrance by the princess in the story. I knew I wasn't a princess, but at that moment, I felt like one.

Kaimi leaned forward, his whiskers scratching my cheek. "You look stunning, Estelle," he whispered. He gently rested his hand on the small of my back and turned me to face the eager men in the Hall.

Hebrus also turned, slowly. It was as if he was the last person to be aware of my arrival. His eyes scanned my body as I returned his scrutiny. He surveyed me in exactly the same way Orontes had. The familiar coldness flooded through me as I was unintentionally reminded of him. Hebrus was as tall as Orontes, but any similarity ended there. He didn't have long, flowing blond hair—he had no hair at all. His head was either shaved, or he was completely bald. He wasn't as dark skinned as the Sachael's, but his whole being exuded a certain mystic, a power which penetrated through me as his green eyes locked with mine.

Kaimi was quickly at his side.

"This is Estelle. She is—"

"I know. I know exactly what she is. I can sense it in every cell of my body." He kept his distance from me, several steps away. I tried to guess whether he was older than Kaimi. His appearance led me to believe he was younger.

Realizing I was staring, I quickly began to speak. "Thank you for coming to see me," I offered, my nervousness causing my voice to quiver.

Hebrus ignored my welcome and spoke to Kaimi. "Well, well, well, Kaimi. I was told the person who summoned me was a female Sachael, but I honestly did not believe it. And yet, here she is."

I held my tongue. I was desperate to talk to him, to appeal straight away for information, but he appeared intent on only speaking to Kaimi. I needed to be careful how I reacted. One wrong word could ruin everything.

"How long have you kept her hidden from me?" Hebrus asked.

"I had the pleasure of meeting Estelle two weeks ago. Although I have known of her existence for over a month."

Hebrus overcame his initial shock at my appearance and slowly circled where I stood. I remained still, not speaking, and not enjoying Hebrus's intense perusal of me. When he had completed his prowl, he stopped directly in front of me and placed his hand against my cheek.

"Oh, she's warm!" he exclaimed. "I have never appreciated the attraction our females have to your kind, Kaimi, but being a male, and presented with such a gorgeous specimen, I'm wondering how my men are managing to control themselves." He gazed at his men, the ones in the black robes. I didn't turn to them—I could feel each and every set of eyes upon me. "The attraction is intense. Her warmth permeates my skin."

Kaimi huffed loudly before walking toward us—to save me, I hoped. "Estelle is already spoken for."

"You have claimed her?" Hebrus turned to Kaimi.

"No. My son has." He narrowed his eyes at Hebrus before crossing his arms.

"Azariah?"

Kaimi nodded.

"Where is he then? I would have expected Azariah not to let her out of his sight. He was always protective of his women, wasn't he, Kaimi?"

"He was, and he still is." Kaimi let his arms drop to his sides, but I still saw the edge of mistrust in his eyes.

"And I should have known you would never dishonor Ianira by taking another lover. My apologies."

"Your apologies are not needed," Kaimi said before glancing in my direction. I noticed the smirk that caught the side of his mouth. "To assume Estelle was mine was a natural progression of thought. But completely wrong."

"How is the beautiful Ianira these days?" Hebrus asked.

"She is resting. It's why I suggested Capheira go to see her. I must say I'm surprised you brought your wife with you."

"She wanted to come and see Ianira. They used to be such good friends until . . . well . . ." He shook his head and sighed. "They were good friends. She misses her."

"As Ianira misses Capheira."

Neither of them made any further comments regarding their wives. They both stared at each other, looking like two wild animals weighing up their opponent before a gruesome fight. Who'd make the first move?

I was struggling not to say anything. It was as if my presence had been forgotten about. While I was relieved not to be the center of their attention, I hadn't lost sight of why Hebrus was summoned. I needed to speak to him about Azariah, about finding the Arcuato Ruins. I wanted to interrupt them, tell Hebrus what had happened and plead for him to help us. And while I waited, I twirled my hair in my fingers, focusing on each of them in turn.

"I left my son, Axius, in charge in Mercivium," Hebrus announced. "He is a fine Oceanid. He will make a great leader when it is time for him to rule. I think we should encourage Azariah and him to meet. It's been a few years since they have seen each other. They are our future, Kaimi. It would be good if our sons could get along the way we used to."

Kaimi nodded before pacing the floor. "And how is Camarina?" he asked.

The words obviously surprised Hebrus as much as they did me. I never expected Kaimi to bring Camarina into the conversation. Hebrus didn't reply immediately. He took a few moments to compose himself.

"She is well, although she still refuses to take a husband. Capheira says she is not ready to commit to anyone. I disagree. If she does not find a mate soon, I will need to intervene."

I rolled my eyes. Hebrus was no better than Kaimi. They should get along brilliantly—they were very similar.

Hebrus turned to me. "So, young lady, you requested my presence. I presume there is a reason for it? Or was it an elaborate plan to get me to see Kaimi, because if it is—"

"No," I stated firmly.

Hebrus raised his brow and chuckled before looking at Kaimi. "And you say the Oceanid females are feisty." He shook his head, then stepped toward me, taking my hand in his. "Please, tell me why you wanted to meet me."

I glanced at Kaimi, seeking his approval. He nodded.

There were too many people able to hear; blond Oceanid men, and dark-haired Sachaels. I didn't know who to trust. I wouldn't discuss Azariah surrounded by strangers.

"Can we take a walk outside? Alone?" I asked Hebrus. "I need to speak with you privately."

Hebrus smirked. "Would that be okay with you, Kaimi?"

Kaimi nodded again, although a thin crease in his brow alerted me to his concern at the situation I'd forced upon him.

I headed toward the doors with Hebrus by my side, fully aware his thumb was lightly rubbing across the palm of my hand. I hoped I wouldn't regret my decision to be alone with him.

But we weren't alone after all. As we walked through the corridors, Chanon followed. He kept a discreet distance, but I was glad he was there.

"So, what did you need to speak to me about? It must be important if Kaimi allowed you to request my presence in Saicean." He looked at the walls surrounding us and glanced at the ceiling of the passageway. "I never expected to see this place again."

I ignored him, continuing to walk away from listening ears. We strolled past the guards and into the gardens surrounding the entrance to Kaimi's home.

"I'm sorry," I said, when we were out of earshot. "I have no intention of ignoring your questions, I just don't want everyone knowing our business. I don't know who to trust."

"So, you don't trust Kaimi—the great Sachael leader?" He sniggered and cocked his head to the side, one brow lifted, waiting for my response.

I shrugged. "I'm not sure yet."

He clicked his tongue against the roof of his mouth. "What about Azariah?" He leaned forward. "Don't you trust him?"

"I would if he was here. But at the moment, he's missing." I kept my focus on him, determined to try and read his reaction. I didn't want to think of the consequences if I got this wrong.

"Missing?" His eyes widened, and he placed his hand on my arm.

I nodded. "Do you know where the Arcuato Ruins are?"

Hebrus nodded before squeezing my arm. "Why would he be there?"

"Orontes has kidnapped him."

"Orontes?" He backed away, releasing my arm. "He shouldn't even be in the sea. I banished him years ago, and I have not granted him permission to return. He always did like to challenge me. But this time, he has gone too far."

Hebrus's hands curled into fists at his sides.

"Why did you banish him from the water?" I asked, curious as to the reason behind his decision. Even though I hated Orontes, I still considered it harsh to be banned from the water when you were an Oceanid. It was where you were meant to be.

"He fell in love with a human," Hebrus stated, no hesitation in his reply. He paced the ground, continually shaking his head.

"And that caused you to ban him from the water for the rest of his life?"

"Yes."

"Why?" I tried to remember if I knew anything to substantiate this.

"My men are not allowed to fall for the charms of a human female. It was a deal sealed many years ago between Kaimi's grandfather and mine. It was agreed that the human women are to be left for the Sachaels." He scratched the side of his head. "It's to protect both our kinds; to keep us a secret. I'm sure you have heard of the many tales concerning mermaids and mermen. That is how it must remain—a mystery, a fantasy even, amongst humans. There has always been a risk that the male Oceanids and the Sachaels would fight for the same woman. Our grandfathers didn't want that. They agreed between themselves that, because Sachaels can only be male—present company excepted—they should be the ones who choose the human women. We have women; therefore, the Oceanid men must stay with their own kind. Orontes ignored the rule."

It seemed a harsh and unfair law. Love was love. You couldn't decide who you fell in love with.

"I don't think Orontes is capable of loving anyone but himself," I said. If he was, I'd never seen any evidence of it.

"But don't you see? By falling in love and living away from the sea, he acted properly. He knew I would never allow him to return to the ocean if he stayed with this woman, but his love for her surpassed anything he had ever known." Hebrus lifted his chin and gave a half-smile.

After the conversations I'd shared with Orontes, I found it difficult to believe he ever loved the woman he originally left the sea for. "Well, he's not kept out of the sea. I know he's been in it numerous times before this happened."

"I guess from your tone that you have met Orontes." Hebrus held his arm out—a gesture for me to take it and walk with him.

I did as he expected.

"Unfortunately, yes. He's working with a group of people on land who are trying to kill the Sachaels."

Hebrus raised his brow, but didn't say anything.

"Only now, it's not only humans who are involved. Many Oceanids have joined them as well. They are unhappy with the Sachaels stealing their women. Did you know it was a group of your men who killed Elpis, Azariah's brother?"

"Young Elpis?" Hebrus stopped walking. "He's dead?"

I nodded.

"I was never informed."

"Should you have been?"

He closed his eyes and sighed deeply. "I was told of the deaths of all Kaimi's other sons. It was always a difficult time for him." He paused for a few moments, as if gathering his thoughts. "You said it was a group of my men that killed him?"

"Yes, three Oceanids."

"Were they caught? And dealt with?" His brows were furrowed and he pinned me with his gaze. "Tell me, Estelle, I need to know."

"Yes. Azariah told me he personally caught the Oceanid who killed Elpis. Other Sachaels caught the remaining two. The attackers were killed."

"Good, good." He sighed as we began to walk toward the lake again. "I never thought I'd see the day it would come to this. The Oceanids and the Sachaels fighting against each other, killing each other. For what? Supremacy in the water?"

"All this hostility could end. I hope when Azariah rules, with me by his side, that we can work together and create a peaceful world in which we can all live. Azariah and I want to change things. We will work with you or your son and start to make a difference. I'd like the Oceanids and Sachaels to be allies, not enemies. And I'm a female Sachael, perhaps there are others. Perhaps we are looking to a future where there will be no need for Sachaels to impregnate land women."

Our conversation had gone full circle; we were back to the reason I needed to speak to Hebrus—Azariah. We had also reached the edge of the lake. "If we don't rescue him, then none of this will ever happen."

"How did Orontes manage to take Azariah to the ruins? Azariah is a strong Sachael, and Chanon is never far from his side." He looked back along the path and nodded. "It seems he is never far from your side, either."

"He drugged him with the venom from the Blue Ringed Octopus. He keeps it in bullets around his wrist. One shot to a Sachael blinds them—it also weakens them considerably. A second shot kills them." The haunting vision of Azariah, pale and helpless when he was slung over Orontes's shoulder, flashed before my eyes.

"And he has managed to do this to Azariah?" Hebrus exclaimed.

"One shot, yes." I looked across the eerily still water. "If he wants to keep Azariah alive but weak, then he'll keep administering the venom. I'm scared he will give him too much. Every hour we spend trying to find him is an hour nearer to his death."

"But why? What is he trying to prove?"

"That I'm a female Sachael."

Hebrus stopped walking. "So when he met you, he experienced the attraction?"

I nodded. "He was the man who ordered my capture. He wanted to prove I was a Sachael, and then use me to bargain with you and Kaimi for his freedom in the water. But he had no intention of releasing me. He threatened me many times, telling me he would take me into the sea and force me to have his children."

Hebrus's eyes widened, and he shook his head. "We need to stop him, Estelle."

His brow furrowed as he glanced across the lake.

"Will you help me find him?" I asked, still unsure of his answer. Nothing he had said gave any indication of his intentions.

"The ruins are well hidden, they lie in a dip in the ocean floor, an ancient city in a redundant crater, but it means we can approach them undetected."

"So you'll help?"

"Of course I will." He smiled at me, and then quickly sobered. "I need to speak with Kaimi."

"Thank you."

He turned and hurried back up the path we had walked along. As soon as he disappeared from view, Chanon rushed to me, pulling me into his arms. "I'm so proud of you," he whispered against my ear. "So proud." His arms held me tightly, and it was a while before he released me.

"We need to follow him," I said. "I want to know exactly what we're going to do, what the plan of attack is."

Chanon stared at me. "You don't seriously think you'll be coming with us?"

"Why not?" I was already marching after Hebrus.

"It's exactly what Orontes wants. It's too much of a risk, Estelle."

"I have to go," I snapped. There was no way I could stay here while they attempted to rescue Azariah without me. "I'm not just going to be used as the bait to get Hebrus here. I have to go with you. Orontes will kill Azariah if I'm not there. Remember, he caught Azariah so *I* would rescue him—he still wants to prove I am a female Sachael. That's what all this is about."

"It's not just about that, though." Chanon grabbed my arm, stopping my retreat. "Orontes wants you. Let's not forget that you are the target in all this, not Azariah. He's gotten caught up in this as a way for Orontes to get what he wants. He doesn't care about proving whether you are a female Sachael or not. It's gone beyond that. He wants *you*, Estelle. That's his only aim."

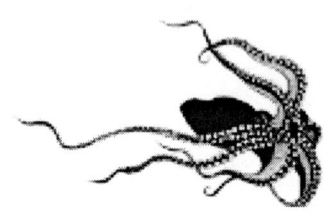

TWENTY - TWO
Battle

Chanon refused to let me follow Hebrus back to the Hall. Which, unfortunately, meant that he missed out on finalizing the plans for Azariah's rescue and providing his input on whether or not I should be included in them. Markos had found us though, and quickly informed him of what was happening. It seemed that Kaimi and Hebrus had decided that I would play an instrumental part in the attack—the possibility of Azariah's death if I was not present too severe to be ignored—and would be sent along with the army after all. It was exactly what I'd wanted, but Chanon wasn't happy with the decision. Still, he had promised to give me a demonstration on how to use a knife in combat after we completed our submergence later that night, just in case I should need it.

When we returned to Azariah's room after our submergence under the yellow moon, Capella, there was a table full of food waiting for us. Chanon sat down eagerly, while I picked at the prawns and the salted seaweed.

"You have to eat, you know," Chanon said. "Keep your strength up. You've got a demanding swim ahead of you in the morning. I'll keep my eye on you, but I won't be able to carry you like I did to get here."

I stabbed another prawn with my fork.

"You should be faster now," he continued, "and the Oceanids swim slower than us anyway, so you'll have no trouble keeping up. But I won't be able to talk to you once we enter the water."

"I know all that," I mumbled.

Chanon frowned at me, his mouth full of food. "What's wrong?"

I placed my fork on the table and pushed the bowl of food aside. "I want to go with you tomorrow, but I don't feel ready. I'm unprepared, and I'm worried I may get in the way rather than be of any assistance."

Chanon sat up straight before pushing his chair back and standing up. "So now you admit that you're not ready? I tried to warn you, but you didn't want to listen, did you?"

I shook my head.

"Right," he said, looking around the room and pushing the table away from me. "Time to learn. You're using Azariah's knife. Get up, show me how you hold it."

I stood, as directed, and he fetched Azariah's knife from the bedside table. When he handed it to me, I gripped the handle tightly.

He nodded. "Good, good, you have a natural grip. But don't drop it, it's all you have. Now, the best way to kill an Oceanid is quickly." He grinned, although I saw nothing funny about what he was saying. "Our speed in the water is a massive advantage. Even you will be quicker than they are."

"So, my training relies on the fact that I'm quicker? That's it?" I asked, dumbfounded.

"No, no. Put the knife down, and I'll show you."

I placed the knife on the table, and awaited further instructions. Stepping in front of me, he gripped my arms and maneuvered me until I stood in front of him, facing away.

"This is the best way to kill them," he said.

With no further warning he brushed up behind me, yanked my chin backward, and pulled the edge of his hand across my neck.

"Or this," he continued, tightly but gently pulling my head back by my hair and repeating the action of pulling his hand across my neck.

"Push the blade deep into the flesh." He pressed on my throat as he spoke. "And then pull it swiftly across their throat."

"Push deep, pull swiftly," I repeated, memorizing the words I would speak if I needed to kill someone. Chanon let me go, and I sat on the edge of the bed. Could I even do it? Could I really kill someone? Did I have the killer instinct it took to issue a fatal knife wound?

"I'm not sure I can do this," I mumbled, not looking toward Chanon. I couldn't bear to see his disappointment.

Chanon tutted and pulled me back to my feet. "Of course you can do it; you may very well have to do it. Now, do to me what I did to you." He moved in front of me, and then turned around.

"Chanon, I—"

"Do it, Estelle. Imagine I'm Melia, that I'm about to kill Azariah. Do it."

Something clicked inside me, and I grabbed his hair and pulled his head back. He swore under his breath, but I ignored him. Pressing my other hand against his throat, I traced it across the exposed skin.

"You can let me go now," Chanon said, tapping the side of my leg.

I immediately released his hair and stared vacantly ahead. "Sorry," I mumbled.

Chanon grinned at me as he rubbed his scalp. "I think you understand." He sat down on the edge of the bed, and I joined him, still unsettled by what we were discussing.

"Slitting their throat is the quickest way to kill them," Chanon continued. "But if you can't get behind them, a series of three stabs to the back or chest, twisting the knife on each, will also inflict severe damage."

"Can you show me?" I asked, hating that this was necessary, but knowing that it could prove vital in the hours ahead.

"Show you?" He shook his head. "You nearly pulled my hair out a few minutes ago. Save your aggression for when you need it."

Tears pricked at my eyes. I was talking about killing someone. And not just figuratively. I was training for the possibility I'd actually have to do it. Kill. Kill someone who had taken Azariah away from me. Who had I become?

Chanon placed his arm across my shoulders and pulled me toward him. He didn't speak as my tears wet his shoulder—he just held me.

It was the middle of the night—time for us to set off for the Arcuato Ruins. An early morning attack had been planned as the perfect time to catch Orontes and his men off guard. I had no need to change my clothes. I still wore the ones I'd changed into for my submergence—a white vest and black knee-length shorts identical to the ones the guards wore. But I needed more than just my clothes. Chanon secured a holder on my lower arm for my knife. As he tightened the same contraption onto both of his forearms, he reassured me that this battle was standard procedure for the army. That I had no need to fear the outcome. I wanted to believe him, I really did. But I couldn't. I knew the man they were going to be fighting. He was incredibly strong, had a hate for Sachaels that drove him forward with passion, and had venom bullets.

I couldn't fix on any one emotion. One second I would be nervous, then excited, then frightened. I had an unsettled presence in my stomach, one which made me feel sick. The moment had finally come, and now that it had, the anticipation was nearly too much to bear.

"We must go," Chanon said, eying me cautiously.

I nodded, unsure of my voice.

With no further discussion, we left Azariah's room and strode through the passageways toward the Hall. The mumbling of voices, audible as we drew near the doors, became deafening as we stepped into the Hall. I viewed the room, aghast at the sight before me. Sachaels—lots of them. They were wearing their customary black shorts, and, from what I could see, they were all equipped with familiar straps around their forearms. They all carried at least two knives. Some of them wore other coverings on their body; some had larger knives in a sheath diagonally across their backs. Many others wore knife holders strapped to their legs, like Chanon. They were fired up, excited, ready to start the journey. Ready to fight.

"Ah, Estelle." Kaimi rushed to my side. "I see you are dressed appropriately. Chanon, have you told her everything she needs to know?"

"Yes, Kaimi." He bowed as he answered him.

"She has only one knife. Is that enough?"

"I feel two knives will hinder her. She will never be left alone to fight. I will be by her side."

"Is it a suitable knife? Have you used it before?" Kaimi reached for my arm, expertly pulling the blade from its protective sheath. His eyes widened at the intricate pattern on the handle. "This is Azariah's."

I nodded. "He left it behind."

Kaimi sighed heavily, returning the knife to me. "Use it, Estelle. Save Azariah, and yourself."

I nodded again.

Kaimi diverted his attention to Chanon.

"Chanon, you are in charge. There are thirty men at your disposal. I would be happier if you took more, but a larger number would risk alerting Orontes to your arrival."

Chanon cast his gaze across the army, staring intently at the men. His gaze widened as they all suddenly quieted and moved aside, creating a gap through the middle of their gathering.

Ianira was walking into the Hall, followed by Hebrus, who held the hand of a woman I presumed to be his wife. I hid a grin as I saw what Hebrus was carrying. The fairy stories I'd read when I was young had got one thing right: the merman king carried a trident.

Coming to stand before Kaimi, Hebrus's wife curtsied.

"Capheira, there is no need for you to curtsey," Kaimi said, stepping forward and leaning to take her hand in his. He kissed the back of it before stepping away and nodding at Hebrus. "May I introduce you to Estelle?" His arm swept in my direction.

Capheira looked toward me, a smile quickly covering her lips. "It's a pleasure to meet you," she said.

Kaimi placed his hand on my shoulder. "Estelle is an extraordinary woman. I have high hopes for her ruling alongside Azariah. I have not seen them together yet, but I have no doubt they will be formidable, a united force, unwilling to be swayed by others."

The noise in the Hall grew louder again, and, as if recognizing the excited eagerness emanating from the men, Chanon cleared his throat and spoke to Kaimi. "It is time. We must leave. Let's bring Azariah home."

"And kill Orontes," Hebrus growled. "If possible, you must leave him to me. I want to be the one to end his life."

"I would like to be the man who ends his life as well," Chanon said.

"So long as one of you kills him," I said. "I'm worried that if he's not, he'll cause even more trouble in the months to come."

"Chanon," Kaimi said. "You must ensure that both Azariah and Estelle come back alive."

"You know I will risk my life to keep both of them safe. I will stay with Estelle, protect her."

Kaimi nodded before raising his arms. "Silence!" he roared above the constant chatter. The Sachaels stopped talking before turning to face our group.

"Men, we are ready. Listen to Chanon. He is your leader for this battle."

"It is time," Chanon announced. "We will travel at a slower speed than normal, so as not to outdistance our allies, the Oceanids. Show them respect. Their king travels with us to show us the place Azariah is being held. He is risking his life to help us. His men travel with him and are being asked to fight their own kind." Chanon nodded toward the side of the room. Six men dressed in black gowns stood looking at the room full of Sachaels. "These men are not to be harmed. They are with us. Observe them now, study them as we swim. You need to know which Oceanids are our friends, and which are our enemies. Our aim is to rescue Azariah and bring him back." He stepped to my side and placed his hand on my shoulder. "Estelle must also be protected and brought back. The Oceanid responsible for stealing Azariah will try to snatch her. Azariah and Estelle are our priorities. I will protect them with my life, and I expect the same from you. Keep your minds as free and clear as possible. I will communicate with you when necessary."

Kaimi stepped forward. "You have been warned about Orontes, the leader of this rebel group of Oceanids. They have all betrayed their kind and their king, but he is especially dangerous, equipped with poisonous bullets. If you are injected with the poison from these bullets, you will be rendered blind, weakened and disoriented. If a second bullet's poison is injected, you will die. I expect him to use this form of attack. Be careful. Look out for your brothers. I want you all to return." He appeared to look at each man in turn. "Now go. May the goddess of our moons protect you on your journey."

The army left the room in a quiet order.

Ianira hugged me, not saying a word—she had no need to. I could see from her eyes how scared and worried she was. Kaimi stepped toward me, his demeanor very different to that he had showed his men.

"Bring Azariah back, and make sure you return as well," he said before pulling me to his chest. "I need you both back here," he whispered, his whiskers once again scratching my ear. "I can't stand to lose either of you."

I nodded, my throat aching with the effort of containing my fear and tears.

With no further words, Kaimi released me. Chanon took my hand and led me from the Hall. Hebrus followed, flanked by the six Oceanids.

No one spoke as we walked to the lake. Maybe it was a time for the army to contemplate what lay ahead of them; perhaps they composed themselves before the journey.

Once there, they slipped wordlessly into formation. It was a well-organized routine. Chanon and I stood aside as a line of five Sachaels walked forward into the water. They carried on walking as Hebrus and his men followed in their formation—two in front of Hebrus, one at each side, and two behind. He was surrounded, protected by his men. Another line of five Sachaels walked calmly into the water, and then Chanon pulled my hand, urging me to walk with him. As we strode forward, Sachaels joined us at our sides. A row of five were at my side, and the same at Chanon's. The rest of the Sachaels followed, another ten men dropping into formation.

Chanon squeezed my hand tightly as the water reached my chest. "Whatever happens, I'm glad we found each other, that I had this time to get to know you, even though it was only a few weeks."

"There are many more to come," I told him, not willing to consider this as the last time I would speak to him. He smiled before sinking under the water, taking me with him.

The stillness and silence of Saicean was left behind as the water flooded my ears. The familiar noise of the sea filled my head. Each ripple of water, every movement of my body created noise—white noise, familiar sounds. They were echoes of my past, my future—my present.

We swam into the depths of the lake before heading through the black tunnel. Chanon released my hand as we reached the exit of Saicean. Ten guards with red bands around their arms were positioned at the opening into the ocean this time, not just the four I'd seen when Chanon brought me here.

The swim upward through the deep abyss seemed to take forever, and as we neared the top, Chanon grabbed my hand again and forced me against the sheer wall of the chasm. High-pitched whistling flooded my ears. With memories of what this had signified last time, I pushed myself against the wall, ignoring the sharp, jagged rocks as they pressed into my skin while Chanon stayed in front of me. His head switched from side to side and upward. The noise became louder, a cacophony of whistles, screeches, and cries. The Sachaels who were initially following us shot past, heading upward into the commotion. Sachaels darted in every direction, swooping and sweeping in large circles before charging fast in diagonal lines. Within seconds, the flurry and the noise died down, and my initial thoughts about us being attacked were confirmed when three lifeless Oceanid bodies floated past, heading to the bottom of the chasm.

Hebrus was frozen in the water. It was the first time I'd had the chance to study him in his full Oceanid form. He was magnificent. His mertail was long and sinuous, silver, each scale tipped with gold. The fin of his mertail was large, easily two meters across, and it quivered as his main body remained still. Protruding from the back of his arms were small delicate fins, matching the color of his tail. They fluttered as fast as the wings of a hummingbird.

He suddenly darted into action and quickly resumed his position, leading the way with his men, and Chanon and I dropped back into the formation we'd set off in. During our journey, we were joined by a large pale-colored and strange-looking octopus, several thin-tailed fish, and a couple of sharks. The Sachaels showed no fear when the animals approached, so I presumed they were harmless, but the sharks unnerved me—they were easily four meters long, and their teeth were clearly visible. The animals were a welcome distraction from the long swim, though. I didn't feel tired, but we could travel for ages without seeing anything. I became bored when there was nothing to see, and, unfortunately, it was at those moments that I tended to contemplate what lay ahead. It was only when we caught sight of magnificent sea creatures that I was distracted about where we were heading and why.

Eventually, Hebrus slowed, gradually coming to a stop in the water. He pointed ahead, and then raised his arms, opening them to each side of his body: the order for the men to circle the edge of what lay before us—the Arcuato Ruins.

Hebrus and his Oceanid men swam along the sandy ocean floor before following the rise of the edge of the crater to wait. I gripped Chanon's hand tightly as we trailed their approach.

Several Sachaels settled themselves at the edge of the crater, positioning themselves alongside us. Chanon shifted forward, peering over the top before sinking back down next to me. He grinned. I guessed from his expression that everything was as he'd anticipated.

Chanon inclined his head toward the crater, and I looked over the edge, taking in the disarranged landscape before me. It resembled a city. The arches and stone buildings were demolished, but there was evidence of a maze of streets running through the rubble. The ruins were completely enclosed within the crater the Sachaels circled. I scanned the area frantically, trying to locate Azariah.

As if reading my mind, Chanon tapped my shoulder and pointed toward the center of the ruins.

I saw him.

Everything in me screamed to swim straight to him, but, as if predicting my action, Chanon's firm hand rested on my shoulder and stopped me from moving.

Held in place, I stared at Azariah. He wasn't moving. His arms were stretched above his head, his wrists bound with rope attached to a tall stone pillar. His head was down, his chin touching his chest, and his legs offered no support. He was hanging by his arms from the pillar.

He was out in the open, almost as if welcoming an attempt for rescue. I didn't like the situation, but my instinct was still to swim to him, to untie him and get away from here. Dead or alive, he had to return to Saicean. I swallowed the panic threatening to overpower me. He couldn't be dead. He couldn't. But staring at the pathetic sight before me, I feared the worst.

A rush of water signified movement from within the ruins, and my focus was immediately pulled away from Azariah. Dreamy, echoing cries filled the water. Before us were two Oceanids, facing each other and rising above the ruins. They were close to where we hid, so close that I had no trouble recognizing Orontes. It took me a few moments to identify the other, though. Its bright scarlet and black mertail was twisted around Orontes's dark blue one. They moved as one through the water, but once they broke free from their passionate kiss, I caught sight of the other Oceanid's face. I recognized who it was—Melia. Orontes and she were in the middle of something pretty intimate, but I couldn't look away, I was entranced by the sight and sound of them. Orontes's golden hair flowed behind him as they moved through the water, kissing, twisting and turning, but he suddenly stilled and pushed Melia away. The distorted rhythmic song stopped, and in its place was an ear-splitting screech. He spun around, jerking as he took in his surroundings, looking for something . . . or someone. His eyes focused on mine when he faced me. He'd sensed I was there.

Chanon realized we had been spotted and must have communicated it to the others. There was a sudden and united movement as the Sachaels surrounding the crater rose from their positions and swooped into the ruins. Orontes didn't move, but Melia quickly turned and followed the Sachaels. The volume of shrieks and whistles increased as Oceanids swam up from the ruins. The sight before me blurred with the movement of attacking Sachaels and fleeing Oceanids, but I was frozen to the spot as three Sachaels swam at Orontes. He didn't wait for them to get near. He reached to his wrist, lifted his arm in their direction, and fired several bullets. All three of them were hit and sank into the ruins below. My eyes widened. Where had he gotten the trigger release for the bullets? Last time I saw him, the bullet had had to be pressed against the skin of his victim. Not anymore. The quick, powerful release of bullets meant that he could fire the deadly venom in quick succession and from a considerable distance. He was more powerful; he was prepared. This was what I'd feared.

I struggled to tear my gaze away from Orontes. He still watched me, seemingly unaware or unconcerned about the battle taking place in the belly of the crater below him. He smirked. It was the look he always gave me when he presumed he had the upper hand.

He curled his finger at me, beckoning me to him, but there was no way I was moving. With Chanon on one side of me and Hebrus on the other, I wasn't willingly going anywhere with him. His mertail flicked, and without any warning, he propelled himself toward me.

Chanon yanked my arm, jerking me from my position. Hebrus moved into my place—his trident pointing toward Orontes. Orontes changed direction sharply. His large mertail displaced the water so much that the force made me tumble backward. When I straightened, I realized Chanon wasn't holding my hand anymore. He had gone. I turned, suspended in the water as I looked for Chanon. Was he injured?

Hebrus swam to my side and pointed in the direction Orontes had gone. Chanon was following him. Unfortunately, seeing my brother chasing Orontes did nothing to stop my building panic. It was only when Hebrus pointed into the ruins at Azariah that I focused.

I dived into the crater with Hebrus right behind me. Swimming low, we darted between the ruined buildings and dodged the crumbling arches before turning into the rubble-covered street that led directly to Azariah. I reduced my speed and focused on the raised platform Azariah was on. Melia was guarding him. My initial panic disappeared, and in its place built a seething anger over the claims she had made toward Azariah. Seeing her stand over him, I saw her protecting him, not guarding him. Was she keeping him for herself? Was this the only way she could have him? I shook my head. He wasn't hers, and he never had been.

A Sachael shot past us, heading toward them. He circled the space, some ten meters or so above, before darting down toward them, a knife in his hand. He headed straight for

Melia. Having witnessed the cold way Chanon had spoken to Melia when on the beach, I wasn't surprised that the Sachael was attacking a female without a second thought, but I was shocked when, after a flurry of movement between them, the Sachael sank to the floor. Red blood swirled into the water surrounding him. Two venom bullets were lodged in his chest. Melia had killed him.

Her grinning features incensed me. She was the woman who had tried to steal Azariah from me. She was the woman who had dismissed Michael. But worst of all, she was the woman who had betrayed us.

I scrutinized her movements. I couldn't let her hit me with a venom bullet. I was convinced I'd only need one to end my life, not two like a full Sachael.

She cut through the rope holding Azariah's arms to the pillar, and he sank to the seabed in a crumpled heap. He was completely still. My eyes widened again, fighting the fresh fear that ran through me. I had to get to him; there was no time to waste.

Hebrus grabbed my shoulder just as I was ready to swim forward. He nodded urgently to the space behind us. Orontes and Chanon had swum down into the ruins, but Orontes had the advantage now. He charged at Chanon, and a silent scream flew from me as he was hurled backward into a building. He slumped to the ground. Like Azariah, he didn't move. I was torn; did I swim to Chanon, or go to Azariah?

My mind was made up when Orontes swam above our heads toward Melia. He handed a spear to her and pointed at

Azariah before looking straight at me. Once again, he knew exactly where I was. His eyes narrowed.

Fully aware of the danger I was about to put myself in, I pushed Hebrus's hand from my shoulder and shot forward. I wasn't prepared to just sit back and watch them kill Azariah without even trying to stop them.

Orontes smirking face remained fixed on me as I approached. I had every intention of knocking him out of the way, grabbing the spear, and killing Melia with it. But Orontes's reflexes were quicker than mine. Years of living in the water had provided him with a distinct advantage over me. He swiftly moved away from my charge. I tried to turn, change my course of direction, but it was too late, and I crashed into the pillar Azariah had been tied to. I screamed as a deep, searing pain shot through my shoulder. Had I been shot? Had Melia or Orontes shot me with a bullet? Was I going to die?

I floated onto the ground next to Azariah, the pain in my shoulder not easing in any way. I waited for my sight to cloud, for my limbs to become unresponsive. It was a fitting end, for me to die next to Azariah. I only hoped we would be taken back to Saicean, that we could be together—if not in this life, then in the next. I groped in the sand for his hand. I wanted contact with him, one last comforting touch for the man I had loved since the moment I saw him. I wrapped my fingers around his, but the icy coldness of his flesh seeped into every bone in my body. All hope deserted me. Tears built behind my eyes as I dragged myself closer to him. Was this the end for both of us? Had we both succumbed to the venom, poisoned by a creature from the sea? The irony was poetic, but the situation gruesome, tragic.

I stayed on the ground, not moving, waiting for my senses to shut down. My shoulder throbbed with each labored breath I took. But I was still breathing. I could still feel the stinging, urgent pain. I was aware of movement around me, bodies rushing, fleeing, attacking. And then there was Azariah and me—frozen in a watery world I had only just discovered.

I lifted my head, wanting to see Azariah for one last time. I didn't care how he looked, for I would always remember him laughing with me, or frowning at something he didn't understand. His grey, life-less features were not him, they were the ghost of his death, a shadow of his existence. But that one last look was all I could concentrate on.

Through tear-wet eyes, I followed the ugly sight of his bruise-covered chest to his blood-spotted neck—the site of the venom injections. How cruel for a man to die like this. He didn't deserve this, any of it.

With all hope gone, I pulled myself closer to him and rested my head on his chest.

And then I realized. I was moving, controlling my own movements. The venom shot into my shoulder hadn't caused any side-effects. I frowned at the pillar I'd crashed into and deduced that maybe I hadn't been hit by a bullet at all, maybe I'd just damaged my shoulder. The pain was still constant, but manageable.

My head rose ever so slightly on Azariah's chest.

Was he alive?

The vein in his neck pulsed.

He was alive.

Filled with renewed hope, I gritted my teeth and pushed myself to my feet. I released the knife from the holster on my arm and focused on Orontes, who was a few meters away with Melia. He sneered as I straightened, but Melia raised her arm in front of her body, pointing her hand toward me. Orontes must have anticipated her intention at the same time I did, for he knocked her hand upward with such force that she flew backward.

He continued to stare at me, nodding slowly as if deciding my fate. I had no understanding as to why he'd left me when I crashed to the seabed next to Azariah. Why hadn't he grabbed me then?

Without warning, he burst forward, coming straight at me. This was it. He would either kill me, or take me away. I held the knife tightly, pointing it toward him.

Everything happened in slow motion. At the last moment, Orontes swooped low, heading for my legs, avoiding the area where I was armed and a potential danger to him. There was no time to change my angle of attack. As I screamed, sure he was going to grab me and carry me away with him, he was knocked sideways. Focusing on a tumbling mass of arms and mertails, I recognized Hebrus. He had knocked Orontes away. He had saved me.

But one solved problem didn't mean I could switch off. Melia had recovered and was, once again, raising her arm, ready to shoot a bullet at me.

Girl against girl. Bullet against knife. Who would win? Who had the most to gain, the most to lose?

I shot forward, grimacing from the pain in my shoulder as I twisted my body above Melia and away from the line of her arm. The bullet just missed my thigh. I continued swimming upward, drawing her away from Azariah, and when there was sufficient distance between us, I swam a zigzag path toward her. She frantically tried to release more bullets, aiming hopelessly and firing them into the water.

When I reached her, I grabbed her hair, pulling her head sideways before twisting her left arm—the one with the bullet bracelet—away from me. A series of short chattering clicks sprang from her mouth before a long wailing cry was released. The sound hurt my ears—within them, not my gills. I cringed as I fought the burning pain, but still she held the impossibly high note. I didn't release my tight hold on her, though, and with a determined shake of my head, I managed to recall Chanon's training. Visions on how to use the knife sprang into my mind as I fought with her. Each jerky movement jarred my shoulder. Her mertail scales scratched my skin as she wriggled frantically, trying to escape my tight grasp. I kneed her in the stomach, the force of it stopping her ear-splitting wail, and took advantage of her weakened state to move behind her. Locking my legs around her waist, I gripped her under the chin, pulling her head back and exposing her neck. She swam upward, but I wasn't letting go. As she twisted and turned, trying to throw me from her back, I steadied myself. Placing the edge of the knife against her throat, Chanon's words filled my head: "*Push hard. Pull swiftly.*"

Her body went limp, and I immediately released her.

Was this how easy it was to kill someone? A split second of force, and they were dead? I stared at her body as it floated into the ruins. A trail of crimson seeped from the open wound in her neck. She drifted toward Azariah, and I swam to them quickly, wanting to make sure she couldn't harm him anymore. My fear was still with me.

And where was Orontes?

Scanning the water in all directions, I couldn't see him or Hebrus.

I placed my knife in its holder and sank to my knees next to Azariah's weak but alive body. Holding his cold hand in mine, I willed him to respond—something, anything that would give me another sign he was alive.

I needed to get him to Saicean, but I had no idea where Saicean was. I debated whether to try and travel to the Faroe Islands with him. We'd be safe there. Michael would help us. But even as I formulated my plan, I knew how hopeless it was. I would never have managed to carry Azariah any distance, even without my damaged shoulder, and I had no idea which direction to swim in to get anywhere.

Azariah was still lying on his back, his eyes open but completely grey, not the luminous white Sachaels usually had when underwater. His lifeless features were partially hidden behind a rough growth of beard. His skin was dry and flaking, and there were several scars across his chest and neck, as well as the darkened areas of bruising on his chest. I held back my tears as I contemplated how many times he must have been injected, and by the state of him, how many times he'd suffered a beating. I stroked the side of his face, but he didn't respond to my gesture.

Someone else touched Azariah's face, and I gasped at their silent approach—Chanon. He was here; my brother was here. He was alive. I cried freely. We were all alive. Damaged, broken, and still in danger. But, at that moment, I allowed myself to trust the glimmer of hope I had. We would be okay.

All around us, the battle continued, the horrendous noise of the Oceanids' persisting. Chanon was focused on something happening above. I followed his gaze, seeing a dark mass above us, swimming high above the crater. Oceanids. Fighting. As they fought, they drifted lower, two mertails thrashing in the water. I narrowed my eyes, recognizing the long blond hair as belonging to Orontes. It was a vicious fight—one where both of them would come away wounded. Orontes suddenly pushed the other Oceanid away, and as it began its slow descent toward us, he swam away.

Orontes had killed again. I had no idea whether it was with the bullets or another weapon, but he had killed one of his own. The man had no mercy, none whatsoever.

The deafening screeches and repetitive whistling drifted away as the remaining Oceanids abandoned the fight. All that was left was the descent of whoever Orontes had killed.

Both Chanon and I stared at the deceased Oceanid's slow fall. It was met by two Sachaels and four Oceanids.

I gasped as I recognized the body.

Hebrus.

Chanon stared at the seabed. His eyes remained fixed on the shifting sands for several seconds. My sadness floated silently in the water. Hebrus had come into battle with us to help the Sachaels. He'd fought his own kind to rescue Azariah. And now one of them had killed him.

Ever so slightly, Azariah's hand squeezed mine—a small gesture, but one that signified he was alive, aware of my presence. Joy mixed with my feelings of sadness. I rested my hand on the side of his face again.

As if in a trance, Chanon carefully lifted Azariah onto his back. The remaining Oceanids surrounded Hebrus. There were other wounded men—Sachaels and Oceanids alike—ones hit by the venom bullets. We were a seriously depleted, battered, and damaged army.

I swam beside Chanon, unable to take my eyes off Azariah. He was alive. He'd responded to my touch, but he looked terrible.

Why did it have to end this way? Why couldn't we all have returned safely?

I knew why.

Orontes. We had all paid his price, and he had escaped. Again.

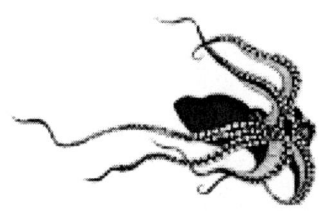

TWENTY-THREE
Return

I broke the surface of the lake, blinking rapidly as my eyes adjusted to the brightness of the moons.

Kaimi, Ianira, and Capheira were standing on the shore. Behind them stood a line of twenty or so guards. Kaimi rushed toward us through the water as Chanon carefully moved Azariah from his back and into his arms.

"Azariah!" Kaimi called.

Azariah lay completely still in Chanon's hold. His head hung, lifeless, and his arms dangled.

"Is he alive?" he asked.

"Yes," I replied. "But he's very weak."

Kaimi was by Chanon's side, staring at Azariah's limp, unresponsive body.

As Kaimi spoke, several guards rose from the water behind us. They, too, carried injured Sachaels. Six of them were in a similar state to Azariah—hit by one of Orontes's venom bullets. Kaimi growled loudly. "Where is he, then, where is Hebrus? I expected him to be the first back, boasting about the way he killed Orontes."

"He didn't make it," Chanon said, his head down, unwilling to meet Kaimi's questioning gaze

"What?" Kaimi gasped.

As if to prove Chanon's words, the remaining four Oceanid men who had traveled to the ruins with us surfaced. Between them, they carried Hebrus's body.

Capheira screamed from the edge of the lake, and Ianira pulled her into her arms.

"We need to get Azariah to his room. Do you have doctors, or someone who can help him?" I asked, ignoring the sobbing from the edge of the lake.

Kaimi glanced at the injured men standing in front of him before giving his orders. "Everybody into the Hall. You," he said, pointing at one of the guards at the edge of the lake, "fetch Solon and the other doctors immediately. Help them!" He gestured sharply to the few guards who stood motionless at the edge of the lake. "Help all of them!"

A guard approached Chanon.

"I will carry Azariah," Chanon snapped. "I need no help. Go and assist the others."

"Why did you not communicate with us?" Kaimi said, looking at Chanon. "We came to the lake because we knew you were on your way back. I had a man in the water trying to communicate with you. You didn't say anything, yet you were ordered to speak. " Kaimi viewed Chanon accusingly. "We had no idea of the injuries or deaths, or whether Estelle and Azariah were alive."

"I apologize," Chanon said, shifting Azariah in his arms, managing to support his head with his forearm. "I was fully focused on returning Azariah home and keeping my eye on Estelle."

"You still should have spoken to me, Chanon. You were in charge, and you didn't do as I ordered." He scowled at him before turning to me. "Are you okay, no injuries?"

"Just my shoulder," I said, rubbing it. Now that it was out of the water, gravity was causing the pain to become increasingly worse.

I walked in front of them, relieved to be back. I wanted to be completely out of the water, free from the reminders of what I had experienced and witnessed. The water pushed against my legs and swirled around me as I moved toward the shoreline. And when I left the comfort of the water, a sharp pain shot up my leg. I stumbled forward, expecting to fall, but Kaimi caught me from behind, his arm looping around my waist.

"You *are* injured, Estelle," he said as I straightened.

"It's just my shoulder." I winced.

"Not just your shoulder, your leg." He pointed to my thigh before pulling my uninjured arm across his shoulder, supporting my weight. A rip in the side of my shorts gaped open wide enough to see a deep cut. "We'll get Solon to look at that as well. It looks nasty."

"Not before he's sorted Azariah and the others," I said hastily. "They need attention before me."

Kaimi smiled, but there was worry behind his eyes. "You will be seen straight after Azariah."

I took a breath, ready to reply, but the sound came out as a loud groan when I put weight onto my damaged leg. Kaimi supported me each time I limped forward, but after a few steps, he scooped me into his arms.

Capheira sobbed loudly as the Oceanids carried Hebrus's body from the water.

"We must take him inside," Kaimi said. "Ianira, help her get there, please."

Ianira nodded, glancing quickly at Azariah before wiping her silent tears and leading Capheira from the lake.

When we reached the Hall, the Oceanids placed Hebrus on one of several rugs which had been placed across the floor. Capheira rushed to his body, sobbing quietly as she laid her hands on his face. Chanon carefully placed Azariah on another rug, and Kaimi released me from his arms. Sinking to my knees, I took one of Azariah's hands in mine.

"Azariah, you're home now. You are safe. We're all here," I said, wiping his hair from his face. Ianira knelt next to me, taking his other hand in hers.

Chanon stood beside the rug, staring blankly at Azariah.

"Chanon," I said. He had received a nasty blow to his back and head when Orontes charged at him. Was he hurt too, and not willing to speak up?

His gaze turned to me, and our eyes locked. He continued staring at me, but didn't speak.

"Chanon!" Kaimi shouted, striding to his side. "I want to know exactly what happened. Everything. Now!"

Chanon snapped from his trance as Kaimi grabbed his arm and pulled him to the side of the Hall. They quickly became involved in a hushed discussion.

The other injured and poisoned Sachaels were being laid on rugs scattered haphazardly around the Hall. The uninjured members of the army who sat on the floor looking dazed. There were numerous Sachaels with cuts and bruises, but it was hard to tell whether they were superficial or something serious. As if to remind me of my own injuries, a renewed pain shot through my leg. I held my breath, waiting for the throbbing to subside.

Ianira crouched down at the other side of Azariah and moved her hands slowly across his chest, lightly touching the bruised and broken skin.

"I have never seen anything like this." Her voice quivered as she spoke. "It's horrendous."

I recalled the way it had affected me. I knew it was nothing compared to what Azariah was experiencing, but shuddered at the memory.

Azariah moved slightly, squeezing my hand. "Estelle," he rasped, a barely audible sound. I leaned over him. "You came for me."

"Of course I came for you," I whispered, my tears making an appearance as he squeezed my hand again.

"Are you okay?" his raspy voice whispered.

"Me? Oh, Azariah. Only you could worry about me when you are in such a state." I couldn't help but press my lips gently against his. "We will both be okay," I told him.

"I know," he said.

Any further conversation was halted as Kaimi appeared at my side, a Sachael I hadn't seen before hovering behind him. "This is Solon," he said. "He's the best doctor in Saicean."

"Can we move Azariah to his room? Settle him there to be examined?" I asked. "I'm sure this rug is not the greatest thing for him to be lying on at the moment."

Kaimi nodded. "Chanon, take Azariah to his room. Let's get him sorted."

I held my undamaged arm toward Kaimi, hoping he understood that I needed his help to stand. He pulled me to my feet, but kept hold of my hand.

"I'll make sure Azariah gets settled in his room," he said, his familiar whiskers tickling my cheek. "Chanon will carry him; he'll come to no harm. He's home now, Estelle. But I need you to speak to Capheira before you join us"

I frowned at him. He must have known I wanted to be with Azariah. I'd only just gotten him back, and I didn't want to be separated from him.

"Please?" he added, nodding his head in her direction. She was crouched over Hebrus's body.

"I'll make sure Azariah is settled comfortably," Chanon told me.

"What do I say to her?" I asked, looking at Kaimi as if he would give me the answer.

"I'm sure you'll find the words."

I sighed before hobbling toward her. I knelt next to her on the floor, my leg burning in protest at the movement. She didn't notice my arrival, and continued to stroke Hebrus's face. This was a private moment between her and her husband. Why had Kaimi insisted I talk to her? I felt like I was intruding.

"I don't blame any of you for this," she suddenly stated, quietly, not turning from Hebrus's body. "But I will make sure Orontes is caught and killed. His life will end for what he has done."

"Hebrus was so brave," I told her.

She turned to me and smiled, taking my hand in hers. "He was never anything else. He told me before he left that he had a feeling this would be his last battle. But he told me he couldn't think of a more worthy reason to fight. He wanted Azariah safe. He wanted him back with you."

"I . . ."

Her hands squeezed mine. "He also told me how you and Azariah see the future of Saicean. How you believe there are other female Sachaels. He wanted a future where the Oceanid men had no reason to hate Sachaels. He wanted peace and harmony. He trusted you to deliver that when your and Azariah's time comes. That is what he died fighting for, Estelle."

I closed my eyes, unable to stop my tears from falling. She was being so strong.

"It must have been hard for him to see his own kind rise and fight against him," I managed to say, my voice breaking on the last words.

"He always believed in doing the right thing. Unfortunately, it occasionally made him an unpopular king. But, like Kaimi, he had to rule his people. You cannot always please everyone, and difficult decisions have to be made." She turned to look at Hebrus but still spoke to me. "I am glad he managed to talk to Kaimi, and that they forgave each other for what happened in the past. It meant a great deal to him to be speaking to Kaimi again, and you were responsible for that. Our families were very close once, and Kaimi and Hebrus were the best of friends. The past few years have been hard for all of us." She sighed deeply. "I know Kaimi can sometimes seem strict and uncaring, but he is a lovely man. He adores you; I can see it every time he looks at you. And Azariah is very lucky to have found you."

"I see myself as the lucky one," I countered softly. "He's a wonderful man."

Her glazed eyes met mine. "Yes. But the future of both of our kinds is ultimately in your hands now. You must do what you know to be right."

I nodded.

"Go to him, Estelle. Go and tend to him. I will be fine. I have several things I need to say to Hebrus." She released my hands and turned back to the body of her husband.

Leaving Capheira alone with Hebrus, I limped to Azariah's room. As I opened the door, I was greeted by Kaimi pacing the end of Azariah's bed. Ianira was at Azariah's side, wiping a cloth across his forehead.

Azariah suddenly arched his back, rising from the bed, tensing his body and groaning loudly before sinking back down. I rushed to him, my own injuries forgotten.

"What's happening?" I asked as Ianira placed the cloth on his forehead again.

"Here," she said as she stood, offering me her place. "Please, you can do this. I'm sure he will feel a hundred times better knowing you are here."

"But . . . but . . ."

"His body is reacting to the venom," Solon informed me, rubbing his fingers thoughtfully on his chin. "Unfortunately, I have no idea how long this will go on for. I know it is not pleasant to witness, but it is a good sign. It means his body is recovering and fighting the venom."

Kaimi growled. "I will personally see that Orontes suffers for what he has done to my son. I will catch him and take the utmost pleasure from torturing him the way he's tortured Azariah"

I wiped Azariah's forehead, noting the cloth was warm. Azariah was burning up. I dipped the cloth in the bowl of cold water next to the bed before tenderly wiping his face and brow.

"I'm here," I told him. "I'm not going anywhere now. I'll be right beside you until you get better."

"Estelle." His voice was clearer than before, but his jaw tensed as he spoke, the pain affecting every part of him.

"Is there nothing else you can give him? Pain killers, or something?" I asked.

Solon shook his head. "I am afraid I have never dealt with this type of poisoning before. His body is dealing with it as best it can. We have to wait. The level of poisoning he has received is severe. I suspect he was injected every six or so hours to keep him subdued. He has also been beaten and cut."

Solon moved to my side before lifting Azariah's left arm. His side was a vile mess of purple, yellow, and black; one huge bruise.

"He has been hit repeatedly. You can see his chest is cut several times, but not too deep. His back though, well . . . it seems they—"

"Enough!" Kaimi shouted. I glanced at him, stunned by his sudden outburst.

"She needs to know," Chanon said firmly.

Kaimi glared at him.

"What? Needs to know what?" I demanded.

Nobody spoke.

"Tell me," I insisted.

Azariah's body went rigid again as he moaned loudly. It made my heart ache to see him like this. I was unable to comprehend how much pain he must be in.

Solon nodded before looking nervously at Kaimi.

"Tell her, then," Kaimi snapped. "Tell her what they did to him."

Solon frowned before speaking. "It looks like they tried to cut out his Sachael mark. It will be heavily scarred."

"No . . ." I couldn't believe anyone would be that vindictive. But this was Orontes we were talking about. Of course he would be that vicious and cruel. I'd witnessed his cold-heartedness when he killed Daniel in front of me. As much as I didn't want to hear what Orontes had done to the man I loved, I needed to know. I needed to understand what he had been through.

"Your leg, and your shoulder," Kaimi said, switching his attention to me. "Let Solon sort you out, then I will release him to go and look at the other injured men." He turned to speak to Solon. "There are several more poisoned with the same venom as Azariah. The other doctors are with them, but I would prefer you to look at them. From what you have told me about Azariah's poisoning, I suspect they will have similar recovery reactions, although none of them as severe as his."

I twisted my body on the chair, not willing to leave my position next to Azariah, but allowing Solon access to my injured leg.

He didn't touch my thigh, though. He knelt in front of me.

"Look at me, please," he said.

I did as directed.

"Just as I thought. Your left shoulder?"

I nodded.

"I noticed you holding it in the Hall. And when I look at you straight on, I can see the difference in height between them.

"Yes, yes," Kaimi mumbled, frustrated. "But what is wrong with it?"

"Dislocated," Solon said. He jumped to his feet and immediately placed one of his hands on my damaged shoulder, the other around my elbow. He pushed my shoulder back and pulled my arm forward, slowly and steady. I grimaced and closed my eyes as I felt the muscles react, but within a few seconds, my shoulder popped back.

Solon smiled before releasing my arm. "Better?" he said.

I nodded, rubbing my newly repositioned shoulder.

Solon was already sorting my other injury. His hands pulled the fabric of the shorts from my skin, and I tried not to wince as it pulled at the dried blood. He stopped after a few moments and reached into his bag to retrieve a knife. With no hesitation, he expertly cut away the leg of the shorts from the top of my leg.

He shook his head as his fingers pressed against my skin, traveling slowly down each side of the wound. It was uncomfortable and sore, and as he pressed on the area just above my knee, I shouted out.

"That hurts, doesn't it?"

I nodded frantically as he pressed harder.

"You are very, very lucky," Solon said. The pain increased as he continued to push on my skin.

"What . . . what are you DOING?" My final word was a scream.

Something metal bounced on the floor.

Solon picked it up. My eyes widened as he wiped the blood-coated object with a cloth.

"This," he stated, holding it up for me and everyone else to see, "was embedded in Estelle's leg. It looks like this bullet didn't release its contents on impact as planned."

Kaimi snatched the bullet from Solon's hand. "This is it? This is the item that caused all this?"

Solon nodded, not taking his eyes off the bullet Kaimi held. "If you don't mind, I would like to examine the venom—see what it actually consists of. Perhaps I can create an antidote so it isn't a threat to us anymore."

"There is no antidote," I muttered, shifting my leg awkwardly. I may not have had a bullet in my leg anymore, but it still hurt.

"How do you know?" Kaimi narrowed his eyes at me, eager for information.

"Orontes told me there was nothing to stop the effects of the venom."

"Even so," Solon said. "I would like to see it."

Kaimi handed him the bullet. "And Orontes may not have told you the truth. He wouldn't want anyone to know what the antidote was, would he?"

I shifted my leg, wincing at the stinging soreness.

"Has anybody got a bandage for Estelle's leg?" Chanon asked. Solon indicated to his bag.

"Here, Estelle," he said, as he knelt on the floor and began to clean my wound with something from the bag. The stinging immediately began to ease, and a coolness spread along the flesh where it had previously burned.

"What is it?" I asked.

"Algaearnum. It was used on both mine and Azariah's scars. It cools the skin and helps to heal the tissues of the wound."

Kaimi came and stood next to me, a frown across his forehead as he inspected Chanon's application of the cream. "You look like you have everything under control in here. I need to see what the injuries are like with the men in the Hall. And I need to speak with Capheira." He paused, looking to Chanon and nodding. "When you've finished playing doctor, come into the Hall. I'm sure Estelle can manage to care for Azariah by herself. She can always call us if she needs anything."

He patted my shoulder, as if offering his silent support, and I was surprised when the bristles of his beard tickled my ear again.

"Chanon has told me how brave you were," he whispered. "You saved Azariah from a certain death. He also told me how you killed the female Oceanid. I told you what a strong woman you were. You are a true Sachael, Estelle."

He kissed my cheek before moving away.

The room gradually emptied. I was alone with Azariah. His knuckles suddenly clenched and his body tensed, but he didn't rise from the bed as he had done before.

"Is it getting any easier?" I asked.

He nodded, but didn't speak. I stroked his cheek, selfishly wanting him to sit up, talk to me, laugh with me, see me. I hated seeing him like this.

Squeezing the water from the cloth once again, I returned it to his forehead. His mouth twitched at the side. His limited response was all I could hope for at the moment. I reached for his hand before holding it in my own.

"I'm not going to leave your side until you are completely better," I whispered, repeating my earlier promise to him.

His body tensed again, and my hand felt like it was breaking in his grasp.

"Don't fight it, Azariah," I said. "Try to sleep. Let your body heal while you sleep. It's what my father always said to me when I was poorly."

I closed my eyes. I'd told Azariah to sleep, but I needed to as well. I was exhausted. I tried to fight my tiredness, wanting to stay awake for Azariah. He needed me. But it was useless. My head sank onto the bed at Azariah's side, and it wasn't long before I was asleep and dreaming. Flashes of what I'd witnessed flew through my mind.

Orontes.

Chanon.

Hebrus.

Melia.

Azariah.

TWENTY - FOUR
Recovery

In the days that followed Azariah's return, I refused to move from his bedside. Meals were brought to me, but remained untouched. I fed Azariah, spoon after spoon of the warm, comforting broth that Kaimi's cook was making specifically for him.

Solon visited regularly to check on Azariah and change the dressing on my wound. And whenever Kaimi visited, his anxious stares and furrowed brow showed his ongoing concern.

Today was no different, and as Azariah drifted to sleep once again, Kaimi sighed.

I understood his frustration. Even though Azariah's lucid moments were becoming more frequent and prolonged, the venom was proving difficult to clear from his system completely.

"This is taking longer than I envisioned," Kaimi said. "It's been three days since he returned."

"He's sleeping less each day," I assured him. "And he's talking more."

He nodded, lightly patting Azariah's arm before turning his attention to me.

"And how is your leg?"

"A bit sore." I didn't feel I had any room to complain about my injury when Azariah was still recovering.

Kaimi headed to the door. "I'll send Chanon to take Azariah to the lake. I had hoped he would let Castor assist him, but, well—you know how strong-headed Chanon is regarding Azariah's care."

"Castor. He's back, is—?"

Kaimi smiled. "Yes. He returned with Xanthe while you were rescuing Azariah. Who do you think is making your dresses? She's enjoying the challenge of the designs Ianira is creating."

"Xanthe makes these?" I ran my hand across the delicate fabric of my dress. I would have to make a point to find her, now that she was back.

Kaimi raised his brow at me before opening the door and leaving.

I sat on the bed next to Azariah's sleeping form. His bruises were beginning to fade, and the cuts across his chest were healing. Visually, he appeared better every passing day, but I had no idea how he was recovering mentally. I still remembered my shock and disgust when I finally saw the deep cuts edging his Sachael mark. He must have been in horrendous pain while Orontes tortured him. He couldn't speak. He couldn't defend himself. It was the worst kind of torture, one which served no purpose other than to maim and provide him with some sick form of entertainment.

I swallowed loudly, halting the tears that were threatening to escape. I needed to get ready for my fifth Saicean submergence.

"Estelle?" Azariah mumbled.

"I'm here," I said. "I thought you were asleep. Kaimi's just left."

"I know. I waited for him to leave."

I shifted nearer to him, careful not to knock his bruises.

His eyes were open, but they stared blindly. The venom still had a hold on his sight. It hadn't yet returned.

"I have many things to say to you," he said. "Things that are playing on my mind. Things I should have said earlier, and did not."

"What things? And why didn't you talk to me earlier, if something's bothering you?"

He turned to face me. Ghostly, milky grey pupils met mine.

"I wanted to see you when I spoke to you. But I cannot wait any longer." His hand reached for mine, grasping openly. I placed my hand in his.

"Then tell me now," I whispered.

He lifted his free hand, feeling for the side of my face. "I need to apologize. I should be on my knees begging for your forgiveness for the stupid way I behaved. If I had not acted so quickly in sending Chanon and the army away, then none of this would have happened. I would never have been caught, and you would not have needed to risk your life for mine. I should have dealt with Chanon, and let the army stay."

"Dealt with Chanon? Why?" I couldn't think of anything Chanon had done wrong.

"I am aware he is still here. Has he shown any unwanted attention toward you?"

"Unwanted . . . oh. That's right. You don't know." I smiled, placing my hand on his chest. "The thing with Chanon—he's my brother."

"Brother? But you don't have a brother." Azariah released my hand and slowly sat up.

"Well, I do now. It explains a lot, actually. Why he was so protective of me, and why he gave you such a hard time for supposedly letting me get caught by The Sect."

"Have you any proof of his claim?" There was doubt in his tone. I didn't blame him. I'd had plenty of doubts when he first told me too.

He shifted his legs around so he was perched on the side of the bed. I took his hand in mine, knowing he craved the contact while his vision was affected.

"Azariah, he is my brother. I need to visit my mother at some point, just to clarify everything, but I'm already sure about what she'll say."

"All these years . . ." A frown pulled across his forehead. "And all these secrets. I am glad he has you. I always wished for him to have other friends, but he is so committed to me. Now he has a perfect sister."

"Perfect? I don't think so, not with my gammy leg."

"I apologize." His frown returned. "I keep forgetting that you are injured. How is your leg?"

"It's fine. Chanon keeps bathing it and bandaging it for me."

He sighed heavily. "You should not be injured, none of you should. And Hebrus should not have died. It is a great pity I will not be able to thank him for his part in my rescue. He was a special man; a true leader of his kind."

"At least your dad and Hebrus made up first," I said, rubbing the palm of his hand with my thumb. "They worked together to devise a rescue plan for you."

"For that, I will be eternally grateful. They made it possible for me to be with you again. I had nearly given up hope of making it back here alive."

"Shhh . . . you can't think like that. You should have known I would come for you."

"I knew you would try. But I had no idea if you would find me. I had no idea where I had been taken. How did you know?"

"I didn't. Well, I knew you'd been taken to the ruins, but none of us knew where they were. It was Hebrus who knew."

Azariah smiled. "Am I to guess you were the reason he came here? I am confident he did not come at my father's request."

"Yes. I released Xanthe on the understanding that she told Hebrus there was a female Sachael in Saicean who wanted to meet him."

"So she is free?"

"Yes. Ixion was killed, as were the others who attacked her." I chose not to tell him about the behavior Ixion had directed at me.

Azariah drew in a breath. "You have been busy."

"My arrival here was somewhat of a shock, you know. You never told me exactly who your father was. He's slightly more that the 'leader of the armies.'" I arched an eyebrow at him even though he couldn't see me.

His expression became serious. "I had intended to tell you before we set off to come here, but with everything else that was happening . . ."

"Why didn't you tell me before? Were you scared about something? Frightened of my reaction?"

Azariah shook his head. "No, none of those things. You had enough to think about. Me telling you that my father was the King of Saicean, that I was next in line to rule . . . it was too much."

I rested my head next to his. "You could have told me, you know. I quite like the idea of you being a prince."

He chuckled, and I kissed his forehead.

A loud knock on the door diverted my attention.

"That will be Chanon," I said.

I stepped to the door to let him in.

"Are you ready?" Chanon asked, striding into the room. He glanced at me, but focused on Azariah.

"Nearly," I responded. "I just need to get changed."

Chanon crossed the room and sat at the table. He tapped his fingers on the wood as I pulled my submergence clothes from the cupboard.

"Estelle has told me that you two are related," Azariah said, lifting his head in Chanon's direction.

"She has?" Chanon said.

"Yes, she has," Azariah replied. "Why did you not say something earlier? You should have told me when I ordered you to leave. I would not have sent you away if I had known."

Chanon frowned before replying. "I'm not sure why I didn't say anything. I suppose I was waiting for the right moment. It . . . well, it just never presented itself."

"You should have told me," Azariah insisted.

"Perhaps. But every time I started to try, I lost my nerve. The subject changed, and then it would have just sounded awkward, forced even."

"It doesn't matter," I said. "We all know now."

"Does Kaimi?" Azariah asked.

"Yes," Chanon and I responded together.

Azariah grinned. "I would have lived to be there for that conversation as well."

"It wasn't a moment I'd care to repeat," Chanon mumbled.

"Why? What happened?"

I raised my eyebrow and entered the bathroom, leaving Chanon and Azariah to discuss my first meeting with Kaimi.

As soon as I'd dressed in my submergence clothes, I returned to the room. Chanon was sitting next to Azariah on the bed, and they were laughing at some shared joke. When Chanon spotted me, he jumped to his feet and proceeded to lift Azariah into his arms. I stayed beside them as we strode slowly through the corridors and the royal gardens to the lake.

The full moon of Procyon shone tonight. It was the moon the Nomen usually submerged under, small and white.

"The colors of the moons are beautiful," I said as we reached the edge of the lake. "Like a rainbow."

"Yes," Azariah responded. "What moon is it tonight?"

"Procyon," Chanon said.

Azariah tipped his head back to face the moons above us. "Then it is like a full moon on land. How I wish I could see it."

I hated that the venom wasn't giving up its claim on his sight.

"You'll see it soon," I promised, taking his hand in mine. He squeezed my hand, locking our fingers together.

"I hope so, Estelle."

As I stepped into the water, I took a deep, calming breath. I loved how alive the water made me feel. I hoped Azariah was experiencing something similar. Chanon stopped moving forward when the water reached his thighs. Azariah's feet dangled in the water and he smiled at the contact.

"Come and stand next to me, Estelle," Azariah said. "Face Chanon. We can do the submergence together."

I faced Chanon, who raised his brow at me. Azariah was in between us, still in Chanon's arms.

"Keep hold of my hand," Azariah requested, as he turned his head toward me.

There was no sign of anyone else, and I was reminded, once again, of the silence of Saicean. It was the one of the many things I was struggling to get used to. I hated it. I wanted to hear the birds singing, the animals rustling in the immense green that rose away from the lake. Neither Azariah nor Chanon had started the mantra, so I did, not willing to stand here all night. As soon as I spoke, both Chanon and Azariah joined in.

"I claim the truth of my existence under the full lunar phase, and submerge within these jeweled waters to keep me safe from harm."

We sank into the water, and, upon surfacing, spoke the mantra again.

After the seven repetitions were done, we headed to the edge of the lake and back to Azariah's room.

As soon as Chanon had removed Azariah's wet shorts and placed him on the bed, I asked him to leave. I quickly changed into my nightgown before climbing onto the bed next to him.

"Hey," I said as I rested my hand on his chest. "How do you feel? Has the submergence helped?"

"I think so. I expect it to help—how can it not?" He turned his head to face me. "My sight is the one thing I am impatient to have return. I am desperate to see you again."

I took his hand and placed it against my cheek.

"I'm still the same. Nothing's changed."

His fingers trailed along the bottom of my jaw before outlining my lips. I kissed his fingertips as they settled upon them.

"Everything has changed. You are in Saicean. You have done five submergences under our seven moons. I know your hair will be lustrous, and your eyes a deeper blue. Your voice has changed. It is richer, fuller . . . sensual. I want to see you."

"I'm confident you'll see again. Your eyes will be the same beautiful, intense blue they used to be. You'll make a complete recovery, Azariah. You're still the man I fell in love with, nothing changes that."

Taking his face in both my hands, I kissed him. I'd told him what I believed, what I hoped for. But even if his sight never returned, I would be here. I had no choice. How could I ever walk away from my soul mate?

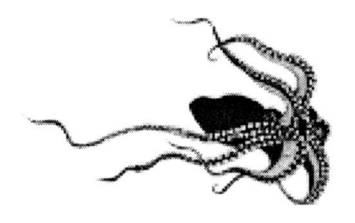

TWENTY-FIVE
Transformation

Azariah had improved dramatically since the submergence under Procyon. It was as if his body suddenly found a renewed determination to fight the venom and the horrendous side effects of his capture.

His bruises were a pale yellow, but they didn't cover his whole body anymore—many had completely faded. His Sachael mark was still healing, the vicious cuts taking significantly longer to fade, if indeed they ever would. But the best part of his improvement was his sight. After the submergence under Procyon, he could see the blurred outlines of things, able to determine light from dark. He was also sitting in a chair rather than on the bed. The strength in his legs was building each day, and he managed to walk around the room with my assistance.

"Can you still only see what's near to you?" I asked him as I changed into my shorts, preparing for our submergence under Spica.

He nodded, shifting on the bed so he was sitting with his back against the wall.

"It is slightly clearer. Perhaps the submergences have already helped."

Pulling on my vest, I noticed tears trailing from Azariah's eyes.

"Oh, Azariah, don't cry." I rushed to his side.

"Estelle, I am not crying. I am frustrated by my situation, not upset."

"Your eyes, you look like you're crying." I frowned at the clear liquid on his cheeks.

Azariah blinked rapidly before rubbing at his eyes.

"Do they hurt?" I asked.

"No, no. I think . . ." He rubbed his eyes again, and then blinked several times before turning to face me.

"I think . . . I think . . ."

"Azariah?" I was worried. "You think what?"

A smile covered his face.

"I think . . . I think I can see you. Estelle, I can see you!"

"Really?"

I threw myself onto him.

"Steady," he chuckled.

"This is brilliant," I enthused, sitting astride him on the bed and wiping the liquid from his cheeks with my thumbs. I wriggled on his lap, trying to get comfortable, wanting to look at his eyes. I hoped the stunning bright blue would have returned along with his sight.

"Be still, please, Estelle. I want to look at you. See if my memory kept your image as a true likeness."

I leaned back a little, watching his expression as he studied me. His hands came up to my face as his fingers explored my lips, cheeks, and ears.

"It didn't," he said, taking in every detail of my face. "You are even more beautiful than when I last saw you. And I was correct in my assumption of your hair being thicker, your skin softer, and your eyes an even brighter blue. It seems the submergences have worked a little magic on both of us."

I smiled, unable to look away from his eyes. He could see again, and his eye color had indeed changed. The greyish-white color of his whole eye, a symbol of his blindness, had been replaced by a pale, blue-covered iris.

"Has your Sachael mark appeared yet? I suspect it will still be very faint." he asked.

"I don't think so. Chanon looks after every submergence, but he's not mentioned seeing it." I recalled my disappointment each time my back failed to show the mark. Somehow, it made me feel like an inferior Sachael. I was beginning to wonder whether the females even had one.

"Turn around. Let me see," Azariah instructed.

I shifted, removing my leg from over his body so I could sit with my back to him.

He sighed as he moved my hair over my shoulder.

"This would be easier if I could see all of your back, not have it partly covered by this top."

His fingers followed the line of my spine, starting at the base of my neck before disappearing under the fabric of the vest. I closed my eyes, reveling in his delicate touch. It was incredibly sensual, more so than normal.

His lips nuzzled the base of my neck, and my skin tingled.

"You were meant to be looking for the mark," I said, my voice barely a whisper.

"My attention has been diverted."

His words were spoken against my skin, followed by another soft kiss.

I tipped my head forward, giving him unhindered access to my neck.

"Check if it's there," I murmured.

His finger ran across my shoulders, trailing along the top edge of my vest.

"No, it is not." Azariah's voice was husky.

I lifted my hair up, piling it on top of my head and holding it in place.

"Are you sure?"

The warmth of his breath swept across my neck as he kissed each of my shoulders.

"It is not there, Estelle. I would have expected it to be by now. You only have tonight's and one other submergence left to do."

"Maybe it'll appear afterward."

His thumbs pressed gently against the side of my neck before pushing into my hair.

"Wait . . . Estelle, I think . . . no, it cannot be."

"What? What is it?"

His hand pushed further into my hair before his fingers rubbed at the nape of my neck.

"You have the mark of a Sachael, Estelle, but it is not like mine, or any other. It is on the back of your neck, within your hairline."

"Really?"

Azariah laughed. "Yes. But it is not the full circular mark. It's like part of the mark, like one of the prongs. I wonder . . ."

"What?"

"I am confident your mark is the same as Chanon's; well, the individual family one. The one that points downward. He has a very distinguishable pattern on the family prong. It would be the same as your father's as well."

"But I definitely have a mark. A Sachael mark?"

"Yes. Most definitely."

I smiled, pleased I finally had a mark to prove I was a Sachael. It was my final confirmation, a brand. The evidence was visual—there for anyone to see. The doubters, the people who claimed I was false. That mark, *my* mark, proved them wrong.

I released my hair, twisting to face Azariah. His grin made me smile even more.

"Am I to assume you are happy with your mark?"

"Yes. I feel like a true Sachael now. And it feels amazing."

He pulled me against him.

"You have always felt amazing to me, Estelle, but never more than when we made love. You were all around me, breathing with me as though we were the same person." He took my hand in his. "I remember how soft your fingers were when they touched me, how gentle your hands were when they caressed me." His lips brushed against mine. "How demanding your lips were when we kissed, how urgently you wanted me, and how wantonly you begged for more."

"You were exactly the same," I replied, gently pushing him backward and regaining my earlier position straddling his hips. "Firm, but gentle fingers exploring every part of my body, seeking and finding the places that sent me over the edge."

"I want to do that again." His fingers gripped my thighs, holding me against him.

"I want you to, as well."

"But we cannot. It is a full moon."

I tried to hide my disappointment as he reminded me of the moon, but he caught the look that must have flitted across my face.

"Oh, Estelle. Do not look sad. I am overjoyed my sight has returned, that we are here together. And I warn you now. Tomorrow, I will insist we make love. I will barricade the door, and we will spend the whole day reacquainting our bodies." He chuckled at my shocked silence. "I am going to find it difficult living here with you."

"Why?" My husky response made me grin.

"Because here, I will not make love to you when there is a full moon, and there are seven of them to avoid. We know what the result of such a union would bring, and it is something I want us to wait for. We have all the time in the world. I want some time alone with you, time together before we start a family." He chuckled, but regained his seriousness quickly. "Living on land, with its single full moon, has never appealed to me as strongly as it does at the moment."

I laughed at his reasoning before moving closer to him, pressing my chest against his.

"The full moons are every four nights, right? That's good. I think we'll need the fourth one to recover."

The deep, throaty chuckle that met my words confirmed his agreement. But as our eyes locked, the smiles and laughter gradually faded.

"I love you," Azariah said, lifting his hand to my face and gently rubbing his thumb on my cheek. I dipped my head closer to his.

"And I love you."

My lips pressed against his, both of us eagerly searching for confirmation of our statements. Our heated bodies molded to each other's as our feelings took hold.

Always the sensible one, Azariah pulled away. "We must stop now, or I will not be able to."

I sighed heavily, understanding.

"And Chanon will be here soon," he reminded me. "Although, I am hopeful tonight will be the last time I will need his assistance to get to the lake."

Talking from outside drifted into the room. Chanon was here. I slid from the bed, straightening my clothes before he entered.

"I'll let you tell him the good news," I said. "He'll be overjoyed your sight's returned."

"I am sure he will. I would like you two to stand next to each other, please, so I can spot the family similarities."

His grin grew as Chanon entered the room. And, as Chanon turned to Azariah, he burst out laughing.

"Your eyes," he gasped. "They're blue. You can see?"

I stepped back as Azariah strode toward Chanon and they hugged each other for a long time.

I wasn't the only one in the room with tears in their eyes when they moved apart.

Azariah's sight had returned, and with it, so had my Azariah. I'd missed him more than I would ever admit.

Four days later, we prepared to submerge under the full moon of Sirius—the royal moon. It was also the one that would make me a full Sachael.

Azariah's sight was back to normal; his eyes were the vibrant blue I'd been desperate to see again. He'd made an astounding recovery, and I grinned when I recalled the last three days. My skin still burned with the heat of his fingers as they'd reunited with every part of my body. We'd spent the majority of our time making love, relaxing in our feelings of complete ecstasy as we slowly gave in to our needs. Azariah was a selfless lover, but he was also demanding. I had met my match.

As we approached the lake, Azariah was quiet, reflective. He leaned on Chanon for support, struggling to walk for any length of time.

"I cannot wait to see Estelle's final transformation," Azariah said, grinning at me as he waited to get his breath back, pausing our journey to the water for a moment.

"You make it sound like I'll change into something different right in front of you."

Azariah chuckled. "Not quite. But I am looking forward to seeing your webbed feet and hands."

I screwed my nose up. Of all the things the final submergence would bestow on me, the webbing was the strangest.

"I have not forgotten your shock when you saw my feet in the water for the first time."

"I'm sure you haven't." I grinned at his teasing. It was so good to have the old Azariah back.

"It is a pity we will not be able to swim properly together tonight. It will have to wait until I am fully recovered, but once I am better, I promise we will do just that."

Chanon supported Azariah as we finished walking to the edge of the lake. Azariah's expression was calm as we headed into the water. I was on one side of him, Chanon on the other as he guided us toward the center of the lake. As expected,

Azariah stopped when the water lapped at his chest. It was higher on me, against my shoulders.

He gazed at the moon.

"Look at the glorious way she spreads her red glow across the land," he said.

Following his observation, I glanced toward the edge of the lake, seeing the colors the red hue created. To me, everything appeared eerie, like a scene from the Devil's underworld—well, minus the fires and prancing red devils. But I understood Azariah's excitement at the color. Tonight was only the third submergence he'd done since his full vision returned. It must have seemed like a miracle.

"You've seen all the colors of the moons now," Chanon said. "Which is your favorite?"

"My favorite?" I ran through the colors: Green, purple, orange, yellow, white, blue and, tonight, red. "It would be either green or yellow."

"Canopus, or Capella." Chanon looked deep in thought. "Interesting, don't you think, Azariah? Why those colors?"

I shrugged. "I think it's because they cast a bright glow across the trees and plants—it reminds me of our father's paintings and the colors he used."

Azariah frowned for a moment. "The Elders should submerge under Canopus, and the guards under Capella. I wonder if your father was a guard. It would make sense as to why Chanon is a strong and worthy one. And you, let us not forget how much of a warrior you have proven to be."

"It would make sense," I mused out loud. I was still curious as to why he'd left his world. "Can we visit the other worlds when you're better?" I asked. "There's no rush, but I'd like to see if anyone knew him. Kaimi said no one called Aaron has ever lived in Saicean. The other leaders should be able to tell me if he lived there. They may have known him, spent time with him."

Azariah smiled and shrugged off Chanon's supporting hold before moving in front of me. "I promise we will find out about your father. But we must find Michael first."

Chanon moved away, giving us privacy, but stayed near enough to get to us if Azariah needed his support.

"I'm looking forward to seeing him again," I said, recalling the last time I saw him, disappearing on Geleon's back. "I miss him."

"So do I, Estelle. Even though he annoyed me at times, I miss his humor. I wonder how he is coping with the Selkies?"

"He'll have them wrapped around his finger, telling them stories and making them laugh, I'm sure."

"That, I can imagine."

"I hope he found them. I mean, how do you tell the difference between a seal and a Selkie?"

Azariah shrugged. "I have no idea, but we will find out when we travel to the Faroes. We will get to meet them, perhaps even spend time with them. I was incredibly surprised when you told me about them, and I am most curious to know why they protect our kind so fiercely, and why they hate Oceanids so much.

"It'll be cold," I said. "It will be February when Michael completes his seventh submergence."

"Ah, but not for us. Remember, you will be a full Sachael, and full Sachaels do not feel the cold either in, or out of the water."

I nodded. I'd not forgotten that piece of information, just the fact it would now apply to me.

My attention was suddenly diverted. Something glistened in the glow from the moon. I stared between the trees at the edge of the lake, at the place the blinding flicker had come from. There was nothing there anymore. Chanon had followed my gaze, and was scrutinizing the bank of the lake.

"Is something wrong?" Azariah followed my gaze.

"No, nothing. I just . . ." I shuddered, quite unexpectedly.

"Are you sure you're okay?" His concerned voice snapped me from my reverie.

"I'm fine. I think I'm a bit nervous is all. All this mention of cold weather is making me shiver."

"Not after this submergence. You'll never shiver again, and you have nothing to be nervous about. Hold my hands."

I turned to face him and placed my hands in his. I blocked out everything around me and concentrated on Azariah.

"Let us speak the mantra together," he said. "Are you ready?"

I nodded, and we both spoke the words that would make me a full Sachael and that would continue to mend Azariah's broken body.

"I claim the truth of my existence under the full lunar phase, and submerge within these jeweled waters to keep me safe from harm."

We sank below the surface of the lake, rising together and repeating the mantra. Seven submergences later, we had finished. I'd never really felt any different while doing the other submergences. Usually, I just felt renewed and full of energy. But tonight, it was different. Each time I came up from the water, my skin tightened, my muscles tensed. My physique was changing—only slightly, but every part of me was altering, completing my final transition to a Sachael. It wasn't painful, more like a tingling tightness, a series of rapid kisses upon my skin.

Once finished, we stared at each other, not speaking immediately.

"Let me see what your hands look like," Azariah said, breaking the silence and lifting our hands in the water between us.

He chuckled. I knew what he was laughing at. He'd seen the webbing, just as I had. Wide-eyed, I stared in disbelief at my hands and spread my fingers open before closing them again. I repeated the action, feeling the resistance of the water as the membrane pushed against it. When I lifted my hands from the water, the webbing shrank away, leaving me with completely normal hands. I dipped them back in the water, and the webbing stretched between my fingers again.

"Unbelievable," I muttered. "And my feet will be the same?"

"Yes, they will, Sachael girl."

"Sachael girl?" I grinned at Azariah's new name for me.

"My Sachael girl," he confirmed.

I looked at the man who had given me so much since I met him, and wondered how it was possible for my love for him to keep growing. We'd dealt with all sorts of craziness since meeting each other, and we both knew there was more to face in our future.

"Are you ready to speak to me through your mind?" he asked.

I nodded and we both sank beneath the surface of the lake.

"Estelle, can you hear me?"

I grinned; his voice was clear in my mind. He sounded exactly how he had when he came to me in my dreams.

"Yes."

Azariah grinned back at me. *"I have no need to hear your inner thoughts, you must keep those private."*

"What do you mean? I only said, 'yes.'"

"I heard everything, not just the 'yes,' Estelle."

Never. There was no way he could hear everything.

"But I can," he responded.

I lifted my head free from the water, joined a few seconds later by Azariah.

"That's unfair," I said, not liking the way my mind was completely open to him. If he heard me, then it meant others would be able to as well. This was a lot harder than I'd imagined. "Tell me exactly how it works, how I can keep my thoughts to myself."

Azariah shrugged. "I am not sure how you do it. It came naturally to me. I cannot remember a time when I had a problem withholding the thoughts I did not want others to hear. The only thing I needed to learn was how to communicate over distance."

"And how did you learn that?"

"I was trained."

I scowled at him. "Who trained you? Maybe they can help me."

Azariah stepped forward, lifting my chin with his fingertips.

"Your brother." He nodded in Chanon's direction. "He occasionally trains the young guards to control their thoughts in the water."

"I'll ask him later, then," I said.

Azariah's lips brushed mine.

"At least we know you can hear other Sachaels when you are in the water, and they can hear you—along with everything you think."

"Stop it." I laughed at the way he was teasing me.

"Remind me never to make love to you underwater. Well, at least not until you've learned to block your thoughts."

He chuckled before pressing his lips to mine again. As he broke away, I noticed the dark shadows under his eyes.

"You look tired," I told him. "We should head back."

"I agree. As much as I would enjoy staying in the water with you, I need to rest. Tonight has been amazing, but also tiring."

As we slowly made our way toward the shore, Chanon walking behind us, I shivered like earlier, although this time, the shivers were stronger. The skin on my back tightened.

"My back," I said, startled.

Azariah stopped. "Spikes!" he exclaimed, but then his features clouded with confusion. "Are you angry?"

"No." I shook my head frantically. "What's wrong with me? Why am I reacting this way?"

Chanon was beside us in an instant.

"Maybe your system is testing its newfound abilities," Chanon suggested, but I wasn't sure. I couldn't shake the feeling of someone watching us. It was just like earlier. I surveyed the lake, searching for any movement on the shore. I couldn't see anyone, but I still felt the uneasy, foreboding stare. It was the same feeling I'd felt numerous times when on the beach at Ravenscar. The shivering, the coldness—that sinister coldness, one which didn't make any sense. And now my back was showing spikes, a Sachael sign of anger.

Or fear?

A warning?

"Azariah." I panicked. What was my body trying to warn me about?

As I spoke his name, the lake behind us began to bubble. Azariah grabbed my hand, while Chanon stood between us and the churning surface of the water.

"What's happening?" I asked.

"I have no idea."

Three men broke the surface of the lake. I immediately spotted the customary red bands adorning two of the men's arms. The other man was taller than both, with short, blond hair that sprang to life as he took in his surroundings.

"Azariah, Chanon, is that you?" he called across the lake.

Azariah frowned before grinning at the man in front of him.

"Axius!" he called. "I hardly recognize you. What are you doing here?"

Axius strode confidently through the water toward us. The water continued to churn behind him as four women surfaced. They were immediately joined by many others.

"Chanon," he said, nodding his greeting before looking to Azariah. "I need to speak with your father." His eyes darted to me. He took in my appearance, his brow rising. "I presume you are Estelle? I heard a lot about you from my father's guards. It's a pleasure to meet you." He bowed, taking my hand in his before kissing the back of it.

"Estelle, this is Hebrus's son, Axius," Azariah said, clear and precise with his introduction. "He has taken over ruling the Oceanids." He placed his hand on Axius's shoulder. "Why do you need to see my father?"

Axius turned to Azariah, turmoil and anger burning behind his eyes.

"There has been a raging battle in Mercivium for the past four days. Many of my men have been killed, the women raped and children slaughtered. I had no option but to bring as many of my people here as I could," he explained.

"I see no men?" Chanon stated, as he looked over the lake at the women who had surfaced in the water. "Or children."

"The men are still outside the entrance. The guards will not let them in unless Kaimi allows it. The children are still hidden under the water. I did not want to come here, but it is the one place I knew we would be safe. I need to speak to Kaimi and ask his permission for my people to stay until I can reclaim my kingdom."

"Reclaim your kingdom?" I asked, puzzled by his words. Why did he need to reclaim it?

Axius shifted his gaze between us.

"Mercivium has surrendered to Orontes and his army. I am no longer the King of the Oceanids. Orontes is."

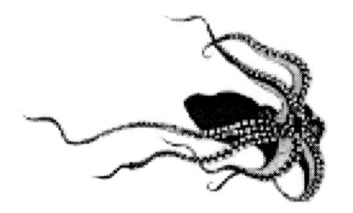

PREVIEW

Jachael Delusions

Prologue – WITCH

KAIMI

"She is a witch!"

I raised my brow and tapped my fingers on the carved wooden arm of the chair.

"So you have mentioned, Pelias. Now, if there is nothing else you wish to say, then please, leave me in peace." I was bored. Bored with his constant accusations, bored with his refusal to listen.

"She has fooled everyone," he shouted. "She has cast a spell, and you are falling into her trap so she can kill you." His brows furrowed, and I was sure he twitched his nose.

I huffed at his ridiculous words and narrowed my eyes at him. How on earth were we related? I didn't even think we looked alike. He was narrow of face, rodent-like with his high-arched brows and his stupid narrow moustache. The beard he had attempted to grow was no longer creeping across his chin and up the side of his face, but even with that pathetic smattering of hairs, he had looked nothing like me.

I stroked my thick beard with my fingers as he continued his onslaught of words.

"I just hope that everyone in this room has heard my concerns!" His voice rose as he looked around at my guards. Did he need witnesses to his paranoid behavior?

He hissed as he returned his gaze to me. "If anything happens to you, then I want it known that I am not responsible."

I held in a laugh. My humor at his seriousness would not be greeted favorably. If anything happened to me, I had no doubt who would be responsible for my death. It wouldn't be Estelle, or any of my guards; it would be him, Pelias, my own corrupt and sneaky brother.

Still he continued; surely he had run out of arguments by now. "She has gained your trust and your confidence, yet she will be the one to finish your life. I would not receive the same treatment if I threatened your life. And I am your brother"

All seven of my personal guards straightened, their hands poised over their daggers or reaching to their shoulder for the handles of their swords. It seemed they had not liked Pelias's somewhat disguised threat.

I hid my smirk. Such loyalty from my men—such unquestionable loyalty. I doubted Pelias had such a reaction from his guards. They appeared as out of place in my Hall as the Nomen did in this world. Untalented, unskilled, and not the brightest of men. Yet still, he constantly surprised me with his accusations and demands. I would not let him see Estelle. I feared that once he saw her, she would become his obsessive target, not me. I would never forget the time he stole Ianira from me, dragging her away to his quarters as his men held me down. Her screams were heard all over Saicean when he placed the branding irons on the soles of her feet. But that was before I was the ruler of this world. He wouldn't dare be so foolish now. He knew I would kill him if he put even one step out of line. I would have killed him when he tortured Ianira if I had been allowed, but it seemed my father thought it amusing. They were two of a kind, Creon and Pelias. I had no love for either of them.

I circled my hand, shooing him away. "Leave me, Pelias. I have had enough of your ridiculous opinions."

He shifted nearer to the steps and crouched down before me. "Please. I beg you, let me see her."

"Get up, you fool." I glared at him as he straightened to his full height. "And no, I will not allow you to see Estelle."

"But I will be able to tell if she is a risk to you and your men!"

"My men? I hardly think she will be fighting with them." I smirked, recalling my last visit to the private training ground. It was where I'd been taught, where my sons had learned, and where any grandsons would be trained. Estelle was a formidable fighter—Azariah's old knife being her weapon of choice. Five months of training with Chanon had made her a fierce warrior. Any man drawn into a fight with her would have met his match.

"Have they seen her? Do they know who she is?" Pelias asked, glancing at my guards, who were still standing with their hands on their weapons. They disliked him as much as I did.

I nodded.

I was hungry, and all that was on offer at the moment was a bowl of apples. I stood, stretching my arms above my head before strolling over to the table with the apples. Pelias followed.

"I really do fear for your life, Brother," Pelias whispered. "Why am I the only one who can see it?"

"Brother?" I raised my brow before biting into an apple.

"You don't like me reminding you of our blood-tie?" His shoulder rubbed against mine, and I shifted away from the unwanted contact.

I sighed before staring at him. "There are moments I wish we were not related. And it's been a long time since you've felt the need to remind me."

"There are many things I need to remind you of these days." He remained serious, like he always did when questioning me about Estelle. Goodness knows what he'd be like if he actually saw her.

"Such as?" His paranoia intrigued me.

"She was responsible for killing four men within one day of her arrival. Your head guard, even. She got rid of Ixion as soon as she stepped into our world."

"Not quite." I turned away from him, smirking as I caught Markos's eye. His hate for Pelias ran as deep as mine.

"That's not what I heard," Pelias said, his eyes flashing with excitement. He thought he was getting new information. Gathering some new glimmer of an unknown story to substantiate his accusations even further. I didn't elaborate and turned my back on him before returning to the steps.

Sensing my refusal to explain, he continued. "Pentheus as well. He was killed by her own hands."

I took another bite from the apple. How wrong he was. Estelle had only killed one person directly. The Oceanid who'd betrayed her and Azariah to Orontes—what was her name? Ah yes, Melia. But, I had to admit, she did give the order to kill Pentheus.

"And then my guards. *My* guards, Kaimi. Not content with murdering two of yours, she wanted mine dead as well. Taras and Diomedes were loyal Sachaels."

I sighed loudly before sinking into my chair. They were nothing but bullies, and bullies of the worst kind. How many innocent Oceanid lives had those men destroyed? Underage Oceanids, even. I understood their appeal, pretty little things when in the water, all their fins glistening with untold hidden secrets, and they were beautiful. I remember Ianira when I first saw her . . .

I cleared my throat, bringing myself back into the present and the pest before me.. "Pelias, you have stated your concerns on more than one occasion. I have listened, I have tried to reason with you, and yet you still continue to come to me with the same repeated accusations."

"It is only through concern that I continually try to get through to you." He dipped his head, glancing from side to side at my guards positioned around the room.

"Then do not concern yourself any longer. I am at no risk from Estelle. None of us are. She is not a witch. She is a Sachael." I pursed my lips and stared at Pelias, narrowing one of my eyes before leaning forward. "Estelle is Azariah's future wife, and therefore, the next leader's queen. You would do well to keep your mouth shut. I have to tolerate you; neither Azariah nor Estelle will need to when he comes to rule. You will be banished."

He stepped backward at my declaration. "Azariah wouldn't dare!"

I leaned back, hiding my smirk as I rested my chin on my hand, surveying him with renewed interest. Had he not given any consideration to how Azariah perceived him? Did he not realize that Azariah *would* banish him if necessary? The man was a fool.

"I think you'll find that he would. I am beyond bored with your nasty smears and quite obvious attempts to discredit Estelle. Azariah, however, is somewhat incensed."

"But ever since her arrival, we have had trouble in the ocean surrounding us." His voice rose, a response to the frustrating situation that had arisen. "Our men die, Kaimi. Every day, we lose one of our own. And not only that, she has forced you to allow Oceanids to live amongst us!"

"She has not forced me to do anything!" I snapped. None of this was Estelle's doing. None of it. My angry stare at Pelias was met by one of his own, and it was only when the door at the side of the room swung open that I averted my gaze.

Azariah strode into the Hall, scowling at Pelias, as he too made his way to the bowl of apples.

"Maybe he is also bewitched," Pelias offered, nodding in Azariah's direction.

"Enough!" My anger burst forth, and I shot to my feet. Azariah had told me many times that I would never put up with Pelias's behavior if it was from anyone else. He was correct. But however much Pelias infuriated me, he was my brother. Part of me was tied to him in a way only he and I could understand.

"Is my uncle bothering you, again?" Azariah asked. "I thought he was only allowed into this part of the house on the night of a full moon. None of them are due to show their fullness tonight. Why is he here?"

"I had things to discuss with my brother." Pelias smiled, but I didn't miss the distaste with which he spoke.

"Which could have waited until tomorrow," Azariah continued. "When you would have been allowed to visit. Not today."

I crossed my arms, knowing Pelias would see the gold bands wrapped around my biceps, the visual reminder of my rule. I didn't speak. I quite enjoyed seeing others tear into him. It saved me the effort.

"Have you parted with the words that could not wait until tomorrow?" Azariah asked, scowling at Pelias as he chewed his apple.

Pelias narrowed his eyes. "I have, but whether I have been heard is a different matter."

"I've heard you Pelias," I stated. "But I see no reason to listen."

Azariah perched on the edge of the table, his eyes permanently fixed on Pelias. He hated him. "You can leave now," he said. "I wish to speak with my father alone."

Pelias stared at Azariah, challenging his dismissal.

"You heard him!" I shouted. "He told you to leave. Remember, Pelias, if you are lucky enough to outlive me, Azariah is your next ruler. Be nice."

Pelias growled before turning sharply. As my guards opened the main doors to the Hall, his two guards joined him.

Azariah's withering gaze followed Pelias. He didn't turn to me until Pelias was out of the Hall and the doors were shut.

"Why are you setting rules which you let him disobey?" Azariah asked.

I indicated for my guards to leave. A short flick of the wrists, and they quickly dispersed. I never liked them being in the same room as me when I was alone with Azariah.

"Sometimes, he is too insistent," I mumbled before nodding at the bowl of apples he was standing next to.

Azariah threw me an apple, which I caught in my hand.

"You promised me you would keep him away from Estelle," he said. "You insist she wears the white dresses when she wanders into the gardens so that he will not view her any differently to the Oceanids. You said he would never come to this area of our home. Yet twice, I have caught him here when he knows he is not allowed. And what do you do? Humor him!"

"Azariah." I spat my bite of apple onto the floor. It was sour. "He is my brother. I do not trust him any more than you. I do not particularly like him. But we are related in a special way."

Azariah covered the floor in long strides and reached his hand to the arm of my chair. "He knows your weaknesses. He knows how far to push you, and he plays with that."

"I know." I patted his arm. "But you have no need to worry. When you come to rule, you can banish him if you so wish. But I warn you now, he may be best staying. At least you have some control over him while he is here. Out in the oceans, who knows what he'll get up to?"

"It will not be my decision, though, will it?" Azariah said. "I am not the next in line to be king. It will be Michael."

I sighed heavily.

Michael.

Menelaus's son was alive, and Azariah had found him. The odds of that ever happening were too indescribable to even try and calculate. I recalled when Azariah had told me of Michael's existence. I'd refused to believe him initially, well aware of the tales and lies human women used to try and catch us into staying with them. But I knew of Menelaus's obsession with the land woman called Morag—he'd told me. I knew she'd been pregnant with Menelaus's son, the future King of Saicean. But I also knew he'd had no intention of returning to Saicean with his son.

I didn't want to be reminded of Michael—I wanted Azariah to be next to rule, with Estelle alongside him. They were what Saicean needed. It was what I wanted. I also feared Michael dead. No one had been able to contact the Sachaels who had been sent to guard him. But both Azariah and Estelle, and even Chanon, believed he was alive. They wanted to go and find him, but I wouldn't let them go.

The oceans around Saicean were not a safe place for Sachaels at the moment. Pelias was right about one thing—the Oceanid army who attacked us daily had only arrived after Estelle's appearance in Saicean. But they weren't her army as he'd ridiculously suggested time and time again, they were Orontes's army, equipped with some sort of gun which fired venom bullets. We were losing too many men. The hunters, the men who brought food back to Saicean, were being picked off regularly. Not a week went by without us losing another man. Even when I sent guards out with them, the result was always the same. Lives lost; a depleted number returning, many of them injured. I wasn't prepared to let Azariah and Estelle go into the ocean while it was full of crazy Oceanids.

They were too important to Saicean. They were too important to me. I wouldn't lose either of them.

My stomach growled, a reminder that food was now restricted. We still ate well, but in moderation. I worried how long we could continue like this. Apples were no substitute for proper food.

Azariah slumped onto the steps leading to my chair, and I sank down next to him.

"Things are difficult at the moment. For all of us," I said. "But I currently have no plans to let Pelias see Estelle."

"But—"

"Let me finish, please." I placed my hand on his knee. "There will come a time when Pelias will discover who Estelle is. One of my guards will mention it, or she herself may bump into him. I can hardly see her being pleasant to him if he talks to her as he does his wife or the other Oceanids. Her response will give her away." I sighed. "But I will repeat my order that he must not enter this side of our home unless there is a full moon. I will ensure he does as I tell him."

Azariah nodded. "And when will you let us leave to find Michael?"

I straightened, my posture no longer relaxed. "You will not be leaving to find him. I will not risk losing you or Estelle to the battle in our ocean."

"But he belongs here. He is the next ruler. We have to find him and bring him back!"

I shook my head. "The only person I will allow to go and find him is Chanon."

"You cannot send him alone. If he was attacked, he would struggle to escape by himself."

"Exactly. Yet you expect me to let you and Estelle go. The most precious people in my life? You know how dangerous it is, you've just told me that one of the best fighters in our world would struggle to escape an attack, yet you ask my permission to go with him? I will not allow it, Azariah. Chanon is the only one I will grant permission to leave and bring Michael back. If he fails, then at least you two are safe."

Azariah jumped to his feet and stepped away from me. My shoulders slumped. I hated arguing with him, but he needed to understand my concern, my fear. I would not let him go, and I would not let Estelle go, either.

"You cannot send Chanon by himself. Even if he did manage to get to the Faroes and find him, he would never get back. You expect one guard to protect the future ruler of Saicean?"

"Why not? He always has before—he's protected you." I paused, letting my words sink in. How many years had Chanon, and Chanon alone, protected Azariah? "I let that happen at your insistence, Azariah, but you also know that I would have preferred you to have more than just Chanon with you whenever you left Saicean. He looked after you quite successfully until you foolishly ordered him away. Then look what happened!"

"I do not need to be reminded!" Azariah's eyes flashed angrily.

So he hadn't liked my reminder of Orontes's attack, and the days we spent fearing him dead. Good. I would never let him forget. He needed to be reminded of his stupidity every so often. It would keep him alive.

"So," I said, "you are telling me that Chanon is not capable of bringing Michael home to Saicean?"

"Saicean is not his home, it never has been. But it is where he rightfully belongs."

I nodded. "And Chanon?"

"I will not allow him to travel by himself and be killed," Azariah said. "I do not think Estelle would be too keen on his solitary departure, either."

"Then Michael will have to remain unfound."

Azariah took a deep breath, looking as if he was preparing to speak, but he remained silent. Shaking his head, he strode from the room, his anger brimming over as he slammed the door.

I scratched my beard, lifting my gaze to the brightness of the ceiling above me. Why couldn't I have been more like my father? If I'd been like him, I wouldn't have cared what happened to Azariah. I know what my father would have done. He would have immediately claimed Estelle as his own when she arrived, and then potentially kill Azariah so he could have her as his wife. She would already be pregnant with a true-blooded Sachael growing within her—his child . . . my child. I shook my head as if trying to clear the inappropriate thought from my mind. I wasn't like him. I'd spent my early years molding myself into a person I considered to be the complete opposite of him. He was a cruel man, incapable of loving anyone. But that was my problem. I loved Azariah and Estelle, and I would willingly sacrifice my own life for theirs.

Lowering my gaze, I placed my hands on either side of my head and closed my eyes. I had an unnerving, unsettled feeling about Pelias and his antics. Huffing loudly, I moved from the steps to my chair.

Markos entered the room, quickly explaining his appearance.

"Kaimi, two of your guards decided to settle a disagreement with one of Pelias's."

"And?" I said, raising my brow, already guessing the outcome.

"Pelias's guard is dead. Pelias is on his way back to speak with you."

I closed my eyes again before nodding my understanding at Markos. No one ever said that ruling Saicean would be easy.

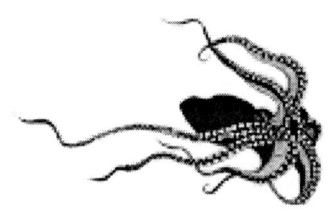

ACKNOWLEDGEMENTS

Once again, I'd like to thank you, the reader, for choosing to read Sachael Desires. I hope you enjoyed it and will continue to join me with the rest of the series.

There are many people to thank in the journey to get Sachael Desires published. Each and everyone of you has helped me get where I am today.

Barbara—still my "google junkie" and background researcher, as well as a sympathetic ear when I need to vent my frustrations or cry on your shoulder. I couldn't do any of this without you and will be forever grateful for your unwavering and continued support. We've still a long way to go!

Denise—you are becoming my marketing and promotion kit whenever I do book signings. If the general public don't know me before they enter a room, you make sure they do by the time they leave. Seriously, everyone needs a Denise when they have a signing. Also, you're always there to bounce ideas off, and your enthusiasm keeps me going when I dawdle to a stop. These next few years are going to be FUN!

Summer—still the first CP I ever worked with and still the person who calls me out on my words when I get carried away (not in the good way). This journey wouldn't be the same without you. Thank you.

I want to thank everyone at REUTS Publications, but specifically **Kisa Whipkey** for taking the chance on me and this series, as it was her desk that my submission initially landed on. Kisa has made my words shine and held my hand through my edits. **Nicole Tone** added her magic to the editing equation this time as well—it was a pleasure working with both of you. **Summer Wier** and **Tiffany Treichel** helped with teasers, trailers, rafflecopters, blog tours, giveaways, and generally anything I threw at them. And **Ashley Ruggirello** once again created a stunningly beautiful cover—I'm very excited to see what the remaining two covers will look like.

And where would I be without all the other people behind the scenes, my writing friends who offer support whenever I need it, and who cheer me on or help out wherever they can. I'm talking about **Kathy Palm**, **Michelle Hoehn**, **Tammy Farrell**, **Julie Hutchings**, **Carys Jones**, **Rae Oestreich**, **Ashley Hudson**, **Ann**

Majory K, Cary Denault, Heather Van Fleet, Cari Dowling, and **Katie Teller**. You guys are THE BEST!

And my other, non-writing friends who I wouldn't be without: **Nicky Tailby, Lorna Jones, Clare Davies Nicholls**. You go, girls—you all sparkle!

My family always play an important part in my publishing journey. I couldn't do any of this without them. **Mum** and **Dad**—you continue to offer encouragement and unwavering support. **Pete**, my husband, you still manage to cope with my regular inability to even form a sentence some days, when I'm in the "zone." My boys, **Joe** and **Matt**, you are the most amazing cheerleading squad around. You are both growing into smart, kind, and compassionate teenagers—I'm so very proud of you.

And lastly, another mention to the place that inspired me to write this series. **Ravenscar**. You're still there, always will be. Unique, untouched, comforting, and full of hidden secrets yet to be discovered. Thank you.

ABOUT MELODY

Growing up, Melody Winter showed a natural ability in art, a head for maths, and a tendency to write far too long English essays. Difficult to place in the world when she graduated, she pursued a career in teaching, but eventually ended up working in Finance. Melody is convinced the methodical time she spends working with numbers fuels her desire to drift into dream worlds and write about the illusory characters in her head.

Melody Winter lives in North Yorkshire, England, with her husband and two sons. When not dealing with football, rugby, and a whole plethora of 'boy' activities, she will be found scribbling notes for her stories, or preparing for another trip to the beach. With an obsession for anything mythical, Melody revels in reading and writing about such creatures. In fact, if she wasn't such a terrible swimmer, she'd say she was a mermaid.